Psycho Psychic Series

Psíquico Loco Serí

Book One

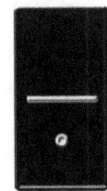

Day of the 15th Party

Día de los Quince Años

By K. del Hierro

Day of the 15th Party ~ Día de los Quince Años
Psycho Psychic Series ~ Psíquico Loco Seri Book One

By K. del Hierro

ISBN-13: 978-0-9857825-0-4 (k. del Hierro)
ISBN-10: 0985782501

TAGS: day of the 15th party, día de los quince años, quinceanera, quinceanous, k del hierro, kathie del hierro, thriller, suspense, psycho psychic, fiction, young adult, action, adventure, coming of age, humor, latino, drugs, violence, gangs, family, psychic, ghosts, death, separation, love, romance, paranormal, spirits, lowrider, car clubs, high school, native american, tonkawa, san antonio, mexico, texas

ACKNOWLEDGEMENTS

To my Family, Friends and Students, past and present-this novel is for everyone I love-without you it wouldn't exist. Thanks to Greg W. for being my backbone--thanks for holding me up my friend. Thank you to my husband, Chris, for your electronic guidance. Mucho gracias Frank R. and Luis H. for accurate local color Spanish (a.k.a., "Texmex") and laughter. Thank you Holle H. for being my mentor--you are brilliant. Thanks to Peggy M. and Patricia G. for truest friendship. A dedication to my brother-in-law, Andrew del Hierro who died from a gunshot wound Easter Sunday, 1995, Dallas, Texas. A dedication to my friend Steve Genovese, who died in the World Trade Center, NYC, on 9-11-2001. Thank you Don P. of the Tonkawa for great phone conversations and blessings! Thanks Jen for the tour of ICU. Thanks Paul for your description of certain chemicals. Thank you to my daughter Jeni and the unconditional love we have for each other. Thank you Dad for letting me, your nutty daughter, bungee cord my laptop to your treadmill to edit and exercise at the same time--love you. Thanks to all of my students for the laughter, love, trust, inspiration and support! Thanks to Meher and Laurel for being my biggest fans before even knowing what you're in for--thank you for your trust!

Meet the characters...

Alonso: birthplace, Mexico City, residence, San Antonio, Texas, tall, dark hair, black eyes, slender, intelligent, loving, fast, psychic, illegal.

Tino: birthplace and residence, San Antonio, Texas, Tonkowa Native American, long black hair in braids, dark eyes, athletic paraplegic, dreamer, psychic.

Tesoro: birthplace and residence, San Antonio, Texas, twin to Tino, dark hair, black eyes, naturally athletic and sexy, shy, honest, fast, smart.

Patricio: birthplace and residence, San Antonio, Texas. Alonso's cousin, brown wavy hair, brown eyes, cunning, charming, law breaker.

Mauricio: birthplace San Antonio, Texas, Patricio's brother, brown wavy hair, brown eyes, joker, reactive, domino player, fast, law breaker.

"K. del Hierro pens masterpiece, Day of the 15th Party."
~Westlake Picayune

"Readers of any age will absolutely love Alonso."
"You have a believable and engaging male lead character."
~ABNA Reviewer

"It is difficult to imagine how the author could have packed more action or variety into one manuscript."
~Publishers Weekly Reviewer

"Take a little trip, take a little trip, take a little trip with me." ~ War

Day of the 15th Party, Book One, Overview

Alonso Mendoza thinks not having his pencil for pre-AP math and competing with Brett for grades is a problem. That being too shy to talk with the mysterious Tesoro is a problem. He has miscalculated problems.

Alonso's papá is deported from San Antonio to Mexico and Alonso must hide his own illegal alien status. His sister and cousins act like they're on a *Teens Gone Wild* film and his mamá's at her wit's end. Overwhelmed by his family, Alonso is convinced he's loco, seeing visions, orbs, and auras. He dismisses it as stress--everything but the repeated dream of Tino, a guy he's never met. That's a crazy problem.

Under duress, Alonso spends his time fantasizing about Tesoro. He's not the only one; the popular athlete, Brett, also has Tesoro on the brain. When the two discover they're crushing on the same girl, the academic rivalry turns fistacuffs. Brett's knuckles up Alonso's nose is an escalating problem.

And...there are those who Alonso wished he'd never seen: the newly dead, those dramatic souls who showing him how they died from cancer, trauma and drugs, also insisting that he *feel* their pain. Just when the game table flips and Alonso's life goes upside down...the dead start to make sense. Now he's on the run with those he loves from a killer calculating problem.

Day of the 15th Party is the first novel in the
Psycho Psychic series.

Day of the 15th Party ~ Día de los Quince Años
TABLE OF CONTENTS

TABLE OF CONTENTS continued…

INTRODUCTION

The Vision

For someone who didn't wish to be noticed, ever, Alonso found it difficult to believe he was holding Tesoro in his arms. He gazed at her in the dank, fresh-water drainage tunnel deep under San Antonio, momentarily oblivious to the looming danger. The strung-out man with the tattoo of the horned skull and the letters "MM" was still deep in the drainage system, trying to locate and kill them.

Tesoro placed her head on the rolled up shirt, still warm from Alonso's body heat. He moved his body next to hers--she was shivering. He reached his arms around her and pulled her in close, placing one leg over her to keep her warm. The curve of the small tunnel forced them into each other. Tesoro brought both of her arms in tight, bent at the elbows, to the front of her body for additional warmth.

"There now." He kissed her forehead as she relaxed into him.

The flashlight app dimmed and the phone powered down from the dying battery. The sight of Tesoro quickly faded into black. His eyes wide open, Alonso could see the softest, glowing gray haze of a figure deep in the pipeline. The sound of his heart quickened to a pace he heard beating in his ears. The familiar static electricity around his mouth and the cold chill up his spine coupled with the cool breeze across the back of his neck caused him to stiffen.

For someone who never wished to be noticed, ever, the attention from the dead was more than he ever bargained for.

Bracing for what was next, Alonso shut his eyes tight, knowing full well it would not stop the visions the dead could induce. They let him know intimately how they died, feeling their pain, fear, their last breath in a barrage of information in clips, pings and metaphors.

A foul stench of infected, rotten tissue rolled through the tunnel and into Alonso's flared nostrils. He could taste this noxious odor in the back of his throat and it gagged him momentarily. Alonso knew the manifesting spirit was moving closer. Pulling his face out of Tesoro's hair, he looked up to see the construction worker taking form from the mist. Showing him tracks on his arms and syringes in his hands.

For someone who tried to hide and not be noticed, knowing that his life was a lie, Alonso smiled in the dark. He could feel Tesoro full length, asleep against his body and thought, "Bring it on..."

~

"Ya párate güevón, ya es hora de irnos." (*Get up sleepy head, it's time to go.*) Alonso heard his papá's voice break through, bringing him into the reality of the school morning.

"Chingado."

"¡Qué no te oiga tu mamá hablar así!" (*Don't let your mamá hear you talk like that!*)

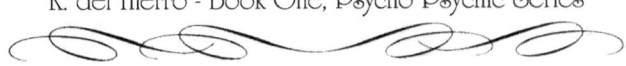

Thomas Stearns Eliot Writer - Poet

26 September 1888 to 3 January 1965

"The communication of the

Dead

is tongued with fire beyond the

language of the

Living."

Memorial plaque ~ Westminster Abbey,

London, England

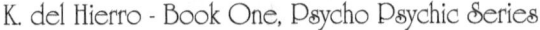

CHAPTER ONE

Barbacoa and INS

"¿**P**apá, te los vas a comer todos? ¿Me das un taco, por favor?" (*Papá, are you going to eat them all? Can I have a taco, please?*) Alonso pleaded from the torn up backseat of the car as old as himself. He leaned forward and placed his hand on his papá's shoulder as the fifteen-year-old Honda Civic labored slowly up the northbound ramp and onto Interstate 10 in San Antonio, Texas.

"Ten. Ya me llené." (*Here, I'm full.*) Alonso's papá responded from the front passenger seat, dangling the taco in the white paper bag over the center console.

"¿Ya lo quieres?" (*Do you want it now?*) Camilo turned back to look at his son.

"Gúardalo adelante." (*No, just leave it up front.*) Alonso shook his head, his black bangs falling across his dark eyes. Camilo placed the tacos on the slightly torn center console.

"¡Si lo dejas adelante me lo voy a comer!" (*If you leave it up front, I'm going to eat it.*) Lisa, Alonso's mamá, teased him in a musical voice, flashing her jet-black eyes at Alonso in the rearview mirror, from the driver's seat.

"¡Déjaselo!" (*Leave it for him!*) Camilo quickly snatched up the barbacoa taco and shoved it in the glove box, just out of Lisa's reach. She shot a playful glance over to her husband and took one hand off the wheel just long enough slap him in a teasing way across the top of his leg.

"No te lo puedes comer, Lisa. Lo necesita para la escuela."

(*You cannot eat it, Lisa. He needs it to be strong in school.*)
Camilo said, not teasing at all.

Lisa let out a sigh; Alonso held his laughter deep in his stomach. He bent down, pretending to dig in his backpack so his parents could not see his expression of suppressed amusement.

"¡Órale, mira ese camión!" (*Wow, look at that truck!*) Alonso said, diverting Lisa's attention from her driving to a pimped-out, dark blue, lowrider sports truck riding beside them. It rode on black rims, Alonso guessed 22s. The back window of the truck bore the words "Royal Riderz" in old English script inscribed in white across the dark tint.

"Aquí te sales." (*Here's your exit.*) Camilo pointed across the dash board. She exited Interstate 10 and rolled the Civic to the red light, where it abruptly stalled out.

"Ay, no." Pushing her dark, silky hair out of her face and with a few frantic turns of the key in the ignition, Lisa restarted the old car. She smiled at her husband with relief. He smiled back, and soon they arrived at Mansiones de Piedra Blanca (*White Rock Estates*) residential area--Camilo's current work place.

The Mansiones de Piedra Blanca was like entering an amusement park fantasy world. All of the plants and flowers lined up in neat rows; the long flat rocks were surrounded by short sego palm trees. The words "Mansiones de Piedra Blanca" were etched elegantly into the great stone entrance. Everything was new, made to appear old world, Alonso's old world, an idealized dream of the world his family left behind in Mexico. The battered Civic, out of place in this environment, puttered over the stone bridge into the newest section of the wealthy community. In the distance, Alonso could hear the familiar sound of nail guns blasting into wood and siding. They were almost there.

Lisa stopped the Civic in front of a castle-sized home under construction. Men wearing flannel shirts, work boots and baggy jeans were carefully selecting limestone rocks to place on the exterior of the home. Camilo leaned over to give Lisa a kiss goodbye; gazing lovingly into her eyes, he ran his rough hand over the back of her head and smoothed down her long, dark hair. He reached for the door handle, but Alonso was already outside opening the door for him. They gave each other a brief hug and Camilo walked toward the men working with the stones. The men waved at him and one worker, with a toothy smile, walked up and gave him a hammer to start chipping the rock with.

Alonso climbed into the front passenger seat beside his mamá. He reached down under the seat and pulled the lever to move the seat back to make room for his long, lanky legs. He immediately reached into the glove box and pulled out the taco.

"¿Quieres la mitad?" (*Do you want half of it?*) Alonso asked his mamá, holding the taco up toward her as they rounded the corner away from the construction site.

"No, no. Nomás estoy jugando." (*I was just joking.*) The Civic let out a ferocious knocking sound as the engine died, again, and the grin left her face.

Alonso placed the taco on the console, leapt out of the car and opened the hood. He looked over the engine, puzzled. He asked his mamá to try starting the car again. Nothing, time and time again...the engine would not turn over.

"¡Ve por tu papá!" (*Go get your papá!*) she yelled out the open car window. Alonso walked toward the new construction, taking a short cut through a house with only the wooden frame up. He wove his way through the pipes jutting up from the concrete slab and turned sideways to fit between the wooden two-by-fours. He stepped over diagonal boards bracing the walls of the home and jumped effortlessly off the tall slab into the mud that would someday be a backyard. In no time at all he was standing by the limestone rock pile in front of the house where his papá was working.

Alonso walked past the busy workers into the open garage. He caught sight of his papá carefully setting a rock into place on a window sill on the other side of the house. Alonso called out through the echoing, empty house. Hearing his son, Camilo placed his hammer on the back window sill and made his way to the garage.

"¿Qué pasó?" (*What's up?*) Alonso's papá asked with concern.

"Otra vez se apagó el coche." (*The car went dead again.*)

"¿Dónde está?" (*Where is it?*) Camilo looked around for the Honda.

"A la vuelta de la esquina, detrás de la casa grande en construcción." (*Just around the corner, behind the big house being framed in.*) Alonso motioned his hand in the general direction of his mamá and their car.

"Bien, déjame avisarle a mi supervisor que necesito salir. Regresa con tu mamá y espera allí con ella hasta que yo llegue." (*Okay, let me tell my foreman I need to leave. Go back to your* mamá *and wait with her until I get there.*) Camilo walked away to talk with the foreman.

Alonso followed the wooden boards placed in the mud up to the concrete slab of the framed home he had walked through earlier. In the same way a swimmer jumps out of a pool, Alonso placed his hands at the edge of the slab and effortlessly lifted his lithe body up to the floor level. He wove through the wooden frame of the home, imagining what the rooms would turn into someday. Walking through what he thought might be the kitchen; he heard the rumble of a vehicle passing by and glanced back over his shoulder.

It was a large white van, unmarked, no windows in the back and two men in suits in the front seat. He knew immediately it was INS, the much feared Immigration Naturalization Service. He knew they were coming for the men working on the large limestone house...and his papá! Terrified,

Alonso's heart leapt in his chest--his papá said to run and hide if this ever happened. He wanted to run to his papá to warn him, but he could not without disobeying his instructions.

He remembered seeing a large garden bathtub wrapped loosely in plastic through the wooden beams. He quickly squeezed through the wooden studs, ducked under electrical wires and rolled sideways into the tub. The plastic lining in the garden tub held water from the heavy rain that had come the week before. It was brown and stagnant and smelly and trash was floating in it. He crouched low into the dark water inside the tub, hoping that no one had used it as a toilet--something he knew happened often on construction sites.

"Hypodermic needle," Alonso mumbled. His attention was drawn to the trash, eye level, floating in the brown water.

"What's that doing here?" He flicked his hand in the water, moving the syringe away from his body. He noticed that the needle was bent back; it obviously had been used. Alonso's skin crawled and his imagination worked overtime with the thought of what else might be in the water with him.

"Repugnante." (*Disgusting.*)

In the distance, the van stopped and men in suits stepped out. They walked toward the foreman, who quickly placed the papers he held down the back of his baggy pants, hiding them. The men started asking the foreman questions. Alonso peered out over the top of the tub as the workers lined were up in a row. He watched as the workers pulled papers out of their pockets; some of them were taken to the van--one of them being his papá! Alonso wanted to scream out. Instead, he held his breath as the van drove past his hiding spot. The van turned away from the road where his mamá waited for him in the broken-down Civic. He slowly stood up, wet and smelly, and gazed down the hard pavement in the direction of the INS van. He knew there was nothing he could do. He knew his mamá would wail. He knew he would not see his papá for a very long time.

Alonso's tears came as hard as the rains that had fallen the week before, dropping from his black eyes into the brown water surrounding his feet in the tub. He watched for a long time as the ripples from his tears moved across the surface. A glimmer of light reflected across the ripples, and for a split second, a young girl with a bald head appeared to be submerged just below the glimmering rings in the water.

She blinked and Alonso jumped back, falling across the side of the tub and onto the concrete floor.

"Mierda." (*Shit.*) He looked deep into the tub again and said, "What was that?"

In the porcelain vessel, there was nothing but filthy water and the syringe floating eerily.

CHAPTER TWO

Polished Onyx and DNA

Alonso was staring at her again. He could tell Tesoro was pretending not to notice him, that she was not comfortable with his gaze. She turned away, reaching for the cold stone pendant around her neck, covering it with her delicate hand. He wanted her to look at him; instead she focused her attention on her art teacher, who was lecturing about abstract expressionism. The room was dim; image after colorful image appeared on the large screen in the front of the classroom full of students. Alonso watched as Tesoro opened her sketchbook and began to nervously doodle.

He could see her struggle to try and disappear away from his stare. She fidgeted in her chair with the occasional fast glance in his direction. Alonso thought she looked frightened. He knew he was being intense. Tesoro leaned over her sketchbook and put the finishing touches on a water bird in flight over a swirling sky. She bent down, her soft black hair slipping across either side of her pale face, further shielding his gaze from her.

He silently counted down the minutes for the bell to ring and quickly left the classroom when it sounded. Once outside of the room, he couldn't help himself. Alonso stopped in the middle of the crowded hallway and turned to look back at the art room door. Students knocked him with their backpacks as they scurried by.

His head was down and his jagged, straight black bangs covered most of his face. He hid carefully behind eyes of polished black onyx that seemed to reflect all of life around him--without allowing anyone to look in. The clear white of his eyes, set in sharp contrast to his stone-black iris flashed directly at Tesoro exiting the art room. He couldn't shake his thoughts of talking to her. He couldn't think of exactly what he would say or how he would initiate a conversation. When he looked at her his words locked up in his throat. He wanted to know more about her in spite of this feeling.

For a second she looked up at him. He pushed his bangs off his winter-pale olive skin as their gazes met. Her nicely shaped mouth opened slightly with gentle surprise. Just as he started to smile at her, a small student with a backpack on wheels tripped him and sent him tumbling down the narrow school hall. His fall was broken by the crowd struggling to make it to their next class on time. When he looked up, the student that nearly took him out was long gone and so was Tesoro.

"Typical." Alonso gathered his composure, smoothed down his un-tucked flannel shirt and quickly put the heavy silver chain that hung from his jeans back into his pocket. Alonso let his bangs fall back over his face, covering his prominent cheek bones and his eyes. He adjusted his black backpack over his strong left shoulder and seamlessly weaved his tall, slender frame through crowded hall to the quiet of the science wing.

In Mrs. Weaver's science room, students were bustling around the back cabinets, setting up their group projects on DNA for grading. Alonso worked his way through the tightly spaced desks as the bell sounded and moved in with his group. He reached into his backpack, just in time, pulling out his part of the group project: to diagram Deoxyribonucleic Acid, using computer graphics to break it down to show its different components. He neatly placed the diagrams in front of the 3-D model made of miniature pom-poms and pipe cleaners that Tracy had hot glued together the night before to resemble DNA. Marcus reached into his backpack to produce a wrinkled, rolled-up baggie filled with bits of cut up paper labels. He haphazardly dumped the entire contents of his backpack on the floor and out rolled a glue stick.

"There it is!" Marcus said, holding the glue stick up in the air as if it were a trophy.

"Okay, let's get the labels on the model--fast," Alonso said. He noticed Mrs. Weaver walking toward the first group with the grading rubric in her hands. Alonso, Marcus and Tracy quickly worked together to put the finishing touches on their project.

"It looks great!" Tracy announced in classic cheerleader fashion, clapping her well-manicured hands together. She reached into her backpack, pulled out her phone and snapped a quick picture of herself standing in front of the project. She stole one more picture of her teammates before quickly putting her phone up, right before Mrs. Weaver turned around. She shot a sly grin at the two boys as she zipped up her backpack on the floor.

Alonso glanced around the room, sizing up the other group projects. It was clear to him that they would receive at least a ninety-five. His team's project was neater, taller, well diagrammed and color coded. No one else had a color-coded project. He knew their project would set the grading curve...this time. Looking at the side of the room, he could tell something was going on. Mrs. Weaver had her arms crossed, close to her chest, over her clipboard--not a good sign. Two students appeared to be explaining their project. When Alonso focused in on this conversation he could tell they actually didn't have a project; they looked desperate and ashamed.

"Is that the group Brett's in?" Alonso bent down, whispering in Tracy's ear.

She nodded yes. "I don't see him, do you?"

"Nope, guess this means he'll have to take a low grade," Alonso said.

Just then, the entire class turned toward the doorway.

Something, or someone, was making a loud racket coming down the hall.

"That's just not fair," Alonso exclaimed as Brett pushed an office cart into the classroom. The cart held a wooden, precisely painted, perfect model of a DNA strand rising like a giant serpent from its center.

Everyone was staring at Brett, including Mrs. Weaver. He walked up to her and handed over an official office pink pass so he would not be counted tardy.

"I bet his dad did that for him," Marcus said under his breath to Alonso and Tracy. They saw their high grade slipping away.

"Yeah, his dad helped him," Alonso sighed, quickly drifting into his own thoughts of his papá with the hum of classroom chatter surrounding him. It had been just over a week since the INS had taken Camilo away. His mamá had not received any word on his whereabouts. He wished his papá was home, or at least what he thought was their home.

"What's that girly thing? Did I hear someone say cheer?" Brett's sarcastic tone broke through Alonso's thoughts. Brett performed a mime of Flores High School's favorite cheer to further poke fun at Tracy, who rolled her big, green eyes at him.

"¡Ya estuvo cabrón!" Alonso spit his words out at Brett louder than he would have liked. He felt a burning at his back and slowly turned around to see Mrs. Weaver staring right at him. She motioned with her index finger for Alonso to come over to her. Immediately he felt terrible; he didn't ever act out in class.

"We need to step out into the hall." A few students who overheard this sounded in unison, "Oohhww, you're in trouble," followed by an audible group snicker.

Mrs. Weaver ignored the students and led Alonso out into the hall. "A few things are concerning me right now. The main thing I want to know is what did you say to Brett?"

"I told him to leave Tracy alone, to not get her into this."

"Not get her into what, exactly?"

"He always has to one up me, Miss." Alonso shuffled his feet, his bangs covering his entire face.

"Mrs. Weaver is my name, I don't respond to Miss." His teacher tried to look through his bangs at his eyes.

"You wouldn't believe me, Mrs. Weaver," Alonso muttered softly.

"Try me."

Alonso looked up; his eyes glistened with the well of emotions built up from the past week of events that he knew he could not verbalize to anyone without getting his family in further trouble.

"He messes up my work..."

"Give me an example, I need something concrete." She had one eye on the class through the small safety glass window on the classroom door as she held the door handle slightly ajar.

"Remember when you asked us to create something usable out of trash?"

"Yes, you turned a gum wrapper into an origami crane. Not your best work, Alonso. You didn't make a very good grade on that."

"That wasn't my real assignment. I made that in art, right before your class. The project I made for that assignment was a pair of shoes sewn together using old tires and plastic bags. It took me two weeks to finish them at home. They were good. Brett took them out of my backpack during lunch and I never got them back. He's always messing with me, Miss."

Alonso blinked back his pent-up emotions, this time looking right at Mrs. Weaver, who let the 'Miss' glide right by without comment. She watched him.

Alonso saw Tesoro and her friend, Sarah, moving down the science hall together, headed toward the girls' room. Sarah pulled Tesoro's elbow and guided her away from him.

He heard Sarah say, "Don't look at that stalker, he's a real creeper."

"Can I give you an opportunity to make this up?" Mrs. Weaver's voice brought him back into the moment.

"There's a contest," she continued. "A science contest, it's in four weeks. I know that's not much time, but I believe in you, Alonso. I see you trying your best every day in my classroom. You have good ideas on paper; it's time to put those ideas into action."

"What do you want me to do?"

"Build a gadget that saves energy." She stooped down to peek in at her class through the window.

"I'll give you the brochure. It explains everything you need to do to qualify."

"How much extra credit will I get?"

"Not only five points added onto your semester grade average, but a chance to compete at a state and maybe national level." Mrs. Weaver looked Alonso square in the eyes.

"Four weeks?" Alonso said.

"Four weeks and five points added to your semester grade average." She opened up the door to the class and directed the snickering students to get back to work.

"Alright, I'm in." Alonso walked past her, glaring at Brett on his way through the room.

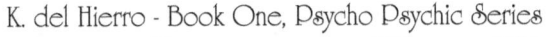

CHAPTER THREE

Dominoes and a Dog

The parking lot emptied out in front of Flores High. Alonso waited for his ride with a few other students perched high on the brick ramp wall in front of the cafeteria. From this vantage point, he had a clear view of his sister driving into the large circular drive just moments after the busses pulled out.

Lilianna didn't look up, or acknowledge Alonso as he slid into the backseat of the golden 1969 Impala next to his cousin Patricio.

"Hola Mauricio, Patricio." Mauricio turned around in the front seat and grinned at Alonso.

Lilianna had her window all the way down. It was a cold day and Alonso knew that Lilianna could not take strong odors. The classic car smell mingled with the odor of cigarette smoke and stale perfume. She was listening to music through earbuds, occasionally singing along and moving her head to the rhythm that Alonso could not hear. Lilianna pulled away from Flores campus, taking a right onto de Zavala.

"Hey, where are we going? I-10 is on the left."

"Whadu say?" Anna pulled one of her earbuds out and looked back at Alonso from the rearview mirror with a bored expression, blinking her long, perfectly applied, heavily mascara'd eyelashes slowly.

"¿Adónde vamos?" (*Where are we going?*)

"Mamá quiere que le ayudes con su trabajo. Te vamos a dejar en la casa que está limpiando." (*Mamá wants you to help her out with her work. We're dropping you off at the house she's cleaning.*) She repositioned the earbud and resumed her singing.

Lilianna pulled into a nice, older neighborhood and parked right behind the family Civic. Alonso got out of the Impala.

"That's it." Mauricio pointed to a small, frame home. Lilianna, Mauricio and Patricio drove off in the golden Chevy. Lilianna's head was bobbing and her hand twirling to the beat.

"Too cool for school," Alonso muttered as he watched them drive off. He didn't enjoy the idea of her hanging out with Patricio and Mauricio. "They're up to no good."

"¿Mamá, estás aquí?" (*Mamá, are you in here?*) Alonso pushed the door to the home wide open. He could hear a vacuum cleaner running from a back room. He followed the sound and found her cleaning the floor of a large empty bedroom.

"¡Alonso!" She turned off the vacuum and went to hold her son. Her closeness felt comforting and he held his mamá in return.

"¿No has escuchado nada de mi papá?" (*Have you heard anything from papá today?*)

"No." She looked up at him and then took her son's chin in hand, brushing back the bangs on his forehead.

"Él va a regresar, está viendo cómo regresarse. Es cuestión de tiempo." (*He's coming back; he's looking at how to come back. It's just a matter of time.*)

Alonso nodded yes, still looking down.

"¿Puedo usar un cuarto para estudiar?" (*Can I use a room to study in?*)

"Sí, los renteros se acaban de mover, y van a renovar toda la casa. Si ves algo que te guste, el dueño dijo que nos lo podemos llevar." (*Yes, this place is a make ready, the renters have moved out. If you see anything you like, the landlord said we could keep it, if we want.*)

Alonso let his backpack slip off his shoulder and placed it on the kitchen counter.

"¿Necesitas que te ayude en algo?" (*You need me to do anything?*)

"Sácate las cosas de los cuartos. Tíralos a la basura si no los quieres. Luego véte a estudiar, para que seas inteligente, como tu tío Frank." (*Just clear things out of the rooms. Take them to the trash if you don't want them. Then go study, so you can be smart, like your tío Frank.*)

Alonso enjoyed going through the make readies and finding useful items to take home. He found soaps, unused shampoos and other bathroom items. Sometimes piles of clothing and shoes were left behind. The last time he helped his mamá clean he found a digital player and an audio book that caught his attention: "Paranormal Advancement." The art on the audio book cover kept him from throwing it out. Stars and more stars, with purple and blue clouds floating across the background cover art. In the center, a man was sitting in a cross-legged position in a bubble with his eyes shut, wearing only what appeared to be a diaper. There was light shooting out from the center of the bald man's forehead, right out of the bubble, across the purple clouds and stars. Alonso hid this from his mamá; he knew neither she, nor Father Fuentes, would approve of his listening to it.

Before his papá had been taken away by the INS, Alonso started listening to the files of the audio book. It started with a man's voice talking over melodic flute music, instructing Alonso how to breathe deeply, to let go of all tension. The deep voice of the speaker was all it took to put Alonso to sleep with his earbuds in. He could not remember anything else from the recording after he awoke. Once, he tried to stay awake to learn more...but the only thing he could think about was Tesoro in his art class: her delicate features surrounded by jet-black, glossy hair, just like his. He went to sleep with an image of Tesoro's face spinning, spinning in his mind's eye. With his papá gone over the past week, he listened to the recording every night; the flute music lulled him to sleep during the relaxation exercise on track one.

He hoped he would find another treasure as interesting as the digital player he found a few weeks earlier. This home contained only food wrappers, a few dirty wash rags and empty cleaning bottles thrown carelessly in a corner of the bathroom. There was nothing he could keep, no matter how hard he tried to think up a use. He gathered up the items and took them to the side yard recycle bin and trash containers. Startled, Alonso stopped what he was doing; he thought he heard something in the backyard. As he looked toward the fence, he saw a black shadow moving past. He moved close to a knothole in the fence and peered through. He was met by a wet nose of a dog, sniffing at his eye.

"Hey, who are you?" Alonso pulled back from the fence and quickly raced through the home, barreling into the back yard.

The dog met him at the back patio and jumped up on Alonso with muddy paws. Happy to see someone, the thin dog let out a few low, rumbling whines as he gave Alonso's leg a hug with his front paws, resting his head on Alonso's hip. He reached down to pet the dog's head and the dog looked up at Alonso with bright, wishful eyes.

"Mamá," Alonso shouted, "¡Mamá, Aquí hay un perro!" (*There's a dog!*)

"¿Un perro, aquí?" (*Wow, a dog?*) She leaned her mop against a corner in the kitchen and followed Alonso out to the back patio.

The dog ran to greet them. Alonso said, "Sit," and the dog obeyed, staying still right in front of them. Alonso smiled; he did not want the dog to jump up on his mamá.

"¡Qué bonito está! ¿Porqué lo habrán dejado?" (*Oh, he's beautiful! Who would leave you behind?*)

She reached down to give him a rub between the ears. Alonso was already in the house, pouring a bowl of water. He took it outside and the dog gratefully lapped it up. Alonso locked his eyes with his mamá. Without saying a word, she knew what her son wanted.

"Alonso, no tenemos ni adónde caer nosotros. ¿Cómo vamos a tener un perro?" (*Alonso, we don't even have a home of our own. How can I take in a dog?*)

"Se puede quedar conmigo en el *garage*. Míralo, no podemos dejarlo aquí. ¿Lo podemos llevar con mi tío Luis, hasta que aparezcan los dueños?" (*He can stay in the garage with me. Look at him, we can't leave him here. Can we take him to tío Luis' home until we find his owners?*)

"Dále un baño primero, y cuando termines limpia la tina." (*Give him a bath first and clean out the tub when you're finished.*) She smiled over her shoulder at her son as he gathered up the black dog and carried him inside.

It was after eleven o'clock at night when Alonso and his mamá pulled up to tío Luis' home on Fennel Drive, in the barrio, just off Vance Jackson. She honked to move her nephews out of her parking spot in front of the small pink, frame house. They looked at her coolly and slunk into the yard, cigarettes in their mouths. Alonso could feel the rhythmic beat of rap coming from the open trunk of the lowrider in the driveway. In the backseat, the dog raced from window to window and Alonso knew he would need to get him out of the car quickly. The dog had the same idea and when Alonso opened the car door he bolted down Fennel Drive, his fluffy black tail flying straight out behind him.

"¡Qué raro! What was that?" Patricio yelled out from the yard as Alonso took off in pursuit. His cousins laughed at the sight of Alonso running and yelling, "Hey dog, hey dog," all the way up the narrow, car-lined road.

Out of breath from the chase and hanging tightly onto the dog's collar, Alonso made his way through the lawn chairs and people playing dominoes in tío Luis' front yard.

He heard comments, "Whose dog?" and "Wuzup dog?" But mostly, he was met with bored glances over the domino tables and the hard beat of the music playing from the "Kaotik Koupé" club car trunk. He carefully made his way through the crowd and into the garage.

"Get off my bed," Alonso said to the strangers in his garage room. They looked at him sideways without smiling and slowly worked their way to the front lawn, pulling up lawn chairs to watch Mauricio beat Patricio at dominoes once again. Patricio knocked over the table when he realized he'd lost and there were peals of laughter from everyone around, including Alonso watching from the garage. He heard his cousins giving each other a hard time, one calling the other "dough boy" and the other stating "you fat."

"Uh-oh, I know where this is going…a wrestling match on the lawn." Alonso knew it was the real reason so many people showed up at tío Luis' home; dominoes just filled the time until the real action started up.

Alonso pulled the rickety garage door shut to muffle some of the noise from the front yard. He turned around to face a very frightened dog, cowering in the far corner of the skinny garage.

"This is my room. Welcome to where I live."

CHAPTER FOUR

Boulder Turquoise and Owls

From the dimly lit back porch, Tino saw a mirror image of the moon as it slowly danced a toenail sliver reflection across the surface of the swimming pool. Nothing else moved; there was no wind in the cedar trees down the hill. It was winter in the Texas Hill Country and all life moved at a crawl to preserve itself for spring. Tino reached into his hand-sewn leather pouch and pulled out a roughly carved wooden flute. Larger than most flutes, it held a deep, haunting pitch that echoed into the quiet night.

He played his grandfather's song, the one he learned when he was ten years old. It was his favorite. He paused for a moment and waited, waited, then he heard it; the faint, familiar, "whooo, whooo" song, drifting in from the escarpment live oak tree in his neighbor's yard. His heart filled with joy as he realized the barn owls were back for the season. With this, a breeze whispered gently from the southeast, soft and humid, sending his melody into the wind, mingling with the song of the owls.

He stayed very still, not playing for a bit, waiting to hear the owls' duet. Placing the flute back into the leather pouch, he reached his hand down and turned the wheel of his wheelchair toward the backdoor.

"There you are," Tesoro said to her twin from the kitchen sink where she stood washing dishes, placing them methodically in the dishwasher.

"You were out there for a while tonight. Are the owls here yet?"

"There are more than two. I heard a younger owl. They brought a fledgling with them this year."

Tino smiled at his sister and wheeled himself across the hard tile floor up to the kitchen table.

"Do you need help with today's English assignment?" She noticed Tino sifting through the pile of papers on the table.

"Can you do it for me?" Tino teased with a glimmer in his bright eyes.

"You wish!" Tesoro placed the embroidered dish towel neatly down at the edge of the polished sink and walked over to the heavy wooden table.

"So, let's look at Mrs. Swartz's web page and see what else she wants from you tonight." Pulling the laptop across the table, Tesoro quickly logged into her brother's student account and found Mrs. Swartz's home schooling assignment for Tino.

"How's Lindsey?" Tino asked.

"She misses you." Tesoro twirled a number two pencil between her fingers as if it were a mini baton, scrolling down with the remote mouse in her other hand, reading the assignment.

Tino had difficulty concentrating on his assignment. His mind drifted off to the owls, the ancestors coming back to visit, his reminder of his grandfather and grandmother. It was almost the anniversary of their death two years ago and the accident that left him paralyzed from the waist down.

They were coming home to San Antonio from a trip to see relatives in Tonkawa, Oklahoma. Tesoro could not go on this trip; her seventh grade cross country team had a winning season that year and she stayed behind at their parents' home to train with her team.

It had been a magical trip. Tino discovered his place with his people, originally from the Edwards Plateau in the Texas Hill Country. A ceremony was held for Tino on his thirteenth birthday. He was given the sacred name of "Racing Raven" and a special silver and turquoise stone pendant. Tesoro was also to be given a pendant that his grandmother wore on her neck. It was made of boulder turquoise, with the silhouette of a wolf naturally embedded in the stone. This unique stone was encased in silver with ancient script surrounding the turquoise. She intended to give this special gift to her granddaughter when they arrived in San Antonio.

That never happened. Tino and his grandparents met with an eighteen wheeler jack-knifing out of control just south of the Red River on Interstate 35. His grandfather could not move the SUV out of the way fast enough, the trailer slammed into the front of the SUV, pushing it through the guard rail and into a ravine.

The small country hospital was not equipped to save his grandparents. Tino thought back to the nurse with the soft smile who brought a few of his grandparents' belongings to his bedside where he lay not able to move, waiting, waiting for his parents to arrive.

Tesoro reached her hand out to gently hold the side of her brother's face.

"Tino, you had a big day. Mom told me you went through four hours of physical therapy. You must be exhausted."

This brought Tino back into the moment, out of his memories that came to him every day, as if the accident had just happened.

"We can finish up your work this weekend." She stood up and pushed his wheelchair down the wide hall, across the woven wool rug and into his bathroom by the garage downstairs. He went through his nightly ritual of brushing his teeth and cleaning up at the end of the day. He thought about the irony of his name, Racing Raven, when he could not run at all. He could not even stand up to take a piss. Tesoro, or his Mom, would sometimes have to help him into his wheelchair.

Tonight, he needed to go away. Far away from the pain of therapists trying to push and move his body around after his latest back surgery. Far away from the friends he missed at school; they never came to see him anymore. He needed to escape the memory of the accident.

He looked out the open window of his room, the white linen drapes blowing gently across the rustic Saltillo tile that covered the downstairs floor. He shut his eyes and listened for the owls. "Whoo, whoo," they echoed into his dark room, "whoo, whoo."

He took a deep breath, then another. He shut his eyes and let out a soft hum upon the exhale of his breath. He could feel the familiar rocking sensation, the gentle, natural tugging from the top of his head. He could see the faint silver line with soft, purple lights leading him out of his pain, leading him to escape from his body for awhile. With no fear he let his spirit go, floating, floating down the wide hall of his home. He floated into Tesoro's room upstairs where she was still up reading, nestled in her lavender bedding with pillows all around and her grandmother's pendant sparkling around her neck. For a moment, he caught a vision of two glowing silvery-grey wolves on either side of Tesoro. One was lying down relaxed, only glancing up to acknowledge his presence in his sister's room. The other wolf stood up and walked to the edge of her bed, hackles up, baring its shining white fangs at Tino.

"Ah protection, Tesoro has protection." Tino thanked the wolves through thoughtful concentration. He focused his energy and let himself feel strong love for his sister. When Tino revealed his intent to the wolf, it settled down beside Tesoro and placed his noble head to rest between his front paws.

Effortlessly, Tino moved to a doorway at the end of the upstairs hall and could feel himself, as light as the ether, running backwards away from the door. Light rushed around him until he felt further and further away from the Earth. He quickly turned around and found himself in a different dimension. Tino knew to stop running. He stood on top of a hill with a clear view in all directions and viewed land formations that danced in staccato, jagged lines across the horizon. A cool wind rushed in suddenly, causing him to shudder. An eerie, whistling sound rose in the wind, racing across the plateaus and through the arch formations. The low sky became brilliant with shades of orange, red and a translucent violet color. This celestial place reminded Tino of the Turner watercolors he frequently viewed online, of the ocean and sky intermingled. He became enveloped in the sense of calm that he can only find in this place--a place he disappeared to every night, as he was taught to do during part of the sacred ceremony with his ancestors in Oklahoma.

He called out for his friends, the strange beings he had become very familiar with since the accident. Tonight he noticed something different; he could see someone in the distance, walking around the arch with the wind in his hair. He appeared to be searching for something, turning over stones and looking into the distance with a confused expression. Tino had never seen this being before in this realm of existence. He kept repeating the same steps, over and over again, as if stuck in a psychic glitch.

"He's lost," Tino said.

"No, he's caught up in an event horizon," a voice sounded from beside Tino. "This is what happens when someone can't let go of a thought and move on."

"How long has he been here?"

"Not long. He is quite alone in his search. I suspect he may not even know he is here. This is just a fragment of a strong emotion from Earth that we are witnessing."

"What will happen to him?"

"That's up to how he responds to the thought that has

him trapped here."

"You're no help," Tino laughed. He wished to go flying through the stars, fast, free, and far away.

CHAPTER FIVE

Flamingos and Shepherds

"**M**amá, Mi tío Frank te está llamando." (*It's tío Frank. He's calling you.*) Alonso said.

He walked past her in the kitchen on his way to the refrigerator.

"Pero mi teléfono ni está..." (*But, my phone isn't...*) and just before his mamá could get the word "ringing" out, her phone rang. Checking caller ID, she answered her phone.

"Hola Frank..." she paused, eyeing Alonso suspiciously.

"¿Sabía Alonso que me ibas a llamar?" (*Did Alonso know you were going to call?*) Lisa held her questioning gaze tight on her son.

"¿No?...Está bien...¿qué pasó?" (*No?...Okay...What's up?*)

She continued her conversation with her brother, a puzzled look on her face. "No, nunca apareció el dueño del perro. Sí, Luis nos va a dejar tenerlo aquí." (*No, we never found the owner of the dog. Yeah, Luis will let us keep him here.*)

He smiled at his mamá, gave her a shrug and slipped past her through the long skinny kitchen and into the garage. He opened the dryer and pulled out the load of clothes he had washed earlier in the day, placing the clean laundry on his bed. Immediately, the black dog jumped onto the bed, sniffed the laundry, turned a few circles and rested on Alonso's fluffy flannel shirt.

"Hey, you'll wrinkle my shirt." The dog looked at Alonso

with raised eyebrows without lifting his head from the shirt. He gave Alonso a "can't you see I'm napping" look. Alonso laughed out loud and jumped onto the bed.

"You need a name..." Alonso let out a deep sigh and reached over to pet the dog between the ears and down the snout.

"You follow me everywhere so I'll call you Sombra!" Alonso smiled at his new dog, Sombra, who moved both of his pointed ears forward.

"Do you like that name? My little shadow, Sombra!" Alonso relaxed as he stroked Sombra and shut his eyes.

He started to drift off into a nap, but just before he went into a full sleep he was engulfed in a fast, full-color image of a boy being thrown from the backseat of a car that had just been in a terrible wreck with a semi. Alonso's entire body wrenched in pain and his heart pounded. He sat straight up in bed and took in a deep breath.

"What was that? Chingado." He climbed off the bed and walked over to open the window on the side of the garage to let in the cool air. He ran his hands back through his hair, pushing his long bangs all the way off his face. He looked up at the ceiling, hands on his narrow hips, rocking from heel to toe, and heel to toe again.

Alonso wished he had a TV in his room, or anything to sidetrack his mind from what just happened. He walked over to the cardboard boxes stacked against the back wall of the garage and opened up a flap. Pulling out a picture of his papá, he clutched it to his chest. He looked up at the ceiling again. One by one, tears slowly fell across his cheek bones, across his sharp jaw line and dropped from his perfectly rounded chin. He ran his sleeve across his face, looked at the picture again and carefully placed it back into the box.

What happened to his papá when the INS took him away, just over a week ago? Why didn't anyone know where he was?

It was not the first time his papá left his family alone at their tío Luis' house. Sometimes he went back to Mexico for work. Trained as a sculptor, his papá was a top mason in Mexico, known for his craftsmanship of understanding rocks and the art of piecing stones together into aesthetically pleasing forms. He went wherever good money was to be made for his craft. Only this time, he did not leave to make money for the family.

Both of Alonso's parents worked very hard to save money. They did not want Alonso to end up like his cousins, or his sister, Lilianna, for that matter. They aspired to send him to an American university after he graduated from high school, and they knew that would be expensive. Determined to see his son get a good education, Camilo asked his brother-in-law, Frank, to mentor Alonso. Frank was the first person in the family to stay in America, become a citizen and finish college. He became an optometrist and opened his own eye clinic in Northwest San Antonio, the Garza Vision Center.

For right now, a college education seemed very distant to Alonso. At the moment, having his papá beside him to talk with seemed much more important. His papá had never been deported before, making this absence very different to Alonso. He feared his papá might be in jail. His cousins enjoyed passing on jail stories from people they knew of that went off to prison. These stories frightened Alonso, even more so with his papá in trouble. He feared his papá might be mistreated. His papá was a kind man--he couldn't bear the thought of anyone doing anything mean to him.

Alonso looked at Sombra, still laying on his freshly washed flannel shirt, and walked back over to him.

"It's okay boy, I just miss my papá." Sombra cocked his pointy, Spitz-shaped head to the side as if he understood and rolled over onto his back, letting his gangly front legs flop over his chest. Rolling his head to one side, Sombra's pink tongue hung out the side of his mouth. He gently pawed at Alonso's face.

Lilianna walked into Alonso's room from the side door to the garage. Her cheeks were flushed and she had mud all over her tight jeans. Her eyes shone bright with excitement; she tried to catch her breath, as if she'd been running. Only two years older than Alonso, at that moment in time she appeared much younger. Her expression of glee quickly changed as she noticed how glum her brother appeared.

"Hey Bro." She walked toward him, her smile fading a bit.

"¿Qué haces?" (*What are you doing?*)

"Nothing," Alonso replied without looking up.

"Do you want to go with me to see something funny?"

Alonso looked up, squinting at her. "What do you mean by funny?"

"Come on, it's right up the road at the church."

He put Sombra on a leash and walked out the garage side door with his sister. They passed the small wooden frame homes with empty flower pots in the front yards. The bare trees had lights and holiday ornaments hanging from them. Front doors were wrapped in reflective foil with decorative wreaths in the middle.

Alonso slowed his pace as they passed his favorite house: powder blue with navy blue trim. It always seemed a little crooked to him, almost as if the old roof was about to slide right off the frame. Each holiday season the elderly couple living in this home placed plastic flamingos in their front yard with blue lights going up and down in waves between the flamingos. This year they placed colorful Hawaiian flower leis around the necks of the flamingos. The couple was out tonight, relaxing on their warped front porch in brightly colored Hawaiian attire, eating their dinner on TV trays from their lawn chairs. The old man waved at Lilianna and Alonso. Alonso waved back as Lilianna gave out a musically cheerful, "Hi."

"Come on..." she said to her brother with a mischievous

grin, quickening her pace. Just as the last bit of dusk gave way to the cool, clear night sky, they rounded the corner to the Catholic Church their mamá and papá attended.

"Shhh..." Anna placed her index finger up to her mouth. "Duck behind this fence, get down low."

Sombra, sensing some type of hunt in the works, crouched low beside Alonso and Anna. They slowly peered around the fence corner to get a clear view of the front of the neighborhood church.

"What?" Alonso whispered in a sharp tone. "I don't see anyone."

"You're not supposed to see anyone. Do you see the church decorations?" He looked at the doorway to the church and initially did not see anything different: the same worn, arched, wooden doors with the rock entry and well-carved keystone at the top. He took a closer look at the oak tree and the nativity scene set up underneath the twinkling, multicolor lights in the branches. This year something was different--baby Jesus and the manger were missing. Only two life-sized mannequins dressed as shepherds stood erect under the tree.

As fast as jaguars on the prowl, his cousins ran from the side of the church, hiding in the shadows, holding something in their hands. Toying with the mannequins, Mauricio pulled the long fabric over the shepherd's head to look like a hood. Patricio rearranged their arms and duct-taped something to their hands. Stooping low in the shadows, Anna put her hand over her mouth to keep from laughing out loud.

Patricio and Mauricio arranged the cloaked shepherds in a head-on battling position instead of the traditional positioning of shepherds gazing lovingly at where the missing manger should be. They extended the toy light swords taped onto the mannequin's hands and turned them on, illuminating them for a galactic battle. The cousins scrambled to the back of the church. The familiar sound of the Impala rumbled around the corner, far away from Anna and Alonso.

CHAPTER SIX

The Test and the Cover Up

The science room was silent as Mrs. Weaver paced slowly between the desks, watching her students bent over, working hard on their tests. Alonso carefully filled in the blanks of a cell diagram, identifying all of its different components: the cytoplasm, mitochondria, nucleolus, nucleus, cell membrane, endoplasmic reticulum, lysosome, vacuole and golgi apparatus.

In his mind's eye, he could see the cell diagram he had drawn over and over again the night before and he was certain he was not missing a thing. Glancing up, Alonso could see Brett three seats in front of him still writing. He became determined to get the test completed before Brett. He wrote his name, Alonso Mendoza, at the top of the page with seventh period carefully printed below and looked around the classroom for his teacher to collect his test.

Alonso's fidgeting caught the attention of Mrs. Weaver. She collected his test with a soft smile, effortlessly gliding up the narrow aisle of desks. Feeling sleepy, Alonso pulled his flannel shirt over the back of his head and placed his head on the hard desk surface, ready for a nap. He felt his body relaxing and he drifted off into his own thoughts of art class last period. Tesoro had been asked to stand in front of the class with her drawing and explain it. He remembered how nervous she seemed in front of everyone. How she did not look up at her classmates and that he could hardly hear her whispering voice. He also noticed the pendant around her neck; it seemed to sparkle at him with a wink. The pendant moved on her chest with the rise and fall of her rapid breathing. He thought for certain he saw the silhouette of a wolf in the brown and blue stone. He squinted his eyes and concentrated his gaze, only to realize that she had quit talking and was staring right back at him. Alonso quickly looked down at his sketchbook, afraid she would think him a pervert for staring so hard. He feared she would think he was staring at her breasts; he couldn't dare look at her the rest of the class period.

Alonso squirmed in his science chair at the memory, pulling his flannel shirt a little further over his head and onto his forehead to give him a soft spot to rest. He tried to picture Tesoro's pendant with his imagination and let himself go into that place between wakefulness and deep sleep. He could see Tesoro in his mind, her gentle features, slight build and delicate hands with black fingernail polish, wearing a silver ring on each finger. Her straight, shiny, jet-black hair, just past her shoulders, cut in a jagged way that he thought resembled an anime cartoon character. Her almond-shaped eyes were framed by heavily applied black eyeliner, Egyptian style, giving the whites of her eyes a mysterious glow. She seemed mythical, poetic, graceful, and untouchable, the most beautiful girl in school. As he focused on holding this image of her in his mind, he caught a glimpse of an old woman with thinning, silver-white hair kneeling beside her, petting a giant silver wolf. Then another wolf walked right in front the old woman to the opposite side of Tesoro and sat down next to her. Alonso's vision came and went in a quick flash. He shifted a bit in his desk, nestled his head into his shirt and drifted into a deep sleep.

"Hey, ya gonna spend the night here?" Tracy's voice in the distance brought him out of his snooze.

"Class is over?" Sleepily, he looked up at her through squinted eyes.

"For a few minutes already. Even Mrs. Weaver tore out of here. The test took me right to the bell, or I wouldn't be here either."

"Oh." Alonso pulled his warm flannel shirt back over his body, stretched in his seat and reached down for his backpack from the floor and stood up.

"Don't you have cheer practice? It's Monday."

"Yeah, I didn't want to leave you to be discovered by the custodians late at night."

She gave him a shove in the arm, turned quickly around, flipped her red hair off her shoulder and danced to the door, singing to herself.

Alonso stepped forward to leave the classroom himself when something tugged at his foot and he tripped, falling loudly into the desk to the side of him. He looked down--the shoelaces of his Chucks were tied together. He heard laughter from outside the classroom door. Marcus and Tracy peered around the corner of the door jam.

"Dude, you were hilarious," Marcus spurted out through his laughter.

"Shut up fool! I know you did this just to get back at me for the time I threw your backpack in the trash," said Alonso laughing himself as he untied the knotted laces. "We're even now."

"You guys still here?" Mrs. Weaver had re-entered the classroom.

"Just bringing Alonso back from dreamland," Tracy said.

"Alonso, I'm glad you're here. Do you have a minute to talk?"

"My ride doesn't come till 4:30. I guess I do." He waved to Marcus and Tracy, who slipped past the doorway.

"Have you given any further thought to the science contest?"

"Nothing's come to me yet."

"You realize I wouldn't have asked you to participate if I

didn't believe that you were capable of coming through on this."

"Yes ma'am." Alonso pulled his backpack tighter across his shoulder. "It's just I'm having trouble coming up with an idea."

Alonso could not tell her how concerned he was for his papá, and how this is what was really taking up all of his thinking time.

"Alonso, ideas, just as life, are all around you. Slow down and look, look and think."

He said, "Okay," although he wasn't certain what she meant. "Can I go now?"

"Yes. Let me know if you have any questions. Why don't you get on my teacher web site. I have a ton of links there to help you get started." She sat at her desk, facing a mountain of ungraded science tests.

Alonso left her room downhearted--how could he get ideas from her web site when tío Luis did not have a computer at his home? Coming to school early was his only access to the internet and this depended on his ride to and from school. His mamá always got him to first period on time and he was grateful for that. His attendance was almost perfect, even with his messed-up home life.

For now, he needed to hurry outside. Lilianna would leave him at school if he was not outside when she pulled up. He would have to call her from the school's office phone and beg her to come back to pick him up. This made her protest and she would give him excuses for not coming back to the school, all the time with Alonso knowing that she went up to road to the local coffee house to hang out with her friends. It was a game they played.

He thought back to the times his sister did not pick him up at Flores. Lilianna went to the school in their neighborhood, not Flores High School. Sometimes she served after-school detentions and could not pick him up on time. Alonso was grateful that tío Frank had signed him up at Flores High School. His tío Frank and tía Ruby lived in the school's boundaries, allowing Alonso to attend school there by placing their address on the school records as his current place of residence. Alonso knew this wasn't right, but his parents convinced him it was the right thing to do for his future. With all of the trouble his sister and cousins got into at their school, he understood that it really was the best decision. He liked Flores High and could not imagine going to any other school.

Alonso reached the stairwell in front of the school just as the Impala pulled up. It was the usual quiet ride home with Lilianna, her listening to songs through her earbuds and Alonso looking out the window across Interstate 10. They pulled up to tío Luis' small frame home just off Vance Jackson in the barrio and parked the Impala behind a car he did not recognize.

"That's Father Fuentes' car." Lilianna looked at Alonso.

"The shepherds battling it out with lightsabers. What should we do?" Alonso asked. Patricio and Mauricio were already in trouble with their papá. Tío Luis let them know if they messed up again they would be out on the streets without a place to live. Everyone in the family was very concerned for his cousins; they knew tío Luis meant business.

"Let me talk," Lilianna said softly, walking in front of her younger brother toward the house.

The heavy smell of picadillo with onions, tomatoes, cumin, garlic and beef slow cooked on the stove top, laden the air of the entire house. The mini-blinds were pulled shut in the front room and there was no light other than the television talk show playing in the background with the sound off. Father Fuentes held his stocky body on the edge of a wooden chair. Lisa leaned back into the well-worn plaid sofa as her children entered. They stopped talking.

"Hola mamá." Lilianna broke the silence with an overly

cheerful greeting. She looked at Father Fuentes, flashing her most charming smile.

"Why don't both of you have a seat with us?" Father Fuentes motioned his hand toward the remaining seats in the room. Alonso and Anna slowly slunk into the hard wooden chairs.

After an awkward silence, Father Fuentes spoke up, "As you may know, I'm here on important business."

He hesitated, peering through his thick, tortoise shell-rimmed glasses.

"There's been an incident at the church. I have reason to believe the two of you were involved."

Lilianna peered down at the worn, tan area rug and Alonso looked at his sister, waiting for her to respond.

"I also have reason to suspect Mauricio and Patricio were involved. It seems someone had a poor idea of a practical joke and rearranged the nativity scene. What do you two know about this?"

"It was me, Father." Lilianna was unable to make eye contact with anyone in the room, her thick black hair falling around her perfectly heart-shaped face.

"Were Mauricio and Patricio involved with this in any way?"

"No." Alonso could not believe his ears. He could not believe that Lilianna was taking the full blame for their cousins.

"No one else?" Father Fuentes leaned forward, his elbows on his knees and his short hands folded in front of himself, as if in deep prayer. He narrowed his eyes, causing his round face to appear even more spherical than usual.

"There were witnesses that saw both of you walking in the neighborhood. Why did you do it?"

"I thought it was funny." Lilianna glanced up, hoping to

gain his favor. She did not.

"Lilianna, I'm disappointed in you. You've left me no choice but to file a criminal mischief charge. I will consider dropping the charges should you change your mind and tell me the entire truth."

Father Fuentes stood up, whispered a quick prayer blessing in Spanish to Lisa Mendoza, as he held her hands in his.

"Father, a criminal mischief charge? Isn't that a misdemeanor? Don't you think that seems a little harsh?" Alonso questioned.

"Were you involved?"

"No sir." Alonso looked down.

"If either of you decide to tell me the truth, I will consider dropping the charges." Father Fuentes let himself out the front door.

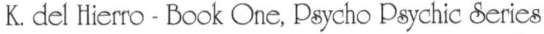

CHAPTER SEVEN

Migas and Eye Exams

Digging deep into his duffle bag, Alonso pulled out his "Paranormal Advancement" recording, shut his eyes and listened. He hoped this would relax him so he could finally go to sleep. He worked through the deep breathing exercises and then concentrated on relaxing with the speaker guiding him, asking him to release tension from the muscle groups in his body. For the first time ever while listening to this recording, he was able to stay awake.

He listened to more of the recording than ever before. The hypnotic voice of the male speaker led Alonso into deep relaxation. There was an odd, pulling sensation from his chest and he felt a rocking sensation. He realized he was floating, looking down at himself. He was out of his body! This felt very natural and somewhat curious to Alonso. Consciously aware that, with just a thought, he could re-enter his body again...and that's exactly what he did.

He opened his eyes and, for a moment, thought he saw a glimpse of the old woman with silver hair pass right by the edge of the bed--the same woman from the sleepy vision he had of Tesoro in art class. The old woman motioned for Alonso to follow her, turned away from him and then disappeared as quickly as she had appeared. He sat up in bed and looked around the large room, so tidy with everything so new. It even smelled different than his room in the garage. All of the bedding was heavily scented with fabric softener and bleach. It smelled clean.

So much had happened after Father Fuentes left that it

left him disoriented and spinning. Alonso's mamá did not hesitate to discipline after she found out that Lilianna had lied about their cousins' involvement with the nativity scene at the church. Her first decision, after she found out the truth, was to send Alonso to live with his tío Frank and tía Ruby in their Northwestern neighborhood in San Antonio. Lilianna did not have it as easy; she had to go to court with her cousins. They ruled eighty hours of community service at the church, doing any work Father Fuentes asked of them. They were also assigned a curfew time of six o'clock every evening and a weekly meeting with a probation officer. Tío Luis allowed Patricio and Mauricio to stay at his home, as long as they met their probation.

Alonso's mamá delivered his sentence shortly after Father Fuentes paid his visit to question Anna and Alonso. After a few phone calls to her brother, Frank, she gave Alonso two hours to pack up his belongings into one of his papá's old duffle bags.

He carefully chose the items he wanted to bring with him: his favorite flannel shirts, the silver chain he hung from his black skinny jeans, boxers, socks, and graphic print tee-shirts. His Chucks were on his feet. He crammed his sketchbook and drawing pencils sideways into the bag. Reaching low into the long boxes under his bed, he pulled out the digital player with the "Paranormal Advancement" recording. He placed it in between a carefully folded pair of jeans in the duffle bag. He knew there was something he was forgetting and then he saw it, sticking slightly out of the corner of a cardboard box--the picture of his papá. He pulled it out, placed it in between the pages of his science book and tucked it into his backpack.

Alonso had trouble getting comfortable in his new room in tío Frank's large house. The ceilings were tall, with a five-blade ceiling fan circling rapidly above. The double window facing the back of the house appeared as if it had never been opened. The entire place felt empty to him: too quiet, too big, and too *clean*. He missed the noise his cousins made playing dominoes with their homies in the front yard. He missed his sister singing and dancing around the house with her earbuds in. He missed riding to school with his mamá and talking with her every day. Alonso realized that things had changed at his tío Luis' home, also. He imagined how quiet the front yard must be with his cousins and sister on probation. Alonso hoped they were doing the right thing so life could return to normal and he could go back to his room in the garage.

Alonso was grateful that tío Frank had allowed Sombra to come with him. He wished they would allow Sombra to sleep with him, but Sombra's new fluffy bed stayed in the laundry room by the garage. Granted, the laundry room was the size of most bedrooms; it even had a sink and a window. Tía Ruby purchased Sombra chew toys and tasty bones to keep him occupied. But Alonso missed him. He felt lonely without Sombra beside him at night and he was certain that Sombra missed him, also.

Alonso opened his science textbook and turned to the page that diagrammed the solar system. He gently pulled out the picture of his papá tucked between the pages, placing the photo upright against the lamp on the nightstand. Would he ever see his papá again? He wished with all of his might that he could travel out of his body and fly to the place where his papá might be...and realized he might possibly be able to do exactly that! He *did* just leave his body for a moment when he listened to the meditation exercises from the "Paranormal Advancement" recording. He didn't think it was his imagination at all; the experience felt real and strangely normal, as normal as breathing itself.

Rolling onto his back, Alonso moved the photo of his papá to his stomach, pressed play on the digital recorder and shut his eyes. Within moments, he cleared his mind of everything but one singular thought: an image of his papá. He felt himself becoming sleepy, as the deep voice droned on through the earbuds. His thoughts drifted to images of Tesoro, her smiling at him. Thinking about Tesoro made him particularly happy and he slipped into a sound sleep with the recording playing deep into the night.

The sound of the alarm clock echoed into his dream of a faraway place. Although he could hear the incessant *beep, beep, beep,* he did not realize it was the clock. In his dream he saw a raven circling above his head, screeching. He felt the wind on his back and teetered on the ledge of a tall cliff. In the far distance, a large cloaked man and a younger person walked side by side. Alonso leaned forward on the ledge to get a better view and toppled off, spinning, falling quickly to the ground below. The beeping of the alarm became louder and louder-startled, he sat straight up in bed, reached over and hit snooze-he wished to stay in bed longer and pulled the crisp new cotton sheet right over his head.

Not able to go back to sleep he tossed and turned, disappointed that he slept through the entire recording without even a hint of his papá's whereabouts. Upset that the only dream he could remember was the one he just had about falling, he pulled out the earbuds and crammed them into the nightstand drawer. Below him on the first floor he could hear faint sounds coming from the kitchen. Tía Ruby was cooking again--she made sure Alonso didn't go hungry. The smell of fresh migas drifted through the house and lured Alonso out of bed.

Tía Ruby stood in front of the giant chef-style stove with double burners. She juggled cut up corn tortillas, cooking them in hot oil in an iron skillet. In the other skillet she poured golden whipped eggs into a mixture of sautéed hot jalapeños, onions and tomatoes. Carefully, she used a spatula to retrieve the crispy tortillas from the oil and stirred them into the hot egg mixture. Alonso's stomach gave an audible growl; Sombra scratched on the laundry room door, wanting to join in the morning breakfast.

"¡Hola! How did you sleep? Any better?" she asked. "Hey, can you get the shredded cheese out of the fridge for me? It's in the second drawer down on the right."

"I slept okay. I would sleep much better if Sombra could stay in the room with me." Alonso said and brought her the cheddar cheese.

Tía Ruby smiled and placed the steaming plate of food on the cool granite island bar in the center of the large kitchen. "Do you want orange juice?"

"I can pour it."

"Pour me a glass, too." Still smiling, she placed the silverware on the colorful, woven placemats.

"Hey, do you have a headache? You keep rubbing your forehead," She noticed.

"No, my skin feels tight right between my eyes. That's been happening to me lately. It's not a headache. It helps if I rub it." Alonso said and bent down to rub his forehead in tiny circles. When he did this, the hand-blown glass light fixture above the kitchen island dimmed.

"Hope that's not a short." Tía Ruby said and glanced up at the flickering fixture.

"When's the last time you've had your eyes checked?"

"Never," he said with a shrug, spooning in another mouthful of migas.

"Can you see the front of the classroom without any problem?"

"I see just fine." He paused, thinking back to the glimpse of the old woman he thought he saw in the room last night.

"Are you sure?"

Alonso stayed quiet for a moment, drinking his juice; he realized maybe he wasn't seeing "just fine." For the past few weeks he had been seeing glimmers of lights, glimpses of little glowing orbs of varying size and color. Sometimes he saw these sparkling clouds of light encircling people. Sombra had a dark blue glow coming right off his shoulders most of the time. Alonso found the lights curious and not frightening at all. It seemed that this is how he should be seeing everything; it felt very natural. But now, talking with tía Ruby, he became concerned.

"Should I have an eye exam?"

"Your tío Frank would be happy to give you an exam. I'll call him later to set up a time after school today." Tía Ruby reached down to give Sombra a pat on the head. "He needs to go for his morning walk."

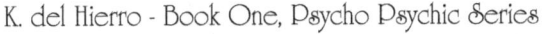

CHAPTER EIGHT

Car Wrecks and Cartwheels

"**W**hy are you pacing?" Tino asked.

"I'm waiting for the bus," Tesoro said, peering through the front window without taking her eyes off the street.

"You've never been worried about the bus. What's going on?" Tino wheeled himself up to the window beside Tesoro.

"I don't want to miss it."

"Why not?" Tino asked. Tesoro gazed blankly down the empty suburban road.

He studied her as she reapplied her lip gloss. "Who on the bus are you trying to impress? Is that what the extra lip gloss is all about?"

"That's none of your business;" she giggled, swatting him lightly on the shoulder.

"Oww, you just hit a gimp," he laughed. "Who is he?"

"Just a guy from school." She picked up her backpack from the living room floor.

"He started riding my bus a few days ago."

"Yeah, do you like him?"

"He's, well, he's different from the other guys, he's quiet and smart."

"Is he hot?" He reached out to thump her on her elbow.

"Owee, you just hit a girl!"

"I didn't hurt you nearly as bad as you hurt me…so, do you like this hot guy?"

"I don't really know him." Tesoro was relieved at the sight of the big yellow bus lumbering up the street. She didn't want to answer any more of her brother's questions; she didn't know the answers herself.

Tesoro boarded the bus, searching for an empty seat close to the front. Her plan was to ask Alonso if he would like to sit by her. All week he had sat with Tracy. She wanted to ask Tracy if they were going out, but she was far too shy to ask. Anyway, what could she do if they were going out? Placing her backpack in the empty seat beside her, Tesoro slumped down in her seat for the next few streets.

"Hey, Alonso!" Tracy yelled from the middle of the bus. Alonso offered a quick smile and walked by Tesoro so quickly that she didn't have a chance to say anything. To distract herself from the missed opportunity, she pulled her backpack onto her lap and started to make certain all of her homework made it into the correct folders. She strained her ears to hear their conversation five seats back. All she could make out was both of them reviewing vocabulary words for their English class. She could see Alonso in the bus driver's mirror. She noticed he suddenly stopped talking to Tracy and was looking keenly out the window at the lane of traffic just beside them.

Suddenly, he jumped up out of his seat and plopped down on the edge of the empty seat right next to Tesoro. He leaned forward into ear range of the bus driver.

"You need to slow down. Do you see that white truck passing us? It's in front of us now, slow down." Alonso said in a firm, low voice. "Slow down!"

"Okay, I'm slowing down. What's up with the truck?" The bus driver looked puzzled.

The moment the bus driver took his foot off the gas, the truck made a sudden lane change in front of a small car, gauging the distance incorrectly and hitting it. The small car spun to the side of the road and the collision caused the truck to lose control--it plowed right into oncoming traffic. The bus driver, with fast reflexes, slammed on the brakes. Cars went flying in every direction around the bus. The sound of tires screeching and metal slamming into metal sounded in everyone's ears. Some of the children on the bus fell to the floor and some crashed into the seat in front of them.

Alonso looked over at Tesoro. "Are you alright?" She did not know what to say; she could not believe what she witnessed. How could he have known something was going to happen with the white truck? If the bus driver had not slowed down, as Alonso had demanded, they would have been involved in the accident, too.

The bus driver turned around to look at the children. "It's alright boys and girls. Is anyone back there hurt?"

"We're all okay," a boy yelled loudly from the back of the bus as the teens pulled themselves onto their seats.

Looking back at Alonso, the bus driver appeared perplexed and simply asked, "How?"

Alonso shrugged. "I just knew, something inside me just knew, when I saw that truck."

Backpacks were strewn all over the aisle of the bus. Alonso bent down to pick Tesoro's backpack up from the floor and smiled as he handed it over. Tesoro took her backpack slowly onto her lap and watched Alonso walk back to his seat next to Tracy.

~

At lunch later that day, Tesoro went to find Alonso in the cafeteria. Weaving between the long tables loaded down with pizza, she made her way to the table where Alonso usually sat. He wasn't there.

Tracy saw Tesoro and stood up as she got closer. "Hey, do

you want to sit with us?"

Tesoro shook her head no. "I'm trying to find Alonso. I want to thank him for what he did this morning on the bus."

Tracy looked confused. "What did he do on the bus?"

"He stopped us from getting into that accident."

"Wow, a superhero. How did he manage to save us from such peril?"

"That's just it, I don't know. It was freaky, it's as if he knew the future. He told the bus driver to slow down right before the accident happened."

Tracy looked up at Tesoro with a serious expression. "Yeah, I wondered what he was telling the bus driver. Weird things have been going on with him lately. I don't even know if he's noticing what's up."

"Yeah, like what?"

Tracy motioned for Tesoro to sit down beside her, within closer ear range in the loud cafeteria. Tracy leaned in closely to Tesoro and whispered: "Flickering lights."

"What?" Tesoro moved back and peered at Tracy with squinted eyes.

"When he is in science class the lights above his head flash on and off. When he leaves, the lights stay on."

"Maybe the bulb is going dead," Tesoro said. "So what does that have to do with the bus this morning?"

"I don't know. I'm just picking up on something peculiar going on with him."

The bell sounded and students whisked around Tesoro, taking their lunch trays to the front of the cafeteria. The coach who worked lunch duty barked over the loudspeaker, reminding everyone to pick up their trash and to remember to cheer loudly for the basketball team at the pep rally this afternoon.

"Go Cougars!" Tracy cheered loudly as she bounced her uniform-clad body across the lunch room floor, away from Tesoro.

Students packed themselves into the old gymnasium later that afternoon. It always smelled sweaty and musty to Tesoro. She sat as far away as possible from the smell of the boys' locker room and the deafening blare of the band. The loud banging of the drums hurt her ears. She climbed up the rickety wooden bleachers all of the way to the upper back wall and found her friends huddled together in a mass of black clothing. Most of the students on the back row had already pulled up their hoodies to hide their earbuds. Tesoro pulled out her earbud set, placed it around the back of her neck and leaned against the cord, her hair covering the wires. Just as she settled in for the hour-long show, her phone vibrated in her pocket.

She read the text from her brother: "Is he hot?" She laughed out loud and she shoved the phone back into her pocket before a teacher could see it.

She spotted Tracy on the gym floor with the rest of the cheerleaders, performing gymnastics on a long mat in front of the crowd. Tracy executed a perfect front flip, followed by three roundoff back handsprings and a cartwheel.

"Impressive," Tesoro said. She continued to watch Tracy bounce to the side of the gym, waving and smiling at the cheering crowd.

As Tesoro gazed at the band far below, something glimmered to the far right of her, a light flickering off and on. Tesoro's heart skipped a beat as she looked down from the light and into the crowd below. It was there, under the flickering light, that she spotted Alonso. He was huddled over something on his lap with his black hair all the way over his face. Tesoro could make out a shoe in his hands; he was in the act of tearing apart a shoe. Not just any shoe, one exactly the same as Assistant Principal Martin wore with coil springs on the heels. She had heard jokes around school about Assistant Principal Martin not being able to move very fast, even with his spring-loaded shoes. Those were the ugliest shoes ever invented, in Tesoro's opinion, completely lacking any enduring aesthetic qualities.

"No, not hot, lukewarm, at best, but not hot," she said under her breath as she watched Alonso mechanically rip the sole right off the bottom of the shoe.

"He's getting a referral for that if he gets caught." Tesoro pointed him out to her friends surrounding her in the bleachers. She leaned back against the wall and directed her attention to the band.

The light above Alonso's head flickered, fizzed and went black--completely unnoticed by the entire school population packed into the old gymnasium.

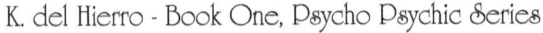

CHAPTER NINE

Shoes and Electricity

The night was deepest black, cloudy, not a star in sight. Perfect, thought Alonso, as he rolled on the sides of his feet from heel to toe in total silence, past tío Frank and tía Ruby's bedroom door and to the laundry room downstairs. Slowly he cracked open the door, hoping he would not startle Sombra. He whispered Sombra's name and the dog looked up at Alonso, slowly wagging his curled tail.

"Hey boy, you're coming upstairs with me." Sombra rose from his designer doggie bed, stretched out his right front paw and yawned, tongue curling in his mouth. After giving his head a little shake, he came to Alonso and placed his muzzle against his leg. Reaching down to pet Sombra, Alonso took off his collar so it would not jangle and they silently made their way upstairs.

Back in his room, Alonso patted his hand on the bed to let Sombra know he had permission to jump on it. Sombra did not hesitate; he leapt onto the fluffy bedding, turned a few circles and nestled onto one of the four large pillows on the bed. Feeling better with Sombra in the room, Alonso set out to finish the task he started at the pep assembly in the gym: tonight he would turn the recycled shoe into an energy producing device.

Alonso removed the torn up shoe from his backpack, his plan completely sketched out in his mind. A few nights earlier, when he fell asleep listening to the "Paranormal Advancement" recording, he had a vivid vision-type dream that woke him up. He dreamt that Assistant Principal Martin was chasing Brett through the school's outdoor courtyard, away from the cafeteria. Every time A.P. Martin took a step in his shoes with springs in the heels he received an electrical shock up his leg. Alonso could see the electricity shoot up his limbs in bluish-white, spider web patterns of brilliant light.

At first Alonso dismissed the dream as nonsense, but he could not get the image of electricity shooting up A.P. Martin's leg out of his mind. Right before gym class the next day, he watched A.P. Martin walk across the gymnasium to the boy's locker room. Alonso noticed how quickly A.P. Martin moved across the old wooden floor and the exertion he exuded with each step he took. Energy was the word that resonated with Alonso from his dream--the dream that now made perfect sense.

From the desk in the bedroom he picked up a pair of pliers and removed the spring from the heel of the donated shoe from tío Frank, the same shoe AP Martin wore. He carefully held one end of the exposed springs and wrapped it from top to bottom in a thin copper wire. Picking up the bottom of the disassembled shoe, he used a powerful glue to hold a magnet in place upright in the center of the heel. Carefully slipping the copper-covered spring over the magnet, he wired the components to a diode that would serve as a rectifier to turn alternating current into direct current. Alonso needed direct current for his invention. He was going to try and recharge the 4.2 volt lithium-ion battery for his phone.

Alonso found his cell phone charger and gingerly snipped the wall plug off the wire. He exposed the two wires coming from the cord and twisted them into place on the diode by the shoe spring. He neatly tucked all of the electrical components into the heel of the shoe and carefully reassembled the heel. This left the power cord for his phone protruding from the side of the shoe. He placed the shoe on his foot and plugged in his phone. Furiously pumping his heel up and down, the power bar on his phone registered a positive charge!

"It works!" Exuberant and exhausted, Alonso pushed a

reluctant Sombra to the side of the bed and fell down beside him. Holding the phone in his hand, the shoe on his foot and still dressed in his school clothes, he fell asleep.

The next morning, the sunlight rolled slowly across the bedroom, over the desk with the tools and onto Alonso's face. A tap-tap, sounded on the door.

"Alonso, are you going to school today?" tía Ruby called through the closed door.

"Do you have Sombra in there? He's not in the laundry room."

"Uh, oh," Alonso muttered. "I'll be out in a minute." Checking the time on his phone, he realized he had fifteen minutes to catch the bus...no time to change clothes. Scrambling, he crammed his study books into his backpack and threw the shoe project on top of everything. He zipped up his bag; Sombra followed him downstairs.

In the kitchen, tía Ruby suspiciously eyed Alonso and Sombra, pulling her house robe tighter around her waist.

"Did you let Sombra sleep with you last night?"

"Are you mad at me?" Alonso looked at the ground, ashamed.

"I can hear the bus! You better get outside, rápido." Tía Ruby threw a breakfast bar at Alonso. "Let's talk about what happened later today. Don't forget your eye appointment with your tío Frank. I'm picking you up from school."

"Thank you tía Ruby!"

He bolted out of the house, ran full speed to the corner and boarded the bus just in the nick of time.

Tracy did not save him a seat; sitting right next to her was Tesoro. They both looked at him strangely as he approached. He took the empty seat just across the aisle from them. Opening up his backpack, he took out the spring-loaded shoe and put it on his foot. Tesoro and Tracy were whispering between themselves. Turning back around in his seat, Alonso took his phone out of his pocket and plugged it into the wire attached to the shoe. He rapidly pumped his foot up and down on the hard metal floor of the bus.

"Yes!" he yelled out, oblivious to the stares of the students around him. Alonso's phone battery icon again registered a fast charge.

"That's what I'm talking about!"

"What?" Tesoro asked.

"Come over here and I'll show you."

With her eyes wide in excitement, Tesoro moved beside Alonso and looked at the phone in his hand. He passed the phone to her, still pumping his heel, but without as much vigor. As his hand momentarily touched hers Alonso felt a tingle rise up his arm and settle deep into the base of his spine. He heard Tesoro catch her breath as she held the phone in her hands, peering at the screen--the battery icon was displaying a power up symbol.

"How are you doing that?" she asked.

"It's the shoe. I built a power source in the heel. My own momentum is creating an electrical current."

"Wow," was all Tesoro said.

"Electrical current," he whispered. She handed the phone back to him. He gently slid the phone from her hand and their gaze met. Incapable of producing words, and with barely taking a breath, they looked deeply into each other's eyes. They were close, closer than they'd ever been, their shoulders touching--Alonso tingled with the vibrant energy between them, completely overwhelmed. Tesoro silently moved back into the seat beside Tracy, who had watched the entire scene between Alonso and Tesoro with a smile she could not wipe off her face.

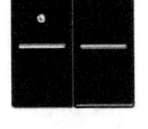

CHAPTER TEN

Portraits and Optometry

The art room was quiet, unusual for this particular class. The art teacher had given a drawing assignment: students had to choose a partner to sit across from to draw while the other person drew them in return. The teacher instructed there was to be no talking during the assignment. After awkward giggling and a few minutes for the students to settle down, the class began to draw each other from across the tables. After about fifteen minutes the teacher asked the students to move to another table and draw a new person. Alonso stood up and looked around the room for an open seat. There were two seats open, one across from the biggest stoner in the school and the other one across from Tesoro. It only took him only a second to grab up the chair across from Tesoro.

"Hi," he whispered, as she put her head down, breaking eye contact with him. The class was still settling in, with students giggling nervously and talking.

"What's on your necklace?" Alonso asked, noticing her squirming and fidgeting in her seat.

"My grandmother left this for me after she died. It's boulder turquoise, that's why it's brown and blue." She reached around her neck, unclasped the necklace and handed it to him. "Do you see the wolf in the stone?"

"It's beautiful, like you," flew out of his mouth before he could stop himself. Tesoro peered anxiously around the class, biting her lip and looked down at the blank page in her sketchbook. She picked up her pencil and held it slightly above the white paper. Her hand shook ever so slightly. Glancing up at Alonso's intense gaze she dropped her pencil and moved her hands under the table. Alonso placed her necklace gently on top of her sketchbook without breaking eye contact. She picked it up and fastened it around the back of her neck with trembling fingers.

"I guess we have to draw each other," Alonso whispered. The room was silent except for pencils scratching across paper and tables wiggling as students squirmed uneasily. Tesoro looked down; she clasped her trembling hands underneath the table out of view.

"I didn't mean to embarrass you," Alonso said. Tesoro smiled slightly, still not looking up.

"You are beautiful," he whispered. Tesoro raised her finger to her mouth and shushed him with a playful grin. Just when he thought she was relaxing, an office aide burst into the room and handed the teacher a slip of paper.

"Alonso Mendoza." The teacher signaled Alonso to the front of the classroom. Alonso took the slip--tía Ruby and the eye appointment. He glanced back over his shoulder at Tesoro, who was now feverishly drawing in her sketchbook. For an instant he saw a soft lavender glow with bursts of luminous white sparks surrounding her.

Rubbing his eyes, he picked up his backpack from the art room floor and walked down the empty hall. At his locker Alonso reached into his backpack and pulled out his energy shoe project, disappointed he would not be able to show Mrs. Weaver his invention next period. He wrapped the cord neatly around the shoe and tucked it on top of his gym clothes in his locker, safe for the weekend.

Tío Frank's optometrist office, the Garza Vision Center, was a quick drive up de Zavala. Alonso and tía Ruby made a grand entrance; the women at the front desk turned their attention fully to Alonso.

"It's so good to meet you finally Alonso! We've heard so much about you." The well-dressed receptionist reached to shake Alonso's hand.

"Your uncle didn't tell us how cute you are," said the doctor's assistant.

"Look at those big, brown eyes--if you aren't just the cat's meow! I bet the girls love you!" the receptionist said.

Alonso quickly escaped their banter and slipped into a side room that held many different types of eye glasses. He tried on a few frames and viewed himself in the mirror. He was a mess. From the full length mirror, a dirty dork with dark rimmed glasses, slightly crooked on his face, stared back at him. He pulled his long, greasy bangs off his forehead, holding them back tight across his head. Amused by his reflection, Alonso pulled his lips in tight until it appeared he had only a dark sliver for his mouth. He realized he had not bathed, nor changed clothes since the previous morning. His garments were wrinkled from head to toe. No wonder Tesoro had looked so frightened.

Directly behind him he heard a rustle, then a click. Whirling around, Alonso caught the last movements of his tía Ruby taking a picture of his reflection in the mirror with her phone.

"Now there's one for the on-line family photo album," she said, grinning ear to ear, as she reviewed the photo on the screen. She was beaming, as if she had just spotted treasure.

"Alonso, you're a mess." She moved in, assessing him closer. "Are those the same clothes you wore to school yesterday?"

"Por favor, tía Ruby, don't put that picture on the internet."

"Too late, it's already added." She tucked her phone into her leather purse.

"Seriously, what happened to you, why didn't you change out of your dirty clothes?"

"I worked on a school project almost all night and then I fell asleep without changing. When you woke me up I didn't have time to change without being late. You just now noticed?"

"Your tío Frank is not going to appreciate seeing you like this; especially after I took you shopping for your new wardrobe." She shook her head with an expression of dismay.

"I suppose it's okay…if you did it for the sake of your studies. I can remember your tío Frank dressing the same way going through college. Just to let you know, that look is most certainly not the way to be a chick magnet."

"Ruby, I don't think he has to try to be a chick magnet, he's one naturally!" The doctor's assistant rounded the corner.

"Follow me, Alonso."

She whisked him away into a dim room with many odd machines on a rotating table. After shining bright lights into Alonso's eyes for the next ten minutes, the assistant took Alonso into a long skinny room and sat him down on a pale-green medical chair. Tío Frank entered and tested Alonso's vision.

"Your tía Ruby let me know that you are seeing spots," tío Frank said, entering Alonso's information into the computer. "Tell me what's going on with that."

"Lights, I'm seeing lights around people and animals, too."

"Your eyes checked out fine, you have excellent vision." Tío Frank turned around in his chair and faced Alonso. "Almost sounds as if you are seeing auras."

"Seeing what?" Alonso was uncertain that he heard his tío correctly. He'd heard about auras from Father Fuentes' mass services. Auras are something holy figures emanate: Saints, Jesus, Angels and Mother Mary.

"People's energy field, auras, some people believe they are seeing a person's spirit," tío Frank said. Pausing, he eyed Alonso carefully for a response. "Nonetheless, I think it would be a good idea to have you checked out by a neurologist." Tío Frank picked up a phone and called the neurology office to establish Alonso as a patient.

"When's the last time you've had a full medical exam?" he asked, placing his hand over the receiver of the phone.

"I can't remember. I don't know if I've ever had one."

"Well then, I'll set an exam up for you. I know just the doctor."

"My art and science classes are at the end of the day and I don't want to miss them. Can you make the appointment for first thing in the morning?"

"Consider it done...are you ready to get out of here? Let's find your tía Ruby and eat dinner together."

When they entered Pirelli's Place, Alonso's eyes widened at the twinkling chandeliers in the entry and the large perfectly arranged fresh flowers on the polished, dark wood round table. He imagined this is where people that live in the Mansiones de Piedra Blanca dine. He felt especially self conscious in his wrinkled, unwashed garments. Girls not much older than he was escorted them through the restaurant to their table. Alonso thought the girls looked unapproachable in their sleek, black dresses as they sashayed through the opulent setting.

Tío Frank asked, "What do you think?"

Alonso looked down from the fresco ceiling of cherubs in clouds surrounded by grapevines. "It's elegant. I like all of the fresh flowers everywhere. How did they get the water to light up in the vases?"

He pointing to the tall, cylindrical glass vases, each holding clear marbles at the bottom with white orchids submerged in water. Light emanated from the bottom of the vases, reflecting a deep blue glow onto the flowers.

"That's a submersible light. Pretty cool looking, huh?" Tía Ruby chimed in.

"Yeah, it's kinda like the glow I see around people sometimes." There was an uncomfortable pause in the conversation. His tío and tía shot quick glances at each other.

"Hey," tío Frank said loudly, clearing his throat to break the silence, "your tía Ruby and I are going out of town for the weekend. I've already spoken to your mamá and she thinks it's a good idea for you to stay with her at tío Luis'."

"For good?" Alonso looked at him in surprise.

"No, just for the weekend. Your mamá misses you and wants to see you. You will need to pack up a few things after we eat and then I'll take you there."

Strangely, Alonso was growing used to staying with his tío Frank and tía Ruby. But he did miss his mamá and his sister and was excited at the thought of seeing them, instead of just talking with them on the phone.

CHAPTER ELEVEN

Airbrushing and Direct Current

"¡**Q**ué onda, primo!"

(*What's up, cousin!*) Patricio yelled from the side of the Impala in the driveway.

"Hola Patricio," Alonso yelled back, getting out of his tío Frank's SUV.

"Where's Mauricio?"

Just then, he noticed Mauricio's feet hanging out from under the 1969 Impala.

"Whatcha doing to the Impala?" Alonso walked to the side of the old car, joining his cousins.

"Taking it to a whole 'nother level, if you know what I mean." Patricio wore a sly grin as he juggled two wrenches.

"Hey fool, don't drop those on me," Mauricio warned from under the car, his voice a high pitch.

"Give me that wrench." He quickly rolled out from under the chassis and grabbed the wrench from his brother's hand. Leaping out of the SUV, Sombra lifted his leg on the Impala's back tire, made a beeline into the garage, jumped on Alonso's old bed, turned a few circles and nestled down onto the covers.

"Hey, control your dog!" Patricio ran to hose the urine off his car.

"¡Alonso, mijo!" his mamá cooed from the open front door.

"Mamá!" Alonso ran up the front steps to meet her embrace. Her arms enveloped him and she rocked him from side to side. He felt a lump come into his throat. How he had missed her.

"¿Tienes hambre? Liliana y yo nos desvelamos ayer haciéndote tamales." (*Are you hungry? Lilanna and I stayed up last night making tamales for you.*) She led him through the small dark living room and into the bright friendly kitchen.

"Ay mamá, mi tío Frank ya me llevó a cenar." (*Oh, mamá, tío Frank already took me out to eat tonight.*) He noticed the disappointment on her face immediately.

"Pero, tratándose de tus tamales, me voy a tener que sacrificar con uno." (*But, I'll sacrifice myself for your tamales!*) She gave him another giant hug.

Unbelievably full from his pasta plate at the elegant restaurant and the tamales, Alonso groaned as he moved Sombra over on the bed. He grabbed the corner of the top blanket and rolled over with it, cocooning his body, too tired to crawl between the sheets. He was still in his clothes from the day before and would wake up in them again, for the third day in a row, but he didn't care. Bone tired, Alonso pushed his laced up shoes off his feet with his toes, kicking them off the blanket and letting them drop to the floor. He immediately fell into a deep, dreamless sleep.

After thoroughly washing up and changing into fresh clothes the next morning, Alonso went outside to find his cousins. Patricio and Mauricio were bent over the open hood of the Impala, pulling on wires and wiggling parts around.

Alonso had not noticed the detailing on the car the night before. In the morning light the car sparkled from a new paint job of glittering gold. The trunk lid was airbrushed with an amazing crucifixion scene. The style reminded Alonso of an El Greco painting he had seen in the art room only a few days earlier: "The Resurrection of Christ." The figures in El Greco's seventeenth century art were elongated, with distinct shadows creating the form of long muscles on the slender figures.

He studied the trunk of the Impala. The three figures were hung on crosses, with a bluish-white band of light creating an arch around the heads of two of the figures and falling just short of reaching the third. The electric light airbrushed on the trunk held Alonso's attention: it was like the auras he had seen around people and sometimes coming off of himself.

"You like it?" Patricio smiled proudly.

"Where'd you get the idea?"

"This friend of mine who's an artist, it was his idea, so I let him do it." Patricio looked up from under the hood.

"You see, it's like this, I'm finding parts for him to fix up his own ride. He did this as payment for parts." He reached deep under the hood to install a new air filter, then screwed the polished chrome cover back into place.

"Where are you finding parts?" Alonso's gut feeling was that his cousins were up to something and he wasn't certain if it was legal. Patricio and Mauricio stopped working and looked at Alonso, then back at each other with sinister grins.

"Should we?" Mauricio asked his brother.

Patricio looked directly at Alonso. "You can see for yourself. You're coming with us this afternoon."

"I have homework to do, I can't."

"Then go do it now. Get it over with so you can hang with us." Patricio flicked his hand in the direction of the house as if to magically move Alonso to follow that path. "Rápido."

Back in the garage, Alonso left the overhead door open allowing the morning light to flood his room. Digging in his duffle bag, he pulled out the older laptop his tío Frank had given him to help with his schoolwork. He needed to look up the assignments he had missed in Mrs. Weaver's science class, but realized he could not get a signal for the internet at his tío Luis' home.

"This is great," he said. He reached for the phone in his front jean pocket and tried to turn it on. It had no power. He had not charged it since the bus ride to school where he had tested it in front of Tesoro.

"Dead as a doornail and no way to charge it." Alosno remembered leaving the power cord for the phone wrapped around the shoe in his locker. Frustrated, he placed the phone beside the computer that he couldn't use either.

Looking at the computer and back at the phone, Alonso wondered if he could use the battery from the charged up computer to power up his old phone. They're both lithium, they both used direct current. Newer phones power up from a USB cable. All he needed was a way to connect the phone battery to a computer DC power source to power up his old school phone. Digging in the duffle bag, he located a USB cord attached to the mouse he used for the laptop. Pulling the mouse all of the way out of the bag, he quickly ran outside.

"Can I borrow the needle-nose pliers?" He pointed to the toolbox beside the Impala.

"Sí," Patricio held the pliers up for Alonso without fully looking up from under the hood of the car.

"Hey, bring those back when you're done!" Mauricio yelled as Alonso ran into the garage, pliers in hand.

Alonso snipped the mouse free from the black cord and cut through the insulation exposing the red and black wires coming from the USB jack. Opening up his laptop, he pressed the power on button. He popped the lithium battery out of the back of his phone, placing the red wire on the plus sign of the phone battery and the black wire on the minus sign. He placed the battery back into the phone, plugged the USB cable into his computer and carefully watched the charging LCD signal on the phone.

"¡Con Madre! It worked!" The phone battery was charging with intensity. As soon as he saw the power reach its peak on the LCD, he pulled the USB jack from the laptop and disconnected the wires from the phone. Scrolling through his contact list, Alonso found Tracy's number.

"Hey cutie!" Tracy's feminine voice sang out.

"Hi Tracy. Do you have time for me to ask you something?"

"For you...of course," she said in a teasing tone.

"What did I miss in science yesterday?"

"Oh, not much. Brett brought in some type of electrical contraption that took up most of Mrs. Weaver's time. She seemed rather enthralled by it."

Tracy yawned as she spoke.

"Did I miss any class work?"

"We started a worksheet that's not due until Tuesday. You can get one on Monday and I'll help you get caught up. Mine is already finished."

"Great. Thanks Tracy."

"Oh, Mrs. Weaver wanted to know where you were at. She mentioned something about an idea for a contest being due soon."

"Yeah, I was worried about that. I hope she'll still take my idea on Monday."

"I've got another call, gotta go!"

"Bye, Tracy," Alonso softly replied into the empty air waves. He pulled out his math textbook and worked out a few homework problems. His attention kept drifting to the sound of the loud Impala engine just outside. Unable to concentrate, he closed his book and, leaving his homework unfinished, raced outside to join his cousins.

CHAPTER TWELVE

Water Pumps and Tamales

"**G**et the tamales out of the fridge and bring them out here," Mauricio said.

"Hang on, let me get Sombra out of the garage." Alonso whistled at Sombra.

Sombra stretched his front paws out and jumped off the rumpled bed. Alonso let Sombra into the kitchen with him and pulled the tamales out of the refrigerator, waving them under Sombra's nose. The dog wagged his fluffy black tail curled tight across his back and sniffed the baggie of tamales, following Alonso outside.

Patricio started the Impala. The V8 engine throbbed out the tune of a well-lubed machine. Mauricio, beside his brother in the front seat, motioned for Alonso to get in the back. He let out a low chuckle as Alonso slid across the torn up seat covers with Sombra by his side.

"You ready to take a little trip, primo? Take a little trip. Take a little trip. Take a little trip and see? Take a little trip. Take a little trip. Take a little trip with me?"

Mauricio laughed as he sang the lyrics to "Low Rider." Patricio joined Mauricio in song and threw the switch on the car's newly installed hydraulics. The old car responded with the front end vigorously hopping up and down. Sombra and Alonso bounced up off the backseat. Sombra let out a whimper and retreated to the safety of the floorboard, gripping the old carpet with his front toenails. The two brothers laughed uncontrollably and slapped each other on the arm in amusement; priding themselves on their accomplishment of installing hydraulic pumps, cylinders, batteries, and switches for the effect. Mauricio lit up a cigarette with a look of satisfaction on his face. They pulled out of the drive and rolled down the street lined with bare trees onto Vance Jackson.

With the side window open, Sombra madly sniffed the fresh air, taking up most of Alonso's view out. He realized he had no idea what part of San Antonio they were in, except that it was somewhere Southside.

"Hey, where are we going?"

"Old Man Gonzales' junkyard," Patricio answered, matter-of-fact. He hand-signed "Southside" by placing three fingers up with two fingers between them, creating an "S" in the negative space between his fingers. He laughed and took hold of the steering wheel again. As they rolled up to a light at a busy intersection, a small blue pickup truck with two girls in the cab pulled alongside. The girls pointed, giggled and waved at them. Patricio and Mauricio both looked at each other at the same time and nodded, Patricio threw the switch and the Impala's front end hopped with a vengeance. Alonso reached mid-air to grab Sombra around the mid-section, but he wasn't fast enough and the dog went flying out the open back window just as the front tires hit the ground with a resounding thud.

Sombra bolted through a strip shopping center parking lot at full speed. Alonso threw the door open, positioning himself in a stance while hanging onto the doorjamb of the bouncing car and leapt to the curb on an upward bounce. He charged in a full-speed sprint after Sombra with the bag of tamales in his hand. Sombra ran around the back of the buildings and bolted toward an open field.

"Sombra!" Alonso yelled.

"¡Sombra, ven para acá!" (*Sombra, come here!*)

He could not run fast enough to catch Sombra. Reaching into the bag of tamales, he whisked one out and with the wind to his back, took a bite. He slowed his pace and let the rich, meaty flavor melt across his tongue and then, without swallowing, he blew several times, down-wind toward Sombra.

It worked, Sombra turned around just long enough to see Alonso waving the tamales in the air. His ears perked up and he ran to Alonso's side. Alonso dropped to one knee as Sombra dutifully sat in front of him and grabbed the crumbled tamal right out of its corn husk. With one fast move, Alonso latched Sombra's leash on his collar and walked the dog back to the Impala.

"Flaco, get in, rápido!" Mauricio reached around to the backseat and pushed the door open.

"Give me some warning next time you bounce the ride!" Alonso said.

"Why don't you leave your dog at home next time," Patricio complained.

Patricio pulled slowly up to a barrio backstreet that bordered the far edge of Old Man Gonzales' junkyard. He brought the Impala to a halt beside a tall chain-link fence with barbed wire running across the top. The fence was completely covered in a thick evergreen vine, completely concealing the junkyard from the street. Alonso and Sombra jumped out of the car, leaving the door slightly open. Mauricio edged his body up to the vine on the fence and peered through into the interior of the yard, between all of the old cars and directly at the front office.

"Come look at this," he motioned to Patricio and Alonso. "See, exactly what I thought. Every day Old Man Gonzales falls asleep in front of his computer after he eats at eleven. He rests his hands on the keyboard, shuts his eyes and goes to sleep sitting up. Look, there's his old hound sleeping by his feet."

"I bet that dog will not stay asleep for long with us making so much noise out here," Alonso said.

"That's why I asked you to bring the tamales. Do you still

have them, or did you feed them all to Sombra?" Mauricio whispered.

Alonso retrieved them and handed one over to his cousin. "Put Sombra in the car. If he sees the yard dog he'll go ballistic."

Alonso signaled for Sombra to follow him and to jump in the backseat.

Mauricio crouched low and lifted a patch of vines up from the bottom of the chain-link fence; he reached down with his free hand and pulled a large, rusty metal muffler from a hole just under the fence. He slid his body through the hole and appeared on the opposite side. Mauricio pulled a whistle out of his front pocket and blew it hard. To Alonso's surprise he did not hear a thing, although the hound dog in the office trotted across the junk yard to Mauricio, his stubby tail wagging hard. Mauricio reached down to pet the dog and at the same time he fed him tasty bits of his tía Lisa's tamal.

"Here, call the dog over when the old man starts moving." Mauricio passed the dog whistle through the fence to his brother.

"We have him trained to come to us silently for food," Patricio said, dangling the whistle in front of Alonso.

"What exactly is Mauricio doing in there?" Alonso asked.

"This is how we find parts." Patricio's eyes were glued to Old Man Gonzales, still asleep in his office chair.

"¿Andas de rata?" (*You're stealing?*)

"You could call it that." Patricio kept his gaze on the office.

"Why did you bring me along? I don't want to be a part of this," Alonso hissed between his teeth. He was furious.

"You look bored, you study too much," Patricio sneered.

Alonso folded his arms across his chest. It was true, he

did study most of the time and something deep inside of him found his cousins' antics thrilling. He moved to the side where the vines were not growing thick and looked directly into the junkyard. He searched for Mauricio amongst the rows and rows of rusty wrecked cars. He spotted the tail of the junkyard dog wagging beside a wrecked Buick. His cousin had to be close.

"Move back, move back." Patricio pulled Alonso behind the vines, out of view. Patricio moved apart a few vines to peek into the junkyard; Alonso did the same. Old Man Gonzales was moving around the office. He lifted his arms up and stretched. He placed his hands across the small of his back and pushed his rotund belly forward in another stretch. Then Old Man Gonzales walked straight into the bathroom.

Patricio pulled the dog whistle out of his front jean pocket and blew hard. The watchdog ran right to Patricio, letting the dog lick his fingers through the holes in the fence. He reached into his flannel shirt pocket and pulled out small round bits of liver treats and offered them a crumble at a time.

Mauricio reappeared from underneath the Buick holding a highly polished water pump close to his body. He scrambled to his feet and ran low, directly to the fence. He quickly passed the pump under the fence to Patricio and then scrambled under the vines through the hole to the other side. As Mauricio and Patricio placed the water pump into the trunk of the Impala, the junkyard dog followed Mauricio and shimmied under the fence. Sombra and the hound barked loudly at each other--Sombra pawed at the interior of the Impala and the hound jumped up on the car door.

"¡No manches pendejo! You idiot, you forgot to put the muffler back to block the dog!" Patricio scolded.

The cousins scrambled to the fence. Alonso struggled to keep the hound away from the car.

"We can't leave the dog outside of the fence. Old Man Gonzales will find our back entrance!" Mauricio frantically looked to Patricio for an answer.

"Hey, flaco, do you have any more of your mamá's tamales?" Patricio asked Alonso, who pulled hard on the hound dog's collar.

"Yeah, I have one more." Alonso reached into his pocket and pulled the last tamal out, wrapped tight in corn husk with a bow. The hound dog pulled out of Alonso's grip and jumped on the car again, scratching the new paint job.

"¡Chingado!" Mauricio snatched the tamal out of Alonso's hand.

"Gonzoles is back at his desk!" Patricio said.

Mauricio held the tamal by the dog's mouth and quickly pulled it back when he had the dog's attention. He lured the hound to the fence. With the skill of a magician, Mauricio slipped his long arm through the thicket of vines and under the chain link fence to the other side. With his body smashed into the vines, he reached with all of his might to wave the tamal in the air. It worked. The hound dog shimmied through the ditch, squeezing past Mauricio and back into the junkyard. The dog quickly lapped up the tamal from Mauricio's open hand. With only seconds to spare, Mauricio shoved the old muffler under the fence, throwing rocks and debris from around the vines into the trench so the dog could not come back through.

"Drive!" Mauricio leapt legs first through the window of the Impala. They pulled away, leaving the hound dog sniffing the ground for tasty crumbs. Alonso turned completely around in the backseat to look at the office as they sped away. Old Man Gonzales was inside typing on his computer. Alonso leaned deep into the old seat cushions, threw his head back, closed his eyes tight and let out a deep sigh of relief.

"¡Chavos locos!" (*You guys are crazy!*)

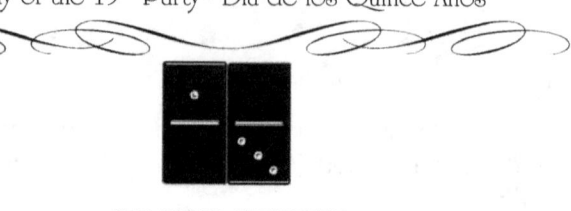

CHAPTER THIRTEEN

The Tattooed Man and Violet Skies

The Impala sparkled brilliantly as golden flecks of light danced off its body in the midday sun. It cruised slowly down Vance Jackson and onto a side street in a little barrio close to tío Luis's home. The sun cast short shadows across the winter brown lawns, giving the unkempt neighborhood a disconcerting feel. Alonso's stomach felt odd, heavy and slightly nauseous. He knew something wasn't right.

Patricio slowed the car to a crawl, stopping in front of a small house with a low, black metal fence across the front yard. Behind the fence dead foliage wept down the sides of neglected plastic planters. A small rock altar in the middle of the yard harbored a faded plastic figurine of the Virgin of Guadalupe. More pots rested on either side of the altar, one knocked over on its side. Two striped tabby cats were curled up by the brown hedges at the side of the front porch; they glanced up appearing bored. A dim blue light from a television flickered through the front window curtain. The silhouette of a thin male figure passed in front of the window, moving towards the front door.

Mauricio and Patricio jumped out of the car just as the front door to the home opened and a tall, gaunt, heavily tattooed man appeared on the porch. In the dim light, Alonso could make out his white wife beater tee-shirt, his black, skinny, straight-fit Dickies with numerous silver chains hanging from the pockets. His cheeks were sunken, his eyes squinty and red. Alonso looked a little harder--the man was only slightly older than his cousins. He reached into his front pocket, pulled out a cigarette and lit it, blowing smoke up into the oncoming night.

The front door opened again and Lilianna stumbled onto the front porch with a bottle in her hands. She rested her weight on the man who tried to push her away. The more he attempted to remove her from his side the more she threw herself on him, laughing and rubbing the side of his face with her hand, cooing at him. He flicked his cigarette to the side, then he reached up and took both of her hands and threw them down by her side.

"Leave me alone, bitch," he yelled.

Alonso wedged his leg out of the barely open back door of the car. Mauricio held his hand on the door frame to stop Alonso from getting out. Through the window of the backseat Alonso could see Anna run to the side yard of the house and out of his view.

"Stay in the car," Mauricio said, furrowing his brow at Alonso.

"No." Alonso slid to the opposite door and jumped out of the Impala. He bolted to the side of the house his sister disappeared behind.

He found Lilianna beside the old frame home on her hands and knees. She was vomiting on the dormant brown Saint Augustine grass. She was drunk. Alonso noticed something dark on the exposed skin of her back, between her shirt and low jeans. It was a graffiti-style tattoo of the "Kaotik Koupé" car club logo. Trouble...the same club Patricio and Mauricio belonged to.

"Lilianna?" Alonso asked for his sister's attention in a soft voice.

"¿Alonso, qué estás haciendo aquí?" (*Alonso, what are you doing here?*) Her words were slurred. She held her long straight hair back and vomited violently.

"¡Estás bien peda!" (*You're stinkin' drunk!*) Alonso had to get her home to safety. Tears streamed down her face, mixing with her black eyeliner and mascara. She vomited again.

Mauricio and Patricio delivered the stolen water pump to the tattooed man.

"What do you mean you can't pay us now?" Patricio asked.

"I'm good for it." The gaunt man slipped back into the house and locked the door. They quickly rounded the corner to the side yard.

"Órale párate, Liliana." (*Come on, Lilanna,*) Patricio said. He pulled her from the ground and held her up. Mauricio placed her limp arms around his shoulder and Patricio did the same thing on the other side. The four of them made their way to the Impala and drove back to tío Luis' home.

Alonso and his cousins steered Lilianna past tío Luis, carefully maneuvering her through the front living room where tío Luis watched college football in the afternoon.

"Algo que comió le cayó mal." (*Food poisoning,*) Mauricio said. He lied to his papá. Tío Luis grunted without taking his eyes off the screen and let out a disappointed yell when his team turned over the ball. Mauricio winked at Alonso as they hurried Lilianna to her room.

Alonso went into his garage bedroom with Sombra, who went immediately to his water bowl to lap up a big drink. Alonso's head was swimming from the events of the day. His face felt flushed with anger at his sister and his cousins for getting into so much trouble. If his papá was present this trouble would not exist. His cousins and sister were meeting their family needs through the car club, Kaotik Koupé. This was not a family he was part of--nor did he want to be.

Exhausted, Alonso propped his pillow against the wall behind his bed and shut his eyes. Finding his papá was all he could think about. A picture of his papá came into his mind. He remembered his kind smile. Again, he imagined finding his papá through traveling outside of his body. Alonso wanted him to know what was happening to his family. He began taking deep, slow breaths, relaxing the muscles in his body and keeping his papá's face in his mind's eye. He could feel himself rocking out of his body into a calm place with soft purple light floating right in front of him. The purple light became larger, sparkling in the center. Alonso sensed he could move very quickly through the light. He pulled himself naturally through one purple light after another and entered seamlessly into the world between wakefulness and sleep.

He accelerated through purple light, to black tunnel, to purple light again. In the distance he heard a faint noise, the sound of metal clinking against metal, like a chime blowing in the wind. Slowing down, he could see small sparks of light going off around him--brilliant shooting stars. He was drawn to one light in particular and he zoomed toward it. Soon, he found himself on the windy, barren place of his dreams.

Standing firm on the high ledge he had grown familiar with he let the soothing, mysterious breeze blow through him. The clinging of metal on metal became more distinguished; the resonating tinkling noise morphed from wind chimes to something more natural, the sound of grackles calling to each other from treetops just as the sun set mixed with the sound of gurgling water rushing over stones.

Over the din of the bird calls Alonso distinguished a voice. He could not determine what it was saying because the words ran together in one jumbled mess of language.

"Hey, I'm down here," a male voice clearly sounded from below Alonso's perch. Alonso peered down and spotted a teen, about his age, looking straight up at him.

"Who are you?" Alonso asked, as he started his descent.

"Tino. Who are you?"

"I'm Alonso. Can you give me a hand getting off this

thing?" Alonso clung to a ledge at least four stories above Tino.

"Jump."

"Jump? The fall would kill me!"

"Okay." Tino walked away.

Alonso's foot dangled below the ledge, trying to find a hold--suddenly his foothold broke and he plummeted downward. Air rushing past his ears, the ground was spiraling closer to him. He shut his eyes. In a split second he was standing upright on the ground, unharmed.

"¡Chin!" Alonso exclaimed as he patted his chest with his open hands to make certain he still existed.

"Hey, Tino, I made it down." Alonso bounded toward Tino, who turned around with the same sly grin on his face.

"How did that happen? Why am I still alive?"

"You're not in Kansas anymore, Dorothy." Tino stopped so Alonso could catch up.

"Is this a dream?"

"No."

"Where am I?"

"You're only here if you should be here. That's why I'm here." Tino gave Alonso a warm, full smile, crossed his arms across his chest and waited for Alonso to consider his words. Alonso was puzzled. He looked at the sky; it was a glowing blue-violet, so transparent the stars shone right through the atmosphere. His hands had a soft inner glow--the same soft glow radiated from Tino. A glimmer of silver light danced from Tino's chest. He was wearing an amulet: metal around the edges, with odd writing inscribed. Inside the metal casing was that odd turquoise with natural brown veins that made the shape of a dark bird, held captive within the stone. It was *exactly* like Tesoro's pendant.

Everything seemed surreal in Alonso's whirling mind, yet

this was more of a reality than anything he'd ever experienced...and maybe life itself was the dream. The glow around his body brightened, his arms, his hands and his fingertips seemed a translucent glow. This strange place was far removed from the hurt he felt from his papá's absence and his family's trouble. Alonso thought intently about his family-- he missed his papá so. He wished his papá were here to see the trouble his cousins and Lilianna were getting into. He wished his mamá would stop crying all of the time. With a rush of emotions welling up, he closed his eyes tight. The next thing he knew he was propped up by a pillow in the open garage of his tío Luis' home with Sombra curled up, fast asleep by his feet.

CHAPTER FOURTEEN

Astral Travel and Memories

Tino took the note Tesoro had given him and unfolded it slowly, reading each word out loud, relishing each syllable.

"tino, school's not the same without u around. hope u r able 2 come back soon. mu lul <3 linsdey"

"Miss you, love you lots." Tino repeated her last words quietly.

"I miss you, too, Lindsey." He smiled to himself, tore a piece of paper out of his notebook and started to write.

"Dear Lindsey, thank you for writing to me. I hope to be back at school soon. I still can't walk, but I hope to very soon. Home school is boring. My therapist tells me I can walk again, someday. In my dreams I walk. Anyway, I don't want to bore you with this. Say 'Hey' to everyone for me. Love, Tino."

He carefully folded the paper and wrote Lindsey's name on the front. He wheeled over to Tesoro's backpack on the kitchen table and placed it on top. He couldn't bring himself to open his laptop to find out what his teachers wanted him to work on. He was behind in school, but he just wasn't in the mood to do the work. Instead, he went to the back deck and pulled his wooden flute out of the fringed leather pouch from the side of his wheelchair. He shut his eyes, placed the mouthpiece to his lips and blew out the slow, melodic notes of his grandfather's favorite song. He felt peaceful; playing music helped him forget that he couldn't be with Lindsey, maybe never. He inhaled deeply and let out a long, breathy melody into the handmade instrument.

Tino's physical therapist had taken a lot of time bending and pulling on his legs to stretch out his atrophied muscles. The therapist had placed him in a parachute-type contraption: a pair of girdle-like shorts that reminded him of a parachute suit. The therapist had fastened the odd shorts with belts and metal loops to an overhead system that took weight off of his body that allowed Tino to move his legs, from his hips, lightly on a treadmill. With the weight off of his legs and his feet barely touching the treadmill belt, he was able to move his legs from his hip joints and walk. Tino felt proud that he was up to ten minutes of moving his legs during this exercise.

He enjoyed the salt water swimming pool more than the treadmill exercises. He especially took pleasure in floating on his back with a pool noodle under his neck, gently moving his arms through the water as his limp legs followed. The sensation of floating felt the same as meditating deeply-- suspended, drifting through space and time. Floating slowly removed the pain from his body and mind. Relaxation exercises stop the brain from producing cortisol, the stress hormone, and he could relax at a very deep level. Floating helped him heal, whether it was in the water or through meditation.

It was late in the afternoon. He would only have Sunday to finish his studies if he didn't work on them now. He reluctantly returned to the kitchen table, pulled out the laptop and looked up his assignments. With no further procrastination, he pulled up his assignment for social studies and started to read from his textbook. Paragraph after paragraph, Tino felt himself moving into the distance...he lost his concentration and drifted into slumber at the kitchen table. The soft blue glow of the computer screen illuminated the side of his face as his head rested softly on his arms over the wooden table top. He entered the state between wakefulness and deep sleep; his theta waves peaked and he moved his consciousness from the kitchen table to the windswept land with the glowing violet sky, far, far away. It was there he met Alonso, teetering on the high rocks, afraid to make his first jump.

"Coo-coo, coo-coo." In the distance the Inca doves gathered at the base of the escarpment oaks. Tino slowly opened his eyes and smiled at their soft call. His vision glided across the contents of the kitchen table and rested on Tesoro's sketchbook tucked just under her backpack. He gently pulled it from the weight of her books, making certain to keep his note to Lindsey in place. Flipping through the pages, there were many images of wolves, wolves on high rocks, wolf faces, wolf pups, and wolves with eyes of magic. He randomly turned to the center of her sketchbook and stared at a page with immense surprise.

"How can that be?" In pencil, right in front of Tino, on the pages of his sister's sketchbook, was a detailed rendering of Alonso--the guy he just met in his astral travels when he drifted off.

How could she know him? Had she seen Alonso in her dreams? Perhaps, he thought further, Tesoro is traveling through space and time in spirit also. He flipped back through her sketchbook to a beautiful black ink drawing of a water bird flying in a sky of swirling lines.

"Cool," Tino murmured, slowly running his hand across the page, feeling its texture and bumps from Tesoro's pen. Suddenly, in his mind he saw Tesoro's hand drawing the bird. Her hand appeared as if it were his own. Looking up in his vision, he saw Alonso in the art room, looking back, in the way that guys look at girls they like.

"Damn, that's how she knows him!" He realized he had just read the vibrations of a past event through psychometry. He placed his hand over the entire page, hoping to get more information...nothing. Just how well did Alonso know his sister? What were his intentions? He was overwhelmed with feelings of protection for her.

He remembered what his grandfather once told him: "If you are strongly bound to something you will receive nothing. If you are silent and still, you will receive everything that is right for you to know."

Tino realized his emotions had gotten in the way of his remote viewing attempt. This always frustrated him. When he wanted information the most, nothing came. It was only with a quiet mind that he could easily receive visions. Sometimes these things made sense, sometimes they were obscure. Over the past two years, Tino had learned to not take every glimmer he received in a vision as concrete proof of anything in the here and now, that sometimes a vision may not make sense until years passed. But this last vision was unmistakably true to the moment.

A breeze blew through the open sliding glass door. Tino felt a sudden chill, this breeze was different--it carried a spirit. He turned around to the door and noticed, for just a fleeting moment, his grandfather in the doorway smiling softly at him. He was wearing his traditional black-fringed blanket over his shoulders, the one he wore in ceremonies. His long silver hair was in braids with white feathers woven into the black leather at the ends. Tino felt an enormous amount of love in the room. He blinked and his grandfather was gone. Only the lonely sound of the cooing Inca doves in the distance filled the silent void between Tino and his vision.

Tino wheeled onto the wooden deck outside. Shutting his eyes to the winter sun reflecting off the swimming pool on the lower deck, he recalled the first time he left his body. He was safe with his grandfather and the Tonkawa people in the sacred ceremony held just for him. On this sacred journey many guides helped him through the process of leaving the earthly plane of existence. He remembered being pulled by the voice of his grandfather, who was just ahead of him. He could hear the fleeting thoughts of the people around him as he journeyed further and further away from Earth. Everything happened as if time itself did not exist. Tino had floated in a glowing cloud of blue and purple light. Something within his psyche recognized that the light emitted great knowledge. He was in awe of the sacred ceremony experience and not quite certain what to make of it at the same time.

The rest of Tino's time in Oklahoma had been spent in storytelling circles with elders. Stories of how his Texas tribe was overtaken by violence and bloody territory disputes. Tales of how the Tonkawa were forced to move north to Oklahoma from the Indian Removal Act signed into law by President Andrew Jackson. Visions of the days when the grey wolf ruled the land and bison roamed freely through Texas. Tino had absorbed their chanting and songs, telling stories of the "real people," his tribe, whom he loved.

Tino remembered their last conversation on the trip back to Texas, traveling through Oklahoma.

"There are very few of us left," Grandfather said.

"How many?" Tino asked.

"Last count, perhaps six hundred real people."

"It didn't seem like many of us were on the reservation."

"That's right--maybe fifteen families live on the res'. Everyone else lives in town. We come together for events."

"Where's everyone else?

"A few Tonkawa fled to Mexico during the violent times. You remember the stories?"

"Yeah."

"Our people come from the Edwards Aquifer, where you live now."

"Really, how come I haven't met another Tonkawa in San Antonio, then?"

"Because there are so few."

"Oh."

"Tino, there's something very important."

"Yes, Grandpa?"

"It's about you."

"Okay?"

"You are a great leader. The elders recognize this in your spirit."

"What does that mean?"

"That you can pull our people back together."

Grandfather suddenly stopped talking, doing everything he could to move the SUV out of the way of the on-coming semi jackknifing out of control. Tino screamed out at impact. The SUV crashed backwards through the guardrail and flew through the air. The impact of the trailer caused Tino's lithe frame to fly out of his loose seatbelt. The intense velocity of the spinning, twisted vehicle forced the back door to fly open and Tino was thrown onto the grassy ravine below. With his grandparents still inside, the SUV sailed through the sky and crashed with a thud onto the ground, far below the highway.

Tino felt no pain as he lay on the grass. He could not move. Just as he realized he was not breathing a slow rocking, spinning feeling came over him, exactly the feeling he had during the sacred ceremony only a few nights before. Tino drifted out of his body and looked down at it from a few feet above. One of his legs seemed to be twisted backwards, and for some odd reason Tino found this sight slightly humorous at that moment, almost as if he was watching a film. He felt just fine where he was at; his body below him didn't seem to belong to him anymore. From the distance, Tino could hear his grandfather's voice telling him to stay where he was, not to leave. Then everything went black, until he awoke in the hospital room just south of the Oklahoma border, in Texas. His body was now riddled with pain and he was unable to move from the waist down.

During his stay in the hospital, Tino learned to project himself from his body with great ease. It was the only way he could escape the intense pain. He discovered he could travel through space and time, experiencing visions. His favorite place to journey was the barren land of violet skies--the place where he had just met Alonso. He was certain he would see him again.

CHAPTER FIFTEEN

Quince Años and Desire

The strong light of the late afternoon sun glimmered through the stained glass windows, creating dappled puddles of color across the congregation in the small church. Alonso glanced over at Lilianna as she moved to her knees during prayer. Her head down, hands folded, the golden light played across her face, her hair, her dress; he thought she appeared angelic. She was in sharp contrast to the drunken Lilianna. If mamá knew what she was doing with the car club, she would ground Anna forever. Lisa gazed with concern at Lilianna. Alonso reached over and patted his mamá's hand, she smiled sweetly at him.

Father Fuentes changed his voice pitch from low and serious to a cheery higher tone. It was time for announcements and prayers for the congregation members, marking the close of the late afternoon mass.

"This evening we have a Quince Años to celebrate; our own Miss Laurencia Castillo is turning fifteen! Her parents Ernesto and Lynette Castillo and her Godparent, Lisa Mendoza, will honor her with this celebration. Alonso Mendoza is the appointed chambelán. Our congregation is invited to join in this blessed event for Laurencia. The Quince Años dinner party will start at seven o'clock this Saturday night at the Community Center Hall, next to our Sacred Heart Church. Please join the Castillo family to celebrate this event."

"¿Mamá, por qué no me dijiste nada?" (*Mamá why didn't you tell me about this?*) Alonso whispered to Lisa as people made their way to the center aisle to leave the church.

"Fue una decisión de último momento, y estuviste fuera todo el día. Anoche fui a tu cuarto para decirte, pero ya estabas dormido." (*It was a last-minute decision and you were gone all day. I went into your room to tell you, but you were asleep.*)

"Mamá, no quiero hacerlo. Tengo que regresar a casa de mis tíos Frank y Ruby el próximo fin de semana." (*Mamá, I don't want to do this, I have homework. I need to be back at tío Frank and tía Ruby's house. I have a large project due in Science on Monday.*)

"Por favor, Alonso, no hay nadie más." (*Please Alonso, there is no one else.*) She gave Alonso her look. There was no way out of this one. Alonso rose from the pew and made his way to the foyer to greet Father Fuentes.

"Alonso." He heard a female voice calling his name, just before he could escape the crowded foyer and disappear into his family's Civic. Laurencia Castillo came bounding toward him, smiling, and wove her way through the crowd. Once by Alonso's side, she took his hands in hers, her expression wide eyed and bubbling over with excitement.

"Alonso, I'm so glad you can do this. We need to practice our dances before my party. Are you free?"

Alonso could not help but to smile at the pretty girl only inches away from him showing him so much attention. Her long, naturally wavy brown hair fell around her round face; her full lips, sparkling with red lip gloss, set in sharp contrast with her perfectly straight, white teeth. He couldn't help but stare at the healthy curves of her body in the tight, fuzzy white sweater she had on. She was so close he could smell her, a rich musky scent, deep and intoxicating. He moved in closer, mesmerized by the brightness in her eyes, noticing how perfect her makeup was with each eyelash lengthened by mascara and meticulously separated. He had not seen Laurencia recently and now realized she had grown up since the last time he was around her. She's beautiful, he thought, remarkably beautiful.

"Come to my house with me, it will only take an hour or so, I promise." She took his smile as a yes and was quickly whisked away into the crowd of elders full of words of wisdom, congratulating her for the pending party. She glanced over her shoulder and coyly waved at Alonso through her admirers.

Alonso smiled back, knowing that he would be holding Laurencia close, dancing the waltzes his mamá insisted he learn through years of lessons.

~

The necktie needed one last adjustment. Lisa reached over to Alonso and moved the perfect knot a little to the right. Gently, she pushed his bangs to the side of his face so she could see her son's eyes.

"Te ves muy guapo. Como tu papá cuando nos conocimos en mis Quince Años." (*You look handsome, like your papá when we first met at my sweet fifteen.*)

She reached over and kissed Alonso on the cheek. He smiled back at his mamá, feeling a bit awkward in the formal suit she rented for him. He let his straight bangs fall back over his eyes. "¿Has sabido algo de mi papá?" (*Have you heard from papá?*)

"No," Lisa said quietly, looking down, blinking back the tears that suddenly welled up in her eyes.

Alonso smiled at his mamá, took her hand and led her up the steps to the old wooden dance hall.

"Ya estuvo. ¡Hay que divertirnos!" (*Let's have some fun!*)

He pushed the door open, only to be greeted by silence. At the front of the hall was Father Fuentes with his head bowed in silent prayer. The great hall filled with guests was frozen in prayer for the Quinceañera. Women moved their rosary beads, one by one, slowly through their fingertips, eyes closed, mouths moving to words not spoken aloud.

Alonso saw Lilianna, Mauricio and Patricio through the

crowd. He led his mamá to seats at a round table with the rest of their family. Taking a seat next to his sister, Alonso winked at her. Lilianna, in turn, pinched her brother on the top of his leg and gently pulled on his tie.

"You're dressed up. You'll make Laurencia look good," Lillianna said.

"Laurencia already looks good." Alonso straightened up his posture and smiled.

"¡Ay güeeey!" Patricio and Mauricio said in a unified voice. Lisa placed her finger to her mouth in an attempt to quiet them.

"There's the Quinceañera!" A woman in front of the hall announced. Alonso turned in his seat. Gliding down the center of the hall, between the round guest-filled tables and wearing an elegant, full-length, white gown was Laurencia. Her long wavy hair was in an up-do, with a few ringlets drifting across her soft, round shoulders. Her shoulders were not all that was revealed by her low cut her dress. Alonso flashed back to a Rubens painting from art class, "Helene Fourment and Her Children," a painting of a woman in a low-cut dress, like Laurencia. Alonso did not realize that girls' breasts could rise so high up and rounded on their chests.

"Bien bonita," he murmured.

Laurencia smiled boldly at Alonso as she sashayed by his table. He caught her scent again, musky, earthy and rich. Alonso held this in his nose for as long as he could without taking another breath. Something funny stirred inside of him. He felt he had to be close to her and would do anything to do so...now. He shifted uneasily in his seat, mesmerized by her presence. He could not take his eyes off of her as he narrowed his gaze through his black spiky bangs, a panther on the prowl. His nostrils flared out in short breaths.

"Come on, Flaco. I don't want to be last in the food line," Patricio said. Alonso broke his stare and followed his cousins to the buffet, ladling a scoop of rice and a tamal filled with creamy, blanco cheeses and green chilies. He filled flour tortillas with rich and meaty carne guisada. He was hungry and piled his plate to the brim. Patricio and Mauricio had moved on to the beer keg. Patricio held their full dinner plates as Maurico filled tall cups with frothy beer.

"Here, you'll need this to dance, güey." Mauricio laughed and handed the beer to Alonso, who took it from him without a word.

"Don't drink too many of those, or you will make a fool of me later when we dance," Laurencia said, flirting in low whisper from behind his left shoulder.

He caught his breath and felt that deep stirring inside of him again. She was so close to him.

"The foolishness comes later, after the dance." The words spilled out before he could stop himself. Laurencia flashed a look of shock at Alonso, turned on her heel and marched defiantly back to her parent's table. She flashed a quick, curious look back in his direction as she took her seat.

"Pendejo." (*Asshole.*) Mauricio said dryly, smirking.

"¡No mamen!" (*Suck it.*) Alonso sparked back.

Back at the table, the food filled Alonso's stomach quickly; he had not eaten well all day. He gulped the beer down thirstily in between bites of food. It helped him feel relaxed, more relaxed than he had been in days. He desperately wanted to loosen his tie, but he knew it would be the undoing of his mamá. He ran his finger uncomfortably between his shirt and his neck and let out a belch.

"Excúse me," he snickered. "Not used to that stuff." Alonso pointed, pistol style at his empty plastic cup, slouching down into his metal folding chair. His mamá rolled her eyes and Lilianna smirked at her brother.

"We're not going to have a repeat of what happened to

me yesterday?" Anna leaned over, questioning Alonso quietly so their mamá could not hear.

"Estoy bien." (*I'm good.*) Alonso muttered under a quieter belch this time, slouching low in his chair, his long legs jutting far under the table top. His attention was quickly averted when señor Castillo called his daughter up to the dance floor to present her with a gift. Alonso straightened his posture and strained to get a better view of Laurencia opening the gift. In awe of her slow, graceful movements, Alonso turned his chair to face the dance floor. Laurencia was holding up a porcelain doll for the crowd to see, her last doll, marking her passage from being a niña to a señorita.

"¡Ya, miedoso! ¡Ya llégale!" (*Come on wus! Go get it.*) Maurico said tauntingly to Alonso. Patricio heard his brother's comment and let out a low, rumbling laugh.

"You're both evil," Alonso responded, without taking his eyes off of Laurencia. She bent down to change from her flat shoes into the high heels her mamá had given her, signifying her rite of passage into womanhood. As she did so, a wealth of cleavage was exposed.

"Chales," Alonso muttered under his breath at the sight of Laurencia spilling out of the top of her gown. He was ready to loosen his tie and dance closely with the beautiful señorita Castillo.

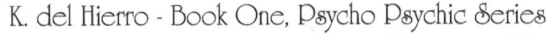

CHAPTER SIXTEEN

Slackers and Silicone

It was Saturday night and Tesoro was ticked off at her teacher and feeling resentful toward the slacker team she had been stuck with for the English project. Brett was taking advantage of her instead of doing the work himself. Marcus and Sarah were just following her lead, taking no initiative. They had accomplished little during class time. Sarah used the computer lab time they had to email friends at school, while Marcus and Brett showed each other sports cars online. So, here she was at Brett's house, trying to motivate her slacker team to finish a project that was due on Monday.

With a sigh, Tesoro looked around the Merrick's luxurious home. The ceilings had to be at least ten feet tall, every inch of the place screamed big money at her. It's not that she felt uncomfortable around money; her family's home was nice enough. This home was pristine, untouchable and seemingly empty to her. Brett's Mom seemed nice enough, possibly overly nice, bordering on fake. Tesoro toyed with the thought of just how much else was fake. She observed Mrs. Merrick moving around in the kitchen: fake nails, fake eyelashes, and obvious silicone injections in her pink, puffy Barbie-doll lips. From the looks of it, her lips were not the only thing that was inflated with silicone. Tesoro could not help but to notice that the woman's breasts were gigantic in her tight, pink spandex workout top, way too big for the rest of her body. She wore an obvious blond hairpiece in a quick up-do and permanent, tattooed eyeliner that was way too dark against her pinkish-white skin.

"Tesoro!" Sarah said sharply, out of the side of her mouth. "Don't be rude, stop staring."

"Sorry. Here, I found the poet that used the lower case 'i' in his poetry, ee cummings. We can use him as an example to back up why we text in lower case. I'm still looking for more examples of military acronyms that are close to the ones we text with."

Looking back at her computer screen, Tesoro added, "Here's what I have so far: '411' for information, and '911' for emergencies. It's the same for police and the military. You know how we just put the number '20' in to find out where someone is at? The police use this, too."

"Duh, ya think that's where they came from?" Marcus said sarcastically, leaning back on the sofa and placing a hand-embroidered pillow over his head, pretending to snore loudly. Brett threw his body over Sarah's lap and forcefully pulled the pillow that Marcus held on his head down tight over his face. Brett's stronghold on Marcus caused him to desperately kick his legs wildly.

"Dude, that wasn't right!" Marcus snarled, as he jumped up.

"What?" Brett sneered, the vindictive type of sneer someone makes when they know they have the upper hand. Marcus flopped down on the sofa again, picked up the expensive pillow and threw it at Brett, who caught it with hands as quick as a lizard's tongue. He placed the pillow comfortably behind his back, still sneering.

"Can we get this thing finished? It's due Monday," Tesoro said.

"We'll get it done, baby." Brett moved in close to Tesoro and pushed her silky hair behind her ear, catching her off-guard. She stiffened, straightened her posture and pulled the laptop closer to her body.

"Don't you mean I'll get it done? You guys should be

paying me," Tesoro said.

Brett laughed and Sarah leaned back into the sofa, picking nervously at the chipped nail polish on her fingernails.

"What do you need me to do?" Sarah continued to focus on her right thumbnail, not looking up as she spoke.

"We need to write a poem using text lingo, we still have to punctuate correctly and spell out words that aren't acronyms."

Tesoro looked back at Sarah. "You can help me come up with something witty that will help us build a case for our research on new uses of language. We have to prove that we still know how to write, even if it's with acronyms."

"So, how 'bout this?" Sarah reached over and typed on Tesoro's laptop:

"4 ur 411, ur gnr8n,

n2k r txt, 2 knw wuz↑ nxt,

kep ↑ wt us f u kn,

b/c d futr s n r h&ds."

(*For your information, your generation needs to know our text, to know what's up next. Keep up with us if you can, because the future is in our hands.*)

"Sarah, that's amazing. That's it, that's what we need! Okay, all that's left is making the slide show look good for our presentation."

"I'm good at that," Brett said.

"Yeah, right," Marcus said. "We all know your Dad does all of your work for you."

"You want me to smother you for real?"

"He has a point, Brett. The only reason the teachers don't call you out on this is because your family donates so much money to the school every year," Sarah said. "Everyone knows you're a cheater."

"So, why don't you show us what you can do on your own, for real?" Tesoro said.

"Give me that computer so I can pimp this thing out--for real." Brett grabbed the laptop right out of her hands.

Brett's mother walked out of the kitchen into the family room. Brett was typing furiously with the computer on his lap.

"You guys seem to have this under control. I'm heading to the gym and then the grocery store. Does anyone need anything before I leave?"

Her smile was way too bright and toothy. Brett, Tesoro, Sarah and Marcus all shook their heads no.

"Well then, I'm off."

Sarah's phone went off with an upbeat little ditty in the backpack by her feet. She placed her hand over the mouthpiece.

"My ride's out front. Do you guys need me for anything else, or am I over it?"

"No, you're over it! Your texting poem really is amazing!" Tesoro said.

"Am I over it, too?" Marcus asked.

"Yeah, I guess. You really didn't do anything though," Tesoro said.

"Ouch, that hurt." Marcus made a face as if he'd been hit and then laughed.

Sarah whispered to the person on the other end of the phone to "hang on" and asked Marcus, "You need a ride home?"

"Sure, I'm of no use here." He winked at Tesoro.

"Bye!" Sarah sang out. She and Marcus found their way to the marble entry and out the palladium style, lead-glass, double door with flanking windows.

"Are you almost finished?" Tesoro glanced sideways at Brett, who had not moved from his position on the sofa.

"Yeah, it's looking sweet. Take a look and tell me if you like what you see." Brett patted on the sofa beside him. Anxious to have the assignment finally finished, Tesoro moved beside Brett and leaned over him to view the laptop.

"Great...now let me see the first page."

"Here, you drive." Brett handed the laptop back to Tesoro for her review.

Brett moved in very close to Tesoro and pressed his leg up against hers. He looked at her intensely. She did not pull away from him this time. Brett shifted his weight slightly and moved his leg slowly up the length of hers. Tesoro pulled in her breath, her nostrils flaring out ever so slightly.

"Finish it." Tesoro abruptly passed the laptop back to Brett, quickly stood up and walked to the chair cattycorner the sofa.

"You're bossy," Brett blurted out.

"And you have a reputation as a player. All I want is for this project to be over. Can I count on you for that?" Being alone with Brett Merrick was suddenly making Tesoro incredibly uneasy.

"Okay, I asked for that. I'm sorry. Can you please come back over here so we can work together to get this done?"

Tesoro moved away from Brett and glanced toward the entry.

"I'm ready to be finished, just like you. I promise I will not do anything to you, I wouldn't hurt you," Brett said.

Tentatively, Tesoro inched her way beside Brett and peered at the presentation, the computer balanced on his lap.

"You can do an 'apply all' to the background to save time." Tesoro pointed to the command on the screen.

"Yeah, but I like variety." Brett said. He looked intently at her from the side of his eyes.

"The presentation needs to go together so it's easy to follow."

"You smell good." Brett picked up a lock of Tesoro's long hair and breathed in deeply. Tesoro started to pull away, but Brett reached his hand up to the nape of her neck and grabbed a large handful of her hair on the back of her head. With his other hand he moved the laptop to the end table. Before Tesoro could scream out his mouth was on hers and he forcefully pushed her down into the sofa cushions.

"Am I interrupting something?" A man's voice burst through Tesoro's moment of terror. Brett instantly loosened his hold on Tesoro. She grabbed her laptop, shoved it in her backpack and without looking back ran to the heavy front door.

"Aren't you going to stay to meet my Dad?" Brett yelled as she fled.

Tesoro closed the large door behind her. With tears welling up she scurried past the open garage toward the iron gate at the front drive.

A nauseous smell was coming out of the garage. The stench wafted up her nose, the rank odor of rotten, over-cooked broccoli mixed in with rubbing alcohol. Tesoro stopped, overtaken from the smell, and peered into the garage, curiosity overriding her fear. The three-car garage seemed normal, a large black, dual-cab pickup parked on one side with bikes, trash receptacles, and an assortment of tools. The pickup had a load of boxes in the bed. Tesoro jumped back with a start as the automatic garage door started to close.

"I'll need to open the front gate for you." Mr. Merrick walked up to Tesoro.

"I'm Brett's father." He reached out his thick hand.

"Nice to meet you." Tesoro did not extend her hand back, keeping her arms crossed at her chest.

He pointed his remote at the gate and it slid open, creating a direct passage for Tesoro to reach the public road by.

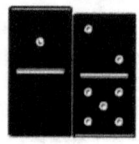

CHAPTER SEVENTEEN

Kissing and Carousing

The lights in the hall dimmed, transforming the mood of the Quince Años into sparkling magic. The spotlights aimed at the tiny mirrored squares on the slowly revolving ball twinkled across the center of the empty, wooden dance floor. The DJ turned up the volume as the chatting guests finished their dinner. Alonso was taking the place of his papá for the first dance, the padrino (*Godfather*) dance with the Quinceañera. He walked to Laurencia's table and took her hand, leading her to the dance floor. Her hands felt cold to him, very different from earlier in evening when they had practiced the dance together at her parents' house.

The first notes sounded for Vals Fascinación (*Fascination Waltz*). Alonso gracefully placed his right hand just above the small of Laurencia's back, holding his elbow out, parallel with his hand. Laurencia placed her arm on top of Alonso's, resting her hand on his shoulder. Alonso took her free hand into his left hand and intertwined his fingers slowly around hers. He looked Laurencia directly in the eyes and nodded gently at her to start the waltz.

"Were your hands clean before you touched my dress?" She leaned in, whispering through a forced smile to Alonso, not missing one move of the box step for her crowd of admirers. Alonso did not answer her; he was slightly offended. Laurencia followed Alonso's lead as he moved her gracefully through the forward balance step, and back balance step, dipping ever so slightly every time their feet slid from step to step.

Briefly glancing over Laurencia's shoulder, Alonso caught a glimpse of Laurencia's mamá dabbing a white lace handkerchief to the corner of her eye. He waltzed Laurencia into the side balance step to the left, then the same to the right, and once again slid into the box step. She felt stiff in her stride and he knew she was nervous and uncomfortable. He moved his hand gently down her back and up again in an attempt to relax her. Instead it threw her steps out of time with his, causing him to bump into Laurencia with full body contact. He backed away quickly, smiled and resumed the lead into the back balance step.

"Don't mess up this dance, it needs to be perfect," Laurencia whispered through her tight smiling lips--lips that did not seem as alluring to Alonso anymore.

"Don't worry. You look beautiful to everyone." Alonso spun her around, her white gown flaring out at the hem, in full swing.

"Do I look beautiful to you?"

Alonso leaned in and whispered into Laurencia's ear: "Sí, bien bonita." (*Yes, very beautiful.*)

She smiled naturally and her step lightened, her movements became fluid and they danced beautifully. The admiring guests applauded as they finished the last steps of the waltz.

The DJ's velvet voice filled the hall as he dimmed the lights, setting the mood for the chambelán dance, "Vals de las Mariposas" (*Waltz of the Butterflies*). Alonso again took Laurencia into his arms; she moved close to him as the first notes gently echoed across the room. He moved slowly and deliberately, leading Laurencia with tenderness through the dance he had memorized from his mamá's many lessons.

The twinkling white lights spun a web around the dancers as they moved in closer to each other, until Alonso held Laurencia against his body. The air seemed still and silent as the crowd lovingly watched the classic sight of poetic motion through dance. Alonso's black suit stood in sharp contrast to Laurencia's white dress; his sharp, chiseled bone structure, and jagged bangs moved from one side of his face to the other as he moved through the waltz with grace. Laurencia's cheeks flushed pink with the thrill of the moment and her expression softened as she gave in to Alonso.

She moved her gaze up to his and, just as the music lowered, Patricio prompted the two young dancers with a loud: "Beso, beso." (*Kiss, kiss.*)

Others joined in. "Beso, beso," they chanted. Alonso was caught up in the moment with Laurencia in his arms, her soft body pressed into his. His heart pounded as he bent down, ever so slightly and placed his lips lightly on hers. She closed her eyes as Alonso tasted tingling peppermint on her mouth and felt her breath mingle with his.

Without warning, Alonso saw Tesoro in his mind's eye and he held his lips still on Laurencia. He loosened his hold from around her small waist. In one fast motion, Laurencia pushed herself back from him, clearly taking offense to his lack of responsiveness. She stumbled back from him with a hurt and puzzled expression.

Patricio quickly moved onto the dance floor, signaled to the DJ to start the party music. He quickly walked up to Laurencia and grabbed her hand, moving her around the dance floor to the tempo of the fast-paced rhythm. The guests took Patricio's cue and hit the dance floor, bumping into each other, spilling their drinks, filling the space of the wooden floor in the hall with happy laughter and dancing.

Alonso stepped backward, almost falling. He did not feel right. It wasn't from what just happened with Laurencia, or thinking about Tesoro. Something did not seem right with the very air itself. A sudden movement caught his eye from the ceiling area. At first he thought he saw shadows between the disco ball lights, but he beheld an unmistakable vision of blacker than black shooting stars moving in a random, chaotic pattern above his head. His body felt prickly; the space between his upper lip and nose tingled with static electricity. He rubbed the base of his nose with the back of his hand, trying to dispel the odd sensation. But it moved to his stomach and filled his gut with waves of nausea.

The music pounded out of the DJ's over-sized speakers and blips of light flickered down on the dancing crowd. Alonso scanned the area for his sister, but she was not at the family table. He glanced over the dance floor, over the leering crowd watching the dancers--he could not see her anywhere. He couldn't shake the feeling of ill ease that came at him faster than a fighter jet.

Alonso spotted his mamá speaking with Father Fuentes and made his way quickly through the crowd, knocking a beer out of the hand of an older man, spilling it all over both of them. As he bent down to pick up the cup off the floor he felt dizzy and disoriented. Then it hit him, hard and fast, a searing pain on the left side of his head, just above his ear--he doubled over. Blipping at him in nanoseconds he saw a vision of Lilianna curled into a fetal position on dormant Saint Augustine grass, blood surrounding her head and running through her hair. He had to find Lilianna now!

Fumbling in his front pocket, Alonso grabbed his phone, pulled up her number and quickly thumbed in "20?" as he wove through the tables to his mamá.

"¿Has visto a Lilianna?" (*Have you seen Lilianna?*) Alonso interrupted Father Fuentes' sentence halfway through.

"Hueles a cerveza." (*You smell like beer.*) Alonso's mamá carefully eyed her son. "¿Estás tomado?" (*Are you drunk?*)

"No, no, mamá. Necesito encontrar a Anna." (*No, no, mamá. I need to find Anna.*) He tried to cover up his desperation.

"Anda afuera con Mauricio." (*She went outside with*

Mauricio.) Father Fuentes answered quickly.

"Gracias." Alonso rushed to the door, tightly clutching his phone.

Lilianna was outside--and so were members of Kaotik Koupé and the Royal Riderz car clubs. Alonso knew how dangerous car clubs partying together on the same turf could be. One sideways look or wrongful accusation could lead to a fight, or worse. He knew his cousins' club played tough and hard. He also knew they had a tenuous relationship with members of Royal Riderz, one of San Antonio's oldest, most prestigious lowrider clubs.

"¿Qué onda, flaco?" (*What's up, skinny?*) Patricio shoved Alonso's shoulder from behind, a push that sent him stumbling down the front steps of the hall.

"You couldn't keep your girl happy? You're lucky I was there to save your ass."

"She's not my girl." Alonso scanned the party of people outside. There were more people outside the old hall than inside dancing at the Quince Años. Lilianna had disappeared into the crowd as rhythmic rap music bellowed from sub-woofers in the open trunk of an '80's model Buick Regal coupe. Again, Alonso was stung by a brief sharp pain on the left side of his head. Thick feelings of nausea rolled over him as he shoved through the crowd, toward the street. His singular thought: find Lilianna before it was too late.

He heard yelling in the distance. Alonso caught a glimpse of Lilianna with the gaunt, tattooed man at her side. The tattooed man suddenly flicked his lit cigarette at one of the Royal Riderz members. Amazingly, the Royal Riderz member walked away calmly, dialed his phone and spoke briefly. The tattooed man walked up to the Royal Riderz member and shoved him, both hands on the chest, to the ground sending his phone flying through the air.

The yelling continued between the two men and Alonso

heard the word "dinero." The fight had to do with money. To Alonso's bewilderment, the Royal Riderz guy did not get up. He stayed on the ground yelling at the tattooed man who kicked him repeatedly in the ribs and arms.

"You said you'd pay me for that water pump TODAY," the tattooed man yelled, kicking the man on the ground again, this time directly on his stomach.

"You still owe me." The man on the ground spit the words out through his teeth, rolling over in pain on the dry grass. Alonso knew they were fighting over the very water pump his cousins had stolen.

"¡LLA Vasta!" Lilianna ran to the tattooed man and grabbed him from behind. He pushed her back and she came at him again.

A car painted flat black, chromeless and without plates emerged from a side street. It crawled down the road to the parking lot. A rear, black-tinted window rolled open reveling a man in the backseat. He wore mirrored aviator sunglasses and a dark blue bandana over his face. He pointed a gun directly at the tattooed man.

"¡Lilianna...no!" Alonso yelled, pushed his way through the fight crowd and lunged at his sister.

It was too late. A deafening shot rang out and she crumpled to the ground--thin, red blood oozed from just behind her left ear onto the dormant brown Saint Augustine grass.

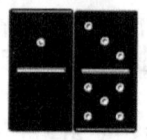

CHAPTER EIGHTEEN

Twins and Tears

"**S**omething just happened to you, something's wrong." Tino met Tesoro at the door, his eyes wide.

"I need some time." She placed her hand out as if to defend herself and ran up the stairs to her room. The door slammed shut behind her.

Tesoro and Tino shared a special connection. Like many dizygotic twins, they frequently completed each other's sentences and knew before anyone else if something was out of kilter with the other. Even though they shared their mother's womb as brother and sister, Tino knew they shared much more than that. Tino could feel his sister's feelings. When she was anxious, and he had no reason to be anxious, his heart rate would go up and he would feel edgy and nervous. When something really good happened to Tesoro, Tino would feel elated before she told him what had happened.

Tino thought back to a time they were in fourth grade: the school placed them with separate teachers to help them concentrate on their own. The school counselor felt they needed to develop as individuals. Tino and Tesoro hated this idea and their parents had to talk them into it. They had never been apart for long periods of time before. Tesoro's fourth grade teacher did not have the same excellent reputation his teacher held. That year, Tesoro struggled with mathematics and was not receiving the help she needed in the classroom to be successful.

They even shared headaches. At school that same year;

Tino could not think clearly, his head hurt, his stomach was in knots and he felt very sad for no apparent reason. Tino asked his teacher if he could go to the nurse's station. On his way to the nurse, he passed the counselors' office and noticed Tesoro waiting in a hard plastic chair in the hall. He asked her what happened and she let him know that she could not finish her math test; she did not understand the problems and that thinking so hard gave her a terrible headache. She was crying as she explained this and his headache began to lift, the knots in his stomach went away and his feelings of sadness disappeared. This was the first time he recognized clairsentience in himself, although he didn't have a name for it in the fourth grade. He just knew he could feel other people, especially his fraternal twin sister.

In grade school, Tino and Tesoro had sometimes been mistaken for each other. They both wore their straight black hair long, past their shoulders. Their mother liked to braid it down their backs and place colorful hair ties at the end of the long braid. The twins were the same height and same weight--even their voices sounding the same when they were young. Both were natural athletes and were always chosen first on sports teams--students fought over who was going to be with them.

The only physical difference was the bone structure in Tino's face. It was thinner, with an angular chin and long, thin nose that came to an almost hooked point on the end. Tesoro's nose was small and rounded; it reminded Tino of their grandmother's. By middle school, everyone could tell them apart. Tino grew tall and muscular. His nose fit his face better, giving him a distinct masculine appearance. He cut his hair shoulder length for football and Tesoro kept her long braid which bounced behind her as she ran with the Crockett Middle School track team. Tino missed seeing Tesoro run at school; he missed them being in athletics together.

Before the accident Tino protected Tesoro. He looked out for her in school, making certain no one messed with her. He introduced her to his friends and tried to get her past her natural shyness. In middle school he became the alpha twin. Tesoro was happy with this arrangement; glad to have someone she could count on to look after her.

Tino had been popular in middle school, one of the most-loved seventh graders at Crockett. Coach K handpicked him as the star running back for the football team that year. He was as fast as a mountain lion on the chase. With the skill of a great warrior, he could maneuver through the opposing team's defense without being touched. It was the best football season Crockett Middle School ever experienced.

After the accident, it all changed. Tesoro became Tino's main caregiver. Their parents had not meant for it to happen that way; it had been a natural progression. In the beginning Tino was angry at everyone and everything. He remembered biting his mom's arm so hard it caused her to bleed. He was hurting and he wanted everyone around him to hurt, too. The only person he did not feel angry at was Tesoro. So his parents stepped out of the way and let Tesoro work with her brother.

Right after the accident, Tino's popularity reached an all-time high. The entire football team paid him a visit one Saturday afternoon. They each signed a jersey with his number on it. Tesoro hung it on the wall of his room. This pissed Tino off even more. He knew he would never be on the field again. He hated looking at the jersey and had Tesoro take it down, placing it in his dresser drawer.

It didn't take much to get rid of his many visitors. All he had to do was be silent, glare and look cross. This was easy because of the immense pain he was in. People took his cue and left him alone. A few brave friends, his real friends lingered, but they received not one positive or kind word from him. One by one, they left him alone also. Except for Lindsey, she stayed in touch with him and he loved her for that.

Many months after the accident, when people had long stopped coming around, Tino longed to have his friends back.

He felt lonely. He would never push people out of his life, never take people who cared about him for granted again. This was the most difficult lesson he ever endured, more difficult than the physical pain. Without that lonely time, he would not have discovered his own spirit. His trip to Oklahoma with his grandparents was the first time he had slowed down enough to consider his spiritual nature. He remembered something his grandfather once told him: "When on a long journey, it's important to stop and rest, to let your soul catch up with you."

"My soul has caught up with me, Grandfather," Tino said to the ceiling of his family's den, as he often did, when in a reflective mood. He pulled his phone from his wheelchair side pouch and quickly texted his sister upstairs.

"r u k?" Although he already knew she was not.

Within a moment he heard back, "no."

"cn i hlp?"

"20?"

"den" He closed the phone and placed it back into his pouch.

"Hey-hey," Tino said slowly. He wheeled to face his sister when she entered the room. He knew to be patient, to wait for her to talk. Tesoro sat down on the overstuffed leather chair by the reading window. She looked down and bit her lower lip; her chin quivered.

"Hey Sis, I'm right here." Tino whispered, placing his hand under her chin, bringing her eyes up to his. "I'm right here." He looked directly into her large, almond-shaped eyes that were welling up with tears.

"Who do I need to beat up?" Tino asked, trying to make her laugh. It didn't work; she let the tears flow.

"I was almost raped."

"What? Who did this to you? Who...that guy you drew a

picture of in your sketchbook?

"What were you doing in my sketchbook?"

"Tesoro, what happened?"

Sobbing she said, "This guy named Brett, you don't know him. He went to a private middle school, his family is super rich. We were assigned group work by our English teacher and we all met at his parents' house to finish it tonight. Somehow, I ended up alone with him and he attacked me. He pulled my hair like a horse's mane and forced me down on the sofa, choking me with his face on mine."

"Do we need to call the police?"

"No, he didn't rape me. His dad showed up and I was able to get out of the house. Plus, he would lie about it and make me look like a fool. He already lied to his dad."

"The asshole," Tino said. He had worked hard over the past two years to move past anger, but this made his blood boil. The intense feelings of helplessness and anger came flooding back and he didn't like it one bit. He took a deep breath and counted backwards from ten to calm down.

"I don't want to talk anymore, just hold me." Tesoro climbed onto his lap in the wheelchair and flung her arms around him. The twins clung to each other, both lost in their own thoughts and unresolved fears.

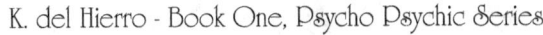

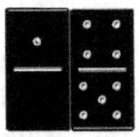

CHAPTER NINETEEN

Nurses and Black Bears

Lilianna's hair, black and board straight, overflowed to one side of the freshly washed white hospital pillow. Bulky gauze covered the left side of her head. Her eyes were closed, not moving, not blinking at all. Alonso reached over his sister and gently moved the flexible, clear intravenous cord that pumped life into his sister's arm over the top of her abdomen. He moved next to her on the bed, lying down beside her comatose body. Shutting his eyes in exhaustion, Alonso fell asleep by Lilianna as he so often had over the past few days.

The dream was always the same for Alonso. She stood in the center of an empty hospital corridor in a gown, feet bare, body skeletal, bald, with black circles under her eyes. She appeared to be about eight years old. Alonso knew she was dead. She looked him directly in the eyes and slowly walked down the long hallway. Each time she stopped in front of a large grey double door. Off to one side was a round metal button. As the dream always played out, she would stop in front of this button and point. Curiosity always got the best of Alonso in this dream. He wanted to see what was on the other side. What was the girl trying to show him? He would press the button and the door would not open. Frustrated, he pressed harder and harder until he was hitting instead of pressing it, yelling, "C'mon, c'mon." He turned around to ask the girl how to get in and each time she was gone.

He awoke to the soft rhythmic beeping of Lilianna's medical devices that held her life. Slowly opening his eyes, the dim light of the hospital room could not hide what he saw next:

a misty, silvery figure moving slowly past the foot of the bed. Alonso blinked and the figure dissipated in that same millisecond. He felt eerily alone in the room. He rubbed his eyes hard, believing he was still trapped between the dream world and the conscious world, not sure of what he just saw.

Propping himself up on one elbow and rolling over to face Lilianna, he wondered where Anna's spirit could be. He wondered if perhaps he could meet her in the barren land of the violet sky, where he met Tino. Abruptly, two male nurses entered the room. Flipping on the lights, they methodically checked Lilianna's monitors, flipping through pages of her files and jotting down notes.

"How are you doing?" the tall African American nurse asked. Alonso slid off the side of his sister's bed and back into the chair beside it. The nurse had a kind face with large compassionate eyes and the smoothest skin Alonso had ever seen.

"Just alright," Alonso said.

"We need to put her on her side now." Alonso moved the large hospital chair away from the bed so the nurses could do their job. They rolled Lilianna to one side and placed specially shaped pillows against her backside to keep her from rolling limply onto her back. Placing a pillow between her folded knees, they rearranged her feet in a running position, one in front of the other, and slipped her warming booties back on.

The older nurse rubbed her arms and legs with his gloved hands, while the nurse with the kind face changed out IV bags. Tubes from underneath the bandage on Lilianna's head drained a clear runny fluid into a bag hanging low from a metal bar off the side of the hospital bed.

"Hey, I haven't met you yet, I'm Jon, I'm new to ICU," said the younger nurse with the compassionate eyes. "You're her brother, right?" Flipping through the charts, he asked, "Alonso?"

"Yeah...Alonso." He was past the initial shock of whether or not his sister was going to live or die. He questioned what they were doing to her, what medicines were being pushed through the tubes running into her body. He felt overwhelmingly protective of her and watched every move the nurses made. He didn't want anyone to make a mistake while she couldn't take care of herself.

"You interested in medicine?" Jon asked.

"Not until three days ago."

"Yeah, you've been here three days?"

"Sometimes my mamá comes, so I can sleep. We take turns. It's just the two of us."

Alonso stepped away from the wall he was leaning on and went to the window, looking outside from the fifth floor at the San Antonio skyline.

"I haven't met your mom yet," the older nurse said.

"It's hard for her to be here sometimes. When she is here, she cries all the time."

Alonso felt relieved to talk with the nurses. He turned around and looked directly into Jon's caring eyes-big, soft, and round-just looking into his eyes encouraged Alonso to open up to Jon.

"My papá isn't with us anymore; he's been gone for weeks. My sister's been with a car club. If my papá were here, we wouldn't have this trouble."

Both nurses looked at each other in one fast glance.

"Yeah?" Jon said.

"Yeah, that bullet wasn't meant for her." Alonso reached over and pushed a lock of long hair off his sister's face. "She didn't deserve this." Alonso walked back over to the window.

"Who was it meant for?"

There was a quiet knock on the door, jolting their conversation to an abrupt end.

"Is it okay if I come in?" a voice asked, thick with a Spanish accent. Alonso recognized the skinny, tattooed man immediately. He looked different in the hospital room lighting, not so hard around the edges.

Jon quickly questioned the man. "Are you family?"

"No."

"What the hell do you want?" Alonso asked.

"I want to give Lilianna a gift." The man stepped forward, placed his hand in his right pocket and pulled out a rabbit's foot on a key ring. He held it up so everyone in the room could see it. He handed it over to Alonso.

"Para la seurte…" (*For luck…*) He stopped and gazed at Anna's motionless body. He put his head down and walked to the door without another word. For an instant, Alonso saw the same fast moving black orbs he had seen at the Quince Años around the man's head as he left the room.

"Do you know him?" Jon continued adjusting the medical equipment and jotted down notes on Lilianna's chart.

"No." Alonso did not want to talk anymore. He felt uneasy and in a dark mood. A deep, confusing anger crept across him; he wasn't sure how to respond to anything, or anyone, anymore. He placed the rabbit's foot in the nightstand drawer and closed it firmly.

"See you around," Jon said. He placed the pen in his front pocket.

"Let us know if you need anything," the older nurse added.

"Hey, Alonso," a familiar voice sounded at the door, just as the nurses left the room.

"Tía Ruby, tío Frank!" Alonso ran to their arms and the

three of them embraced. Tía Ruby held Alonso's face in her hands and kissed him on the forehead. It seemed an eternity had come and gone since he had last seen his tía and tío over dinner at the elegant restaurant.

"How is she today?" Tío Frank asked, moving to Lilianna's bedside.

"The same, she's not waking up. Her face is not as swollen as it was."

"How are you doing?" Tía Ruby looked hard at Alonso.

"Tired, I'm tired."

"Tired! Every time we've been here you've been asleep in the waiting room up the hall! I can't imagine how on earth you can be tired."

Alonso chuckled. He had been sleeping a lot more than usual.

"I went by the school today to pick up your work from the front office. They had something for you."

Tía Ruby handed him a large, folded-over piece of bright yellow construction paper. Alonso opened it slowly; the paper was filled with colorful notes, doodles and signatures from everyone in his art class. In the lower left-hand corner of the page, a small pencil drawing of a wolf caught his attention. Tesoro's signature was beside it and he anxiously read what she wrote:

"To Alonso, I hope your sister gets well soon. My brother almost died once. I understand. Take care of you, too, Tesoro"

Reaching into her large designer purse, tía Ruby pulled out a small item wrapped in lavender tissue paper.

"This is for you. A girl brought it to the office while we were there today." She handed the small package over to Alonso. He took it and held it in his hand for a moment, unopened. He knew it was from Tesoro, he could feel it was from her. He held his breath as he opened the soft paper. A note dropped from the package to the floor. Tía Ruby picked it up for him.

"This is for your sister. It's from my tribe. It's a black bear made of onyx, it reminds me of your eyes. Place it by her facing the east. It will help her through the transition back to the land of the living. xxoo Tesoro

P.S., I hope you don't think I'm weird for giving this as a gift."

Alonso held the small stone in his hand. Only an inch long, it felt heavy, cool, and its energy felt good in his hands. The hospital window faced the east. Alonso placed the bear on the window sill, facing downtown San Antonio.

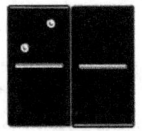

CHAPTER TWENTY

Closed Doors and Backseats

"**C**'mon, open, open damn it." Alonso screamed at the grey double door. He body slammed the door; he pounded the round, silver button...and nothing. It would not open. His frustration was more than he could tolerate, so he screamed, low at first, from the gut, then up, louder, into his throat, a tormented, scratchy, rough scream.

"They can't let you through, you know," a calm male voice sounded from behind him. Alonso whirled around to find nothing but an empty hospital corridor. He ran in the direction of the voice, ran as hard as he could, his Chucks squeaking as they hit the highly polished linoleum floor. Without warning, the same locked door appeared right in front of him. He did not have time to slow down. Alonso threw himself to the ground as if he were sliding into home plate, pulled his elbows over his head and his hands behind his neck. He was going to hit hard and he knew it. Instead, he blew through the closed door, sliding feet first on the floor, as if mass and matter didn't exist. He opened his eyes and he was back at the Quince Años, lying in the middle of the crowded dance floor in his rented suit.

He pulled himself up thinking he could run outside and keep Lilianna from being shot in the head, thinking somehow the universe was offering him another chance to save his sister. When he made his way outside and looked for his sister through the crowd of car club people, she was nowhere to be found. He walked to the street, half expecting to see her on the ground, bleeding. But, she was not there.

Then he saw something that stunned him--Tesoro! She was leaning against his cousins' Impala looking right at him with a Mona Lisa smile. She looked amazing. Her jeans were tight and fit just right, showing her feminine curves and athletic legs. Tesoro's large, dark, almond-shaped eyes cut a hole right to his heart. She slowly reached up to brush a lock of black hair out of her face as a breeze swept past. He loved the way her mouth curved up at the corners when her nicely shaped lips rounded into a smile. Tesoro's loosely fitted, pale lavender cotton blouse draped across her chest in a low swoop, with a gathered small string tie that held the shirt together in the front. The fabric was also gathered under her breasts and again at the short cap sleeves. The silver and turquoise pendant rested gently on her chest, rising and falling with each breath. She was a goddess to Alonso, feminine and alluring beyond his wildest dreams, a contemporary Athena Nike.

Tesoro reached behind her and pulled a piece of folded paper from her back pocket. She slowly unfolded it and showed it to him. Alonso moved in a little closer to read it: "xxoo" was the only thing written in the center of the notebook page. Tesoro smiled even bigger at Alonso, who instinctively, knew exactly what he had to do. He'd never in his life felt so attracted to a girl. He gently pushed her body up against the gold Impala and kissed her hard, gently biting at her lips. She kissed him back, fast and full. He felt out of control as he placed his hands up the back of her shirt, the small of her back curving in toward his body. Her skin felt soft, as if it were warm silk and all he wanted was to feel more of her. He squeezed his hands around her bare waist, under her loose shirt, pulling her in even closer. He was overcome and overwhelmed with strong emotion for her.

They moved into the large backseat of the Impala and shut the door, out of the din of the car club activity, the loud, rhythmic pulse of rap reverberating through the cool night air. She was breathing hard through her mouth, her eyes wild and large, searching his face.

"You're beautiful," he whispered. He placed his hand across her cheek, running it down to her neck and undoing the loosely tied, gathered string bow at her chest. Her shirt fell open a bit, exposing the rounded tops of her breasts. He looked at her for a moment longer and placed his mouth gently on hers, lowering her body onto the wide car seat. He kissed her mouth, her cheek; he sucked and bit gently on her neck. She ran her hands through his hair and down his back. He lowered himself and lightly kissed the top of her chest. Pushing his body up from hers with one hand and looking her directly in the eyes, his jagged black hair falling around his face, he moved her shirt lower and lower with his other hand...

Suddenly, a blinding light shone and Alonso opened his eyes to see Jon, the nurse, standing beside him in the otherwise empty hospital waiting room.

"We heard screaming, are you okay in here?" Jon asked.

Alonso had una grande erección; he quickly pulled his graphic tee over his jeans and rolled over on his side to camouflage it. His breathing was shallow and his entire face glowed in a fine mist of sweat. Alonso cleared his throat.

"It's alright, that happens to me every morning," Jon laughed as he casually sat down in the chair across from the sofa Alonso rested on. "She must be hot." John said. Alonso laughed harder than he had in a long time--harder than his grande erección.

"You can't even imagine," Alonso said.

Jon reached around to scratch the back of his neck and said: "Man, to be your age again."

He shook his head slowly back and forth. He was quiet for a moment and then looked at Alonso seriously.

"You know there's the possibility that your sister may never be the same again."

"She's going to be fine," Alonso said. He had run this same

question through his mind many times before. He would always shake this thought, keeping a picture of his sister in perfect health in mind.

"You seem so certain, how is that?"

"I just know it. There's no other way for me to think about her."

"That's fair. You don't want all of the medical details, do you?"

"Why should I? You guys do your job and I'll do mine as her brother." Alonso sat up as he bluffed Jon in as tough of a tone as he could muster. He did want to know everything; he was just afraid.

"What's your job?"

"To be here for her..." Alonso said.

"What about your life, your school, the hot girl?"

"My aunt and uncle are bringing my school work for me. I'm keeping up just fine." Alonso lied about his school work; he had not opened a book.

"This could go on for a while."

"Then I'm here for a while."

"This place can get to you."

"What do you mean by that?" Alonso wondered if Jon meant all of the death he felt here, the intense dreams he was having.

"Hospitals, they get to people after a while. Make people depressed. You need to get back to your life, is what I mean by that."

Alonso didn't want to leave Lilianna. His family was falling apart; losing his papá was hard enough. There was no way he was going to lose his sister, too. He felt scared.

"I can't leave her alone. What if she wakes up and no one

is here?"

"I'm here, and so is our entire staff. This is what we do." Alonso stiffened, his arms crossed over his chest, head down in a frown and knees drawn in together.

Jon asked. "Do you have a phone?"

"Yes." Alonso popped the phone out of his pocket and held it up.

"Let me put your number on file and I promise you will be the first person we call when she wakes up. Put my number in your phone. You can call me anytime I'm on night shift."

"I don't know how to get a ride back to the hospital."

"Your aunt and I have already talked about that. She let me know she can bring you back here at a moment's notice."

"You've already talked to her about all this?"

"She let me know they have your dog at their house and they've been taking care of him." Jon said.

"Sombra," Alonso muttered under his breath. He had not thought about Sombra much over the past few days. How could he have forgotten about his dog? The reality of losing touch with his responsibilities came crashing in.

"When are they coming to pick me up?"

"Tomorrow before school starts."

"Guess I better get my school work done." Alonso looked at the stack of untouched school papers and books on the table next to the sofa.

"Trust me, it will keep your mind off of everything else," Jon said. "You a coffee drinker?" Alonso smiled and shook his head 'no.'

"Okay, I'm going to let you be. Don't forget, I'm right up the hall if you need anything."

CHAPTER TWENTY-ONE

Basketball and Baseball Caps

At the front desk, Assistant Principal Martin personally checked Alonso into school after his absence.

"Let's go talk in my office for a minute."

"Sure." Alonso wondered if the hospital or the police had told the school that his mamá doesn't live in this district.

"How are you doing?" A.P. Martin asked, shutting the door behind him. Alonso knew this was not a good sign. He'd never seen an administrator's office before; it was bare with nothing on the walls. Beige file cabinets and piles of paperwork were everywhere.

"Have a seat," A.P. Martin said with squinted eyes.

Alonso was ridged with tension. He sat on the edge of the hard wooden chair.

"We're glad you're back at school. How's your make-up work going?"

"I stayed up last night and finished most of it." Alonso relaxed, relieved that he was still a student at Flores. He moved back in the chair.

"That's good. I have something for you." A.P. Martin reached into his center desk drawer and pulled out a light-blue laminated hall pass with "counseling" printed clearly in the center. He passed it across his cluttered desk to Alonso.

"It has an expiration date of two weeks from today. I want you to feel free to use it at any time to visit your counselor. If you make a poor choice to use it for something other than the counseling office...there are consequences. Do you understand?"

"Yes sir." Alonso tucked the stiff slip deep into his black backpack. He knew what the pass meant. He'd seen other students use them to get out of class; usually the emos and the students who were picked on all of the time. He didn't foresee pulling out this pass not even for an emergency.

Something suddenly caught Alonso's eye. He looked just past A.P. Martin to the small, fast moving black orbs, the same ones he saw at the Quince Años and around the tattooed man. He narrowed his vision in on A.P. Martin and gave him a suspicious once over. The Assistant Principal pushed back from his desk and leaned back in his chair, as if to distance himself from the student sitting across from him.

"I'm not going to have trouble with you, am I? We have a zero tolerance policy for any type of violence at Flores. If you're upset, go to counseling--don't take it out on anyone here. Do you understand what I'm telling you?"

"Yes sir."

"We're in first period now, you may go to class," A.P. Martin said.

Alonso went right to his locker, trying to shake off the funny feeling of static from the inside of his nose and across his upper lip. He knew the meeting with the Assistant Principal did not go well, that A.P. Martin did not trust him...with good reason. Alonso was living a lie by attending this school, outside of his real district.

"Chales, mi mero mole está en México DF." ("*Hell, my real district is Mexico City.*")

A pale blue glimmer of light floated just to the left of Alonso's open locker, just within his peripheral vision. The light suddenly disappeared; in its place, a student was walking in the hall. At first he thought the light was merely a reflection-

-but maybe it wasn't a reflection after all.

Something seemed odd about the guy coming toward him. He seemed too thin, plus he broke school rules and wore a baseball cap. He didn't have a backpack with him, nor could Alonso see any type of hall pass in his hands. As he moved in closer Alonso noticed the boy had the same dark circles under his eyes as the dead girl in his dreams. Alonso locked eyes with him and turned around from his locker as he walked past-- neither breaking the intense stare.

The teen's mouth was not moving, but Alonso heard him say something. He could not understand the individual words, but he recognized the voice. It was from the dream he had at the hospital. Alonso glanced up at the ceiling in disbelief. When he looked back down the hall, the student was gone.

"¡Dios mío me estoy volviendo loco!" (*Oh my God, I'm going crazy*.) Alonso placed both of his hands flat on top of his head, elbows out on either side.

"I'm hearing things and seeing things." He stood in front of his locker, moving his hands to grip high up on the door and on the opposite side of the open locker for balance. Slumped over, head down, staring at the floor Alonso tried to make sense of what was happening to him...what was happening to his life. He remembered studying the effects of stress in his health class. Could it be he was having some type of breakdown? Or, even worse, could it be he was really seeing the dead? If he was, what was he supposed to do about it? Why did they choose him? It wasn't as if they were giving him some type of profound message, like the psychic shows on television. It was all gibberish to Alonso. This had nothing to do with his life right now.

Louder than a game show buzzer the school bell sounded. Within seconds the halls filled with students. Alonso pulled his morning textbooks from his locker and started up the hall to his second period class. Rounding a corner he spotted Tesoro. Then he spotted Brett, pushing and shoving his way through the sea of students, right toward Tesoro. Alonso looked on curiously as Brett caught up to her and started talking, using a lot of exaggerated hand gestures. They disappeared into an English room together and Alonso lost sight of them.

Second period math class always came easy to Alonso. He liked his math teacher, Coach Rodriquez, and always knew what to expect with the organized structure of the class. Students stayed in the room past the regular class time each day to watch "Student News" with the local "FBTV" or "Flores Bobcat Television" clips put on by students in the film production class. Usually, this was a time for Alonso to finish his math assignment so it didn't turn into homework. But today the student clips caught his attention.

"Today we are going to have a moment of silence for Skye Peterson. Skye, a sophomore at Flores, died last Sunday at Christus Santa Rosa Children's Hospital after his four-year battle with Leukemia. This moment of silence will be accompanied by a photo tribute of Skye put together by his friends here at Flores. Will everyone please take a moment with us to stand in silence in honor of Skye Peterson."

Alonso stood up with the rest of his class. He had trouble holding himself together--the student on the screen in his math class was the same guy he saw in the hallway wearing a baseball cap during first period...the same guy whose voice he had heard at the hospital. His mind reeled. What he had seen was real. He had seen a dead student walking up the hallway of Flores. He wanted to tell someone. He was internally freaking out, but everyone would think he was crazy. Neither Alonso, nor anyone else in the room, realized that his own energy caused the fluorescent light above his head to flicker alternately dim to bright.

Alonso placed his head down on his desk as soon as the moment of silence and picture tribute was over. The florescent light tube above his head went completely out.

The routine was to pull his afternoon books from his locker before lunch, but nothing felt routine about this day to Alonso. He wasn't hungry, so he skipped eating and went directly to the gymnasium to shoot hoops with the guys.

"¿Qué paso, chaparro?" Marcus yelled from the loud, crowded gym floor. This always made Alonso laugh. He was already six-feet, one-inch tall, far from being short. Marcus rifled a basketball right at Alonso's face. He caught it cleanly and placed it under one arm, allowing his backpack to slide off his other shoulder. He caught the strap in his hand right before it fell off completely and threw it into the massive stack of backpacks on the bottom steps of the bleachers. Alonso eyed Marcus as he dribbled the ball right past him, put up a long shot at the hoop, only to have another boy throw a ball at the same time. Their balls collided mid-air, both missing their shot.

"Nice one." A.P. Martin said from the sidelines. He reached down to pick up Alonso's ball and threw it back. Alonso gave A.P. Martin a low, quick acknowledgement wave, honed in on Marcus and took off dribbling to the other side of the court.

Moving quickly to the right to avoid Marcus' steal attempt, Alonso tripped over someone's foot and was sent reeling to the wooden floor. Landing with a hard thud, Alonso felt the wind knocked out of his lungs. Gasping for air he rolled over to the bleachers. He could feel the rhythmic thud of feet thundering past him on the ball court floor. Alonso looked to the bleachers; sitting on the third row up was Skye Peterson. Alonso stood quickly not taking his eyes off Skye this time.

"What do you want with me?" he asked. Suddenly a student slammed into Alonso's side, knocking his attention away from Skye. When Alonso looked to the bleachers again the newly dead teen was gone.

CHAPTER TWENTY-TWO

Double Dipping and Dog Kisses

"**C**ome sit by me, pretty please with sugar on top!" Tracy beamed a wide smile at Alonso as he boarded the bus. Tracy ran her hand across the empty vinyl seat beside her and bounced a few times, her smile widening, red hair dancing around her face.

"Sure." Alonso slid in next to her, not taking his eyes off his phone, carefully scrolling for text messages that may have come in from the hospital. There were none, so he took this as a good sign that Anna was doing well, or, at least the same.

"How's your sister?" Tracy asked. Alonso placed the phone in his front jeans pocket instead of his backpack where he usually kept it.

"The same, I guess." Alonso's attention was diverted; he spotted Tesoro and Brett talking outside the bus. Her back was to him. Brett smiled and reached over to help Tesoro pick up her backpack from the ground. Tracy noticed, too.

"He's talking to her a lot lately."

"Are they a couple?" Alonso tried to play it cool.

"I don't know, yet. I'll find out for you." She winked at him.

"You don't have to find out. I don't care." Alonso slumped into the hard bus seat. Tracy backhanded him across his shoulder.

"Yeah, right! You do so care!" They laughed. Tesoro

boarded the bus and walked right past Alonso without glancing his way. She took a seat far to the rear of the bus and stared out the window.

"Like I said, I don't care and I don't think she does either."

"She looks upset." Tracy glanced over her shoulder at Tesoro. "I'm going to talk to her."

"Whatever." Alonso slouched deep into the bus seat, arms crossed over his chest.

"Hey, can I sit here?" Tracy said, sitting down beside Tesoro without waiting for a reply. "So, what's up?"

"Hi." Tesoro smiled at Tracy.

"Hey sweetie, you look upset, what's up?" she asked again.

"Oh nothing...really." Tesoro glanced back out the window and turned back to Tracy. "What do you think of Brett Merrick?"

Tracy laughed. "He's a major player. Why?"

"He never leaves me alone."

"Yeah, I've seen him around you a lot lately."

"It's like he hunts me down at every corner. He's overbearing and makes me cringe at the sight of him."

"You seem to be laughing when he's around. Why so glum now?"

"He does make me laugh. He does these stupid magic tricks with money."

"Like what?"

"Take today, he showed me a quarter, slapped his hands together and it disappeared, then he pulled a quarter out from behind my ear. Next thing I know he's all up in my face holding two quarters end to end, like they're floating between his index finger and thumb. That just bugs the crap out of me."

Tracy laughed, "Seems he's trying to impress you."

"Well, he's just getting on my nerves. Right before I got on the bus he ran in front of me and pushed a pencil right through the center of a quarter. I mean, how does he do that?" Tesoro made a scrunched up face.

"That's not so bad, just tell him to go away."

"Wish it were that easy. I don't want to like him or laugh at him."

"And you do?" Tracy asked.

"No, that's not the only reason I want him to go away..."

Alonso looked into the bus driver's large mirror. He had a clear view of Tesoro and Tracy talking. She was looking down as if in deep thought. She was so beautiful. He could not stop himself from staring. He wondered how he could get her attention. Was she even interested in him? He didn't think he stood a chance with Brett after her. In the high school jungle Brett was popular and he was not. Then he thought back to the bear she gave as a gift and smiled.

Tracy bounded up the bus aisle beside Alonso. "They're not a couple," she whispered in his ear. The bus stopped at the corner close to tío Frank's home. Tracy gave him a hug around the neck "I hope your sister's going to be okay."

Alonso glanced back at Tesoro, who was watching intently as he hugged Tracy. She quickly looked away. He hopped off the bus and looked back as it pulled away. Tesoro was looking directly at him through the window. She smiled ever so gently and slowly lifted her hand in a wave.

"You're beautiful," he said directly at her, hoping she could read his lips. He saw her laughing through the glass.

"Damn." He shrugged, smiling to himself. He remembered the tingles he felt when they sat next to each other watching his phone charge from his invention. Alonso wished to feel those tingles again, the very thought gave him goose pimples up and down his arms--he shuddered with a thrilling rush. Alonso walked briskly to tío Luis': his shoulders back, posture straight and his long legs moving with purpose and speed.

"Tía Ruby, it smells good in here. Have you been cooking all day?" In the kitchen tía Ruby was busy smashing pinto beans with the flat bottom of a ceramic coffee mug in an iron skillet. The smell of the food was too much for Alonso. He was starving. Tilapia fish filets were turning a light golden brown in the skillet beside her. She poured a bowl of diced tomatoes, serrano peppers, onions, green olives, lemon juice and capers over the filets. Popping a lid on the skillet, she turned the heat down to a simmer.

"There!" she announced proudly. Alonso had already located pico de gallo and flour tortillas on the kitchen island and was helping himself.

"Don't double dip. I don't know who you've been kissing!" Tía Ruby laughed and gave him a gigantic hug.

"It's good to be back here." Alonso hugged his tía in return.

"There's someone else that's missed you." Tía Ruby pointed to the laundry room door and Sombra scratched his paw from the other side.

"Sombra!" He flung the door open and the jet-black, pointy nosed, fluffy tailed dog bounded into the kitchen. Alonso and Sombra rolled around on the wooden kitchen floor for some time, Sombra licking Alonso's face all over and nipping at his nose. Alonso pet Sombra all over and rubbed his ears. For Alonso, it felt so good to be laughing again. It was good to feel safe.

"Hey, I took Sombra to the vet yesterday. He's about two years old and a purebred Swedish Lapphund. A fine example, according to the vet, show dog quality!"

Sombra's ears perked up and he stood a little taller, all of the sudden appearing regal.

"We took him to the groomers and had him bathed, too. Doesn't he smell good?"

"Do you smell good?" Alonso grabbed Sombra, buried his face in the dog's ruff and smelled him. This had both of them joyfully rolling on the floor again.

After eating, Alonso ran upstairs with Sombra to his room. He leapt through the air directly into the center of his bed and the covers flew up around him in a soft heap as he rolled over onto his back, smiling. Sombra hopped next to him on the bed, with his black front paws over Alonso's stomach. Sombra gave Alonso a doggie kiss on the chin and rested his head between his paws. Alonso pulled out his phone and checked for messages--nothing. He wanted to call Jon, but it might still be too early for him to be on night shift. He stared at Jon's phone number on the blue screen while he slowly petted Sombra and both dozed off to sleep.

Alonso was in his hospital corridor dream again, facing the large door that would not open. He hit the chrome button repeatedly with no results, then with all of his might and will he body-slammed into the heavy double door. Like before, he flew right through as if matter and mass didn't exist.

When he sat up he was in the garden tub of the home under construction at Mansiones de Piedra Blanca. He stood all of the way up and looked down into the filthy brown water. Something stirred just underneath the surface. It was the girl, the bald girl from his dreams. He froze as she pulled her body up into a sitting position, right from between his legs in the tub.

He was immobilized, frozen, as she stood up and stepped outside of the tub and onto the concrete floor. She left wet, bare footprints behind her as she walked into what would someday be the kitchen. The girl squatted down and placed her wet hand on the dry concrete. She looked at the floor and ever so slowly looked up, staring hard at Alonso. With fervent eye contact, suddenly only her face filled his entire field of vision.

She was talking to him, fast. Alonso could not distinguish the words that filled his brain. It was as if her mouth and her words were out of sync, or as if she were speaking in another tongue.

Alonso heard his phone ringing. He opened his eyes to find Sombra crouched at the edge of the bed with his hackles up. A chill brushed across his bare arm, it caused him to shiver. He looked to his side and nothing was there. He looked at Sombra again and ever so briefly caught a glimpse of the bald girl at the end of his bed. His phone went to message. The room fell silent. Although he could no longer see her, he could feel the girl in the room, frightened, alone, and very, very dead.

"I don't know what you want with me?" He waited for a response, then in a little louder tone said, "I don't understand. What do you want?"

He let out a fast, frustrated sigh and Sombra rushed up, licking him on the face. He still felt the girl's presence, but his need to listen to the message was stronger than his need to talk to some possible figment of his imagination.

His phone let out two short blips, letting him know that he had a voice message saved. He pressed play and listened to his message:

"Hey Alonso, this is Jon, the nurse from the hospital. My shift just started and I wanted to let you know that Lilianna is the same. She's resting, and so is your mom. Your mom is spending the night here. Both she and I agree that you should stay at your uncle's house and get some rest. I'll call you back if anything changes."

Jon's voice was soothing to Alonso; he closed his phone, reached into his backpack and pulled out his homework.

CHAPTER TWENTY-THREE

The Raven, the Owl and the Falcon

"So...he's G.T." Tino scrolled quickly down the web pages he brought up from his research on Brett Merrick. Glancing over the Sacred Heart private middle school web site, Tino had discovered that Brett had taken a first place award in eighth grade at the regional Destination Imagination exhibit. He deduced that only students in the Gifted and Talented program could receive this award--so Brett must be G.T. Tino surfed over to the Flores High School site. It didn't take him long to find Brett on this site, too. His name was all over the place, student of the month for October; "A" honor roll list, Student Council member and quarterback for the football team.

"Dang, I'd be playing ball with him this year." The screen held a picture of Brett in his Flores jersey. Zooming in, Tino thought that Brett might be of European descent, probably Czech Republic or Polish. He looked a little harder and thought, maybe Austrian with a little Italian in him. He had a wide, muscular, stocky build. His hair was brown and wavy; his eyes, bright blue. Looking harder, Tino noted Brett's serious expression, the narrowing of his eyes and the two distinct vertical lines between his eyebrows. His straight eyebrows were low on his forehead, pulled down into a scowl, reflecting no sense of happiness whatsoever.

"This guy's an asshole." Tino closed the laptop. He had seen enough to know Brett Merrick could cause serious problems for Tesoro. What had happened to Tesoro at the beginning of the week was deeply under his skin more than he wanted to admit.

Tino wheeled across the Saltillo tile to his bed, frustrated that he could not go to school to personally kick Brett's ass anytime soon. He amused himself with the thought of wearing Brett's scalp as a necklace.

An idea rolled across his brain as swift as a lightning strike in the southern sky and he started to think out loud:

"Tesoro knows Alonso from school. Tesoro knows Brett from school. Alonso and Brett go to the same school--they could know each other." He pulled up onto his bed, leaned back and placed his hands behind his head. "If not, they need to know each other...Alonso can protect Tesoro from Brett...IF I can trust him to stay away from her."

Tino shut his eyes and focused. He needed to know if he could truly trust Alonso.

"Grandfather, I need your guidance. I need all of my spirit guides to work with me tonight," Tino said to the ceiling in his bedroom. "I need to know more about Alonso."

He shut his eyes and took a slow, deep breath; he felt his body relaxing. He took another slow, even deeper breath, imagining his breath running up the core of his body and out of the top of his head. He let himself go into a completely relaxed state, where the brain settles into quiet theta waves...the place between sleep and wakefulness, where anything can happen.

Tino floated comfortably just outside of his body. He could see the black raven and the owl sitting side by side on his window sill, both watching him. From his open window they flew away together and Tino followed them into the star-filled heavens, just as he had done countless times before.

The raven was Tino's main spirit guide and his Tonkawa namesake, Racing Raven. It is said that the raven has the ability to see into the future by racing his eyes out in front of where he is positioned and back again. This is not for the faint of heart; the raven only chooses humans capable of seeing the dark side of their own nature with no fear. The raven is always present when a person is experiencing a transformation. With the help of the raven, Tino had the ability to see clearly into the spirit world and understand his dreams.

As Tino followed his guides, faster and faster, a third bird emitting brilliant, yellow-gold light joined them. As quickly as Tino wished to be with them in the place of the violet skies he was there, and so were his guides. Perched on a ledge were the raven and the owl. From the golden light, the falcon emerged and perched beside the owl. Tino glanced down at his own ethereal body, admiring the glow radiating from his inner self. He could see his own aura very clearly in this place. From the boulder turquoise pendant hanging from his neck an electric streak of purple light bolted across the surface. He felt a light, tingly, floating sensation...as if every part of him was wide awake for the first time.

The raven placed his head down and pulled his wings forward, his shape morphing into the shape of a man wearing a long black wrap with a fringed hem. His recessed eyes were as black as the raven's feathers; his wispy, black hair fell to his waist line. The wind rose and blew his thin straight hair and his shawl to one side, giving him a brooding, haunting appearance. Difficult to see at first, Tino blurred his focus and detected a faint, dark-purple light emanating from the man.

Tino turned to look at the barn owl which had turned snowy white while his attention had been on the raven. An elderly man emerged through shimmering white light, replacing the owl. His long, pure white hair crisscrossed in many overlapping braids; even his beard was made up of many silken, white braids, pulled together into one. All of the braids intertwined to create a neat point at the end of his beard. His mustache braided neatly into the beard, creating an intricate design. The owl man's eyebrows were severely arched, creating a perfectly braided, crescent moon shape over transparent, light hazel eyes surrounded by white eyelashes. His face resembled a full moon with a crooked, pointed nose and thin pale lips. A large white blanket covered the body of the old man and wrapped around his waist. Another swath of white fabric was thrown across his shoulders. The owl man radiated a deep turquoise glow around his entire etheric auric body.

A golden light shone from the area the falcon had occupied just moments earlier. From this light, the shape of a younger man emerged. He wore a light, golden-tan jacket with fringe and long, loose pants of the same color. His hair, parted on the side, fell across his forehead in golden wisps. He smiled gently at Tino, golden light dancing right off his very skin. His light brown eyes, flecked with gold, bore friendliness that made Tino feel safe. His grandfather taught him about the falcon, a telepathic messenger from human to human and human to spirit. The falcon is a junior guide with many ties to the Earth, called into action when communication is difficult.

Tino's guides had never before taken on human form. They always came to him as animals, speaking through telepathy. He felt a sense of awe and privilege seeing them in this form.

"Thank you, Grandfather, and all of my ancestors." His plea to the spirit realm had been fully honored. He knew he had to use this power wisely. Before him he had the best guides to journey him through the dark unknown, to face his fears, and to communicate within the human and spirit world.

The guides smiled and nodded as they acknowledged Tino, "Welcome."

"What is it that you need to face?" Owl spirit asked in a low, deep voice.

"I need to know more about Alonso."

"Why do you need to know about him?"

"For my sister's welfare." The guides went silent.

"Can I communicate with him?" Tino looked directly at falcon guide, the messenger.

"I am the one who led him here to meet you in your travels. He does not know that he has called me to work with him in the deep secrets of his dreams. Do you wish to meet him again?"

A wisp of golden light suddenly spiraled past Tino and disappeared into the violet sky. The falcon does not hesitate and moves with great purpose and speed. Tino remembered this from his grandfather's lessons. Raven pointed to a bright point of light through the deep violet sky and Tino was whisked along with him into Alonso's upstairs room at his tío Frank and tía Ruby's home.

Sombra awoke, ears and hackles up at full attention. He ran to the closed door and pawed at the base of it, trying to get out of the room. Alonso lay in deep slumber, utterly unaware of the activity around him. He was dreaming of Tesoro again, touching her stomach, running his bare hands slowly across her silken, bare skin. Falcon spirit stood upright in human form by Alonso's bed, laughing.

"I'm not sure if you want me to pull him out of his dream!" Falcon said. Raven immediately raised an eyebrow and grinned at Falcon, seeing for himself Alonso's dream.

"What is his dream?" Tino asked.

"He is dreaming about your sister. He is in love with her," Falcon said. Alonso suddenly let out a moan and said Tesoro's name, still sound asleep.

"What?" Tino said loudly.

Alonso quickly came out of his dream, sat up in bed and gasped for air. To his left was a fast-moving, golden light flying across his room; right beside it a large violet orb and little shooting specks of pure, bright, white light attached to the purple orb.

"Who's here?" Alonso was breathing rapidly. The lights disappeared and Alonso yielded again to the comforting blackness of night.

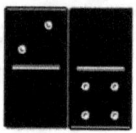

CHAPTER TWENTY-FOUR

Angels and Auras

The school bus rolled through the winter fog to the street corner, two houses up from tío Frank and tía Ruby's. Alonso, still in a fog himself from a night of restless sleep, lumbered head down, up the steps of the bus. He took an empty seat at the rear of the bus and slumped over onto his backpack.

"Go sit next to him," Tracy whispered to Tesoro. "Go on." Tracy pushed Tesoro to the edge of the vinyl bus seat.

"Nooo, he's sleeping. I don't want to bug him."

"All that much better, a surprise when he wakes up!" Tracy gave Tesoro another playful push on her leg.

"C'mon, just get up." Giving one final shove with her body this time, Tracy pushed Tesoro right off the seat into the aisle.

Tesoro stood up in the aisle, glaring at a smug Tracy. The bus driver, at the same time, gave a disapproving glance in the large mirror. Tesoro walked past the bored students, some asleep, some doing last minute homework and stopped at Alonso's seat, looking down at him. Taking a deep breath and, ever so quietly, she slipped into the seat next to him.

His head was bobbing up and down with the bumpy ride of the school bus; he had drifted off quickly to that place between deep sleep and wakefulness. He let himself go, still hearing the noises of the chattering students in the background. His mind became a movie screen of broken images, pieced together, not making any real sense--nor did he care if it made sense. He just watched it go by as his mind drifted further away. Skye appeared in his mind's eye, his entire face filling Alonso's field of vision. Alonso could hear Skye's voice, but it was jumbled, distant, broken. Skye's mouth was moving, but not in sequence, the jumbled words making no sense at all. Then he felt Skye, he felt his last struggle for breath, his desperation to live, his fear; he felt his lungs, tight, filled with fluid, his heart skipping about madly and a conscious panicked inability to get air.

Pulling quickly back into full consciousness Alonso gasped for air, sitting straight up on the hard bus seat, his eyes wide, still reeling from panic. He bent down elbows on his knees and threw his head into his open palms, covering his face, breathing...breathing. Then he felt warmth, more of a tingle, right beside him...Tesoro. He turned his head slowly to his left and peered at her through his long bangs and fingers.

Her mouth was open, not knowing what to say. Her eyes...her eyes; he thought he saw fright there. He scared her, he had scared himself.

The bus jolted to a stop in front of the large, brick school. Tesoro raced to grab her backpack off of Tracy's seat and mixed in with the students scurrying to first period. Alonso waited until the bus was almost empty to get out of the backseat. He could see Tesoro through the bus windows, her head down, clinging tightly to her backpack, moving quickly through the crowd. He also saw Brett moving directly toward her, a giant smile on his face.

"Great impression I just made," he mumbled. He made his way to the boys' gym for his first class, glad to have the track and field to run off what just happened on the bus.

The run around the track did Alonso good. He felt wide awake for his second period class.

"Alonso Mendoza," his math teacher called out. He looked up from an algebra word problem. His teacher moved to the side of his desk and handed him a folded pink office pass.

Alonso opened it, quickly noticing it had A.P. Martin's signature and the "immediately" box was checked off. He jumped up from his desk and bolted to the door.

"You might want to take your backpack." His math teacher caught him right before he stepped out of the classroom.

Alonso made his way up the long hallway; he could see Patricio and Mauricio through the safety glass windows in the administrative office. He broke into a full run and flung open the office door. The office ladies scowled at him for his abrupt entrance.

"Is it Lilianna?"

"Your mamá needs you at the hospital," Patricio said.

"Don't forget to sign out, put the time down beside your name." The shorter of the two short office ladies stood up, sternly pointed to the school sign out sheet and handed Alonso a pen.

"Lilianna's okay? Right?" Alonso asked. Mauricio shrugged out of view of the office aides and motioned for Alonso to follow.

Racing, they vaulted over the low brick ramp wall just outside the front of the school and jumped into the gold Impala.

"What's up with Lilianna?"

"She's on a new machine...you'll see."

"She's going to be okay?"

"Yeah." Patricio glanced back at Alonso and turned the key in the ignition. The Impala's engine sounded out a rhythmic, guttural whop-whop-whop and then growled, mountain lion in attack mode, when Patricio accelerated.

"What did you do to the car! It's pimped!" Alonso leaned forward.

"She made for da street, ain't she sweet, not your average trick-r-treat, da girl got me 'n heat, jus' lisin' to her beat, yuh."

Mauricio sang out deep and loud, in rap time, riding low in his seat as he moved his head back and forth, turkey style.

"You just made that up, fool," Patricio chided. Mauricio took off his baseball cap and wacked Patricio across the back of his head with it.

"Don't hit me with that again, or I'll own it."

Alonso laughed hard from the backseat. It was good to see his cousins.

Patricio pulled the Impala into the parking lot under Interstate 35 in downtown San Antonio. Alonso could see the tower of the Christus Santa Rosa Hospital. He gazed up at the gigantic mural on the side of the hospital tower. It was made out of tiles by the talented local artist, Jesse Treviño. Once his art teacher brought in a guest speaker to represent Jesse Treviño and shared stories from his life as a Latino artist with the students at Flores. Alonso loved Treviño's artwork, especially the oil painting "Mis Hermanos." The downtown mural depicted an image of a large angel sitting behind a little boy who holds a dove cupped in his hands. Alonso noticed the dove's golden aura; this aura also reflected onto the face of the boy and the angel.

"Aura," Alonso whispered. Taken by the fact that he was not alone in his visions, if this artist could have visions, so could he.

"Lock it. I don't want no one messin' with my ride," Patricio said. They took a short cut through the large parking lot, using the corners of hoods and trunks to jump as hurdles, setting off car alarms as they went. They jaywalked across the access road through fast traffic and whisked quickly through the hospital's side door.

"¡Mijo, Alonso!" Alonso's mamá was waiting for them in the hallway by Lilianna's room.

"¡Mamá!" Alonso held onto his mamá in the wide corridor of the hospital ICU wing. "¿Cómo está Anna?" (*How's Anna?*)

"No muy bien." (*Not so good.*) She cradled her son's face between her hands, looking deep into his eyes. She pulled her arm around his shoulders and led him into Lilianna's room.

It took a moment for everything to register in Alonso's mind. He looked at the room, filled with equipment attached to his sister, looked at his mamá, and back at the equipment again. A new machine was by Anna's side; a tube led to her mouth. A balloon filled with air and then decompressed rhythmically from the machine. He noticed she had two additional intravenous fluid bags hanging from the metal pole beside her bed. One bag was heavily labeled.

"Es una respiradora artificial." (*It's a breathing machine,*) mamá said, looking down. "Tiene una inflamación cerebral y una infección. A lo mejor no se recupera." (*She has swelling of her brain and an infection. She may not recover.*)

Alonso went to his sister, while Patricio and Mauricio waited nervously beside the door. Reaching down, Alonso rearranged the covers on his sister, tucking her in. He sat on the edge of her hospital bed.

"Anna, no me dejes." (*Anna, don't leave me.*) Tears filled his eyes and slowly ran down his cheeks.

A slight movement from the corner of the room caught Alonso's attention. The tattooed man was leaning into this dim spot of the room. He pushed himself up from the wall, head down and walked right past Alonso and out the door.

"Él viene aquí aveces," (*He comes here sometimes,*) mamá said.

Clearing his throat, Alonso looked at his mamá. "¿Hay alguna forma de encontrar a mi papá?" (*Is there any way we can find papá?*)

His mamá slowly shook her head no and looked at the

ground. Alonso rose from his sister's side, walked past his mamá and his cousins to the public bathroom up the hall.

As he stood at the urinal, Alonso saw someone standing behind him through the reflection of the shiny metal. He did not hear anyone enter the room. He turned around, finding no one else in the room. As he washed his hands, Alonso felt an odd chill across his back. Looking up into the mirror he saw a young man with golden blond hair, parted on the side and wearing a tan jacket with fringe standing directly behind him. The man flashed him a warm smile, pushing off the wall he casually leaned against. Alonso turned around and the man was no longer there. In his place, Alonso saw a golden flicker of what appeared momentarily to be the wings of a bird in flight-- like the mural of the dove with the golden aura outside of the hospital. Alonso bent over the sink, splashed cold water on his face and rubbed it across the back of his neck.

CHAPTER TWENTY-FIVE

Scout Dues and Caldos

Mauricio rounded the corner of the empty hospital corridor. The coast was clear of cameras and people, allowing Patricio, Mauricio and the tattooed man to have a private talk.

"Do you have the money for the water pump?" Patricio asked.

"Yeah." He reached into the front pocket of his Dickies and pulled out a roll of cash. He flipped through it, holding it inside his fist and slid it over to Patricio.

"We're square."

The tattooed man reached over and snatched the large wad of bills back out of Patricio's hand. Mauricio reached past his brother and grabbed the man's shirt at the neck pulling it down into a twisted wad. A tattoo marked his chest. Ink covered the area just above his heart: two large capital "M's," a skull with horns coming out on either side was centered between the letters.

The tattooed man followed Mauricio's eyes as he stared at the tattoo. The man laughed. Mauricio's fist loosened from the waded shirt and he took a step backward. The tattooed man held tight to the wad of bills that he grabbed from Patricio and counted out twenty dollars, stuffing it into his deep front pocket. He handed Mauricio back the rest of the money.

"That's ten percent. Consider it scout dues." The tattooed man turned and walked up the hall, the soles of his black metallic, Nike Air Jordan CK's, soundless on the tile floor.

Mauricio and Patricio watched silently from the corner of the hall as the man stepped onto the open elevator.

"¿Lo viste?" (*Did you see that?*) Mauricio said.

"Yeah." Patricio's expression was grim.

"See what?" Alonso walked out of the hospital bathroom overhearing the tail end of his cousins' conversation, hoping they had seen the strange blond guy with the tan jacket, too.

"Nothing," Mauricio said.

"Here." Patricio placed the wad of bills into Alonso's hand.

"What's this?"

"It's for Lilianna's hospital bills," Patricio said.

"I can't take this." Alonso shoved the money back at his cousin. Patricio stepped back with his hands out to either side making it impossible for Alonso to hand him the money.

"Where did you get this? Is this Lilianna's blood money?" Alonso shook the wad of cash in his fist. Alonso saw a deep red glow with a palpable static sensation coming from Mauricio.

"Is this the money for the pump?" His fists shook at his side.

"Alonso this isn't our fault. That man has a price on his life that is more than the cost of that pump," Patricio said.

"You don't get shot for a pump, Alonso," Mauricio said.

"This is the best we can do for Lilianna. Give the money to your mamá, por favor," Patricio pleaded.

Alonso stuffed the bills into his front pocket and the three of them walked back into Lilianna's room in silence.

Alonso's mamá had her head down. She wiped her eyes with a white lace handkerchief. Her small fragile frame was perched on the wide hospital window sill, the light silhouetting her upper torso creating a soft white halo. No one spoke. There was only the sound of the breathing machine rhythmically filling the thick air in the room and an occasional audible sob from Lisa.

Father Fuentes walked into the room with two glasses of water.

"Alonso, Mauricio, Patricio." He acknowledged them with a nod and direct eye contact. He walked to Lisa, placed his hand on her shoulder and gave her the icy water. She looked up and attempted a smile of gratitude. Father Fuentes sat down next to Lisa on the window sill and whispered prayers in Spanish. Lisa took out her rosary beads out and counted through them. She followed Father Fuentes as he led with prayer. Alonso sat at the edge of Anna's bed, took her limp hand and held it between his hands.

Mauricio and Patricio slipped out the door quietly, just as tío Luis slipped in. He went to his sister and Father Fuentes and handed Lisa a letter. Pulling out of her prayer, she slowly opened the envelope and burst into tears.

"I'm taking your mamá to the chapel on the first floor." Father Fuentes supported Lisa as they got up from the window sill, the letter clutched tightly to her breast.

"What did you just show her?" Alonso asked.

"Your papá sent a letter…" tío Luis looked down, "…he's found work in México. He's working to come back to you, Lilianna and your mamá, working hard."

"Did he say when?"

"No."

"He's okay?"

"Sí." There was an awkward silence. "Do you need anything?"

Alonso shook his head, not looking up from his sister's face. He felt confused and exhausted from the restless night before. Left alone with his sister, he curled up next to her on the hospital bed and stared blankly at the tiles on the ceiling. The day nurses came into the room and silently worked their way around the siblings, checking the monitors and busily writing down readings. They flipped the lights off and left Alonso napping.

"Hey, hey." Alonso could hear the voice of his tía Ruby. He felt disoriented for just a moment. Perhaps he was waking up at their home in Northwest San Antonio? He felt nauseous when he realized he was in the hospital room. All of the emotions of the situation came rushing back as he looked at his sister, barely alive, right beside him on the bed. He rolled off the edge of the bed and into the green chair by the window.

"I brought a bowl of pozole caldos for you," tía Ruby said, pulling the hot container out of a fabric grocery bag and placing it on the nightstand with a spoon and neatly folded paper towel. She pulled out a baggie filled with chopped red radishes, lime slices, fresh chopped onions, with bright green cilantro sprigs and placed it beside the tightly sealed container of pork soup with hominy.

"Your mamá called to let me know that you were at the hospital. How's your sister doing?"

She moved in closer to Lilianna touching the side of her face gently with the back of her hand, making a soft 'mmm' humming sound.

"She's not so good. I'll need to talk to the nurses to find out more."

"Hey, remember your tío calling to make an appointment with a doctor for you?"

"Yes."

"That doctor has an office right next door to this hospital. He's got you on the schedule for this afternoon. I was going to pull you out of art class, but you're already here."

"I'm fine. I don't think I'm the one who needs a doctor right now." Alonso's brow furrowed. He looked down at his sister.

"You're still seeing lights?"

Alonso reached over and uncovered the soup container, added the radishes and stirred. Yes, he was seeing orbs and dots of light almost all of the time now. More than that, he was seeing ghosts.

"Do I have time to eat?"

"Si, Alonso, you have time to eat. Are you going to eat the onions and cilantro?"

"No, I just like radishes." Alonso slurped down the first spoonful of broth, thick with pork and hominy.

"This is really good." He smiled back at tía Ruby and finished the rest of the soup.

Tía Ruby pulled out her phone and left a message for Lisa to come back upstairs to be with Lilianna while she took Alonso to the doctor.

As tía Ruby and Alonso crossed the parking lots between medical buildings, Alonso was surprised to see that the Impala was still parked in the lot, but his cousins were nowhere in sight. Alonso hoped they weren't getting into more trouble. He didn't like the red aura he saw around Mauricio earlier. It didn't feel right or look right. It was jagged around the edges. He knew his cousins could run into real trouble downtown. As upset as he was with his cousins, he didn't want anyone else in the family to get hurt, or taken away.

"What is it?" Tía Ruby asked. Alonso had stopped with his back turned to her.

"Nothing." He crammed his hands deep into his front pockets, past the silver chain that hid inside and caught up with her.

The neurology waiting room was tiny with no windows. It had stiff blue chairs lined up in four neat rows. Behind a sliding glass window a receptionist paid no attention as tía Ruby penciled in Alonso's name on the register.

"Are you okay here? I'm going back to Lilianna's room to be with your mamá."

"Yeah...bye."

"Alonso Martinez," called out a rotund nurse with a round face and black hair streaked with coppery-red highlights. "Follow me please."

Alonso followed the nurse through narrow corridors into a small room with a set of scales and other medical equipment. She weighed him in at one hundred, sixty five pounds and measured his height at six feet one inch. The nurse placed a blood pressure cuff on his arm and sealed up the Velcro with her chewed up half-painted nails.

"109 over 68." She wrote down her findings and pulled the thermometer out of his mouth.

"Am I normal?"

"You are as normal as they come, a little sleepy maybe." She smiled and asked him to remove all of his clothes and step into a gown.

"The doctor will be with you soon." She shut the door and left Alonso to change.

Alonso was apprehensive. He was afraid he wasn't normal at all. He was afraid that he had something wrong with his brain and that was why he was seeing things no one else did. He wasn't sure how he was going to tell the doctor he thought he was losing his mind, seeing lights and dead people. He was scared.

Alonso heard papers being shuffled just outside the door. The doctor walked in and quickly put Alonso through a series of coordination tests.

"So, your Uncle Frank let me know you're seeing dots?"

"Yes sir." He wanted to tell the doctor everything, but felt frozen with the fear that he might really be going crazy. He wondered: who sees auras around people, anyway?

"Does this happen to you every day?"

"Yes."

"Have you ever heard of migraine headaches?"

Alonso wanted out of the room. He wanted to be back with his sister. He started to shift nervously on the edge of the doctor's table. The fluorescent bulb above Alonso's head flickered furiously, completely unnoticed by the neurologist.

"Well, sometimes headaches can cause visual disturbances. They can cause you to see lights. I'm not going to risk that this is what is causing you to see 'dots.' I'm writing up an order for you to have a MRI."

The doctor walked out the door.

"Headaches," Alonso mumbled. "I don't get headaches...headaches don't cause you to see, hear, and feel the dead."

CHAPTER TWENTY-SIX

Anger and Inquisitions

"**Y** ou!" Tesoro heard a yell from across the school sidewalk; it was Brett. He was running toward her with a big grin on his face. "How's the sexiest girl in the school doing today?"

She wanted to slap him for talking to her that way. What a jerk, she thought. She reached her hand up to her armpit to grab onto her backpack strap a little tighter. Looking straight forward, Tesoro made a beeline to her bus. She went into a light jog in an attempt to lose Brett. He wove through the students and caught up with her.

"Stop, stop," Brett said laughing. "I need a dollar." He jumped directly in front of Tesoro, put his hand out and raised one eyebrow with a smirk on his face.

"C'mon, I know you have one, cough it up."

Tesoro pushed past him through the crowd. She pursed her lips and moved quickly. He jumped in front of her again.

"What!"

"Give me a dollar. I'll give it right back, I promise," Brett said.

"Will you leave me alone after that?"

"Yeah, yeah, just give me the dollar," he said holding out his hand. Tesoro reached into the front zipper pouch on her backpack and pulled out a bill.

"Now, stop walking, don't move," Brett placed his hand

directly in front of her as if he were a traffic cop. She stopped. He flipped his hand palm side up and Tesoro reluctantly, still squinting at him, placed the dollar bill in his empty hand. He took the bill into his hand slowly, slowly, not breaking eye contact.

"What?" Tesoro was losing patience with him.

"Just watch." He folded the bill three times, cupped the bill between his hands and pulled them apart. The folded bill levitated just between his hands.

"How'd you do that?"

"It's magic, baby. I have more where that came from."

"I would imagine you do," Tesoro said dryly and stomped to her bus, Brett beside her.

"Can you leave me alone?" Tesoro stopped walking and faced Brett directly. "I'm mean seriously, where do you get these things from? Do you stay up all night practicing? Is your daddy paying someone for you to learn this crap? Seriously, I bet you are hooking into some cheesy online site?

"'Seriously...'" Brett mimicked Tesoro. "...damn, you are so hot." He reached to place his arms around her waist and she back stepped out of reach.

"Are you sure you don't want to go out sometime?"

"I'm sure. I bet you learned your stupid magic tricks on YouTube. You, Brett Merrick, are a player-dork! Leave me alone!"

"I don't give up without a fight!" Brett ran away from her backwards and into the crowd boarding the buses.

The bus ride home was slow for Tesoro, she had missed seeing Alonso. She was lost in her thoughts of Brett's magic trick as she walked through the front door of her home.

"You look as if you've had a good day," Tino said to his sister.

She reached down to give him a quick hug and made her way toward the kitchen. He followed her as she rummaged through the pantry for an afternoon snack. "Do we have any cereal left?"

"It's still on the counter from this morning." Tino pointed at the box by the sink.

"Hey, can we talk?" Tino turned serious.

"Yeah?"

"There's no good way to say this...how are things going at school with the guy who pounced you last Sunday night?"

"Don't worry, I can handle Brett. He's just a big dork."

"How did your therapy go today?" She asked, trying to change the subject.

"Good, I'm still believing the miracle."

"I'm believing it, too." Tesoro held up the cereal box. "Do you want some?"

"No, I'm not hungry, Mom stopped for a burger on the way home."

"And she didn't pick one up for me?" She slid into the seat next to her brother.

"Tesoro," he said quietly, "I can't get over my own anger at what happened to you."

"I know, I'm mad too." She reached her hand over to her brother.

"He's harmless. He just likes me."

"How are you handling your anger?"

"I mostly ignore him when he comes up to me. He does these weird magic tricks, gets in my face and tries to impress me. I'm not impressed." She rolled her big brown eyes, lying to both herself and her brother. Deep down, Brett was getting to her. He was making her laugh. She looked carefully at Tino. She could read that her brother was still concerned, that he wasn't comfortable with the situation.

"Plus, I know not to be alone with him, E-VER." She emphasized the word 'ever'--separating it strongly between syllables.

"I don't like being this angry. He is a real enemy to me, Tesoro."

"Just let it go. He can't hurt me."

"I haven't been this angry since the accident."

"Tino, remember what Grandfather taught us about enemies?"

"Yes, to wait at least eleven days before attacking and if the attack is still necessary to perform a sacred ceremony first. This way everyone would have time to consider other options and possibly make peace with the situation."

"It hasn't been eleven days," Tesoro said.

"It sucks being stuck here. I want to help you. What if you are alone with him again? What would you do?" Tino asked.

She made her voice go low and gruff. "I'd kick him in the nads!"

The twins laughed harder than they had in a long time and settled into the routine of schoolwork. Tesoro tutored her brother in social studies as the moist southern wind blew through the open dining room window.

Tino reached into Tesoro's backpack and pulled out her sketchbook. He turned to the page where she had drawn Alonso. "So, tell me about this guy?"

"That's Alonso, he's just a guy in my art class. I had to draw him for an assignment."

"Yeah, does he like you, too?"

"I don't think so. I'm pretty sure he likes a cheerleader

that I know, Tracy."

"Your drawing of him, it's so...tender."

"Give that to me." Tesoro snatched the sketchbook out of her brother's hands, accidentally ripping the drawing of Alonso in half.

"Oh, no," Tesoro cried out. "Where's the scotch tape?"

"Where it always is." Tino pulled back watching Tesoro carefully. She pulled the tape out of the drawer underneath the recharge area for their phones. Running back to the table she carefully pieced the sketch of Alonso back together, making certain it matched up perfectly before pressing the tape firmly into place.

"You really like him." Tino placed emphasis on the word really. Tesoro gently reworked the shading that smudged from the tear and repair. Her eyes welled up as she looked at her brother seriously.

"But I don't think he likes me back." She bent her head down until it met the top of her arm, using her sleeve to wipe the moisture out of her eyes.

"That's quite a predicament you're in. Brett likes you, but you don't like him. You like Alonso, but you don't think he likes you--seems complicated."

"It is." Tesoro forced a smile for her brother.

"How can you be so sure this guy doesn't like you?"

"He never talks to me, but..." Tesoro reflected, "...when I'm close to him, there's this weird sensation, like static electricity."

"What do you mean?" Tino sat upright in his chair.

"Oh, he's just a weird guy. I don't know what it is I'm seeing in him."

"Maybe it's not what you're seeing. Maybe it's what you're feeling."

"I just feel alive when he's near me, more alive than I've ever felt before." Her demeanor shifted to pensive.

"But I think something's off with him. Strange things happen when he's around."

"What's up with that?"

"Lights...lights seem to go out around him. Plus, he stopped the bus from getting into a wreck by knowing it was going to happen before it happened. That's just weird."

"I knew it!" Tino spoke loudly, snapping his fingers in the air. "He's opening up!"

"Opening what up, exactly?" Tesoro said.

"He may be psychic."

"You mean like real magic? He can predict things and move things with his mind--that kind of psychic?"

"Something like that, but I suspect he doesn't know what's going on yet."

"Why are you all of the sudden the authority on a guy I like?"

"You might not understand this; I met him in a dream I had recently."

"Let me get this straight, you're dreaming about a guy I like, that you don't even know? You're as crazy as him."

Tesoro grabbed her backpack and marched upstairs to her room with the lavender bedding.

CHAPTER TWENTY-SEVEN

To Die and To Live

Alonso could see his body below him, asleep in the ICU waiting room, curled up on the hard sofa, but he could not return to his body. He felt as if he could not breathe. He could not move from this spot. Concentrating, he tried with all of his intention to slip back into his body as easily as he had previously. It didn't work. A high-pitched scream built up in his throat, but never made it out.

His astral field of vision quickly filled with the face of a man. He appeared translucent, filling all of Alonso's sight and thoughts. The man's face was wrinkled with sun and age, his eyelids sagging over his bloodshot, grey-blue eyes. Alonso quickly made a connection--the word 'construction worker' jolted his mind. The man's blond hair was mixed with grey, thinning in the front. He was unshaven with stubble the same color as his hair. Alonso thought he could smell the man. He smelled like old sweet beer. He could not get this smell out of his nose.

The man's thin lips started to move, slowly at first, and then a voice entered Alonso's head. He knew it was the voice of the man coming through exactly as it happened with Skye Peterson at school and with the bald girl. He could not understand what the man was trying to say. The voice became louder and louder. The man was screaming, desperately trying to tell him something. Alonso could not comprehend because the man's mouth was out of sync with his words.

Against his will, Alonso felt himself being rapidly pulled

backwards by his head through a tunnel--only this time it didn't feel right. His mind screamed in silent searing panic.

He looked up at hallway lights above his head moving at warp speed. He was on a gurney racing through a narrow hall. He was losing control of everything around him. He was dying, he was sure. He had pain on the side of his head, dull, throbbing, and pinching at times. He felt a warm trickle of liquid flowing down his neck, settling in a sticky pool at the base of his head. Had he been hit in his sleep? Did the tattooed man come into the waiting room to kill him while he was sleeping? Or, was the man he just saw-the man whose voice he could not understand-his murderer?

He tried to cry out, but he could not make a sound. The movement stopped. He was beneath a bright round light, the type of light depicted on television shows where doctors save traumatized patients in operating rooms. He could hear the voices of doctors, technicians and nurses surrounding him. They were in light green gowns, with light green masks across their noses and mouths. He could only make out their eyes and couldn't understand what they were saying. It sounded foreign, as if they were speaking Latin.

A doctor leaned over him, tilted his head back and sliced his neck open. It pinched and burned at the same time--a sudden, dreadfully sharp pain that did not match the pain on the side of his head. A technician handed the doctor a clear plastic tube and they inserted it into the front of his neck. He could feel the tube going down his throat, into his bronchial tube, his lungs suddenly filling up with air. The pain worsened with oxygen running into his brain again.

Tilting, I'm falling, tilting off the table, Alonso thought. The room rushed by in sideways waves, everything moving from left to right in quick, dizzying bursts. He felt a jab in the fold of his arm and saw an IV bag beside the stretcher. One of the bags contained blood. The vertigo intensified; Alonso felt himself growing weaker and weaker, slipping away.

The vertigo became a rocking sensation, from his feet to his head. He was being pulled again against his will. Only this time it did seem natural, peaceful, quiet and right. As automatic as breathing normally is, he slipped away from his body that was riddled with pain and moved beside the light in the room. He could hear the chatter of the hospital staff below him and the constant hum of a machine alarm sounding loudly, flat-lining. All of these sounds grew more and more distant. Alonso wanted to see himself. He wanted to see if he had really died. He could not believe he was dead. How did this happen? He could not stop thinking about his mamá. She could not bear to lose him right now. Oh, he loved her so much.

In the background chatter, he heard something, or someone say, "Fully charged, stand back, administering shock to patient." The pain seared through his body, a jolting white hot blast. His head and body convulsed uncontrollably. The pain in his head, his throat, the sickening spinning of the room...he was back in his body. This time, he wanted out of his body, he wanted out of the unbearable pain, this treacherous and all-consuming pain. His chest tightened up in agony and he tried to scream out to no avail.

"Morphine, fast," a male voice commanded as he slipped away into a dreamy, drugged, unconscious state. He heard the voices of the hospital staff echoing and far away. He felt himself gently lift into the ether. Turning over slowly, he looked down and saw the dead body of the construction worker on the operating table below him. One of the nurses pulled the scraggly man's eyelids closed over his fixed, blue-grey eyes.

Alonso felt confused and relieved at the same time. He realized he had just experienced the death of the construction worker as his own.

"Over here." He heard a loud feminine voice and he realized he was not in the operating room any longer. He was back in the hospital hallway, at the grey double door with the bald girl, the chrome round push button by the door gleaming like a diamond. She wore a loose crumpled hospital gown. It was light yellow with little teddy bears creating a patterned print across the fabric. Her feet were bare and her legs so thin he could see her bones sticking out.

She pointed to the shining button on the wall and moved her head to the side, looking at the button and back at Alonso. As always in this dream, his curiosity got the best of him. Again he was compelled to press the button over and over again with the same result; the door would not open. Frustrated, he body slammed the door again, as he had many times before in his dreams, hoping to get out of the hospital hallway. Whatever was on the other side of the door had to be better than the cold corridor he shared with the bald girl.

Another thought occurred to Alonso. He slowly turned around and asked the bald girl, "Who are you?"

She pointed to the door on the opposite end of the corridor.

"Oh no, I'm not playing another game with you. Who are you?" Alonso asked again.

The girl turned and slowly walked away from him, her skeletal frame moving silently up the long well-lit corridor. A new corridor appeared to the right of the girl. She looked back briefly at Alonso and turned into the new hallway. He followed her.

At the end of this hall another grey double door started to open of its own accord. The bald girl walked through the door and Alonso raced through behind her just as the door started to close again. This hallway seemed less dreamlike--it seemed real. There were more doors on either side of the hall with numbered plaques. Paintings of calm idealistic landscapes adorned the walls. Alonso looked up and saw ceiling tiles and fluorescent lights. He looked down at his hands and they were his own, much to his relief.

Slowing down, the bald girl pointed to another large double door. She stopped and motioned for Alonso to look through the safety glass window. He could see more hallways and a symbol that he didn't recognize: a bright yellow circle with a black dot in the middle and three black triangular shapes coming out of the dot.

"What is that? What are you trying to tell me?"

As he asked this question, Alonso abruptly found himself in another hospital room. This one was quiet. He felt weak, his bones ached, his muscles ached and his heart felt like it was barely beating. People he didn't know were pacing around the room. A plump young woman with rosy cheeks walked up to him and touched his face with a moist washcloth. It felt good.

"I love you baby," she said, tears slowly rolling across her ruddy face. She walked away and a man about the same age as the woman, walked up to him.

"You're my inspiration and my angel. I love you so much," he said as he took Alonso's hand and kissed it: wet, scratchy, whiskery kisses. He walked away and held onto the woman as Alonso watched, his eyes slowly opening and closing in utter, uncontrollable exhaustion. He felt he could not look at the couple in the room any longer. He fought to keep his eyes open, and he could not. He went into an unconscious state and peacefully slipped away.

He could see the couple, their heads on the edge of the hospital bed holding each other, crying. A minister was in the room with them. He was praying out loud. Alonso moved his viewpoint to the edge of the bed and looked. It was the bald girl in the bed. She appeared to be struggling, breathing roughly, like a fish out of water--short, fast gasps for air. She stopped breathing for a moment as the couple held each other tighter and the minister's praying became louder. She took two last slower gasps for air and stopped breathing.

Alonso felt a presence beside him. It was the bald girl, holding her mother from behind.

"It's alright Mommy, I'm right here. Mommy look." A little

more desperate, "Mommy, Daddy, look at me, I'm here, I'm here..." she cried, "...why are you crying?"

Slowly, she turned her head to the side and looked directly at Alonso with a perplexed expression and asked: "Who are you?

CHAPTER TWENTY-EIGHT

Doorways and Elevator Rides

Lilianna was the same. After four hours and what seemed as an eternity to Alonso in the ICU waiting room her condition was unwavering. What should have been a good rest left Alonso confused and somewhat overwhelmed. Looking down at his sister, he wondered what could be going on inside her head in such an intense level of unconsciousness. Could she be haunted by experiences of the dead at this hospital, also? Was she out of her body? Perhaps visiting a beautiful world far away? Or, was she simply out cold, held captive, suspended, as her body aged involuntarily, with no awareness of her condition? He wanted to know if he could reach her, to tell her to come back to them...to live.

"Alonso, good to see you buddy!" It was Jon, his voice rich and warmly congenial.

"Hey," Alonso said looking up through his haze of thoughts.

"She's hanging in there; your sister's a fighter." Jon moved over to her breathing machine and checked the electronic read-outs, taking note.

"How are you doing?"

"Alright, I guess. I'm having a lot of strange dreams."

"I told you this place would get to you. What are you dreaming about, that hot girl?"

"I wish," Alonso chuckled. "No, I dream about people that I think may have died here."

"Yeah?" Jon raised an eyebrow at Alonso. His smile disappeared.

"Stress can do strange things to people. Do you have a doctor to talk to?"

"I'm already talking to one. My uncle Frank knows this guy that works across the street. I had an appointment with him just this afternoon."

"Did you tell him you were having strange dreams?"

"No, I don't want him to think I'm loco." Alonso grinned a little.

"Alonso, they have good medications for stress. You should consider telling this doctor everything." Jon finished checking on Lilianna. "Promise me you'll think about what I just told you." Alonso acknowledged with a nod.

"Take care buddy." Jon smiled and left Alonso amidst his own thoughts.

He was restless. He could not stay in the room with his sister any longer, but he didn't want to leave the hospital, either. He walked to the elevator, closed his eyes and pressed a random button. With his eyes closed, he blindly walked out of the open door into a hallway. Opening his eyes, it was exactly the same as the hallway he had just left: highly polished light grey granite, with stripes of darker granite inlay on the floor with an area rug of muted green, commercial quality carpet under his feet. He ventured off to the right, down an empty corridor and spied a long glass window. He peered into a room filled with nurses and plexiglass bassinettes. The clear bassinettes cradled the smallest babies Alonso had ever laid eyes on. Some of the babies had tubes attached to their tiny bodies. A few of the smaller babies were in completely enclosed plexiglass cases, with armholes and gloves that allowed nurses to reach through to administer care.

Alonso gazed in amazement. Their little hands were perfect and no more than an inch long, they even had fingernails and wrinkles at the knuckles. He watched as their little faces made scrunched up expressions and then relaxed again. He realized he enjoyed watching the tiny babies.

Alonso could feel a presence just to the left and behind him; a cool breeze rushed across the back of his bare neck. He looked into the glass that reflected as a mirror directly in front of him and saw the bald girl in her yellow hospital gown with the teddy bear pattern. He froze, not wishing to frighten her away. She was watching the babies with him.

"I can see you," Alonso said in a low voice to the girl's glassy reflection.

"What do you see?" She whispered, barely moving her lips, her eyes large, staring right back at his reflection. Alonso was frightened to breathe, not wanting to break his communication with her. She was eight years old at the most at the time of her death. Her height was the only clue to her age; she was incredibly skeletal from being sick for so very long.

"What's your name?" He softened his tone a bit. Underneath her large eyes he could see she was frightened.

"Amy. What's your name?" She smiled briefly and seemed happy to have someone to talk to.

"I'm Alonso. Do you remember meeting me earlier?"

"Yes, in the hallway. I want you to open a door for me that I need to get through. I can't open it by myself."

"The door with the big chrome button!" Alonso grew excited.

"You can help me, you know how."

"Do you know you're dead?" The idea that Amy could have died years ago flashed through Alonso's mind. As he thought this, Amy moved toward him.

"Yes."

"When did you die?"

"That doesn't matter. What does matter is that you can help me."

"What do I need to do?"

Her voice became low. The chill on his neck was becoming a frozen blast.

"Get me through the door," her voice screamed in his head. Alonso whipped around to look at her, but she was no longer there. He turned back around to look at the reflective glass: only babies and nurses. Amy was gone.

"Loco," he muttered and walked back to the elevator with his head down. He pressed the button to ICU to return to his sister's room. The metal door closed. He felt the same chill on his neck.

"Amy?"

Without warning, the lights flickered and Alonso felt the sudden jolt of the elevator stopping between floors. The chill in the room became colder yet. Alonso froze. The fine hairs on the back of his neck and on his face were tickling and prickling. He felt a tingling around his mouth and inside his nose so strong that he had to rub his face.

The lights flickered again. Alonso knew he was not alone.

"Who's here?"

Silence echoed back from the pitch black, empty void of stalled cube suspended in mid-air by cables.

The construction worker's voice filled his ears. He could not see the man anywhere. He could only hear the resounding tones of the man's disjointed words echoing through his brain.

Alonso desperately pushed on the elevator buttons, but they were dead. Then he noticed a dim red light and a button that had the word 'alarm' written on it, just below the elevator panel. He pushed it, but the alarm didn't sound. Instead, a phone rang through the small speaker beside the red button.

"Do you need help?"

"I'm stuck," Alonso said into the dark.

"I'm calling a maintenance crew for you right now," said a bored male voice on the speaker.

"What's your name?"

"Alonso Mendoza."

"Alonso, we'll have you right out of there. How old are you?"

"Fifteen. Where are you at? Are you in this building?"

"No, I'm not in this building. I'm not even in your state."

"Oh, you just call for help?"

"That's how it works. How long were you in the elevator before you called?"

"Not long, three or four minutes."

"That's not bad, just stay with me on the phone and you'll be out of there in no time."

The lights above Alonso's head flickered again. He felt the eerie chill strengthen on his neck.

"Are you still there?"

"Mmm-hmm." Alonso said quietly, afraid if he spoke too loudly, something might happen.

"Yes, you sound a bit nervous. Just take a deep breath. You're going to be okay."

Suddenly the elevator slipped and jolted to a stop. Alonso's knees buckled. The lights went off.

"Hello..." Weak with fright, Alonso called out into the pitch black, empty elevator. A flicker caught the corner of his eye. A hazy grey cloud that seemed to glow faintly from the inside out appeared directly in front of him. The cloud slowly took the shape of a large man.

"Who are you?" Alonso asked in a whisper. Waiting in the silent space of the suspended elevator--no sound came back. The grey cloud dissipated before his eyes, the elevator lights blinked back on and the elevator moved through the shaft.

"I lost contact with you for a moment, are you doing alright?" It was the voice through the speaker.

"I'm moving, everything seems normal," Alonso said.

"That's good, someone must have reset it from within the building. Our crew is not there yet."

Something reset alright, Alonso thought as the elevator came to a stop and the door opened onto the ICU floor.

Alonso vacated the elevator with a little more speed than usual. He glanced behind at the open doors. What just happened to him? One part of his mind wanted to believe that he was making contact with dead people; another part of this mind thought he was going totally crazy, stressed out and not able to function. Perhaps he should tell the doctor everything that was happening to him. Maybe it all was too much, with his papá gone and Lilianna's coma. Maybe he was going insane.

CHAPTER TWENTY-NINE

Nuclear Blasts and Energy

Mrs. Hamilton's soft voice faded into the background of Alonso's mind as he drifted into thoughts of Lilianna and his mamá for a moment. He wanted to leave the social studies classroom and call his mamá from the boys' room, but he resisted. For now, it felt good to be back in the classroom, something normal, something to remind him of his own life, something far away from the death that had pursued him through the hospital corridors.

He refocused his attention to Mrs. Hamilton as she showed a model of an atom on the screen in the front of the room, explaining how it contains energy. Another diagram came up on the screen. It showed the molecular structure of a nuclear reaction diagramed with lithium, hydrogen and helium atoms, with the sphere-shaped protons in red and the neutrons in blue. Below it was the mathematical formula for a nuclear reaction: $6/3Li \div 2/1H \rightarrow 2\ 4/2He$. Alonso studied the equation. He had memorized the periodic table of the elements in seventh grade and he knew that lithium was a metal, that hydrogen and helium were gases. He was intrigued with the thought that it took only three elements to either create usable nuclear energy or destroy everything.

Mrs. Hamilton asked Marcus to turn the lights off and started a DVD on nuclear energy. The film was grainy and old. It showed test bombs going off in the desolate Nevada desert, clips of underground bunkers and images of the Cold War.

Alonso's thoughts drifted off again, this time to Tesoro.

He smiled, knowing that he would see her next period in art class. He only saw her from a distance on the bus and during lunch. He needed some private time with her, to thank her for the note and the bear. Art class would be the perfect chance to do just that.

From out of nowhere, Alonso felt the familiar rush of goose bumps across the back of his neck and the brush of a cold chill. He looked up at the film just as it showed the use of nuclear energy for modern medicine. A symbol flashed across the screen, a bright yellow circle with a black dot in the middle and three black, triangular shapes coming out of the dot. The same symbol Amy pointed to--the symbol for radioactive material.

The cold chill caused Alonso to sit straight up. A glimmer of light caught the corner of his eye from the left of the film screen. Behind the glimmer was Skye Peterson, seated at a desk with his baseball cap. Skye turned around slowly in the seat and looked straight at Alonso, who stayed as still as possible, even forgetting to breathe for the moment. Skye pointed to the film being shown on the overhead screen. A CAT scan machine, x-ray machines and other diagnostic radiology equipment were being shown. Once again, without warning, Skye's face appeared in Alonso's entire field of vision. He was screaming and Alonso could not understand a word of what Skye was trying to say. Alonso knew to freeze and not to make a sound. He knew he was the only person in the classroom able to see the dead.

Slowly slipping out of the side of his student desk, Alonso quietly asked Mrs. Hamilton if he could go to the restroom.

"You look pale, are you okay?" She smiled kindly.

"Yeah, just tired."

"Let me know if there's anything I can do."

Alonso took the light-green hall pass and walked into the empty hallway. He looked both ways, perhaps Skye Peterson would again appear out of nowhere. Alonso's long bangs fell onto his face as he walked past the large restroom to the small restroom in the science hall. He knew the large restroom in the social studies wing was used for smoking cigarettes and sometimes pot. Occasionally the girls came into the boys' room to stand on the toilet lids with the guys to blow smoke through the narrow, open windows above the stalls. He even heard rumors that people had sex in that bathroom, although he had never witnessed it himself. Alonso didn't feel like being in the party bathroom, around a lot of people who were skipping class.

Slipping around the corner to the quiet science hall, he pushed the bathroom door open so hard that it hit the wall on the other side with a slam. Alonso stood in the middle of the empty room and called out for Skye Peterson.

"Where are you, Skye? Show yourself. What are you trying to tell me?"

Nothing. Alonso waited, spinning, looking around the room quickly.

Still nothing.

"¡Hijo de la chingada! ¿Qué pedo te traes conmigo?" Alonso spit the words out through his teeth, his fists clenched in anger.

"He doesn't speak Spanish, he can't understand you and that's good. He does understand that you just insulted him."

Alonso turned around quickly to find the man with the blond hair and fringed jacket. He appeared quite bored, leaning up against a sink with his legs crossed at his ankles and casually inspecting his fingernails.

"Who are you?" Alonso asked.

"I'm Sha." The blond man let loose a gleaming, toothy smile.

"You obviously need help, Alonso."

He sounded Alonso's name out slowly, carefully pronouncing each syllable with his eyes ethereal and bright.

"What's happening to me?"

"Kind of intense, huh?"

"So you...you know about...?"

"I know what you just went through, yes, that is what you want to ask me." Sha's voice was peaceful and full of understanding.

"Are you...dead?"

"You could call it that." Sha's brilliant smile even seemed to brighten the lights in the room for a moment.

"Are you an angel?" Alonso asked, remembering the glow around the angel in the mural on the side of the hospital. Sha was surrounded by a soft golden glow.

"In a way. I'm your guide, Alonso."

"What kind of guide?" Alonso moved in closer to Sha, close enough to touch him and that's exactly what Alonso did. He felt warmth and a rush of strong energy simultaneously; his hand went right through Sha's arm.

"You're not real?" Alonso jumped back with shock.

"I'm as real as you are. I'm in a different dimension, Alonso." Sha smiled softly and knowingly.

Alonso felt the peaceful energy emitting off Sha as he tried to wrap his mind around the idea that he was talking to a spirit.

"Am I crazy to see you--to be talking to you?"

"No, Alonso, you opened yourself up to allow my presence. Everyone has a guide, sometimes more than one. I've been with you your entire life."

"Why can I see you and no one else can?"

"Everyone is capable of seeing their guides. People have lost touch with their open spiritual nature and have become logic minded over the past few hundred years. It's the most ancient of cultures. The Aborigines, the Native Americans and many African tribes have held onto the idea that we live in spirit. What you are witnessing with me is nothing new to humankind. It's as ancient as the Earth itself."

"Yeah, but why me, why am I seeing dead people?" Alonso whispered.

"Because you allowed yourself to be open to the possibility. It's really that simple."

"I did? When?"

"Remember when you wanted to leave your body to find your pádre? That's called astral projection, or journeying. It was then that you opened yourself up to possibilities outside of the Earth plane."

"Okay, I'm not sure I'm following you. You're telling me I asked to see dead people?"

"Yes."

"How do I stop it? I don't understand it, I don't understand them."

"Do you want it to stop?"

Alonso looked down. He stayed quiet for a long time, rubbing his forehead.

"No," he answered in a contemplative voice. "I want to understand what the dead are trying to tell me."

"Good." Sha moved in a little closer to Alonso. His energy filled the small ceramic tile bathroom. Alonso could feel warmth and tingling around his mouth, a slight electrical pulse encircled him. As Alonso turned around to see if anyone else was present, Sha disappeared, leaving only a glimmer of brilliant golden light in the shape of a bird bolting past Alonso's periphery.

Alonso's focus turned to the sounds in the bathroom, of water slowly dripping from an old school sink, stained from years of use. He could hear someone in the girls' room on the other side of the wall flush a toilet. The bathroom seemed dim without Sha present...like the grainy, black and white film he had watched earlier in Mrs. Hamilton's room.

CHAPTER THIRTY

Playing Chicken and Love Letters

Tesoro did not look up at Alonso when he entered the art room and slid behind his table, pushing himself low into the hard plastic chair. He reached his long arm across the table and picked up a pencil with his right hand. Instead of drawing with it, he spread out the fingers on his left hand and methodically jabbed the sharp pencil down between each of his open fingers, playing chicken. He quickened the pace, his right hand thrusting the sharpened tool mechanically between the flesh of his fingers, his long bangs dancing across his face. He stabbed the pencil down so hard on the table between his knuckles he broke the tip clean off. The entire class stopped working and watched him, including Tesoro. Alonso was unaware; he didn't care. All he cared about was taking his mind off of what happened in the boys' room last class period with Sha, taking his mind off of what happened with Skye and Amy.

Alonso hit the table so hard with the pencil that it split down the middle, splintering in his right hand. He grasped the broken pencil with his fist and placed it flat on the table in front of him, looking at it for a spell. The class went silent--then slowly resumed its low rumble of chatter.

Students refocused their attention on their art project, except for Tesoro. Her gaze was fixed on Alonso. She watched his every move, not taking her eyes off of him for a second. She was breathing shallowly, her nostrils flaring ever so slightly at the sides. Her eyelids and cheeks flushed pink at the sight of Alonso losing control. Shifting her weight in her seat, she pushed her perspiring hands down the tops of her thighs to move her pants down her legs a bit.

Alonso lifted his head and sent a piercing stare through his tousled bangs right at her. Tesoro caught her breath. How beautiful she looked to him, how hot, intense and sexy.

Alonso pulled his arms over the table top, folded his hands together and leaned forward slowly, maintaining his gaze with her. He noted her obvious flush, the rise of her chest with each shallow breath with her lips slightly parted. He felt something stirring inside of him, something primal. They stared at each other for a very long time, an intense, deep stare.

The teacher walked between them to work with a student whose hand was up, breaking Alonso's trance. He quickly looked down at his blank sketchbook page--he had not worked on the assignment at all. They were studying two-point perspective and architecture. He was to draw a building using a horizon line and two vanishing points. His heart was not in the assignment at all; he could only think of his strong feelings for Tesoro and everything he wanted to tell her.

Alonso looked at the page for a moment longer, pulled his favorite ink pen from his backpack and wrote Tesoro's name neatly at the top left-hand side of the page.

"Tesoro," Hesitating for a moment, running his fingers over her name, the words poured out.

"For months now, I have listened to the wind blowing through the trees outside my open window at night. Whenever I hear this sound, it leads me to thoughts of you. Only the wind can hold witness to my feelings toward you. Whispers from the wind blow through me, my thoughts about you, my needing you, my dreams of you. Only the wind catches these moments and carries my thoughts of you through the leaves of the trees as they sway and bend in the breezes, moving with my desire. It's the wind that sweeps across both of us, our skin, our hair, our breath as we take it in. I want to be the wind at night, flowing through your open window and bending down over you in a soft caress, as my heart touches yours, my skin touches yours, our hands

intertwine, our lips meet for the first time.

I envy the wind...it is able to touch you, and I am not. Alonso"

With a tan pencil, Alonso lightly drew an image of a tree behind his words; he placed swirling, light blue lines between the branches with small hearts between the spaces of the swirls. Tearing the page carefully out of his sketchbook, he folded it up and placed it in his tee-shirt pocket.

Alonso gazed at Tesoro working on her assignment, using a ruler and concentrating to place each line in the correct place. A soft lilac light radiated from her in all directions. The area right above her chest appeared to glow a soft pink color. She looked up at Alonso and the colors around her deepened, became larger and brighter. She smiled at him and the bell sounded.

The students pushed to the front of the room, placing their assignments on the shelf by the door, holding Alonso back. Tesoro was already far ahead in the hallway. Sighing deeply, he knew he would have to wait to give her the note after science class.

The last hour of the school day ticked forward in slow motion; three fifty-two, four-ten and finally, four-twenty. The bell sounded and Alonso made his way quickly through the crowded hallway, wedging himself between students talking and texting. The halls resembled a busy airport to Alonso and he pushed his way through as if he were about to miss a plane. He spotted Sarah and Tesoro talking and laughing. Alonso hesitated for a moment and then moved in.

"Hey," he said, gently reaching out to hold Tesoro's upper arm. She stopped, looked down at his hand on her arm and looked back at him.

"What are you doing, you creep? Did she give you permission to touch her?" Sarah yelped.

"I have something I want to give you."

Alonso reached into his front tee-shirt pocket to pull out the note, but just as Tesoro reached for it Brett jumped in between them and snatched it out of Alonso's hand.

"What's this?" Brett backed up through the crowd, out of Alonso's reach, and opened the note. He let out a loud, menacing laugh as he read it. Alonso jumped through the crowd and lunged at Brett trying to retrieve the note. Brett shoved Alonso backwards into the crowd and onto to the floor, his fall barely broken by students around him. Just as Alonso pushed up off the hard tile floor, Brett jumped on top of him and tried to punch him in the face.

Alonso had seen enough fights with his cousins to know what to do. He shoved Brett hard in the chest, pushing him back just far enough for Alonso to pull his legs up from under Brett's weight. Forcefully, Alonso pulled his legs up to his own chest. Just as Brett was recovering from the shove to the chest, Alonso kicked his feet, full force, into Brett's solar plexus and threw him backwards, knocking the breath right out of him. The note went flying into the air and Sarah quickly scrambled to grab it off the floor. Before Alonso could get up and Tesoro could take it from her, she read it.

"You perv. How dare you give my friend something like this!" Sarah screamed. She shredded the note into tiny pieces and threw it up into the air. It was further scattered by the feet of students racing for their rides.

"¡Culera!" (*Bitch,*) Alonso yelled. He picked up his backpack and ran to the front of Flores High.

Alonso glanced behind and could see Brett's friend pulling him up from the floor. He could hear yelling. "Wetback, we're taking you down!"

Alonso raced down the concrete ramp in front of the school, hurdled the brick retaining wall and bolted to his cousins' Impala, waiting at the circular drive for him. The back window was down. He threw in his backpack and seamlessly slid through the open window without opening the door.

"¡Písale!" (*Hit it.*)

Without even a glance in the rearview mirror, Patricio slammed the gas and squealed out of the crowded parking lot.

Alonso hung his upper torso out the back window and saw Brett on the curb with his friends, his fist raised in rage in the direction of the Impala.

"Chales. Glad to see you guys, you saved my ass." Alonso smiled at his cousins, grabbing and squeezing their shoulders at the same time in gratitude.

"Who was the gringo at the curbside?" Mauricio asked.

"You don't miss a thing, do you?"

"No. Who was he? ¿Le partimos su madre?" (*Do we need to beat him up?*) Mauricio persisted.

"Maybe, just maybe." Alonso smiled at the thought of his cousins going after this rich jock.

"You still mad at us?" Patricio glanced in the rearview mirror.

"No."

"Did you give the money to your mamá?"

"Not yet."

"Your nose is bleeding." Mauricio handed Alonso a wadded up rag from the glove box.

CHAPTER THIRTY-ONE

Mustangs and Poetry

"**W**hy did you tear it up? That was mine, it was meant for me!" Tesoro yelled at Sarah in the empty hallway.

"Get out! You're acting like you want it from that emo freak!"

The note was scattered to the winds. Only a few pieces remained. Tesoro reached down and picked up two jagged pieces that were covered with brown sneaker prints from fast moving students. She could make out only a few words: "my needing you, my dreams of you" and "when our lips touch." She clasped the papers and moved her hands tightly to her chest; her heart pounded and it was hard to breathe after reading his words.

"How could you have taken this from me? What did the rest of the note say?" A lone tear rolled down her cheek as she stared at Sarah.

"C'mon Tesoro, I don't remember it word for word. We're going to miss our bus if we don't run for it."

"I don't care." Sarah grabbed Tesoro by the arm and pulled her into a trot down the hall and outside to the bus lane.

"There's my bus!" Sarah broke away from Tesoro and ran as fast as she could and jumped aboard just before it pulled out. Tesoro looked for her bus, but it was nowhere in the lineup. She watched Sarah's bus round the corner in dismay.

"That bites, that really bites." She sat down at the edge of the curb and pulled the ragged bits of Alonso's note out of her pocket.

A car with a loud racing engine pulled up beside Tesoro. It was Brett in the backseat of a new Mustang convertible with two seniors from the football team riding up front.

"Need a ride home?" Brett asked with a wide smile.

"I can manage just fine on my own." Tesoro stood up and started to walk up the sidewalk, away from Brett. She pulled her phone from her backpack.

"I'm not going to hurt you. Plus you've got these two big bodyguards in the front seat to protect you."

"Didn't I tell you to leave me alone?"

"What, are you mad that I tried to protect you from that creeper-stalker?"

"He's not a creeper-stalker."

"You like him don't you?

"Leave me alone!"

"You do need a ride home. Right?" Brett said.

"I don't mind taking you home." The driver turned around and gave Tesoro a wink and a smile.

"C'mon, we'll get you home before the bus can. Call someone if you like and let them know what you're doing."

Brett slid over in the backseat, offering Tesoro a place to sit. Tesoro raised one finger in the air to signal for Brett to wait and speed dialed Tino.

"Hey, I'm catching a ride home with three guys from the football team." She was quiet, listening hard to hear her brother. She placed her free finger in her ear opposite the phone to block the sound of the music and the muffler.

"I'll be fine. Here's their license plate, PLY-BLL," she announced loudly. "Yeah, I think it means play ball, too. Okay, I'll see you in a bit. Love you, too."

Tesoro jumped into the backseat and buckled in. The driver turned up the music and peeled out of the parking lot.

"So, you like that guy?"

Tesoro held her hair back from the wind and looked away.

"The emo, spick in black." Brett said.

"You're prejudiced. How dare you call..."

"Just protecting you baby," Brett interrupted.

"Stop the car!" Tesoro leaned forward to the driver. "This was a mistake."

The driver pulled the Mustang over to the side of the road. The guy in the passenger seat jumped out of the car, leaving the door open.

"Here you ride up front," he offered.

"She can stay back here with me," Brett said.

"She needs to give directions to her house so she's better off up front."

Tesoro glared at Brett and moved to the front. She pulled her hair back, twisting it into a braid and focused her attention on the driver, giving him instructions. The Mustang roared down her street and came to an abrupt stop in front of her house. Tesoro could see Tino pulling the curtain back on the living room window, peering out at her.

"Hey, I'm having a party next Friday," Brett said. "Everyone will be there. Do you want to come?"

"Next Friday?"

"Yeah, can you make it?"

"I...I don't think so." Tesoro reached for the door handle. "Hey, thanks for the ride." She was grateful to be home.

"I'll see you around." Brett yelled. The Mustang turned a

tight circle in her street and sped off.

Tino met her at the door.

"That's Brett Merrick! What the hell are you doing?"

"How do you know what he looks like?"

"I ran a search for him the other night. He's all over the web."

"Oh, for what?"

"He's a jock. He's won a few awards for GT stuff, Destination Imagination awards."

"I didn't know that he's in GT. He doesn't seem like someone who would be."

"Tesoro, after what he did to you, you trusted him enough to ride home with him? What's up with that?"

Tesoro turned her back to him. She was crying silently, head down and shoulders heaving with each breath.

"What happened?" he asked gently. "Tesoro, talk to me."

"I can't take you being mad at me right now." She reached into her front pocket and pulled out the small slips of torn paper with Alonso's handwriting, handing them over to her brother.

"What's this? Who wrote this...Brett? I'll take him out, gimp style."

Tesoro momentarily laughed at Tino between her crying. She turned to her brother, her face wet with tears.

"It's from Alonso."

"Alonso?"

Tesoro nodded yes and, biting her lower lip, she let her tears fall freely down her flushed cheeks.

"I've never felt like this."

"So if you like this guy so much, how did you end up riding home with Brett?"

"I missed my bus. Brett was there." Tesoro looked her brother in the eyes.

"Why are you crying, then?"

"Alonso and Brett got into a fight this afternoon."

"Over you?" He hardly gave Tesoro a chance to finish her sentence.

"I guess. They were like two bears wrestling for territory. Alonso's so skinny and he kicked Brett right off of him. He's fast."

"Who won the battle?"

"Neither."

"Let's try this again. It's Alonso that you like, right Tesoro? I'm not letting you off the hook this time."

Tesoro stayed quiet for a long time, looking at her right foot as she traced small circles across the Saltillo tile floor with her big toe, her hands gracefully folded behind her back.

"I've never liked a guy like this before."

"Yeah, you in love?"

"No!" Tesoro laughed. Picking up her backpack from the sofa, she ran up the stairs, leaving Tino alone and perplexed.

Tesoro pulled the torn sketchbook paper out and flattened it across her lavender bedding. She rested on her stomach and propped her chin up with her hands, her elbows making deep imprints on the downy bedding. Touching the frayed paper, Tesoro read aloud: "My needing you, my dreams of you...when our lips touch...when our lips touch..." she spoke in a whisper and reached her fingers up to her mouth, gently touching her lower lip.

Reaching into her backpack, Tesoro pulled out her

sketchbook and a glue stick. Finding a clean page in the sketchbook she carefully glued down the torn bits of paper from Alonso's note. Opening her marker bag, she selected a pink highlighter and drew a heart around his note. She took her pen and wrote the words, "I am waiting for your kiss..." carefully at the bottom of the page. Folding this page over on itself, she closed her sketchbook and pulled out her English homework, reading the poetry assignment.

"being to timelessness as it's to time," e.e. cummings

"being to timelessness as it's to time,
love did no more begin than love will end:
where nothing is to breathe to stroll to swim
love is the air the ocean and the land

(do lovers suffer? all divinities
proudly descending put on deathful flesh:
are lovers glad? only their smallest joy's
a universe emerging from a wish)

love is the voice under all silences,
the hope which has no opposite in fear:
the strength so strong mere force is feebleness:
the truth more first than sun more last than star

--do lovers love? why then to heaven with hell.
whatever sages say and fools, all's well"

CHAPTER THIRTY-TWO

Gifted and Talented

"**A**lonso, Patricio is on the phone for you," tía Ruby chimed up the stairs and through Alonso's open door. Alonso pulled his worn black tee-shirt over his slim, muscular frame, clipped his silver chain to his dark skinny jeans and raced bare-footed down the stairs, taking the steps two at a time with Sombra right by his side.

Alonso quickly picked up the phone from the granite kitchen bar.

"Hola."

"Hola," Patricio said somberly. "I have news."

"Yeah. ¿Qué pasa?"

"Lilianna's friend, the man with the tattoos, he's tagged by the Royal Riderz," Patricio said quietly and quickly.

"And...?"

"Lilianna took his bullet; he's a marked man."

"I've already figured that much out."

"The Royal Riderz pull jobs for another outfit. They're hired to take him out."

"What other outfit?"

"That's the part of the puzzle we're trying to put together. Me and Mauricio are trailing him today. Are you in?"

"I have school, I can't."

"We'll pick you up right after school. Are you in?"

"Whatever...can you take me to see Lilianna?"

"We'll be there. Be ready, flaco!"

Alonso pressed the end call button and placed the phone back on the bar.

"What did he want?" Tía Ruby asked.

"Nothin'," Alonso replied. He went into the laundry room, pulled a pair of socks from the dryer and laced up his Chucks.

"I might be back late today," he yelled over his shoulder, running to catch the bus as it pulled up to the corner.

~

Alonso went to his locker first thing, pulled out his shoe invention and smiled. He didn't want to miss the science fair deadline and he couldn't wait to show it to Mrs. Weaver during class. Just beyond the wall of moving students, Brett studied Alonso as he placed the shoe in his backpack. Smirking, Brett walked up to Alonso in the crowded hall and slammed him through the crowd into the side wall. Several students tumbled in all directions, all glaring at Alonso and Brett as they regained their stride.

"Culero." (*Asshole,*) Alonso said under his breath.

"Come to the office with me, Alonso." The voice of Assistant Principal Martin crept up from behind.

"What did I do?" Alonso hoped A.P. Martin did not understand the Spanish word he had just let loose.

"Come with me."

"I'll be late for first period."

"I'll write you a pass."

Alonso walked just behind A.P. Martin through the long corridor. He shut the office door behind him and motioned for Alonso to have a seat.

"How's your sister?"

Alonso looked down. He was not expecting this.

"She's still in a coma," he said, not looking up.

"She doesn't go to Flores."

Alonso shook his head without looking up.

"I know about you, Alonso. You live with your uncle in this district some of the time."

Alonso felt a deep fear rise up from his stomach and into his throat.

"Where do your parents live?"

Alonso knew he could not stay quiet any longer. It would feel good to tell the truth, even if it meant losing everything.

"My papá has been deported."

"That must be hard on your family," A.P. Martin said.

"Yes sir." Alonso's bangs hung like a curtain over his face.

"You're a good student, Alonso. You are the type of student Flores likes to have, you...you bring our scores up."

Smiling, A.P. Martin leaned back in his chair. Alonso cocked his head to one side, as if he just heard A.P. Martin wrong.

"There are two teachers at Flores that have noticed you and they are recommending you for the advanced placement classes." He concluded.

"What two teachers?"

A.P. Martin laughed out loud.

"Science and math. Mrs. Weaver and Coach Rodriquez."

"Science and math, yeah, I like both of those classes. Does this mean a lot of extra work?"

"It just means you will have another teacher, the Gifted

and Talented Coordinator for our district, Mr. Bushel. You will be able to go to his room to work on your assignments. We will need to pull you out of one elective to make time to attend his class once per week. You will need to take a few tests and your family and teachers will need to fill out paperwork on your ability. You will also need to present a project that reflects advanced thinking."

"I already have the project!" Alonso reached into his backpack and pulled out the shoe.

"Those are like the shoes I wear. That's already been invented, Alonso." A.P. Martin leaned in closer to look at the shoe.

"No, it's not like that, this one produces direct current for powering up phones...look."

Alonso placed the shoe on his foot, pulled his phone from his backpack and plugged it in. He handed his phone to A.P. Martin as he stepped repeatedly down on the shoe springs.

"See, it's powering up." Alonso reached over and pointed to the battery icon.

"You did this?" A.P. Martin's tone went from low to high.

"Yeah, yeah." Alonso tapped his foot with the spring-loaded shoe to an inaudible rhythm. His long bangs swayed in time from side to side over his face as the battery continued to gain strength.

"It's my project for the science contest."

"Has Mrs. Weaver seen this yet?"

"No, I'm turning it in this afternoon," Alonso replied, still pumping away on the shoe.

Assistant Principal Martin handed the charged phone back to Alonso and wrote a pass for his first period teacher.

"We'll start testing you tomorrow. Counseling will call you out of class. Keep that phone turned off and in your backpack. I don't want to see it back in my office. Not all teachers allow students to use phones in their rooms."

"Yes sir."

Alonso switched out shoes, placing his project shoe in his backpack. On his way out the office door he waved a quick goodbye to A.P. Martin.

Walking into the empty boys' locker room to change, Alonso realized he had an opportunity with the pass from A.P. Martin to buy some time out of class. He intended to find Tesoro next door in the girls' gym. He quickly pulled on his gym clothes, leaving his backpack on the locker room floor, the hall pass clutched in his hand for Coach. He strolled toward the girls' gym and looked sideways through the open double doors. He spied Tesoro in the crowd of girls running laps around the perimeter of the large room.

"Hey," he whispered as she passed the open doorway. Tesoro stopped right beside him, breathing hard from the run.

Alonso noticed her muscular, athletic legs and her tight white athletic socks, pulled up just below her knees with a band of pink at the top. He took in her knees, angular and well shaped. His eyes traveled up the long defined muscle on the side of her leg, up her thigh and to the rounded quadriceps that showed through the top front of her tight gym shorts.

"What?" Tesoro stopped short.

"Hi!" Alonso smiled at Tesoro.

"What are you doing here?" She looked through the crowd of running girls. Her coach was distracted and did not see her standing by the door.

"I wanted to apologize to you."

"For what, putting Brett in his place?"

Alonso laughed. "No. For grabbing your arm when I didn't have your permission to."

"For real, you're apologizing for that?" Tesoro laughed. Coach's loud whistle sounded in the background. It was time for a new exercise. Jogging backwards, away from Alonso, she looked him straight in the eye and said just loud enough for him to hear: "You have my permission to grab my arm."

Alonso lingered in the doorway as Tesoro turned and ran away, full speed. For a split second, Alonso saw the shadow of a silver wolf running beside her. Shaking off his flash vision, Alonso went outside to join his class running laps around the track.

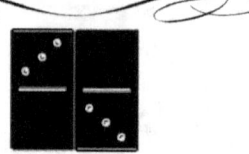

CHAPTER THIRTY-THREE

Coaches and Hall Passes

Brett noticed Alonso's grungy backpack leaning up against the gym locker. He looked both ways to make certain the coast was clear. Alonso was nowhere in sight. Bending down to look into the abandoned backpack, he saw the odd shoe with springs: Alonso's science project. He took the shoe out. Walking out of the locker room into the gymnasium, Brett flung the shoe high up into the interlacing ceiling beams. The shoe caught on top of a metal bracing beam, far out of reach.

Brett ran out of the gym right as Alonso came through a side door from the field. Alonso saw Brett and slipped into the shadows of the locker room to avoid any further conflict. His backpack was right where he left it against the locker. Picking it up, he left the locker room and walked through the gym, oblivious to the shoe right over his head.

On his way to class, all Alonso could think about was the glimmer he noticed in Tesoro's eye when she gave him permission to touch her arm. The thought of this made him feel weak, short of breath and light as a feather at the same time. He felt as if his heart were going to sing itself right out of his body.

Mr. Chang stood just outside the door of Alonso's second period advanced placement algebra class. He smiled and shook each student's hand as they entered the room, something he did for each class. Mr. Chang's thick, rough hands reminded Alonso of his papá's hands--warm and comforting. Alonso looked through his dark bangs at his new math teacher, almost expecting to catch a glimpse of his papá.

"I need to talk with you right after class," Mr. Chang said, letting go of Alonso's hand. Alonso took his seat in the back of the small room packed with desks. He reached into his backpack to pull out his notebook and realized something did not feel right--something was missing.

Alonso pulled his backpack up from the floor and onto the small desktop. His heart pounded: his shoe invention was missing! Making his way to Mr. Chang, who was still holding the door open for students, he asked if he could go to the restroom.

"Alonso, you just got to class, why didn't you go during passing time?"

"I was in a hurry to make it here on time. I didn't want to be counted tardy on my first day with you."

"Okay, just make it fast."

Alonso's charm with his teacher worked and he sprinted in the direction of the closest boys' room and let the door slam behind him. He was alone and he needed a moment to breathe and think about what could have happened to his project.

"Brett!" He flashed back to Brett leaving the gym during first period.

Alonso cracked open the door to the boys' room and looked down the long hallway toward the math room. The door was shut and his class was in session. Alonso cut around the corner to the side door, avoiding the security camera. Once in the courtyard, Alonso ran full speed to the boys' gym locker room. The seniors were changing out; many of them were on the football team. They eyed Alonso suspiciously as he pushed his way past them to his locker.

"Did anyone find a shoe? It has springs on the bottom," Alonso announced loudly to the group. They stopped what they were doing for a moment, stared at him blankly and continued their routines.

Alonso put his hands in his pockets and walked into the empty gym. He thought back to Brett's presence in the gym. He must have taken his shoe project out of his backpack. Going to the large trash can in the corner of the room he started to dig.

"Cold." The voice startled him. He spun around, but the empty gym only echoed with the squeaks from his Chucks. The bleachers were pushed up against the wall, creating a perfect hiding place for almost any small object. Alonso looked at the edges of the bleachers first. He heard people entering the room; it was a group of seniors cutting through the gym to the track. Quickly, he ducked down between the wall and the bleachers. There was just enough room to squeeze between the back wall and the underside of the folded up bleachers. He wedged himself low and stooped down to travel the length of the back gym wall under the folded bleachers. He did not see his shoe anywhere in this poorly lit space.

"FREEZING!" The voice was loud. Alonso jumped and hit his head on the metal rod that held the wooden bleachers in place, knocking a paper bag from above that landed right by his feet. He picked it up and opened it. Inside he found another bag, smaller and clear. Inside the bag were pills--hundreds of small, white, round pills.

"Ay, Cabrón," he exclaimed under his breath. His hands began to tremble: he could be taken out for this! He rolled up the bag and stuffed it down his pants. He'd flush the contents down the toilet at the first opportunity.

Shimmying through the rest of the bleachers, Alonso emerged on the opposite side only to meet up directly with Coach Johnstone, the head football coach. The formidable man placed his hands on his hips, making him appear larger than he already was.

"Who are you?"

"I'm Alonso. I've lost my shoe sir," Alonso said humbly,

which was easy because he was so nervous that he could hardly speak. It took everything he had in him to keep his voice from quavering.

"What do they look like?"

"It's just one shoe. It has springs in the bottom; it's for my science project."

Coach Johnstone looked up at the ceiling and slowly pointed to a rafter by the basketball hoop. "Would that be your shoe?" he asked with a slight grin.

"HOT!" the playful voice caused Alonso to jump back. It was the same jumbled voice he heard coming from Skye Peterson, only this time he could make out the words. Coach Johnstone flashed Alonso a curious look.

"Yes sir. That's it. How do we get it down?"

"I'll call the custodians. Do you have a hall pass, son?" Coach Johnstone questioned.

"No sir. I told Mr. Chang that I was going to the restroom and came here to find my science project."

"Any idea who threw your shoe up there?" Coach Johnstone pointed up.

"I have a suspect, but I don't want to blame him. I didn't exactly see him do it."

"Do I know 'him?'"

"He's on the junior varsity team. Brett Merrick."

"You're being honest with me and I appreciate that." Coach Johnstone winked.

"I'll write a pass for you. You're lucky you caught me on my conference period."

Alonso wasn't quite sure what to make of Coach Johnstone's kindness. Why would he listen to someone he didn't know accuse his top player of doing something? Coaches usually took after their players and defended them.

"Here's your pass. I'll have your shoe project held for you in the front office. Now get on to class," he said with a thick southern drawl.

As Alonso left the gym, he spotted movement under the basketball hoop out of the corner of his eye. Skye Peterson was leaning against the wall. Skye tipped his baseball cap in acknowledgement of Alonso's presence. Alonso nodded in return. Alonso concentrated with all of his might on the word "Thanks" and directed it at Skye. Skye said "You're welcome," just as clear as the cobalt Texas sky on a cloud-free day.

Lunch rolled around and Alonso made his way to the office where his shoe project was waiting behind the front desk. After showing his school photo identification card, Alonso had the project back in his hands. He decided to place it in his locker, safe and secure until science class. He reached into his locker and pulled out the sandwich that tía Ruby made. He downed the sandwich on his way to the gym to see who was playing basketball.

"Hey, Alonso, catch!" Marcus yelled from inside the crowd of guys running across the court.

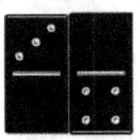

CHAPTER THIRTY-FOUR

The Fight and the White Pills

Alonso missed the ball Marcus had thrown his way. His eyes were fixed on Brett, who was walking directly toward him with his arms open and his head and chest jutted forward.

"What?" Alonso yelled at Brett from ten steps away. Brett moved with more determination, his fists clenched at his side, the two deep vertical creases between his eyes etched deep into his lower brow. His piercing blue eyes narrowed as he closed in on Alonso.

"What do you want with me, culero?" Alonso stood his ground.

Brett bolted forward and pushed Alonso hard in the chest. Alonso jolted backward without falling.

"What?" Alonso challenged again.

In the distance, Assistant Principal Martin and Coach Johnstone were taking in the entire scene. They looked at each other, had words and moved directly across the crowded court in the direction of the altercation. A.P. Martin pulled a portable radio from his belt and spoke quickly into it.

Brett slammed Alonso in the chest again, this time knocking him off balance and onto the ground.

Brett jumped on top of Alonso and yelled, "I finish what I start and you're about to be finished, bitch."

Alonso quickly twisted out from under Brett's wrestling hold before Brett could punch him. Jumping to his feet, Alonso took off toward the gathering crowd of boys who were ready for a fight. A large boy pushed Alonso back into the ring of students naturally forming a fighting pit at the far end of the gym. Brett lunged at Alonso, grabbed him around the waist and tried to take him down. Alonso elbowed Brett in the face causing him to topple. Brett pulled on Alonso's pants to maintain his balance. The paper bag Alonso had forgotten about spilled from the front of his jeans and the small white pills bounced across the wooden gym floor.

No one in the crowd moved as Alonso turned a full circle, taking in the amount of drugs that had just poured from his pants. Brett's mouth opened and his jaw dropped in a look of pure shock. His eyes narrowed and he clenched his fists.

"You emo thief, that's what you were doing in the gym. I'm taking you out."

Brett lunged at Alonso, shoving him back into the crowd which fluidly morphed into a new shape to make more room in the fight pit. Alonso tumbled backward, stunned by Brett's verbal slip: he knew about the drugs behind the bleachers.

"You put them there. ¡Pinche Narco!" Alonso yelled.

"Dude, it's 'Oxy,' flowin' everywhere," a loud voice sounded from the sidelines.

"Get it up, get it," another voice sounded out in excitement. It was the barbiturate Oxycontin they were yelling about. Alonso saw three guys that he knew were heavy users scrambling on the floor, sweeping up the barbiturates that had dropped out of his pants seconds earlier. They were laughing like they had discovered gold. Brett saw Alonso off guard watching the scramble and sucker-punched him square in the nose, sending Alonso to his knees. Brett kicked his left shoulder, causing him to fall to the right on his side to the floor.

"I'm finishing you," Brett yelled. He kicked Alonso in the kidney just as Assistant Principal Martin and the school police officer suddenly appeared.

"Break it up!" A.P. Martin yelled. Brett ran the other way.

"Flat on the floor--NOW." The officer yelled. Coach Johnstone pushed out of the crowd directly in front of Brett.

"Do what he says." Coach Johnston's girth was twice the size of Brett. Stepping back, Brett dropped to the floor.

"I want you to get up and walk to the office with us with no further trouble. Do you understand?" The officer said. Brett slowly got up and the officer escorted him through the scattered crowd.

"Hey guy, get up." Alonso heard Coach Johnstone through the crowd. He looked across the quickly clearing floor. All of the little white pills were gone, and so were the druggies. Alonso rolled over to his side, curled up into a painful ball and groaned.

"I'm taking you to the nurse, you're bleeding everywhere." Coach Johnstone pulled Alonso up from the floor by the arm. Alonso felt weak, his head was swimming and he saw white flashes of light going off everywhere. Suddenly, he felt he was being pulled backwards through a tunnel and everything was going black around him. He heard a loud roaring noise like a large ocean wave moving directly over head. The last thing he remembered was the construction worker's death...and now it was his turn.

The sound of the school buzzer going off awoke Alonso with a start. The bag of ice on his head fell to the side of the hard vinyl bed in the school nurse's office.

"How ya doing?" a kind female voice asked. She placed the ice bag back over Alonso's nose. "That was quite a punch you took."

"Can he be moved?" Alonso heard the serious voice of Assistant Principal Martin.

"Alonso, can you get up slowly for me?" the nurse asked.

"Yeah, my nose hurts. Is it broke?" Alonso slid his lithe

frame to the edge of the vinyl bed and moved into a sitting position.

"It's not broken. You did bleed a lot and we had to clean you up." The nurse moved the ice bag into Alonso's hand and then moved his hand to his nose.

"Hold it there for another hour."

Alonso could not breathe through his nose. He reached up with his free hand and felt the opening to his nostrils. Gauze was rolled up and neatly tucked inside.

"When can I take the gauze out?"

"I'll take it out for you in just a bit. For now you need to walk to the office. Right Andy?"

Alonso caught the way she smiled and called him Andy instead of Assistant Principal Martin and wondered if they were perhaps friends, or more?

"Come with me, Alonso." A.P. Martin led Alonso to the hard wooden chairs that lined either side of the administrative hall in the main school office.

"Have a seat and wait for me to call you in." A.P. Martin shut his office door leaving Alonso alone in the hall.

Alonso had never been in any type of trouble in school. How had all of this blown out of control so quickly? He rested both hands over the ice bag on his nose and leaned forward in the chair. He closed his eyes and his bangs fell over his entire face. Alonso could feel the last of the blood shift in his nose, moving forward, moving into the gauze. It felt good and gave him some relief from the pressure in his head.

The door to A.P. Martin's room quietly opened and closed again. Peering to one side through his bangs Alonso saw Brett take a chair across from him.

"Not such a pretty boy now, are you?" Brett muttered under his breath.

Alonso pushed the ice bag further up on his nose, partially blocking his eyes and his view of Brett. He knew they were both in enough trouble and that Brett was smart enough to not try anything in the office.

"Brett Merrick, I have your mother on the speaker phone. You need to come into my office. She wants to talk to both of us at the same time."

Brett grudgingly went into the office, shutting the door behind him.

Alonso felt suddenly sleepy; he wanted to lie down and take a nap. With his eyes closed he could make out soft purple clouds of lights coming at his head, ever so slowly. He relaxed into the lights and let them engulf him. Something about this felt comfortable and familiar. He remembered the land of the violet sky and wished he could disappear into that place to escape his current reality.

"You can heal yourself," Sha whispered in Alonso's right ear.

"Follow my lead..."

He continued: "You are focusing your energy into your heart and your heart glows with a brilliant pink light made up of total love. This light is growing through your entire body. It's working its way to your nose and sealing the blood vessels and shrinking the swelling."

Alonso could feel warmth spreading across his entire body. He could feel an embrace of love in his chest moving out to the rest of his body. His nose started to feel light and less achy. There seemed to be a magnetic pull from his hands, lifting the pain right out of his body. Instinctively, Alonso put the ice bag down and shook his hands out on either side of his body. He moved his hands back up over his nose, without actually touching it, and imagined light energy mending every part of his face.

"Nice," he said softly, playing with the magnetic pull he

felt between his two hands, extending to his nose. He felt a draining from his forehead and all through his sinus cavities, providing relief from the swelling.

"Alonso, come on into my office." A.P. Martin's voice pulled Alonso out of his trance.

Grabbing the melting ice bag from the wooden chair beside him, Alonso took a seat in A.P. Martin's office right next to Brett. The odd realization of again being in this same office during first period, but for a very different reason hit Alonso. He was remorseful for having been in a fight.

"Tell me what is going on between you two." Assistant Principal Martin leaned across the large desk cluttered with papers. Neither boy said a word. They stared at A.P. Martin with blank expressions.

"I see how it's going to be." He pulled a referral form from his side drawer and wrote Brett's name across the top.

"Brett, I am giving you an at-home suspension for the next three days, just as we discussed on the phone with your mother. I need you to spend the rest of today in school suspension. You may wait in the hallway for me. Shut the door behind you."

Turning his attention to Alonso, A.P. Martin softened his demeanor.

"Why does this guy dislike you so much?"

Alonso smiled at A.P. Martin's directness and honesty.

"We both like the same girl."

"Alonso, I saw what happened to you. I saw Brett start the fight."

Alonso held his breath and wondered if A.P. Martin had seen the bag of pills fall out of his pants. His throat went dry and he started to perspire. His hands were shaking. The thought of being busted for drugs that did not belong to him was overwhelming, especially when his intention had been to flush them down the toilet.

CHAPTER THIRTY-FIVE

Consequences and Invitations

Alonso pushed open the door to the nurse's office. Two students were waiting to see her and she was on the phone. He went to the mirror above the sink and looked at his nose for the first time since the punch.

"Not bad," he mumbled lifting his nose up to get a better view of the gauze stuffed up his nostrils. Very carefully, he pulled out the gauze. It was covered in clotted blood. Dampening a paper towel, he cleared the dried blood from around his nose. Other than a little swelling around his eyes on the bridge of his nose he looked almost normal.

The nurse stepped out of her office and all three students simultaneously looked her way.

"Have a seat and I'll pull that gauze out for you in just a minute," she said to Alonso. Turning her attention to the first student in line, she pulled open a drawer filled with diabetic snacks and handed a bag of animal crackers over to a rather pale girl. With her back turned, Alonso quietly slipped through the open door without being noticed.

The bell sounded and Alonso didn't realize what period he needed to attend next. The empty halls filled with students within seconds. Alonso spotted Marcus about ten students ahead in the crowd. He used his height and long legs to maneuver through the crowd to move right beside Marcus.

"Hey, what period are we in?"

"Dude, you're here! I thought for sure you'd be

suspended or in juvie, especially with the pharms. Where'd you get those?"

"They didn't see them and the bandana boys sucked them up like a vacuum cleaner," Alonso said.

"Man, I thought for sure you'd be suspended, or worse."

"Me too. I didn't even get a referral."

"What the hell were you doing with oxy?"

"I found it in the gym. I was going to flush it."

"Flush it--damn, that shit's worth a fortune. Who did it belong to?"

"It may be Brett's."

"Is that why he came after you?"

"No," Alonso said.

"Did he get a referral?

"Yeah, he's suspended for three days. I don't know why I didn't get one, too."

"Did you make some kind of deal with A.P. Martin?"

Alonso shook his head 'no.'

"I need to know what period to go to next."

"We're in sixth," Marcus said.

Alonso reeled around in the opposite direction. He had missed his entire fifth period social studies class. He bolted to the art room just as the bell sounded and slid low into his seat He pulled his sketch book out of his backpack to do the required five-minute drawing warm-up. He hoped no one in this class knew what had happened in the gym over lunch. The fight would be the hot topic of the school for the next few days. He knew to lay low and stay quiet until the next big thing happened, or until no one cared anymore about what happened today.

Drawing the warm-up still life set up in the corner of the art room for what seemed the hundredth time, Alonso shut his eyes; he was bone tired. His nose felt somewhat better, but his head was swimming and he needed to shut it down. The art teacher was busy setting up supplies for the next lesson on the far side of the room. Alonso saw a chance to catch some shut eye and was too tired to care if he got in trouble.

After moments of quick, dreamless sleep, a loud thud in the art room pulled Alonso back into consciousness. A large boy had tripped over a backpack on the floor and landed on his side right beside him.

"Here." Alonso reached his arm out to give the guy a hand-up.

The boy squinted his eyes in recognition and boldly stated: "You're the guy that fought in the gym today."

Every eye turned on Alonso and the room fell into total silence.

Without missing a beat, Alonso said, "Hey--that was a big tumble you just took. Are you okay?"

"Yeah." He brushed himself off and returned to his seat.

Alonso looked for Tesoro to see if she noticed. She was looking his way. He questioned if Tesoro heard students talking about the fight; if she heard the drug rumors that were flying all over school. The swollen nose under his dark bangs confirmed the fight. She had to wonder why he would have such a large stash. He hoped she would believe him; he knew he didn't fit the image of a dealer. Surely she knew who the dealers were at Flores. He needed to talk with her soon, in private, to tell her the truth beyond the rumors.

He rose to sharpen his pencil on the opposite side of the room and walked right past Tesoro. As he did she quickly flipped her sketch book open to a new page, as if she were hiding something. Alonso's untucked flannel shirt caught on the sketch book and it fell to the floor. He reached down to pick it up and noticed the page that fell open was folded over. He flipped it open to find the torn bits of his note glued into her sketch book with a pink heart drawn around the fragmented words. His heart raced as he read, "I am waiting for your kiss..." at the bottom of the page.

He slowly folded the page back over, closed her sketch book and placed it on the table. He brushed her hand and looked directly into her eyes. He felt the electricity again, the tingling her touch sent through his entire body. She drew in her breath, he suspected she felt the same electricity between them. Alonso backed away from Tesoro slowly, not breaking eye contact and sharpened his pencil, amazed at what had just been revealed to him.

The bell sounded faster than Alonso expected. He needed to collect his shoe science project out of his locker and still make it to seventh period on time. Mrs. Weaver was expecting his project and he couldn't let her down. He also felt relieved that Brett would not be in science class the next four days. He could give the shoe to her without interference.

The white board in the science room was color coded for assignment types and it appeared today was going to be active. Mrs. Weaver had the room set up for a lab, group work, and then a quiz over the main topics from the lab. Alonso finally found a moment to pull out his shoe and take it to Mrs. Weaver, who was engaging a group of students to discuss the experiment on gasses. Alonso held up the shoe in front of her face and announced: "This is my project!"

"You will need to show that to me later. Do you have your report on the function of the project written out yet?" Her tone was sharp.

"No, Mrs. Weaver, I don't." Alonso looked down and dropped the shoe to his side, feeling deflated.

"See me after class." Mrs. Weaver turned back to the students.

Quietly placing the shoe into his backpack, Alonso settled into completing his worksheet on gasses and memorizing them from the periodic table of the elements. Just as the rest of his group put the final touches on their worksheets, he felt his phone vibrate in his pocket. Alonso asked Mrs. Weaver if he could go to the restroom and he slipped out of class.

The text message was from Patricio: "out front" is all it said. They were already in front of the school waiting on him, at least fifteen minutes before the bell. The phone vibrated in his hand again. The text read, "apúrate."

The bell sounded as Alonso bounded back to the science room to grab his backpack.

"Alonso?" Mrs. Weaver caught him at the door.

"Can I talk to you in the morning?"

"I'll be here."

As he raced through the hallway, he didn't notice Tesoro behind him calling his name as she pushed through the students to catch up to him. Rounding the exterior corner of the cafeteria, Tesoro suddenly stopped running. Alonso was running at top speed, easily and faster than anyone on the track team. Breathing hard, Tesoro bent down with her hands on her knees and, looked through the crowd toward the busses, her eyes fixed on Alonso.

"He's fast, really fast," she panted. She walked toward her bus, still looking over her shoulder as Alonso wove way ahead of her, through the yellow busses toward de Zavala Road where his cousins waited.

"Hey beautiful." Brett's voice sounded just to Tesoro's left. She kept walking.

"Hey, that druggie emo needed to be taken down," Brett continued in a loud bragging tone as he took hold of her elbow. Tesoro pulled away from him and quickened her pace. Brett jogged and moved in beside her.

"Say 'yes.' I'll leave you alone if you say 'yes.'"

"Yeah, right." Tesoro moved away from him through the crowd.

"Great, I heard a 'yeah' in there. That means you'll come to my party Friday night. I can have the guys you met with the Mustang pick you up from your house at eight," Brett said smiling and his blue eyes sparkled.

"She can make it, for sure!" The overly zealous voice of Sarah broke through the crowd as she moved in next to Brett.

"What?" Tesoro exclaimed as she spun around to face both Brett and Sarah.

"Hey, I thought you were suspended?" Sarah questioned.

"I am...couldn't get an early ride outta here. I was stuck in ISS."

"You're so good at arranging rides. Imagine that!" Sarah said with a sly grin. "Have your friends pick both of us up at Tesoro's house."

"Sarah! What if I don't want to go?"

Sarah reached out and hooked arms with Brett, still smiling at him. "She's going and so am I," she winked.

"Be ready by eight." Brett darted through the school busses and the parking lot to join his friends in the Mustang.

"Sarah!" Tesoro yelled.

"You are so going to his party!" Sarah said.

"No, I don't want to, I don't like him."

"Yeah, but I do. You're going to get out of your house and have fun. That's that."

CHAPTER THIRTY-SIX

Fandaza and Handshakes

Moving slowly in school traffic, the glistening gold Impala turned a few heads. Alonso jumped into the backseat through the open window, catching his breath from the run. Mauricio pulled the gear shift into drive and crept into traffic on de Zavala Road. Patricio slouched low in the passenger's seat, hand hanging out of the window, patting the side of the door to the low bass rhythm reverberating from the sound system. He eyed a group of girls waiting to cross the road at the light. The girls giggled among themselves, talking behind their hands as they exchanged glances.

Mauricio and Alonso turned to look at the girls just as one turned around and bounced her rear end. Patricio slouched down lower in the seat, pulling his shades over his eyes and jutted his lower lip out. He bobbed his head to the beat of the music and continued to tap the side of the car door.

Mauricio pushed the switches on the hydraulic system and crouched down low, pulling his cap low over his forehead. The Impala bounced at the light and the girls laughed in delight. They imitated the car by jumping up and down and clapping their hands to the beat. Alonso was smiling at the girls at the light.

From a distance, Tesoro peered at the scene from the bus window. "Hey Tracy, why he would leave school so quickly in a lowrider?"

"Don't know? It doesn't make sense, does it?" Tracy questioned back from her seat beside Tesoro.

"Do you think he has a secret life of dealing drugs with hoodwinks from another school?"

"Who knows? Guys like to think they're all that, bad ass and all, you know."

"I didn't think Alonso was like that. I misjudged him."

"Nah, he's just a guy." Tracy reached into her bag and pulled out glittering pink lip gloss. "Like my new shade?" She applied the shiny gloss liberally to her mouth.

"That's pretty on you." Tesoro smiled.

"What's the interest in Alonso, you like him?" Tracy asked and held the lip gloss out for Tesoro to try.

"No thanks, not my shade. Not my type of guy either," Tesoro said. The bus turned onto de Zavala Road.

"What about that guy? Is he your type?" Tracy pointed to the new convertible Mustang with Brett and his friends inside as it pulled up next to the Impala.

"That fandaza should be in the junk yard." Brett's voice carried across the traffic and through the open bus windows.

"Uh-oh." Tesoro kneeled on her seat and hung her head out the window looking at the two cars filled with guys.

"Hey, get down in your seat," the bus driver yelled. She ignored him. The other students were starting to lean against the windows with her, realizing some type of action was about to go down.

The Impala stopped bouncing and the dark tinted windows rolled up. Alonso and his cousins crouched low in their seats. Loud bass rhythm from the rap music boomed from the Impala, blocking out any further insults Brett yelled out from the Mustang. The light changed to green and the Mustang burned bluish smoke from the tires as it squealed from the intersection, jumping ahead in traffic.

The Impala lingered behind the rest of the traffic, moving

into position to follow the Mustang from a distance. It looked like a gangster car next to the small, later model cars on the road.

"¡Síguelos a ver que onda!" (*Follow them, let's see what's up.*) Mauricio tightened down on the steering wheel as he rounded the corner, four cars behind the Mustang that entered the southbound lane of Interstate 10.

"Aren't we going to the hospital? I want to see Lilianna," Alonso said.

"Your friend is going that way." Mauricio said and glanced back at Alonso.

"If they drive too far past the hospital, I'll stop trailing them." The Mustang was gaining speed in front of them on the interstate and he turned his attention back to driving.

"Trust me, Brett and his friends are up to no good. We don't need to follow them to know that," Alonso said.

"Yeah, I want to know what type of 'no good' they're up to." Mauricio pressed his foot down on the gas.

"Why does this guy have it in for you?" Patricio looked back at Alonso.

"He's jealous of me."

"Yeah, jealous of what, flaco?" Mauricio laughed as he changed lanes to hide beside an eighteen wheeler, just out of sight of the Mustang.

"We both like the same girl."

Mauricio took off his cap, reached back and slapped Alonso across the head with it. Alonso responded with a quick duck and cover of his already injured face.

"You mean to say that idiot wanted to take you out because of a girl?" Mauricio's voice pitched high as the Impala swerved toward a semi and rocked back and forth dangerously as Mauricio regained control of the large car.

"¡No, no!" Alonso shouted. "I think he's dealing...big time...and we like the same girl."

"Just stay on him. Let's find out." Patricio pointed to the right and Mauricio followed the Mustang off the interstate and into downtown San Antonio.

"Don't lose him, he turned under the highway." Patricio pulled his body up in the seat and hung his head out the window to get a better look.

"They're parking under the highway. Stop here or they'll see us."

Mauricio pulled the Impala behind a large SUV and they jumped out.

Brett was talking with a guy under the highway. The man and Brett shook hands and a tall skinny man discreetly slid a small item to Brett. Patricio and Mauricio were very familiar with this tactic. They'd seen it many times previously in the school halls when students exchanged drugs for money. The two guys in the Mustang appeared nervous and kept inching the car forward, away from Brett.

"Yeah, what do you make of it?" Mauricio said.

"It's Jorge Cobos he's dealing with! Look...see? His pinche eskeloto arm is covered with tattoos," Patricio said.

"That's the guy Lilianna took the bullet for!" Alonso spit through his teeth, his anger rising as he fought to stay out of view. His face was getting hot; he inched forward, ready to pounce. All of the anger that he had held back over the past few weeks surfaced. He wanted to take Brett and the tattooed man down at the same time. Mauricio grabbed his arm to keep him from blowing their cover.

Brett placed the small baggie in his front pocket and jumped into the Mustang without opening the door. The driver burned rubber, tearing out of downtown San Antonio onto Interstate 10 northbound, too fast for the Impala to follow.

"¡Mira este güey! What's he doing now?" Mauricio said. Jorge Cobos opened the door to a late model black pickup. He looked over his shoulder, then pulled what appeared to be a yellow tennis ball from under the backseat of the dual cab truck. Looking both ways, he stuffed the tennis ball into the front pocket of his work pants.

"¡Chales que troca chingona!" (*Damn, what a truck!*) Patricio said.

"That's not his ride," Mauricio whispered.

Patricio, Mauricio and Alonso moved into the shadows of the monolithic concrete pillars that supported the interstate overpasses. Jorge Cobos walked away from the slick truck, right toward the pillar that hid them. They skirted around the pillar in stealthy silence to avoid being seen. It worked; the tattooed man walked right by them. Patricio and Mauricio glanced over at each other. They both recognized that something was still going down and they wanted to be part of the action. Following Cobos from a safe distance, they made their way through parking lot, traveling north through the perimeter of Columbus Park paralleling San Saba.

"Hey, I know where we are!" Alonso exclaimed.

"There's the hospital." He pointed to his right, to the back of the towers.

"Are you coming?" Patricio asked.

"Yeah," Alonso said.

"Shhh." Patricio ducked behind a shrub. "Get down." Cobos pulled the tennis ball out of his pocket and clasped it in his hand, speeding up his pace.

"Look at how he's moving. He's into something big. Remember his lame tattoo with the 'MM'?" Patricio glanced over at his brother.

"What do you think he's into?" Mauricio said.

"No good, that's what he's into. Let's keep hanging tight so we can find out why Lilianna took his bullet."

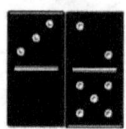

CHAPTER THIRTY-SEVEN

El Mercado and Empanadas

Mauricio, Patricio and Alonso followed Cobos, ducking behind trees and kneeling down between shrubs. Cobos moved quickly, not looking back. He jogged across a small parking lot just past the Piazza Italia fountain and sprinted through a field of dead grass. He was holding the yellow tennis ball tight in his right hand.

They ducked in front of the San Francesco di Paola Church, peering around the red brick corner of the building as the tattooed man jogged down San Saba Street right beside Interstate 35. Cobos crossed a bridge over a waterway as San Saba changed names to Quincy Street. He suddenly ducked off Quincy Street and under the network of aerial concrete roads that make up the highway interchange of Interstate 35 and Interstate 10. The hermanos and Alonso made a break for it, bolting full speed through the open parking lot and field.

Following Quincy Street to the Cameron Street underpass, Mauricio spied the man through the interstate concrete support pillars and motioned for Patricio and Alonso to follow. They moved quickly, creeping through the shadows of shopping carts, empty MD 20/20 bottles and weathered cardboard boxes requisitioned by the homeless.

"Get down fool," Mauricio hissed at his brother and cousin. The man had stopped and turned his head to listen. Mauricio pulled Alonso by the elbow to the hard concrete below and into a large cardboard box. Patricio crawled in behind them.

"Dang, what's that..." Patricio lifted his hands from the bottom of the box and placed his fingers up to his nose..."smell?"...wrinkling his nose in disgust.

"Callate," Mauricio hissed. The brothers crouched in the box until they heard footsteps again. Mauricio peeked out from the side of the box and saw the tattooed man dart across Blevin Street to the north side of the interstate junction. He walked casually eastward to a small neighborhood. They scrambled out of the box quickly, their hands and the knees of their pants wet with the smell of urine from the box.

Cobos' skinny frame entered a barrio long forgotten by the hustle and bustle of the city. They ran across Blevins and into the barrio, but lost sight of Cobos. He had disappeared into the dilapidated homes with peeling paint and decaying roofs. Some of the homes were boarded up with gang graffiti filling the weathered planks in staccato, spray-paint marks. The brothers knew immediately from the dark blue tags that they were deep in old school Crips turf. They looked apprehensively at each other and continued on between the old homes.

Just up the road, Patricio heard sounds coming from an open one-car garage attached to an old brown home with burglar bars all the way around. Inside the garage, an old television with a rabbit ear antenna blared Mexican television programs into the stillness of the downtown 'hood. They ran to the home next door and ducked behind a car parked in the driveway. In the garage, two men bent over an old sofa with staple guns. There were many other pieces of old furniture stacked atop of each other in a jumbled mess.

"It's an upholstery shop," Patricio said.

"I bet it's a front," Mauricio said, without taking his eyes off the action in the garage.

"Yo, Cobos, Jorge Cobos, que no se te olvide."

(*Don't forget this.*) A voice sounded from the back of the garage. Patricio, Mauricio and Alonso silently slipped underneath the old car in the driveway, out of sight.

Cobos quickly walked beside the car and suddenly stopped beside the trunk. Patricio carefully rolled his head to the side to look at Cobos. He was holding a rolled up baggie containing rolls of hundred dollar bills instead of the yellow tennis ball. Cobos was into something big and it had to do with the owner of the black pickup truck and the tennis ball. Jorge stuffed the bills into the front of his pants and broke into a light jog, crossing the street, traveling back in the direction of the interchange.

"C'mon." Patricio elbowed his brother and they slid backward under the chassis of the car. Crouching, they ran between the old houses in pursuit.

"Where'd he go?" Alonso stopped, looking toward the interstate junction. Slowly, they crossed back over Cameron and under the interstate. They stopped in an open area under the concrete maze hanging low above their head, the roar of city traffic whizzing by. They heard a metal clank, loud and sharp, echoing through the pillars. Patricio ran to the sound; a metal manhole under the bridge was circling into a seated closed position, creating a racket, and the tattooed man was nowhere to be seen. Patricio carefully pulled off the manhole cover and crawled inside first. They climbed down the small metal rebar ladder. Alonso hesitated at the edge, peering into the dark hole.

"Put the lid on, fool," Patricio whispered.

"No, we need light," Mauricio said. Patricio continued his descent into the small shaft.

"Ouch...get off my hand dough boy! Me estás pisando la mano." (*You're stepping on my hand!*) Patricio said.

"Sorry..." Mauricio quickly moved his foot back up the next rung.

"¿Quién anda ahí?" (*Who's there?*) A voice echoed through the tunnel. Mauricio quickly climbed back up the rebar ladder, Patricio directly behind him. They pulled themselves out of the shaft, just in time to see Cobos at the base of the shaft pointing a flashlight directly at them.

"¡Chale tamale!" Patricio spit out. He and Alonso quickly moved the large metal cover back over the hole.

"¡Córrele güey!" (*Run fool!*) Patricio yelled, pushing his brother in the back.

"¡Ay mamacita, se me atoraron los dedos!" (*Mamá, my fingers are stuck!*) Mauricio yelled as he fell sideways to the ground from his brother's shove.

"¡Sácalos pendejo!" (*Get them out, you idiot.*) Patricio and Alonso pulled the manhole cover up slightly, to free Mauricio. Patricio took off in a full sprint, Mauricio and Alonso directly behind him. They skirted across San Saba and back into the trees of Columbus Park on the north side of the hospital.

"Do you think he recognized us?" Mauricio asked as they walked through the shrubs on either side of the park pathway.

"No, we move too fast," Patricio snickered and Mauricio joined his laughter.

"Chales, me dio hambre vamos a al Mercado." (*Damn, I'm hungry, let's go to the Mercado,*) Patricio said.

"I can't, I have to see Lilianna," Alonso said, waving goodbye and jogging to the front entrance of the Christus Santa Rosa Hospital.

Mauricio and Patricio made their way south of the hospital and into la Mercado, a mall filled with the sights and sounds of Mexico. Colorful blankets, rugs and hand woven purses were in one shop and talavera plates adorned with flowers and fruit filled the stores. The merchandise spilled from the stores and was stacked in the mall aisles. Tejano music filled the air from the live band on the stage in the center of the mall. The band broke into a peppy rendition of "Vals de las Mariposas," the same song that played at Laurencia's

Quince Años. Mauricio took his brother's arm and flamboyantly danced with him in the center of the aisle.

Mauricio pulled Patricio close to him and yelled: "¡Ay, Laurencia, te amo Laurencia!"

"¡Pinche maricón!" (*You girl. Let go of me.*) Patricio pushed away from his brother, grabbing his brother's baseball cap off his head and slapping him across the side of his head. Mauricio quickly pulled his hat out of his brother's hand and secured it back on his head with a grimace.

"Hey, that store has empanadas."

"Do they have pumpkin empanadas?" Mauricio asked.

"Can't you read, burro? Look, that's what the sign says." Patricio pulled his brother's hat from his head, again.

"Do that again and I'm taking you down." Mauricio grabbed his cap right out of Patricio's hand midswing.

"We need to get out of here," Mauricio said seriously.

"Let me pay for these at least. What, are we missing curfew?"

"Yeah, it's getting dark out. We need to run." Mauricio pointed to the door at the end of the long mall aisle where the sun rested low in the sky, casting long shadows from the buildings across the city street. The hermanos backtracked through the market, bolted through the door and sprinted full speed to the parking lot where they left the Impala.

"Why are you always hungry? We're going down in juvie over a stupid empanada."

Patricio grabbed Mauricio's hat again and threw it at him, hitting him in the back.

"You mess up my lid and you're going down," Mauricio said and picked up his hat. Mauricio gave his brother a swift knee in the side, causing Patricio to stumble to the ground and right on top of the bag of pumpkin empanadas. Mauricio reached down to give his brother a hand up. Patricio reached up and pulled his brother to the ground with him, quickly pushing him face down into the concrete. Sitting on top of Mauricio, pinning his arms in a wrestling hold, Patricio held up the bag of flattened pumpkin empanadas to the side of his face.

"See what you did? We don't even get a last meal before we go to juvie."

"You smell like piss." Mauricio made a scrunched up face as he pushed his brother off of him. The two brothers rolled on the ground, laughing and scrambled to stand up. They raced fast and low back to the Impala. The setting sun rolled deep into the western sky and reflected hot orange highlights into the golden mirror finish of the car.

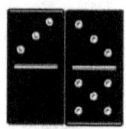

CHAPTER THIRTY-EIGHT

Sub Sandwiches and Healing Energy

Lilianna's hospital room appeared the same as it had two days before. The stiff white hospital sheet was pulled neatly up to Lilianna's waist. Her arm was by her side with tubes running crisscross from the I.V. bags dripping life into her body. The room was quiet except for the incessant beeping of the machines by her bed. Alonso ran the back of his fingers across Lilianna's cheek; he bent down to kiss her on the forehead. He felt pangs of guilt for not coming sooner, but what could he do? She didn't even know he was there.

Alonso sat at the edge of Lilianna's bed, looking at his sister for a very long time. His eyes became heavy, his head hummed with exhaustion. Gently moving her I.V. tubes out of his way, he nestled down beside her and stared at her face, at the rise and fall of each breath she took. He closed his eyes as tears welled up and rolled down the side of his face onto the bleached linen. All he really cared about at that point in time was his sister living and his papá returning to the family. His tears flowed freely...his mind drifted off.

"Hi." A quiet female voice moved across Alonso's consciousness. This awoke him and he glanced sleepily around the room. At the end of the hospital bed there was a hazy light. He gazed curiously into the misty glow--the figure of the bald girl formed in the light. The girl dissipated and so did the light. Alonso drifted again; just as he was fading off, he experienced a flash vision of a large, expensive home in the older section of Mansiones de Piedra Blanca where he had last seen his papá.

Rolling onto his back, Alonso rubbed his eyes. Why this

neighborhood? It didn't make sense. He moved off Lilianna's bed and opened the drawer in the nightstand to find something to write with. Moving to the vinyl chair, he sketched a drawing of the home in his vision on the hospital stationary with the Christus Santa Rosa logo. He did not complete his drawing. Alonso was exhausted--he fell asleep with the pad of paper on his lap, the pen in his hand and his head bobbing down.

Jon made a soft shuffling noise, working quietly as he adjusted the controls on Lilianna's equipment.

"¿Qué pasó?" Alonso muttered in a low sleepy voice.

"Hey, I didn't mean to disturb you." Jon's smile warmed the room.

"Yeah, what time is it, anyway?" Alonso looked at the stationary on his lap and tore out the sketch, placing it into his pocket.

"About two a.m....how long have you been here?"

"Since after school, I'm not really sure. Guess I slept for a while."

"From the looks of you, you needed it. You been at school?"

"School and my aunt and uncle's place. I'm caught up on all of my classes now." Alonso sat up a little straighter.

"That's great news. Hey, what about that hot girl, have you seen her?"

"I've seen her."

"She still hot?"

Alonso turned to face Jon directly.

"¡Ella es chisporrotea caliente!" (*She is sizzling hot!*) Alonso grinned and made an exaggerated hissing sound and slapped his own rear end. They both burst into laughter. Alonso looked at his sister and stopped laughing.

"How's Lilianna...really?"

"She's the same, Alonso. Her brain swelling is starting to go down just a little with the drainage shunt. We may be able to take the shunt out in a few days."

"That seems like a good sign. Is it?"

"Alonso, we can't ever predict these things. She may wake up tonight and then there's a chance...well, coma patients don't all make it through."

"Has my mamá been with her today?"

"She was here all of last night and most of today."

"I miss my family." Alonso looked down. How much his life had changed within a few weeks, he thought.

"That's a big thing for you to admit. I'm proud of you. Hey, I have a sandwich in the fridge, if you want it?"

"Is it stale and moldy? I only like stale and moldy food!" Alonso teased.

"I made it before coming in tonight. One of the pharmaceutical reps brought dinner in for our team. It will get stale and moldy if you don't eat it."

He briskly stepped out of the room with Lilianna's chart in his hand.

Alonso found himself lost, gazing at his sister again. He was startled when Jon re-entered the room.

"Here." Jon handed Alonso the sandwich.

"Thanks." Alonso quickly ate the sandwich.

"So, it's good to hear you're keeping up with your school work."

"The best I can. I guess I'm doing better than I expected; the assistant principal placed me in advanced placement math today."

"Wow, so you're one of those naturally brainy guys. I remember going to school with guys like you. Bet you don't even need to study to make all "A" honor roll, do you?"

"Yeah, I study hard just like everyone else. I'm good at math and science. I just don't want a lot of extra work right now, that's why I'm not sure of this class."

"That could be a problem. I certainly understand your uncertainty. What do you have to gain by being in the program and what do you have to lose?"

"I could lose time and it could be too hard for me right now. There's so much going on with Lilianna, my papá..."

Alonso caught himself and stopped.

"Yeah, what's up with your dad? He's never here. Are your parents divorced?"

Alonso wanted to tell Jon everything, wanted to share his life and what he was going through, but he couldn't. It might mean the rest of his family could be deported back to Mexico. He slowly shook his head no and looked back at his sister.

"Don't want to talk about it now?" Jon got up and walked to the door. "I have one more round tonight. Let me know if you need company and want to talk. I'm right down the hall."

"Thanks for the sandwich."

The man-sized sandwich rested heavily on Alonso's stomach. He rubbed his eyes, reclined in the hospital chair and drifted off into quick restless visions of the house in Mansiones de Piedra Blanca. The disturbing slideshow kept Alonso from sleeping. He barely opened his eyes and gazed at his sister in the dim light.

"Qué hermosa." (*So beautiful.*) His eyes welled up with tears and he had an odd sensation of pressure in his nose. It didn't feel right. He slowly reached up and felt right where Brett had punched him. He pushed down on the bridge of his nose and was met with a sharp pain that shot to the top of his head.

"¡Chiuhua!"

"It's not broken." Sha's voice gently penetrated the dim room.

"Where are you?" Alonso peered around the room.

"Use your hands to heal." The light wispy tone of Sha's voice seemed to be right beside Alonso. He wasn't sure if it was his imagination or if Sha was really with him. Alonso held his hands together, as if in prayer, and slowly pulled them about an inch apart. He felt it again, that odd magnetic pull, almost a heat between his two hands radiating from the center of his palms.

"Oddest thing," he said aloud and tested the energy by extending his hands even further apart. Still feeling the warm magnetic tug, Alonso moved his hands two feet apart. He could still feel the energy. He moved his hands back together and concentrated on what he was feeling. The more he concentrated the stronger the sensation between his hands. Alonso closed his eyes and slowly moved his right hand over the bridge of his nose with his left hand slightly over his right hand. He could feel the warmth of his hands radiating into his pulsing nose. Once again, he imagined his nose mending, the swelling going down. He felt an electric tingling from the center of his palms and into his nose. The pressure he felt in his nose gave way to soft warmth and his pain disappeared. For the first time since he'd been punched, Alonso could breathe gently through his nose and it felt good.

Settling deeper into the vinyl recliner, Alonso relaxed and looked again at Lilianna. He wondered if this energy could heal his sister. Then he slipped into sleep.

"Hey, Alonso." The soft voice of tía Ruby tripped through Alonso's mind and the light from the hospital window caused him to squint.

"Híjole. ¿Qué hora es?" (*Oh, what time is it?*) Alonso asked as he pulled himself stiffly from the chair. His eyes were rimmed with dark purple circles from the punch he had taken in the nose the day before.

"Jon called me and let me know you were here. I was worried about you when you didn't come home last night. C'mon, you can still make it to school on time."

Tía Ruby reached down and picked up Alonso's backpack from the floor.

"Hey, what happened to your nose?"

"I was in a fight."

"Did you win?"

"No...tía Ruby, I don't want to leave her." Alonso reached over to rub his hand across his sister's forehead. He bent down and gave her a kiss on the cheek.

"I understand, Alonso."

"Would you mind bringing me back here this afternoon?"

"Sure, you need to come back this afternoon anyway, for your MRI scan appointment. Remember?"

"Oh yeah, I forgot all about that."

"I'll pick you up during last period." Alonso walked beside her to the car, lost in his own thoughts. How could he help Lilianna out of her coma?

CHAPTER THIRTY-NINE

Sticky Rice and Warm Lips

By the time Tesoro made her way through the cafeteria line, only wilted wok food-piled high in a metal tub by a tub of sticky rice with the oddest sulfur odor-remained. The smell alone was enough to flip her stomach. It wasn't the description she had read on the school's web site the night before when she decided to wait in the hot meal line instead of the sandwich and pizza line, as she normally did. Stir fried vegetables and chicken with lemon grass was the description: it was more like a compost heap made up of leftover vegetables from the day before. She set her tray down and cut through the line to grab a cookie and milk instead.

As Tesoro waited to pay she saw Brett and Sarah walking together through the crowd. She stood on her tip toes to get a better look. Brett and Sarah had their arms around each other, laughing and trading little love kisses. They made their way to the table where Tesoro usually sat.

"Guess I don't need to worry about him anymore." Tesoro handed the lunch lady a few bills and wove her way to the same table.

A strange sensation came over Tesoro, warm and tingling. She recognized this sensation at once--Alonso's touch. She held her breath, turned and was greeted by Alonso's smile. His hand reached out to wrap around her elbow. He took her lunch to carry and pulled her out of the crowd.

"I need to talk with you," she said breathlessly.

"I know, come with me."

Tesoro followed Alonso across the courtyard and into the two-story academic hall. He cut down a side hallway, into the science wing and then the narrow social studies hall. Tesoro wasn't sure where he was taking her and why he was moving so quickly. She had to jog just a bit to catch up to him.

Without warning Alonso stopped and held out his hand, "Let me go in first, wait a second, then come in." Alonso slid around the corner into the make-out bathroom.

Tesoro never went in that bathroom! She had heard the stories of druggies hanging out in there and students smoking and sometimes having sex. Her heart pounded, her hands trembled and her legs moved her to the door. Holding her breath, she reached out and pushed the door open.

"Nervous?" Alonso was leaning against a sink, his arms crossed over his chest. "Me too. This isn't a place I usually hang in." He grinned as he walked toward her, his dark unblinking eyes locked on hers. Reaching out, Alonso took both of Tesoro's hands and pulled her toward his chest. He wrapped his arms around her and placed one hand around the back of her head, pulling her in tight.

Tesoro trembled; she was light headed, short of breath and dizzy. With each breath, Alonso pulled her in a little tighter. He started to sway from side to side, rocking her slowly as he moved his hands through her hair, across her neck and back. He buried his head in her hair and breathed in deeply.

Tesoro melted into his warm, comfortable arms, so strong and secure around her. It didn't matter at the moment that they were in the make-out bathroom at the school. It didn't matter that a boy had just flushed a cigarette down the toilet and walked out of the stall right past them, barely paying them any mind. Tesoro wanted this moment to last forever. She wanted to see his eyes and pushed back from Alonso just enough to look at him.

"Eres un ángel." (*You're an angel,*) he whispered, pushing her hair off her cheek, off the side of her neck. He took her chin gently in his hand and pulled her face up to meet his. Reaching down, Alonso softly kissed Tesoro's forehead. She felt the lingering warmth of his mouth on her skin and a dizzying, tingling sensation coursed throughout her body. She knew what was going to happen next and she couldn't stop it. She felt Alonso's breath on her skin, hot moist breath that smelled sweet to her. His mouth kept continual contact with her as his lips lightly skimmed her eyelid, her cheek, over her nose, her upper lip, tingling the entire way. She let her mouth open slightly as his mouth joined hers, softly, gently. She reached her arms around him and started to pull on his shirt, pressing her lips hard into his and kissing him deeply.

Alonso pushed Tesoro into the tile wall, kissing her hard and fast as he pulled her shirt up and ran his hands across her bare back. Both gasped for air as they pushed their bodies into each other, their hands frantically discovering each other. Tesoro felt lost, spinning and overwhelmed. She placed her hands under his shirt and pulled it up. Alonso moaned as he kissed her. She became weak and started to sink to the ground. He pulled her up by the waist, reached his hands up to her bra strap and unclasped it.

Tesoro opened her eyes in surprise; a sudden awareness of her surroundings came flooding in. She was at school, in the make-out bathroom. Anyone could walk through the door any second, including a teacher. She could feel herself stiffen. She had not had the chance to talk to Alonso.

"What?" Alonso stopped kissing Tesoro.

"I can't, I can't." Tesoro pushed Alonso gently back from her, shaking her head back and forth, her long, dark hair swaying around and sticking to her wet face. Her eyes were wide, glistening and searching.

"I understand," Alonso reached over to the sink and picked up her cookie and milk carton. He handed it to her, smiled with a wink and checked his hair in the mirror, pulling his bangs over his eyes like a hood. He walked out the door bringing her fully back into chilling reality, away from the most searing thing that had ever happened to her. With urgency, she wished him to suddenly reappear through the closed door. It didn't happen.

She was alone...not certain what to do with the tingling sensation that was running all over her body, pulsing up and down her spine and settling into deep places. She looked at herself in the mirror. Her face was red, her pupils large and her nose flared as she took in air quickly.

"I'm a mess." She turned the faucet on cold, splashed water onto her face and looked at herself to make certain she was still the same girl. She dabbed the stiff paper towel over her face; it softened as it picked up the moisture from her skin. It felt good to her. Tesoro looked at herself in the mirror, slowly moved the damp paper towel across her lips, moved her finger across her lower lip, slower yet still trembling ever so slightly, fresh with the memory of Alonso's kiss...a memory she did not want to ever let go. Placing the paper towel in the cold water and bringing it to her warm lips again, she whispered:

"being to timelessness as it's to time, love did no more begin than love will end: where nothing is to breathe to stroll to swim love is the air the ocean and the land..."

She smiled at herself in the mirror: she had remembered the words of e.e. cummings. The poem finally made real sense to her. She touched her lips, wishing the sensation of timelessness from Alonso's mouth touching hers to stay with her forever.

CHAPTER FORTY

Friendships and Waiting Rooms

"**A**ssistant Principal Martin called me today." Tía Ruby didn't take her eyes off the interstate directly in front of her.

"Yeah," Alonso sighed. "What about?"

"He mentioned placing you in a program. He said he's already talked with you about it."

"Oh yeah, advanced placement, he wants to move a few of my classes around. I've already started A.P. math." Alonso watched a red Mustang whip by them to the left.

"Sounds as if you're in, then? You want me to leave you off here? Do you know where the radiology wing is?" She pulled up to the front entrance of the hospital.

"Yeah, I can find it." Alonso jumped out of the car and bolted into the Christus Santa Rosa hospital. He was ready to have this appointment over. From the moment he had been pulled from art class to meet tía Ruby, he couldn't stop thinking about Tesoro. Alonso reached into his pocket and pulled out a tiny slip of paper. He replayed Tesoro handing over her phone number to him as he walked past her when he left the art room earlier. After gazing at it for a moment, he slipped it back into his front pocket.

Alonso followed the signs for the radiology wing. He smiled at the large woman behind the counter.

"Do you have an appointment here?" she asked. "You need to sign in and then have a seat in the room to your left."

There were a few people in the waiting room, most of them wearing hospital gowns. For a split second, he thought he saw the bald girl looking up at him. He signed his name and when he looked back up she was not there anymore. The room was unadorned, simple and poorly lit. The people appeared bored as they flipped through six month old magazines.

Alonso cleared his throat and took a hard chair next to a boy in a wheelchair. The boy seemed to be about his age. He had his head down, using both thumbs to text on his phone. Something about him seemed familiar. Alonso reached back into his pocket and pulled out Tesoro's phone number. He glanced at the clock; school was in session for the next ten minutes, too soon to call her.

Pulling his phone out, Alonso plugged in the number so he wouldn't lose it. Instead of typing her name in, he typed in "<3" as a heart.

"Antonio Torres," a voice echoed across the waiting room.

"I go by Tino." The guy in the wheelchair inched forward.

"No way!" Alonso said. It had to be him, it was his voice, it was his long, black hair, and it was his face. Alonso jumped out of his seat to walk beside Tino.

"It's okay. I can get myself to the door just fine." Turning around in his wheelchair, Tino looked directly at Alonso.

"Do I know you?"

"I was about to ask you the same thing," Alonso said.

Tino looked down, shook his head, sighed and wheeled himself closer to the door where the nurse waited. He turned his wheelchair around, just in front of the doorway, looked directly at Alonso and said:

"I told you that jump wouldn't kill you."

Alonso walked toward Tino, extended his hand and said,

"Hi Tino, I'm Alonso, I didn't think, well, I didn't recognize, um..." he stammered.

"You didn't expect me to be real, or a gimp." Tino shook Alonso's hand.

"No, neither."

The nurse motioned for Tino to follow her down the corridor. Tino waved casually at Alonso and wheeled himself through the door.

There's no way that just happened, Alonso thought. How could Tino exist here, if he came to him in a dream first?

"Alonso Mendoza," the same nurse called. Something about this section of the hospital reminded him of yet another dream, the dream of the bald girl and the empty corridors with the slick floors. The nurse led him into yet another waiting room, this one less crowded. She instructed Alonso to change into a hospital gown in one of the changing rooms just off to the side of the waiting room.

"This can't be right," Alonso said, pulling the baby blue gown over his body and tying it in the front.

"I can see your stuff with it tied like that." Alonso heard Tino's voice from the changing room waiting area.

"It ties in the back," Tino said louder, laughing. With a crooked grin, Alonso re-entered the dressing room and switched the gown around.

"So, what are you doing here?" Tino asked. Alonso slid into the chair next to him.

"Getting an MRI."

"Obviously, that's why everyone comes here. Let me ask again, what's wrong with you to bring you here?"

"Strange dreams messing with my head," Alonso replied, causing both of them to burst out in laughter.

"Seriously, what's going on?"

"I'm seeing things, dead people, glowing orbs of light," Alonso said.

"Doesn't sound like a good reason to have an MRI." Tino looked curiously at Alonso.

"Yeah, it's strange, I feel fine."

"You are fine. For me, it's a normal way of life."

"You see dead people?"

"Dead people, dead animals, ancestors that I didn't even know. I even know my spirit guide." Tino looked back seriously at Alonso.

"So, I'm not crazy?"

"Is that what you're thinking?"

"Yeah."

"Seeing in the spirit realm is part of my culture; it's part of how I was raised." Tino looked at Alonso with a kind face.

"Not me, my Catholic mamá would think I'm muy loco and call the priest out for an exorcism if I told her what was happening to me." Alonso looked down, thoughtful.

"You're not crazy, you're walking in two worlds."

"Yeah, I know this is real. It's just that I've gone through a lot and I'm not sure what's happening to me."

Alonso felt he could tell Tino anything, as if he'd already known him for a long time.

"See that girl over there?" Tino pointed to a girl with a slight build, walking away from the waiting area.

"Yeah, what about her?" Alonso was surprised. It was the dead bald girl from his own visions and dreams.

"She's dead," Tino whispered. "Watch this." Tino turned to the woman with her toddler two rows of seats behind them.

"Hey, did you see a young girl, maybe eight or nine just

pass by?"

"No. No one has walked by in a while," the woman casually replied.

"You see her, right?" Tino whispered; Alonso nodded yes.

"That lady didn't see her and you and I did. That girl is dead."

"I've seen that girl before. She comes to me a lot. Her name is Amy."

"I've seen her in my visions, too! She's a confusing one. She's an earthbound spirit and I'm not certain why she hasn't left yet. Usually children don't hang around for long, if at all."

"She has talked to me," Alonso said. "I felt her die. It's like I was inside of her, feeling everything."

"Yeah, that's the way they get your attention sometimes. The newly dead can be dramatic," Tino said.

"Hey, how could I have met you, before I actually met you? How did that happen?"

Alonso moved in even closer, his eyes rooted into Tino in a dead serious gaze.

"We met in the dream realm, a place where spirit can travel."

"Why do you know so much about this?"

"My grandfather started teaching me the ways of my people early in my life. These teachings are sacred and secret, but somehow, you have broken through and you have come to know our ways through your dreams."

"How could that happen? I'm an illegal alien from Mexico City. I'm not American, not one bone."

"I thought you were from San Antonio," Tino laughed.

"I thought you were from outer space," Alonso chuckled.

"Hey, you're the one who called yourself an alien, not me. I don't know why you were able to travel to the land of the violet skies?" Tino pondered. "That is a place of knowledge my ancestors created long ago."

"So, you're saying I don't belong there?"

"Yeah, only the 'real people' can make it there."

"'Real people'--say what?"

"'Real people,' exactly what it sounds like.'" Tino's tone was humble.

"Oh. I still don't get it," Alonso shrugged.

"We're native."

"That's obvious. So am I, native to Mexico."

"Okay, it's like this, we were the first to live here, in San Antonio. Our tribe name is Tickanwatic. It's what we call ourselves--it means 'real people.'"

"Wouldn't know how to spell that!" Alonso laughed.

"You've probably heard of the Tonkawa, right?"

"No."

"Well, that's who we are. Tonkawa means 'They all stay together,'" Tino said.

"If you're all together in San Antonio, why haven't I heard of your tribe before?"

"That's the irony. Our name means we're together. Most of our people live in Tonkawa, Oklahoma. There are a few of our tribe, like my family, who live off the reservation."

"Is there more of your family in San Antonio?"

"Like I said, there are not very many of us left."

"Tell me again, what does you being a real person have to do with that weird dream where we met? I'm a real person, too!"

"It's a spiritual meeting place for my ancestors and spirit guides."

"Oh."

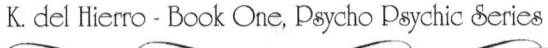

CHAPTER FORTY-ONE

Sisters and MRI's

Tesoro, you told me you would go tonight!" It was Sarah on the phone. "You can't back out now. You need to come to this party with me!"

"I don't trust Brett," Tesoro said.

"You promised."

"I didn't promise anything, Sarah. Plus, Tino's not home yet and I need to be here for him; I don't know what his day was like."

"Tesoro, please, please. You are always taking care of your brother. You need to get out more. You need a life."

"Sarah, I have a life, stop it," Tesoro said.

"Everyone knows you like that emo creeper. No one is going to mess with you, Tesoro. Brett isn't going to mess with you." Sarah added in a sing-song voice, "He's messing with me now."

"Will you stop calling Alonso names. I like him."

"You don't like my boyfriend."

"No, Sarah, I don't."

"That makes us even. Brett's not even the slightest bit interested in you. He thinks I'm all that. He calls me 'baby.' We've kissed." Sarah said smugly.

"Yeah, I've seen the two of you all over each other at school."

"Trust, let me come by to get you." Sarah pleaded.

"Okay Sarah, okay, come by at eight."

"Earlier! I'll see you at seven. My mom can drop me off so we can get ready together. This is going to be a blast. I can't wait!"

Tesoro held the phone in her hand, looking at it for a while. She auto-dialed Tino and held the phone close to her ear with her eyes shut.

"Hey, hey!" The familiar tone of her brother's voice rang through the speaker.

"Are you still at the hospital?"

"Yeah, I'm still here. They're doing an MRI on me today. It's slow going."

"Why are you getting another MRI? You're not having another surgery, are you?"

"Tesoro, hope, please hope. I want to walk again someday and there's a new neurosurgeon that might be able to fuse things back together for me."

"You know the risk."

"Yeah, I know. I'm willing to take it."

"When are you going to be home?"

"I'm not sure. I'm still in the waiting room."

"Okay..."

"What? Is there something you're not telling me? You have a hot date tonight? Is someone coming over and you don't want me around?" Tino teased his sister and looked over to Alonso, who was listening to every word with great interest.

"No, I don't have a hot date, but I am going to a party tonight."

"Whose house?"

"Brett Merrick's. I think his parents will be home."

"You going by yourself?"

"No, Sarah is going with me. She and Brett are an item," she said, her voice calm. "I'll be home by midnight. Don't worry about me."

"Just stay away from Brett in case he changes his mind and decides to like you again instead of Sarah." Tino was using his joking tone again.

"He likes Sarah, not me. You should have seen them all PDA in the cafeteria today." She stopped laughing and sighed deeply, pushing the hair off her face.

"You okay, sis?"

"Yeah, I'm just hoping to see someone at the party."

"And, who would that someone be?" Tino turned around and looked directly at Alonso, who pretended to not be listening by texting his tía Ruby. He was convinced he heard Tino say Tesoro's name and was not going to miss a word.

"You already know who," Tesoro said.

"Yes, I do...bye sis, love you."

"Bye."

"You have a sister?" Alonso's heart was beating fast. The realization struck him like lightning: Tino could be Tesoro's brother! Alonso looked at Tino closer. He noticed a distinct likeness, as if they could be twins.

"Yeah, I have a twin." Tino smiled.

"I knew it! Tesoro, right-it's Tesoro-I know your sister from school!"

"Small world," Tino said.

"Dude, how can that be? I like your sister."

"I know, she's told me about you," Tino said, laughing.

"What did she say?"

"She likes you too, Alonso," Tino said matter of fact.

Alonso put his head down in quiet amazement of Tino's words. "She likes you..." His heart felt warm and light, quite unfamiliar, quite wonderful.

"Do you have any brothers or sisters?" Tino's question got Alonso's attention.

"Yes, Lilianna is my sister. She's been injured, in fact she's in this same hospital right now."

"Well, let's go say hello to her when we're finished with this."

"We can see her, but...." Alonso cleared his throat and looked down, "...she's in a coma. She was shot in the head."

"That's serious. Can I see her?"

"Yeah." Alonso looked up at Tino. "She's a mess, tubes everywhere. I'm friends with the night nurse. He'll let you in with me."

Tino picked up his phone and dialed his mother.

"Mom, I'm at the hospital for a while longer...into the evening." He looked at Alonso. "I'm with a friend...a new friend...I'll call when I'm ready for you to come get me...love you too."

After hanging up the phone, Tino said, "So...let's go meet your sister. You've already met mine. Plus, I think you've made a big impression on her all on your own." Alonso laughed with Tino. "Alonso, you should come over to our house sometime."

"That would be great!" The nurse called Alonso's name. "Guess this is it."

"No worries. It's easy, just remember to breathe."

Alonso made his way to the room that contained the loud MRI machine.

"Hey, let's wait for each other here," Alonso said.

"They only have one machine, Alonso. There's no choice. I'll see you when you get out of the hole. You'll have a magnetic personality!"

Alonso stepped into the room with the MRI machine. It was cold, white and sterile. He sized up the technician, who appeared slightly bored as he prepared the settings.

"Hi, I'm your flight attendant today...Paul." The technician reached out to shake Alonso's hand.

"You want me to lay down in that?" The ominous, gigantic, hollow magnetic instrument was not anything Alonso wished to be a part of.

"Do I have to go through with this?"

"It's really easy. We do have medicine we can give you to help calm your nerves, if you want."

"It's okay. What do I need to do?" Alonso's nerves quickly settled down. This is something many people go through, including Tino.

"The machine pretty much works itself. It doesn't hurt you in any way. All you have to do is lie down and follow the directions you hear once you're inside. Some people even start to go to sleep."

The technician placed his hand on Alonso's shoulder and guided him to the platform bed that enters the MRI machine.

"I don't think I'll sleep through this."

Alonso sat on the hard platform and moved onto his back. The technician disappeared behind a wall on the side of the room.

"We are only doing a scan of your head. This shouldn't take too long," the technician's voice echoed through the speaker.

Alonso relaxed. It was somewhat cave-like, nearly

comforting. He began daydreaming about Tesoro, their moment in the make-out bathroom...how his instincts took over as he pulled her toward him, how warm, soft and sweet it felt to have her next to him. He remembered the pull he felt, starting in his abdomen and moving into the rest of his body, up into the pit of his stomach, his heart, his mouth. An almost liquid energy that took over everything he knew, as he touched her, kissed her, held her, his fingertips electrified with each new experience.

The loud whir of the MRI machine faded into the distance as Alonso mechanically answered the commands of the pre-recorded voice over from the machine. His mind was completely filled with Tesoro...what she felt like, smelled like, tasted like. He felt his abdomen grow warm as he realized what had happened to him. With this development, the machine came to a stop and the bed he rested on moved out, exposing just how relaxed he had become.

"¡Ay güey!" He said, quickly rolling over on his side. He wondered if Paul had noticed his condition. He tried his best to cover his erection under the flimsy gown.

"That's it," the technician said. Alonso sat on the edge of the platform and pulled at the gown, further covering his embarrassing moment.

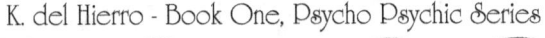

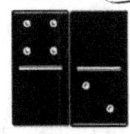

CHAPTER FORTY-TWO

Designer Jeans and Tee-shirts

"**S**arah, you look fine, stop fussing," Tesoro said. Sarah wiggled on her tip toes as she peered across her shoulder at the backside of her khaki shorts in the mirror.

"Do I need to wear heels?"

"No, shorts and heels together look slutty. Flip flops, that's the way to go. If you're showing off in one area, downplay another."

Sarah turned to face herself in the mirror. "Seriously Tesoro, is it too cold to wear shorts?"

Tesoro laughed. "We're in Texas; it's never too cold for shorts!"

"You look so classy, your jeans...they just fit you so well. I wish I looked that hot in jeans."

"Sarah, you look hot no matter what," Tesoro said.

Sarah ran her hands down the front of her long shirt as she admired her friend's reflection. Tesoro's slender, muscular frame was perfect for the designer jeans and low, strappy turquoise and brown leather heels that adorned her feet. Her simple, v-neck tee-shirt that fit her in all the right places held just a touch of femininity with slightly gathered, torn fabric around the plunging neckline. The same torn fabric of the shirt made up a loose tie just above a key-hole in the neckline. The white shirt was in strong contrast to her jet-black hair that framed her neck and shoulders. Her boulder turquoise necklace rested dead center on her décollegage. It was accentuated and made exquisite by the low white shirt with the keyhole neckline framing the pendant. Tesoro was wearing more eyeliner than usual with a slight exaggerated line from the edge of her eyes applied the same way Egyptians did in ancient times.

"I like your makeup. It's more than what I'm used to seeing on you. You look simply beautiful," Sarah said. Tesoro twirled around in the mirror, lifted her shirt and looked at the back pockets of her jeans.

"It's there because I run. It's the only reason I have an ass. I don't think I'd have one, otherwise."

She extended her rear out toward the mirror and shook it. Sarah playfully slapped Tesoro on the butt. Laughing, they grabbed their purses and darted downstairs.

The growling Mustang came to a stop in front of Tesoro's living room window. Sarah's phone played a peppy ring tone and a picture of Brett appeared on the screen.

She smiled, reached into her purse and teased, "I'm running late, Tesoro doesn't want to come, after all."

"Hey, don't tempt me," Tesoro whispered as she adjusted the strap of her fringed leather purse on her shoulder.

"No, no, I'm just playin'...yeah, they're outside...I just heard them pull up. We'll be out in a sec." Sarah winked at Tesoro as she dropped her hot pink phone, covered with rhinestones, back into her purse.

"You ready for a party?" Sarah flitted out the front door with Tesoro close behind.

Tesoro slid into the front passenger seat of the Mustang. She smiled at the driver, the same senior from the football team who had driven her home with Brett. He looked her up and down in a way that made Tesoro feel self-conscious; she immediately reached into her purse to text Tino.

"On my way to the party at Brett's house. I'm with Sarah."

She typed slowly, trying to avoid the driver.

"Be careful," Tino replied.

"Yeah, yeah." She sped up her typing.

"Seriously, be careful. One of your friends is with me."

"Who?"

"I'm not telling. ☺"

"Tell me!"

"Nope!"

"Okay then," Tesoro texted and speed dialed her brother's number.

"Who's with you?" She asked impatiently. The wind from the Mustang created white noise in the phone speaker.

"What? You're hard to hear."

"Tino, don't do this. Who is with you?" She used her higher pitch voice, saved just for her brother in times of frustration.

Tino's laughter was broken by the sight of Alonso stepping through the door of the MRI room. He appeared disheveled. His hair was tousled, his shirt hung unevenly around his hips and his cheeks were notably flushed.

"Hey, there's someone who wants to talk to you," Tino said loudly enough for both Alonso and Tesoro to hear. He held out the phone to Alonso.

"Tino, stop messin' with me. Who is with you? You're just playin' with me. Stop it now!"

Alonso's smile grew broad as he held the receiver out enough for both Tino and himself to hear Tesoro's protesting voice, followed by silence.

"Tino? Tino, are you still there...Tino, stop this. Tell me who it is. I'm going to hang up on you if you don't talk to me."

Alonso cleared his throat and said quietly, "Tesoro?"

"Who is this?" Tesoro felt her heart jump into her throat-- it was Alonso's voice. She held her breath as she waited for his response, reaching her free hand to pull her long hair out of her face and into a makeshift ponytail held together by her fingers. She leaned forward to break the wind in her face and listened.

"Tesoro, this is Alonso..." he paused, waiting.

"I don't understand. Why are you with my brother?"

"We know each other." Alonso gave Tino a slight punch on the shoulder as they grinned at each other.

"This is awkward," Tesoro said, recalling the bathroom episode earlier in the day.

"Hey, what are you doing later?" Alonso asked.

"I'm on my way to a party right now. I'm not sure when I'll be home tonight." She sounded more flip than how she really wanted to come across.

"Is there a chance I can talk to you tonight?"

"Maybe, I don't know how loud it's going to be...house party. Can I call you when I get a chance?"

The wind was whistling loudly between her mouth and the receiver.

"I can't hear you very well."

"I'll call you later," she yelled.

"Sure. Do you want to talk with Tino?"

"Yes." She wished she could see him instead of going to Brett's house with Sarah.

"Did that surprise you?" Tino said.

"How do you know Alonso?"

"We're both having our MRI's at the same hospital. He's

in the waiting room with me."

"Oh. How did you find out he knows me?"

"He heard us talking earlier and figured it out, Tesoro."

"What all did he tell you about me?"

"That he knows you from school."

"...and that's it?"

"That he likes you." Tino laughed and winked at Alonso.

Tesoro fell silent.

"Hey, be careful at the party. Alonso and I are going to hang out," Tino said.

"Can we trade places?"

"Go have fun, Tesoro. I'll talk to you later."

"Okay, love you..."

The Mustang stopped directly in front of the Merrick mansion which appeared much more inviting than the last time Tesoro had visited. Lights were on in every room, giving it the appearance of a polished jewel glowing in shades of amber and gold. The trees were wrapped in small white lights and twinkled like small fairies dancing throughout the leaves. DJ dance tunes pulsated through the warm winter breeze mixed with the sound of laughter and talking from the party going on inside.

Brett stepped out of the house followed by an entourage of girls that whisked right past him and ran to the football player in the backseat with Sarah. They escorted him by each elbow, up the stairs and into the house. Two other girls latched onto Brett and whisked him back into the house, right behind the first group.

Sarah looked at Tesoro and winked.

"I'm his date, you know."

She skipped up the stairs behind him, unescorted, leaving Tesoro and the car's driver behind.

"Do you need help out of the car?" He turned around to face Tesoro.

"Oh, so sorry...no, I can get out myself." She smiled at him, realizing she had not communicated with him the entire way to the party.

She reached over the console and shook his hand.

"I'm Tesoro, by the way--hey, thanks for the ride out here."

"My pleasure, I'm Joey...by the way," he said. He hopped out of the car and opened the door for Tesoro, holding her elbow as she stood up.

"Thank you." She was still taking in the grandeur of the party. Joey placed his hand at the small of Tesoro's back and guided her up the stairs, through the palladium doorway and into the large entry with marble floors. Tesoro got a chill up her spine and recalled the last time she was in that grand entry. This party seemed a little too loud with a few too many people.

Turning to Joey, Tesoro asked, "Where are Brett's parents?"

Joey laughed. "Do you really think he would allow his parents to be here tonight?"

Am I in over my head, Tesoro wondered? This crowd was far more developed than she could fathom from her wildest dreams. Some of the people in the next room appeared old enough to be in college. She had made a big mistake. She backed up to the doorway only to be met with Joey's hand touching the small of her back.

"I'm going to the bathroom, you need to go meet people...go on!" Joey pointed to the people in the dance area and slipped down a side hall.

CHAPTER FORTY-THREE

Vendors and Reiki

"**W**hat's that guy up to?" Alonso noticed a tall man in a dark suit talking with Paul, the radiologist. Something about this man seemed familiar. Alonso leaned to get a better look.

"Oh, I've seen that guy hanging out here before. I think he must be a hospital vendor," Tino said.

"What's a vendor doing in a hospital?"

"Business."

"Right."

Alonso walked to a water fountain. He was able to move closer to the man.

Returning to Tino's side, he said in a low voice:

"That's Brett Merrick's dad. I'm almost certain of it. I've seen him a few times at the school."

"The same Brett that Tesoro's at the party with?" Tino questioned.

"She's with Brett? That's why she didn't want to talk to me!"

Tino looked at Alonso with a sideways glance.

"What do you mean, she didn't want to talk?"

"Brett's been after her for a long time. I've seen her talking to him at school."

"What part of me telling you that Tesoro likes you did

you not understand? Plus, she let me know that Sarah and Brett are an item."

"Brett's a player...trust me when I say he's still after her. She's a hot number."

"I should take you down for that. Don't talk about my sister like that."

"My bad. I'm just sayin'..."

"...that Brett's a loser. Seriously, do you think she's safe? You know him better than I do."

"No."

"Should we get a ride out to his house tonight?"

"I can one up it-watch this footwork-the party is about to be over." Alonso worked his way over to Mr. Merrick's side.

"Hi, you're Brett's father? I know you from school." Alonso extended his hand toward Mr. Merrick, who shook it with a firm grip and an otherwise expressionless posture.

"Oh..." he paused, looking Alonso up and down, "...you're in his science class."

"Yes sir, you have a good memory." Alonso flashed a great smile at Mr. Merrick.

Tino moved in a little closer, leaning forward in his wheelchair to hear, pretending to be pre-occupied with his phone, trying not to smirk.

"What was your name, again? I don't believe I caught it."

"Alonso Mendoza. Nice to meet you, sir."

"Nice to meet you...what brings you to the hospital?"

"MRI."

"First one?"

"Yes sir. Funny coincidence meeting you here. Brett invited me over to your house tonight."

"Oh yeah? Do you have a class assignment to work on with him?"

"No sir, he invited me to the big party he's having. I'm surprised you're not there. You must really trust him."

"It was nice to meet you...Alonso, right?" Mr. Merrick smiled as he shook Alonso's hand again.

"You must excuse me. I have business with the hospital."

Mr. Merrick quickly worked his way out of radiology. Tino and Alonso caught a glimpse of him pressing the elevator button.

"Do you think he's going home to break up the party?" Tino winked at Alonso.

"No doubt in my mind." Alonso placed his hands in his pockets and leaned back.

"Hey, what room is your sister in?" Tino asked.

"Are you finished here?" Alonso pointed to the MRI room.

"Finished 'til next time."

"She's upstairs, just follow me." Alonso started for the elevator in the hallway. Tino moved so quickly behind him that the black feathers tied with leather onto the back of his wheelchair flew directly out behind him.

"She looks peaceful," Tino said, moving to Lilianna's bedside. Alonso walked over and brushed his sister's forehead with the back of his hand, then reached down and took her limp hand into his.

"How long has she been like this?" Tino wheeled in a little closer.

"I've lost count of the days."

"I have to ask this: how is she still alive? She had a bullet go into her brain. How does someone live through that?"

Alonso looked at Tino in surprise. He couldn't imagine

his sister dead.

"She's not dead, she's in a coma," Alonso spurted out in a defensive tone.

"Hey, hey, it's okay. I didn't mean to upset you. Of course she's alive. I shouldn't have said that."

"No, it's okay, I didn't mean to come off so upset. I've just never considered her as dead." Alonso pushed his bangs off his face.

"Hey, what happened to your nose, it looks bruised? Did you get in a fight?" Tino scrutinized Alonso for a moment.

"Yes, I did get in a fight...with Brett Merrick!" Alonso laughed.

"No way!" Tino laughed even harder. "I hope you kicked his ass."

"More like he kicked mine," Alonso pointed at his nose.

"That's not your ass, that's your nose." Their peals of laughter broke the tension.

Jon, the night nurse, walked into Lilianna's room.

"What's all the commotion? You two are so loud you're going to bring the entire wing out of their comas." Jon extended his hand to Tino, "Hi, I'm Jon."

"I'm Tino, I'm a friend of Alonso's. Is it alright for me to be in here?"

"No one needs to know. Seriously, keep it down a little. You two are in after visiting hours. I heard you all the way up at the nurses' station."

"Did my mamá come by today?" Alonso asked. Jon went into routine, checking all of the equipment in the room.

"For a little while this morning. She seems to be doing better. This has become a second home to her...that's how it goes. Why don't you call her and find out for yourself. She misses you."

"I'll do that, Jon. Thanks."

"Okay, that's it for my rounds. Is there anything you two need?"

"No, we'll keep it down. Let me know if anything changes with Lilianna."

"Great...bye...nice to meet you Tino."

"Good to meet you, too." Tino reached to shake Jon's hand.

"He seems pretty cool, for a hospital employee, that is."

"Yeah, I like Jon." Alonso sat beside Lilianna, again hoping that her eyes would suddenly open and his family would come back together.

"Had something weird happen, maybe you know about this?" Alonso looked directly at Tino.

"When Brett punched my nose, it was messed up and it was bleeding. I got this, well, message, that I could use my hands to heal my nose. Have you ever heard of such a thing?"

"That's Reiki, Alonso, hand healing. Energy work is sacred to my tribe...perhaps not so sacred anymore. It's an ancient art and now it's all over the internet like everything else. Seems nothing is sacred anymore..."

"Do you know how to do it?" Alonso asked with a serious tone.

"Yes. You don't mean?" Tino looked down at Lilianna.

"That's exactly what I mean. Do you think it's...possible?" Alonso lowered his voice.

"I know how to do it, Alonso, but I've never done it before on anyone but myself...and that's not working out so good for me."

"Wait, feel this." Alonso held out his hands, palms up,

parallel to the ground. "Put your hands over mine, don't touch me."

Tino held his hands over Alonso's. "Wow, dude that's strong, your aura is strong."

"That's so cool, I felt yours, too. It's like a magnet and electricity all mixed together, right?"

"Yeah, that's it. But I see auras." Tino pulled his hands slightly away from Alonso's.

"See, it's still strong, like we're soul brothers or something. You're freaking me out."

"What does this look like to you?" Alonso asked.

"Little white balls of light, mixed in with diamonds that pull up from the center of our hands."

He pulled his hands even further away, still keeping his palms parallel to Alonso's hands.

"I've never meet anyone with such strong energy before. Are you sure you're not Tickanwatic?"

"I'm sure I'm Mexican."

Tino put his hands down.

"I need to meditate before I try to do this on your sister. There are no guarantees. I need to ask her spirit permission in my meditation."

Tino wheeled himself away from Alonso and began to chant in a low, monotone voice...

"Ra, Ma, Da, Sa...Sa Say So Hung..."

CHAPTER FORTY-FOUR

DJ's and Grinding

"**T**esoro, over here, over here!" She heard Sarah over the thud-thud-thud of the music and saw her jumping up and down in the crowd, waving at her.

Making her way through the party crowd of dancers, Tesoro moved quickly to avoid bumping into anyone.

"Ooooh, there you are!" Sarah reached out through the crowd and grasped both of Tesoro's hands in her own. Still dancing, Sarah started to move Tesoro's hands around to the rhythm of the beat that pounded out through the sound system of the DJ.

"Why aren't you with Brett?"

"He's being a host and I'm making the most!" Sarah laughed loudly as she reached for her drink.

"Here, taste this, it's sooo good!"

"No, that's okay."

"Try it; it's exactly like lemonade, only better!" Sarah screamed over the tunes.

"I don't want to drink," Tesoro yelled, pulling her hands back from Sarah.

"Great party, huh? Hey, let's go find Brett."

"Sarah, I don't belong here. This doesn't feel right to me."

"Just loosen up, that's why I'm drinking. It's fun. C'mon." Sarah took Tesoro by the hand and led her through the crowd into the large kitchen.

"Brett!" Sarah screamed out as ran to him and threw her arms around his neck. Brett reached around Sarah's small waist and pulled her up into the air. They kissed as Brett crossed his arms around her back and squeezed Sarah's upper thighs. They swayed back and forth to the loud tunes.

Tesoro flashed back to what had happened between Alonso and herself in the make-out bathroom. No different than what Brett and Sarah were doing. She flushed and turned to the sink, pouring herself a glass of water. The water felt cool going down, icy and smooth, smoldering the embers left behind from thoughts of Alonso. Her lips tingled slightly as the music faded into the background. Tesoro reached to touch her mouth with her finger tips, remembering his kiss.

"Did that make you hot?" Brett whispered in Tesoro's ear.

"How long have you been beside me? Where's Sarah? Where'd everyone go?" Tesoro whirled to face Brett, angry. Brett laughed. He grabbed Tesoro around her the waist of her tight white shirt and started to dance in place.

"Loosen up babe, this is a party."

"Let go of me right now," Tesoro hissed in a quiet, firm voice. She narrowed her eyes, backing away from Brett.

"Where's Sarah?"

"She's in the bathroom. She said I smeared her makeup. Loser."

"You're the loser."

"Jealousy looks good on you." Brett pulled Tesoro from the waist directly into his body and kissed her hard.

Tesoro pushed with all her might against his chest, clenching her jaw shut. She could smell the liquor on his breath. Only muffled desperate "hmmmhhh, hmmmh" sounds exited her nostrils; she fought hard to break free of his muscular arms.

"Brett, leave her alone." Joey's voice broke Brett's grip on Tesoro.

"Piss off." Brett turned around to confront Joey. At that point, four senior football players stepped into the kitchen.

"I said leave her alone."

"Hey, you guys can get out of my house." Brett pulled back from Tesoro to fully face the seniors.

"If we leave, we're taking her home, too." Tesoro turned back to the sink, wet a paper towel and wiped her face. She was breathing hard, angry and fighting back tears. Her lips felt bruised.

"Tesoro, do you want to go home?" Joey's voice softened as he asked her this. She nodded yes, afraid that if she spoke her voice would crack and she would start to cry.

"Hey, what's going on in here?" Sarah's voice broke the silence; her eyes darted from person to person.

"Nothing you need to know about," Brett said.

"Actually, Sarah, we were asking Tesoro if she wanted to go home right now," Joey said.

Sarah ran to her friend's side, "Tesoro, baby, I shouldn't have left you." Tesoro could smell that Sarah had just swallowed more alcohol. Her words were a bit slurred and her language slowed.

Concerned with her friend's frame of mind, Tesoro forged a smile for Sarah. "It's okay. I'll stay if the guys stay."

She glanced at Joey for safekeeping. No way could she leave her friend alone with Brett. She needed to devise a way to get Sarah to her house safely. They had planned to spend the night together after the party.

"I'm fine, really. We can stay, Sarah." Tesoro held Sarah's hands reassuringly.

"Oh goody! Brett, another one of your special lemonades. Get Tesoro the same."

"You don't need to drink anymore tonight." Tesoro continued to hold Sarah's hands.

"C'mon, just one little drink, please Tesoro. It'll be fun."

"Sarah..."

"It's the best drink E-VER!"

"Okay, I'll try it. I'll take a sip of yours."

"I'll get it for you, Tesoro," Brett said.

"A small one." Tesoro pinched her finger and thumb to show an inch of height. She managed a fake smile at Brett.

"You've got it." Brett moved from the kitchen into the dance area and disappeared into the crowd.

"Hey, you're alright, really?" Joey took Tesoro's elbow and looked her square in the eyes. "I can take you home right now."

"Yeah thanks, I'm fine. I may need to take you up on that a little later. C'mon Sarah, let's go dance, I love this song!"

They made their way into the center of the dance pit where the people were grinding to the beat of the bass.

"Look, there's Brett!" Sarah jumped above the crowd to get a better look. "Tesoro, who's he talking to?"

Tesoro jumped up to the beat of the music, as if her spying was intentional dancing.

"Looks like he greeting some guy at the door. They're shaking hands."

"Probably dealing," Sarah sang out as she turned on her heel and spun around, waving her arms wildly in the air.

Tesoro laughed for the first time since they had arrived at the party. She mimicked Sarah's dance move and threw her arms above her head and twirled around. It felt good to be lost in the music, to be swallowed up by the crowd of dancers. Tesoro shut her eyes for a moment and let the music move through her as she picked up the natural rhythm in her body and began to feel the music as never before. She could feel the bass in her chest, the lyrics in her heart and head. Her legs, hips, arms and hands moved with flawless synchronization and effortlessly timed rhythm.

"Nice moves, rock star," Tesoro heard Joey's voice beside her as she opened her eyes. He was smiling and dancing beside her. Tesoro smiled back as he stepped into her rhythm, gently placing his hands at her natural waist and they danced together, step by step, mimicking each other's newly made up movements.

The song ended and another one quickly took its place, overlapping, leaving little room to rest in between. Tesoro picked up the tempo of the new song and lined up with Sarah, who was grinding with a crowd of people. She started to move her hips around with Sarah's as they laughed. Joey watched only momentarily before moving in between Tesoro and Sarah. Grinding with them he stood behind Tesoro and moved with her lead, Sarah danced behind him.

Tesoro could feel Joey behind her and somehow, even with his sexual dance moves, she felt safe with him around.

"Hey ladies, here are the drinks you ordered," Brett sounded off above the beat.

"Oh good, I'm so thirsty. Thank you sweetie." Sarah tiptoed up to give Brett a quick kiss and he handed her a drink.

"Here, I made one just for you...it's weak." He smiled at Tesoro as he handed over the smaller glass. "Only this much alcohol..." he made a small pinching gesture with his fingertips, mimicking what she showed him in the kitchen.

"You will not feel a thing," he said.

The dancing had made her thirsty and she took it from

Brett. It was cold and tart. It did taste exactly like lemonade, but there was a distinct burning in the back of her throat as it went down. She stopped and looked at the glass. Something was very wrong with it; she should not be drinking it at all.

"Go ahead. I made it weak, just for you," Brett said.

"Don't you like it?" Sarah asked.

"It's different, I don't drink," Tesoro giggled.

"Neither do I," Joey laughed and downed the rest of Sarah's drink in one large swallow.

"Gross, dude." Sarah made a funny face and Tesoro laughed out loud.

"Your turn," Joey said to Tesoro. He started to move his hips around in a grind.

"Finish that so we can dance again." His toothy smile was contagious. Tesoro tilted the glass back and let the drink slip easily down her throat. Brett took her glass from her hand, looking at her in a way that didn't feel right to Tesoro. He and Sarah left the dance floor, leaving Joey and Tesoro grinding with the crowd.

CHAPTER FORTY-FIVE

Light and Energy

Alonso's phone rang, breaking the self-induced trance necessary for Tino to perform Reiki on Lilianna.

"Hey, Mauricio. ¿Cómo estás?" Alonso listened carefully to his cousin. "¿Qué pasó?" (*What happened?*)

Tino glanced over at Alonso with concern. He could tell that something wasn't right.

"¿Dónde estás?" (*Where are you at?*) Alonso shrugged at Tino and placed his hand over the receiver. "My cousins, they're in trouble."

"Yeah, I'm at the hospital...You want me to pick up your car? ¡Ni madres! ¡Estás loco!" (*No way! You're crazy!*) Alonso blurted out. "I can't, I don't have my driver's permit."

He shifted his feet and listened hard. "Ya, hombre. ¿Dónde está el carro?" (*Okay man, where's the car?*)

"What's going on?" Tino asked.

"My cousins left their car downtown and they're at my uncle's house just off Vance Jackson," Alonso sighed. "They want me to drive their car back up north."

"How did that happen?"

"You really want to know? They've been chasing this guy, the guy my sister took the bullet for." Alonso peered over at Lilianna. "It turned out he discovered them and turned on them, then he started to chase them. They freaked out and hopped on the closest city bus. They are laying low at my tío

Luis' house."

"Where's the house?"

"Just south of 410, off Vance Jackson." Alonso looked at Tino, puzzled.

"Why do you want to know?"

"That's a way to get home without having to wheel myself the entire way."

"No, I'm not driving illegally. My mamá would kill me."

"But you can drive, right?"

"Yes, I know how to drive."

"Good, let's do it then. It's Friday night, let's have a little fun."

"If I'm caught, I'll never get my license."

"Look at me, I'm a gimp. I'm your excuse. You can tell the police you're taking me to the hospital."

"That's messed up." Alonso made a face at Tino.

"There's no way we're getting caught. Have you driven on a highway before?"

"Yes, my mamá lets me drive on the highway and so does my tía Ruby. You don't think we would get caught?" He asked.

"No way, all you have to do is drive the speed limit and look like you know what you're doing. Plus, if we get pulled over I'll tell the cops that I fell out of my wheelchair and injured myself. I'll pretend to hurt, which doesn't take much acting for me."

Tino dialed home. "Mom...yeah...I have a ride. Don't worry, I'm with a friend." Tino smiled at Alonso. "Tesoro is at a party. Yeah, I know we're all the sudden popular...Love you, too."

Alonso picked up his phone: "Mauricio, I'll bring your

car...yeah, yeah...más al rato." (*later on.*) Without putting his phone down for even a second he speed dialed his tía Ruby. "Hola...I have a ride from the hospital, you don't need to pick me up."

"Now we can stay out as long as we want to." Alonso turned to look at Lilianna and then back at Tino. His eyes filled with hope, a hope that hadn't existed for a long time.

"Let's do this together." Tino wheeled over to Lilianna's side. "Can you chant with me?"

"How does it go, teach me."

"It's like this: 'Ra, Ma, Da, Sa, Sa Say So Hung'." Tino chanted and Alonso joined in.

"Ra, Ma, Da, Sa, Sa Say So Hung." The words made Alonso feel sleepy and relaxed. They were calming, peaceful words that seemed attached to his very spirit.

They chanted together. "Ra, Ma, Da, Sa, Sa Say So Hung."

A soft golden light filled the room...Alonso could sense Sha close by. His hands tingled and pulsated with energy. When he looked down at them there appeared to be tiny, rolling diamonds moving across his palms, sparkling like a river on a bright sunshiny day. He could see the same thing on Tino's hands. They placed their hands on Lilianna--Tino's on her forehead and neck, Alonso's on her hands which crossed over her stomach. The light from their hands sparkled across Lilianna's small body; in the dimness of the room she appeared luminescent.

"Wow," Alonso murmured.

"Ssshh," Tino said softly, "Ra, Ma, Da, Sa, Sa Say So Hung." He sang in a low, rhythmic voice, his eyes shut. Soft energy filled the room. When Tino reopened his eyes a distinct glow had filled the room. The glow turned into a mist and the face of Tino's grandfather appeared. The apparition was looking down, shaking his head back and forth slowly and somberly in a "no." Alonso's eyes were shut tight focusing on his sister. Alonso did not see Tino's grandfather. Tino nodded at his grandfather with his silent message. His spirit faded into the dimness of the room.

Tino slowly pulled his hands off of Lilianna. Sensing a shift in the energy of the room, Alonso opened his eyes and pulled his hands gently off Lilianna. The ethereal energy dissipated and the sound of the beeping machines returned to the foreground.

"Is that it?" Alonso said.

Tino nodded yes. Tino didn't look Alonso in the eyes.

"What's wrong?" Alonso felt the air itself as heavy energy.

"I don't know if we were able to reach her."

"Hmmpf," Alonso muttered under his breath. "You can't tell me what I saw and felt was fake. That wasn't my imagination."

"Depends on what you thought you saw and felt, Vaquero."

"Lights, I saw lights like rolling diamonds moving across our hands and onto Lilianna. Just like you said when you told me about how you see auras." Alonso squinted at Tino for reassurance. "The air didn't feel right, that's the best way I can explain myself. Things felt heavy, almost hard to breath." He paused, "I didn't like it."

"Yeah, don't worry, sometimes energy work does that. Let's leave. You ready to drive?" Tino said.

"Not really." Alonso stood up and walked over to the window, looking out to the gleaming city lights set in sharp contrast against the night sky. A familiar chill brushed Alonso's bare neck. Looking up he quickly recognized Amy looking back at him in the reflection of the window. He stopped breathing and slowly turned to Tino, who was also looking at Amy's form in the glass.

"Open the door," she whispered.

"You can open it yourself," Tino said.

Alonso thought Tino was being rude and scowled at him. "She wants you to press the button on the door."

Tino ignored Alonso, focused on Amy and continued, "You already know the way home."

"I'm scared," Amy admitted.

"Of what?" Tino asked.

"I don't want to leave yet."

"It's what you have to do. It's easy."

"How?" she asked.

"Feel love and let go," Tino said. Amy's reflection was translucent and the twinkling lights of the city shone a little brighter through the glass. Palpable warmth of radiant love entered the room and in an instance Amy vanished.

"Tino, I felt her spirit. I felt Amy go." Alonso said and contemplated what happened. "Wow, just like that, huh?"

Tino nodded in acknowledgement to Alonso and looked back at Lilianna. They both gazed at Lilianna for a long time and silently worked through what they just witnessed with Amy's departure and with performing Reiki on Lilianna.

"Your sister is beautiful," Tino said softly. "Her spirit felt light, safe and happy. She did let me flashback to when she had been shot. I felt her pain, the falling to the ground, the confusion she felt as she slipped away into a coma. She knows you were there."

"Thanks for letting me know that. How did you get so much information?" Alonso asked.

"Lot's of practice getting out of my own body, I guess. Wish I could see her awake, she really is beautiful."

Alonso relaxed and let out a chuckle. "Your sister is

beautiful too!"

"She'll be glad to hear that, coming from you." Tino wheeled himself over to the window beside Alonso.

"You think? I'm not sure if she likes me. Does she talk about me?"

"I already told you she likes you. How many times do I have to tell you this for it to sink into your head?"

"Does she talk about me?"

"Yeah, why?"

"What all has she said?"

"Why do you ask like that? Is there something I need to know about Tesoro and you?" Tino hesitated, "You haven't...you haven't...you know, done it with her? Have you?"

Alonso looked down, embarrassed; he knew to tell the truth. "No, we have not 'done it'." He looked back up and smiled at Tino. "We did make out for the first time ever, today at school."

"Today?" Tino yelled.

"Shush your mouth. You're going to wake my sister up!" Alonso said deadpan and straight faced. Tino's inquisition gave way to amusement and they burst into laughter.

CHAPTER FORTY-SIX

Shakespeare and Roofies

Tesoro made her way through the crowded kitchen, past the kissing couple grinding to the music and past a boy with glasses talking on his phone with a desperate look in his eyes. Tesoro could hear his pleas to stay out later, one finger in his ear and the phone pressed tightly against his other ear. She felt extremely light and happy from dancing with Joey and slightly dizzy from the drink Brett had given her. All she could think about was Alonso; she wanted to talk to him. Reaching past her lip gloss into her small purse, Tesoro pulled out her phone. She propped herself up onto the dark granite counter top, sitting on the edge with her back up against the maple cabinet doors.

The battery was about to go dead. Quickly, she looked up Alonso's number that she had entered earlier in the day and listened hard to the ringing. His voice message played and she quickly hung up, not wanting to communicate through phone tag. Tesoro turned off her phone, reserving the last bit of battery power.

She felt funny; the dizziness was worsening. At the same time she felt especially light, tingly and giddy. As she moved off the counter top she lost her balance and fell to the floor, landing with a thud on her side.

"Ooohh." Tesoro lifted her head from the hard tile below and saw Brett reaching his hand out to help her up. She squinted; her vision was crossed. She was losing control of her coordination.

"Too much to drink?" Brett pulled Tesoro from the

ground and wrapped his arm around her waist to hold her up.

Tesoro tried to talk, to tell him she only had one drink, but the words did not make it out of her mouth. She uttered a mumbled, undistinguishable groan instead.

Brett pulled her close to him, wrapping his arms around her waist as he pushed his body into hers. He rocked her slowly from side to side and pushing his lips into her dark hair he whispered into her ear:

"To-morrow, and to-morrow, and to-morrow,

Creeps in this petty pace from day to day,

To the last syllable of recorded time;

And all our yesterdays have lighted fools

The way to dusty death. Out, out, brief candle!

Life's but a walking shadow, a poor player,

That struts and frets his hour upon the stage,

And then is heard no more. It is a tale

Told by an idiot, full of sound and fury,

Signifying nothing."

Tesoro pulled back, placing her hands on his chest to keep her balance. She managed to look him in the eyes and uttered:

"You're creepy." She collapsed into his chest with a sigh and he held her up, pulling her tightly in.

"Not creepy, wrong play dear. That's Shakespeare, MacBeth, Act 5, to be exact," Brett whispered.

Tesoro slumped and started to slowly fall down the front of his body, toward the ground. Brett lifted her up into his strong arms, took her purse from the counter top and walked her through the crowd. The party goers watched as Brett casually explained that she had too much to drink and needed to rest. He made his way to the back part of the house and placed Tesoro on the guest bed on the lower floor by the garage. She moaned as her head hit the pillow.

Fighting her double vision and dizzy head, Tesoro asked, "What's wrong…" and faded deep into a feathery white, linen pillow. She struggled hard to focus on Brett, to make sense of the moment, flipping between great fear and a giddy sense of false well being.

Tesoro struggled, "Please, what's happening?" A lone tear gathered in the corner of her eye.

"Just a little roofies, you know, Rohypnol. Date rape time, dear."

Brett pulled himself on top of Tesoro and whispered in a harsh voice:

"You'll enjoy this, but not remember a thing." Laying full length on Tesoro he kissed her hard on the mouth.

"Just don't lay there playing dead," he said angrily. He grabbed her chin and pushed her face hard against his. "Move like you want it."

"Mmmfff." For a moment she felt a little stronger and with all her might she moved her arms between Brett's body and hers and tried to push him away. But the drug had taken full effect. She was too dizzy and disoriented to fight anymore. She slid into a state of giddy amnesia and started to kiss Brett back with great passion.

"Damn it!" Brett rolled off of Tesoro to pull the ringing phone from his pocket.

"Dad! Are you still at work? Yeah, everything's fine, just have some guys over…watching a movie. You're on your way home? Where are you now?"

He covered the mouthpiece, nervously clearing his throat.

"No, no Dad, everything's fine. See you in a bit." He hung up, placing the phone in his pocket.

Tesoro was trying to open her eyes. Her eyelids fluttered as her mouth tried to move to speak. She attempted to raise her hand, but it fell limply to her side.

Leaning over the bed, Brett reached to pull her cheeks up, causing her mouth to pucker and gave her a smack of a kiss on the lips. He stood straight and buckled the belt that he started to loosen only moments before, staring at her angelic face. He pulled down her shirt and buckled her sandals back on her feet.

"Damn you're gorgeous, babe."

Brett picked up Tesoro, her hair falling back from her face, her arms around his neck. He slipped out the door, down a short dark hall, past the large laundry room and into the three-car garage. In a semi-conscious state Tesoro rolled her head on Brett's chest and bit at his shirt and giggled. Brett let Tesoro's legs drop to the ground as he held her upright. She pulled her arms up around his neck and reached up to kiss him.

"Oh, now you want to play, I see how it is." Brett used his free hand to lift the lid off of a plastic storage container, removing camping gear, lanterns and green butane tanks off to the side. At the bottom of the container was a nice, soft sleeping bag. He moved Tesoro's arms from around his neck and ordered: "Stand right here." In her hypnotic state she obeyed.

Brett quickly unrolled the army green flannel sleeping bag and fluffed it up into a makeshift bed at the bottom of the large container.

"Get in the box and lie down." She did.

"I'm going to count backwards from ten to one. When I reach one you will be in a deep sleep. You will remain in a deep sleep until you hear my voice again. I'm saving you for later, a sweet midnight dessert." Brett started to count from ten to one and closed the lid on the container. Tesoro was sealed in, curled up in a ball, fast asleep.

Brett raced back into the house, directly to the DJ. He stopped the music, grabbed the microphone and belted out: "Party's over, everyone get out fast."

The dancers groaned as they fumbled around, looking for their personal belongings.

Brett leaned into the microphone again, "Everyone clean up your stuff. Let's move it people."

Sarah pushed toward Brett. She screamed over the crowd, "Where's Tesoro, where's Tesoro?"

"Sarah, baby." Brett grabbed Sarah around the waist and pulled her close.

He whispered in her ear. "Calm down, I just saw Tesoro leave with Joey--she's fine. Hey, you need to get home, too. Sorry, my pop's on his way."

Brett escorted Sarah to the front lawn and asked friends if they could take her home. He reached around Sarah's small waist, pulled her in and kissed her hard on the mouth.

"That's for later, baby. I'll call."

He gave her a pat on the rear of her khaki shorts and a wink as she walked out the door.

"Damn, damn, damn." Brett raced around the emptied house, frantically picking up trash. He positioned himself on the sofa with the remote control in hand, flipped to a movie and awaited his father's arrival.

CHAPTER FORTY-SEVEN

Orbs and Accidents

Alonso retrieved the keys from under the Impala's front bumper hidden in a magnetic box and unlocked the doors, just as his cousins had instructed. Tino maneuvered out of his wheelchair and into the front seat. Alonso folded the wheelchair and placed it in the large trunk, careful not to puncture the sub-woofers.

"Okay, are you ready for this?"

"Sure, I trust."

Just as Tino got the word "trust" out of his mouth, Alonso accidently pressed the hydraulic switches and the car started to jump and bounce wildly in the parking space. The Impala was way too close to the surrounding parked cars.

"Dude, make it stop," Tino yelled as he bucked helplessly, unable to balance himself with his legs.

Alonso slammed the same switches again and the car jolted to a stop.

"What the hell was that?" Tino said.

"My cousins...they installed a hydraulic system. Are you okay?"

"Yeah, yeah, I know what hydraulics are. I'm fine. This is a freakin' weird ride." Tino smiled and pushed himself up from the center console, lifting his tangled legs with his strong arms.

"Great start." Alonso glanced tentatively at Tino and started the engine.

"Keep an eye out for police cars and I'll try and get us to my uncle's house."

Alonso carefully maneuvered the car along the highway, minding the speed limit.

"Hey, watch out, over there." Tino pointed to an accident about half a mile ahead on the side of the road. Alonso could see the flashing lights of the three patrol cars. He pulled over to the opposite lane of traffic and parallel a large truck to avoid being noticed.

Suddenly, a car on their bumper furiously flashed its high beams directly at their car.

Tino turned around. "Not cops. They must be going to a fire."

Alonso sped past the semi and pulled in front of the truck, letting the car pass. A multitude of small black orbs blacker than the darkest night in the mouth of a cave whipped out from the car beside them. Alonso glanced quickly at Tino.

"Black energy," Tino warned. "Lay low--don't look at that car and slow down."

The glossy new Cadillac coupe pulled alongside the Impala, mirroring its speed. Alonso crouched down low, just as Mauricio and Patricio had taught him to do to look cool for girls. This time it was not about looking cool. Alonso felt a chill up his spine and that familiar cold prickle across the back of his neck. The Cadillac CTS-V picked up a speed; it was like a glistening black raven with the city lights reflecting in all directions. Alonso looked over from his hunkered down position, his bangs hanging low over his face.

Through the tinted glass he could make out the shapes of four young men, not much older than the two of them. One of them placed his arm up against the dark glass and flipped off Alonso, middle finger pressed hard against the glass. He could see a tattoo on the guy's forearm--a skeleton wearing a sombrero. Alonso swore he saw the eyes in the skull turn into an eerie glow as the black orbs spiraled around the car. He faced traffic directly and let his foot off the accelerator, pulling into the far right lane for slower traffic. The Cadillac sped into the night and vanished out of sight. Tino looked at the highway sprawling out in front of him and shook his head in dismay.

"You should not have looked at them, bro," Tino said. Then his expression changed to pure terror.

"Get off the highway, NOW!" he screamed, looking at the traffic behind the Impala.

"This isn't our exit," Alonso said and at the same time jerked the wheel to the exit ramp.

"Holy tomole!" Tino yelled. Alonso glanced over his left shoulder back at the highway from his position on the access road.

In the place where the Impala would have been on the interstate, a large pickup truck with a fifth wheel pulling a horse trailer was jack knifing. It would have made a direct hit on the Impala. Cars were spinning and crashing into each other from every angle. It was a massive accident. One car flipped on its side and skidded into the concrete barrier, blocking the traffic on the southbound side of the highway. Alonso let out a loud groan. The noise from the squealing tires and crashing metal was more of a memory than Tino could stand. He pulled his elbows up over his head, arms locked against his ears and hands clasped behind the base of his neck. He closed his eyes tight and grimaced.

Alonso guided the big car onto the access road and pulled into the nearest gas station. He reached out and put his hand on Tino's arm still locked tight over his head, eyes still shut.

"Are you okay?"

"That was meant for us." Tino pulled his arms down and gave Alonso a slit-eyed stare.

"What?"

"We offer powerful medicine," Tino whispered, staring straight ahead out the front windshield, his voice barely distinguishable.

"That was close...how did you know? Did you see it before it happened?" Alonso asked. He recalled his own experience on the school bus with the truck that swerved and caused an accident.

"No, I heard my grandfather scream, 'Get off the road.'"

"Mucho gracias, Grandfather of Tino!" Alonso looked up to the sky through the windshield and smiled. They laughed together, lightening the air in the old car.

"Hey, I know where we're at. I'm taking a short cut through the mall parking lot to get home." Alonso pointed to Crossroads Mall ahead in the distance. "I ride my bike here sometimes."

"Okay," Tino said.

Alonso pulled out of the gas station and crept back onto the interstate access road toward the mall. He turned off the headlights and slowly cruised the back way down Fennel Drive, toward Vance Jackson and into the familiar barrio to his tío Luis' home.

Mauricio and Patricio were exchanging heated insults over a game of dominoes on the flimsy card table in the driveway. They barely noticed their car as Alonso pulled up to the curb, lights off.

"This is where I live sometimes. My mamá will be here." Alonso pulled the key from the ignition and exited the car. "Hang on for a second."

"I have no choice." Tino motioned a wide gesture with his hands over his legs.

"I'll be right back."

"Hola flaco. ¿Cómo estás?" Mauricio stood quickly at the

sight of Alonso and knocked over the card table--the dominoes went flying.

"Hey, I was winning, you loser!" Patricio yelled.

"¿Qué alegata se traen?" (*What's all the ruckus*?) Lisa came running to the front door. Her furrowed brow quickly turned into a smile as bright as the full moon above.

"Alonso!" Lisa embraced her son.

"Mamá! Es bueno verte." (*It's good to see you.*)

"¿Cómo llegaste? ¿Y quién es esa persona?" (*How did you get here? Who's that in the car?*) She looked directly at Tino, who was looking back at her.

"Es mi amigo Tino. Tengo que ayudarle a salir del carro." (*That's my friend, Tino. I need to help him out of the car.*)

As Alonso gently pulled from his mamá's embrace, he turned around and saw that Patricio and Mauricio had already made it to the Impala. They were setting up Tino's wheelchair and opening the door for him. He knew he was home.

CHAPTER FORTY-EIGHT

Mansions and Syringes

"Ohhh..." Tesoro moaned as she tried to stretch out from her crumpled position in the storage box where Brett had dumped her. She came slowly into consciousness, not knowing exactly where she was. The Rohypnol, running hard in her bloodstream, made everything seem dreamlike and surreal.

She opened her eyes, reached out and pushed the plastic lid off the container with ease. The garage was dark; only landscape lighting shone through the windows of the three-car garage. As she stumbled out of the container, headlights hit the garage door. Even in her drugged condition Tesoro knew to hide. Her deepest intuition told her everything was wrong. She wedged between bookcases on the side wall that were piled over with boxes.

The garage door opened and an F-150 dual cab truck pulled into the empty space right in front of the container from which Tesoro had just escaped.

Brett's father climbed out of the cab with dark tinted windows, his business suit crumpled on his tall frame. He was on the phone.

"No, it's not the same place, I gave you the address earlier...that's the place. Yes, I need it done before five this morning, like I told you before. Yes...it must happen before daybreak."

Merrick opened the back door of the dual cab, exposing more cardboard boxes, exactly the same as the boxes she was hiding behind.

"I'm bringing more out right now. I have about ten more boxes for this job before we put the concrete down."

He pressed the automatic button to shut the garage door.

"Just needles, nothing hot this time. Yeah, all bio haz…just have the damn concrete there. Yes, pour it right away…third site on the right. Be there when I tell you to or I'm cutting you."

Tesoro was weak again from the Rohypnol. She felt foggy, dreamy and she wanted to sit down. She bent her knees and slid her body to the floor as quietly as she could. Her elbow caught on a box lid and it fell to the floor. Plastic bags marked 'biological hazard' tumbled down with a loud crash. She came out of the drug-induced haze for a moment: I'm in deep trouble, she thought. In the bag she could see syringes and biological waste, items that must be disposed of according to legal protocol. Why would that be in this garage, she wondered? Merrick suddenly threw his phone onto the seat of his truck and stormed directly at Tesoro.

"Oops," Tesoro whispered, still giddy and grinning at the sight of the large man lurking above.

"Don't I know you?" Merrick bent down to Tesoro, eye level, and squinted at her.

"What? Are you drunk girl? Talk to me."

Tesoro could only giggle. Merrick held out his hand and helped her up.

"How long have you been in here?"

"I'm not really sure…" Tesoro turned a circle, spinning on one foot as she answered him.

"Shhh, don't tell anyone I'm in here. Brett told me not to tell." She put her finger to her lips to seal the secret.

"Ah, Brett. I do remember you now. You're the girl who bolted from our house. Do you need a ride home?"

"Yes."

"Get in the truck and I'll take you there." Merrick climbed in and buckled up his seatbelt.

"Why do you have medical waste?" Tesoro looked at the boxes in the backseat.

"Moving offices, those are empty boxes. Know anyone that can use them?

"No."

"Too bad."

"Why do they have the bio-haz label?"

"They're just boxes."

Tesoro craned her neck to look behind.

"How much did you hear?" he asked.

"Hmmmpph?" Her grip on the moment was slipping; things were not making sense.

"Stay here for just a second, I forgot something." Merrick climbed out of the cab and pulled a black fabric bag from one of the boxes on a top shelf in the garage. He had his back to Tesoro and she could not tell what he was doing.

He placed something in his front suit pocket and got back into the truck.

Giggling, Tesoro pointed forward, "Home, James..."

"Right," Merrick said. He started up the truck and backed out of the garage and into the street.

"Hey, my house is the other way..." Tesoro pointed again, right across Merrick's chest this time. "...it's the other way." She looked at him, puzzled.

"I know a short cut," he said.

"You look just like Brett," Tesoro said. "What was I doing at your house, anyway?"

"You don't know...really?"

"I'm at a party and next thing I know I hear you talking to someone on your phone."

"What do you remember hearing...Tesoro, right?"

"You were talking about a delivery and something being done by five. That's all I can remember. Just business talk, I guess."

Merrick's posture stiffened and he sped up, gripping the steering wheel tightly.

Tesoro didn't feel so giddy anymore. She looked at Merrick and with the roofies wearing off felt truly frightened.

"Where are we going? This isn't the way to my house."

"I told you this is a short cut. Plus I have something to drop off first." Merrick turned up the main drive of a large subdivision. He was no longer making eye contact with Tesoro. Something was very, very wrong.

Merrick abruptly stopped in front of a home construction site. Boards surrounded what would be the foundation of a house, with PVC and copper pipes protruding from the rock and rubble.

"Here, help me carry the boxes out."

"It's okay, I'll wait in the truck. I don't feel so good right now." She was telling the truth. She was frightened and feeling extremely sick to her stomach, the same type of stomachache she had felt right before the accident that killed her grandparents and crippled her brother.

"I don't want you throwing up in my new truck. Get out and wait for me."

Tesoro wrapped her arms around her stomach, watching Merrick carry the boxes to the center of the home site. She knew he was dumping medical waste illegally. Filled with a mixture of anger and fear, Tesoro bolted, running as hard as she could up the center of a muddy street.

Merrick hopped into the truck and soon roared up beside her.

"Get in or I'll run you over."

Tesoro turned on a dime and nimbly jumped a wooden horse set out as a road block into an undeveloped section of the neighborhood. She had open territory and ran as hard as she could. Merrick blasted through the road block, through the field and pulled up next to Tesoro.

"Get in." She kept running. He slammed the car into park and jumped out, chasing her on foot. Tesoro's shoe stuck in the mud, she stumbled and lost her balance--she was still off center from the roofies. He grabbed Tesoro around the waist and pulled her to the ground.

"Let me go, let me go!" She threw elbows, kicked wildly and tried to bite his hand. Merrick locked her in a wrestling hold, reached into his coat pocket and pulled out a partially filled syringe.

"You know too much, little girl." He pushed the needle into Tesoro's neck, straight into her jugular and emptied the contents. Merrick held tight watching her eyes as the drug took effect.

"What are you doing to me?" Tesoro's vision crossed and her words slurred out; she could not fight any longer. Her head fell back, she gasped for air and blacked out.

CHAPTER FORTY-NINE

Virgin of Guadalupe and Bones

"¡**M**amá, tamals!" Alonso exclaimed as he opened the steamer.

"Here, Tino, you have not lived till you've tried one of these!" He reached into the pot with tongs and pulled out tamales. The pork tamales surrounded by a generous portion of masa were neatly wrapped in corn husks. Lisa's signature was to find a smaller piece of corn husk and tie a little bow around the center of each tamal.

Patricio, Mauricio and Tino were gathered at the kitchen table covered by a torn vinyl table cloth bearing pictures of fruits and vegetables. In the middle of the table, a candle was burning in a glass container illuminating a printed prayer and an image of the Virgin of Guadalupe.

The flimsy paper plates were barely a match for the mound of tamales Alonso piled up for everyone. Patricio got up from his fold-out chair and pulled out Topo Chicos from the refrigerator. He grasped the bottle necks between his fingers and carried all four at once to the table.

"Looks like a party to me," Tino said. He felt happier than he had in a long time. It was good to feel so welcome, to have friends.

"How did you like flaco's driving?" Patricio asked.

"He did great, even got us out of a bad accident." Tino grinned at Alonso.

"He did that? No?" Mauricio took off his baseball cap and

hit Alonso across the shoulder; they all laughed.

"Hey, do you know how to play dominoes?" Patricio asked.

"No, but I can learn," Tino said.

"It's an easy game, just watch for a little while...see, you start with seven bones and add up the dots that you can find a match on," Mauricio said.

"Don't let them fool you, Tino. They fight over this game all of the time." Alonso laughed and Mauricio slapped him on the back of the head with his cap again.

"Stop hitting me with your damn hat!" Alonso swiftly reached up and pulled the cap out of Mauricio's hand.

"When did you learn to be that fast?" Mauricio held out his hand in a gesture to get his cap back. Patricio also took note of the look in Alonso's eyes, a determination he had never seen.

"C'mon, gimme my lid back," Mauricio said.

Alonso passed the cap back to his cousin. "Don't hit me again." Alonso kept his eyes on Mauricio.

"Who's going to show me how to play dominoes?" Tino said.

"There's four of us playing, so that means we get five bones each," Patricio said.

"What's a bone?"

"You *really* haven't played this before, have you?" Patricio asked. "Okay, a bone is a tile. You have to put your bone by an open bone with a matching number. If you have a double, the numbers on both sides are the same, you can put it in the center and the next play can move from both sides. When you don't have a bone, you have to pick one out of the bone pile, here. You add up the amount of numbers you've placed and the lightest hand wins everyone else's points...but not his own points. Got it?"

Patricio demonstrated the game quickly.

"Not really, but let's play," Tino said laughing.

"Here Tino, look, you can play a three off my three/six bone," Mauricio said.

"Okay, I have a double three. How do I place it on the table?" Tino asked.

"Sideways." Mauricio reached over the table and took Tino's game piece out of his hand.

"Hey, you can't touch his game piece!" Patricio stood up, almost knocking over the flimsy table filled with dominoes, Topo Chicos and tamales.

"Sit down fool." Mauricio placed Tino's bone by his three/six.

"Here we go," Alonso muttered and turned to Tino. "Don't say I didn't warn you." Alonso and Tino burst into laughter as Patricio and Mauricio glared at each other.

"Another tamale?" Alonso held the plate up for Tino.

"Those are so good. Your mamá makes great tamales. They're not too spicy." Tino reached over and helped himself to another tamal, grinning widely.

"Whose play is it? I've lost track," Alonso said.

"Mine." Mauricio reached over and placed an attaching three/one bone down next to Tino's double.

"¡Madre mía! Did you see that?" Patricio stood up again, yelling.

"See what?" Mauricio's tone was taunting.

"Mauricio, pinche tramposo, I saw you." Patricio pointed to the bone pile.

"I did nothing, nothing I tell you. I don't cheat. Sit down fool." Mauricio's voice was high pitched as he motioned for his brother to take a seat.

"No, no, no, not this time. There are witnesses." Looking at Alonso and Tino, Patricio said: "Did you see him drop one of his bones into the bone pile as he put his three/one down?"

"I wasn't paying that much attention to those bones," Alonso answered nonchalantly, drinking his Topo Chico.

"I saw you watching him. I know you saw him drop that bone."

"Tino!" Alonso screamed suddenly. Tino was slumped over in his wheelchair. His short, fast breath was coming out with audible wheezing noises.

"Get mamá!"

Tino's head flopped forward; he had quit breathing. Mauricio pointed to half of a tamal in Tino's hand.

"He's choking! Someone call 911!" Maurcio yelled.

Lisa ran into the kitchen.

"¿Me podría alguien explicar lo que está pasando?" (*Can someone explain to me what's going on?*) Lisa saw Tino slumped over, the half-eaten tamal in his hand. She immediately went to him and put her fingers down his throat.

"Nada." There was nothing lodged in his throat.

"Ayúdenme a recostarlo en el piso." (*Help me put him flat on the floor,*) she said. Alonso and Mauricio immediately moved Tino to the floor as Patricio held tight to his phone waiting for 911 to pick up.

"Háganse a un lado para darle primeros auxilios." (*I need to do CPR, stand back.*)

Lisa placed one hand on top of the other, right in the center of Tino's chest. Before she could press, Tino gasped for air and opened his eyes wide.

"¡Mamá! ¡Ya, ya está respirando!" (*Mamá! Stop, he's breathing.*)

Tino looked up at Lisa. "What just happened?"

Lisa looked at Alonso for the right English words. "You blacked out and stopped breathing. We thought you were choking," Alonso said.

Tino pushed up into a seated position.

"My sister, I have to call my sister. Someone help me up." Tino's words flew from his mouth. They helped him back into his chair.

"Where's your phone?" Alonso asked.

"In my bag, I can reach it." Tino pulled his phone from his buckskin bag and speed dialed Tesoro. He cleared his throat repeatedly as he listened to the recording that her voice mailbox was full.

"She's not picking up."

"What's going on?" Alonso asked.

"Something's not right with Tesoro. She's in trouble of some type." Tino dialed his home number.

"What happened? Did you have a vision of Tesoro?" Alonso asked. Lisa, Patricio and Mauricio stood by, puzzled.

"She can't breathe. It's dark and hard to tell." Tino held the phone away from his ear. "My mom's voice mail...c'mon, someone pick up." He waited for the recording to finish. "Hey, Tesoro, if you're there, pick up..." he paused, waited, and hung up.

CHAPTER FIFTY

Game Tables and Playing Straight

Tino had his phone to his ear, repeatedly listening to the same recording on Tesoro's phone.

"¿Nada?" Alonso asked.

"Nothing."

"What do you think is going on? Do you really think she's in trouble?"

"It's hard to say. I get these senses of things all of the time and half the time I don't know what to make of them."

Alonso laughed, "I know exactly what you mean."

"If I jumped every time my intuition kicked in I'd be a basket case. Sometimes these things pan out, sometimes it's nothing."

"Does this feel like nothing?"

"No. I've never blacked out from a vision."

They watched as Mauricio set up another domino game.

"Who was she with earlier? You know, at the party?"

"Other than Sarah, I don't know, she didn't say."

"Remember when you told me Brett and Sarah are an item? Do you think she went home with Sarah?"

"That's highly likely. I don't know how to reach Sarah."

"Hey, are you two in?" Patricio placed the bones out for a

game.

"Yeah, yeah." Alonso turned to Tino. "I can call my friend Tracy. She might have Sarah's number."

"What are you waiting for?" Tino said. Alonso pulled the phone out of his pocket and dialed Tracy.

"Hey...yeah, sorry to wake you up...do you have Sarah's phone number? No, I'm not crushing on Sarah...I need to ask her something...you're the best...thanks."

Dialing Sarah's number, Tino reached over and grabbed the phone out of Alonso's hand.

"Hey!" Alonso said.

"She's my sister. I'll talk to Sarah."

"Alonso, your play," Mauricio said. Alonso picked up the six/one bone and placed it sideways next to the one/one Mauricio started the game with.

"Hi Sarah, this is Tesoro's brother...yeah, her twin...Tino, that's right. I know it's late, but do you know where Tesoro is? What do you mean you've been blowing up her phone? Who did she leave with? You're not sure? Joey, you think? I don't know him. Do you have his number? No. Okay, thanks...hey, call me back on this number if you hear from her."

"That didn't sound promising," Alonso said.

Tino picked up a six/three bone and placed it by Alonso's six/one.

"Who's Joey?" Alonso asked.

Mauricio slapped down a three/blank and at the same time stealthily slid one of Alonso's bones off the edge of the table with his elbow. It fell onto his lap and he hid it under his leg.

Tino wheeled back from the table, again dialing his sister's number.

"What did you just do?" Patricio questioned his brother. "I know that look on your face."

"What?" Mauricio said. "I did nothing. You crazy."

"Hey, stop fighting. I asked Tino something."

"I don't know who Joey is." Tino put the phone away.

"Pass," Patricio said as he pulled a bone from the pile and placed a blank/two down. Alonso placed a two/one. Tino a one/five and Mauricio placed a five/five.

"What the hell! Where did that come from?" Patricio asked.

"That was my five/five. He had it under his leg, primo," Alonso said.

"You saw that and didn't say anything!"

"I'm not going there." Alonso pushed away from the table.

"I need to get home," Tino said.

"Will you let me take the Impala?" Alonso looked at Patricio.

"Hell no!"

"Can you take me to my house?" Tino asked. Mauricio and Patricio exchanged glances.

"Come on." Patricio pulled the Impala keys from his pocket.

"You live northwest, right?"

"Close to tío Frank," Alonso said.

"Point the way. Tino, you should be in the front seat instead of this fool," Patricio said.

"Watch who you callin' fool." Mauricio crossed his arms across his chest and sank low into the seat. He stared blankly out the side window.

"Who crawled up your butt and died?" Patricio said.

"You did and it stinks. Lay off, will you?"

"Turn here. It's five houses up on the right."

"Hey, gimme the keys so I can pop the trunk and get the wheelchair," Alonso said.

"Come into the house with me," Tino said.

"Sure." Alonso reached around the door and positioned the chair for Tino. Alonso pushed him up the sidewalk. Not a light on or a sound to be heard. Tino put the key into the door of the seemingly empty house. Opening the door, he flipped on the living room lights and wheeled quickly to the kitchen in the back of the house. His mom had left a note on the bulletin board--playing Bunko with the girls, love mom.

"Can you run upstairs to my sister's room to see if she's there?"

"Sure."

"It's the room to the right at the top of the stairs."

Alonso noticed the photographs of Tino and Tesoro hanging in the stairwell. They were both younger, standing at about the same height, skinny, with braided hair. One picture showed them wearing athletic track gear, holding up a trophy. There were pictures of Native American celebrations with people in long black cloaks, black lines drawn down the center of their faces.

Alonso reached the top of the stairs with the geometric runner covering the hard wood steps. His heart pounded and he walked quickly to the edge of the bed. In the dim light he saw Tesoro was not there.

Without warning, two flashes of light shot across the darkness and quickly turned into misty figures. Two silver wolves appeared at either side of Tesoro's bed, growling at Alonso. He backed out of the room as he kept his eyes on the wolves, slammed the door and ran down the stairs.

"What?" Tino asked.

"She's not there. Wolves, there are wolves in her room."

"Ah, my sister's guardians. I saw them in the vision I had of Tesoro."

"Yeah...I keep having visions of Skye. He's showing me a house. Here, I drew a picture of it." Alonso retrieved the crumpled paper from the hospital stationary.

"Do you know where it's at?" Tino asked.

"It looks like the neighborhood my papá used to work in, Mansiones de Piedra Blanca."

"Those are expensive homes. In my vision, I was running with two wolves through a nice neighborhood. Do you think it's the same place?"

CHAPTER FIFTY-ONE

Grandmother and Gravel

"**H**ey now little girl," Merrick said to Tesoro. "That shot wasn't supposed to kill you."

He carried her to the truck in the chilly Texas wind. He tossed her in the truck bed and drove back to the home site with the gravel and pipes.

Merrick backed up to the edge of the wooden frame-out for concrete, jumped out and opened the cab doors. He pulled the last two boxes out from behind the driver's seat and made his way across the gravel, placing them beside the others. He emptied the contents--bags and bags of medical waste with the bio-hazard symbol printing ominously on the sides--into the hole dug in the center of the home site. A few of the bags burst open: used syringes, latex gloves, bloody gauze and human tissue from biopsies rolled out, glistening in the moonlight. Merrick's tall frame created a heavy silhouette against the black night sky.

"Mmmfff." The sound of metal being kicked erupted from the back of Merrick's truck. He tucked the boxes under his arm and ran to the truck, throwing the boxes into the bed beside Tesoro.

"Back from the land of the dead?" Merrick grabbed her by the ankles and pulled her to the edge of the tail gate. "We'll have to do something about that."

Tesoro tried to open her eyes. Her head hurt, her stomach hurt, everything was spinning and nothing seemed real. Somehow, she found the strength to flip onto her side in the truck bed. The sudden movement caused her to throw up all over herself.

"Now why would you go and do a thing like that?" Anger lines etched into Merrick's face as lines in the center of his eyebrows deepened, creating distinct elevens. "You've just become a serious liability."

He pulled Tesoro out of the truck and threw her across his shoulder, her arms and head swinging wildly across his back as he ran to the dump site. He flung her into the pit and she landed with a thud. She groaned and tried to open her eyes, but she could not. Her lids fluttered as her eyes rolled around in her head as if she were asleep and in the throes of a bad dream.

Gravel hit Tesoro flat and hard on the side of her head, her ribs, her legs. She groaned and pulled herself into a fetal position, placing her arm over her head.

"Time to go nighty-night little one." Merrick threw her purse on top of her and continued to pummel Tesoro with gravel until she was completely covered.

The phone in Merrick's front pocket broke the silence of the night.

"Damnation, what next?" He reached into his pocket and put the phone to his ear. He picked up the shovel and walked back to the truck.

"Brett, yes, I'm on my way home...late night."

"What did you do?" Merrick asked, rising anger in his voice.

"Why would you do a thing like that? Why in the hell would you give a girl Rohypnol? What do you mean she's disappeared?

He glanced back at the job site.

"Stupid, stupid, stupid...I've got another call...we'll talk

more when I get home." Merrick flipped to the incoming call.

"Yes. The job site is ready for the pour, the sooner the better. The gravel is in, the pipes are in, everything is prepared...get the concrete truck out before five this morning. Yes, it's important that we stay on schedule."

He ended the call and said, "Idiot."

Merrick pulled away from the site with the lights off. He traveled down the long stretch of empty road before stealthily traversing the streets filled with large homes and sprawling, well-manicured yards. He turned on the lights as he exited the neighborhood.

~

Tesoro's survival instincts were strong. She had created a pocket of air with her body while curled up in the fetal position as Merrick had shoveled gravel on top of her. The rubble weighed heavily on her body, making it difficult to take a full breath. She tried to move her elbow, but each time she did more rocks closed in on her cocoon.

Tesoro's heart was racing and she was choking on dust. She slipped into uneasy near unconsciousness, only to reawaken to a hazy awareness of her situation--one of unquestionable death. As panic melted away into dizzying theta waves, Tesoro's link to the in-between worlds opened up in her mind. She visualized, as clear as a movie on a large screen, her grandmother holding her hand when she was eight years old...just the two of them walking through the woods behind her parents' house in the late summer. Yellow flowers bloomed profusely at the edges of the dirt path. Rabbit ear cacti heavy with red-violet fruit pods jutted up between partially buried limestone boulders. Twisting escarpment live oaks and brushy cedar trees filled the land.

Long white and black strands of her grandmother's hair flowed straight across her simple, off-white muslin dress, cascading in unison with the wind. Grandmother's aura shone brilliant white. It emanated from her like soft clouds swirling with the wind. Inside her glowing aura were sparks of crystal bright light moving vertically from the crown of her head. Close to her skin, sparkling transparent diamonds rolled like a thin film of water, glistening in the sun. As she walked, the surrounding land swirled and moved, also taking on the light of grandmother's aura. Her kind face emanated wisdom. She turned to Tesoro and without moving her mouth, telepathically said:

"You will not walk this path any further with me...not now. Use your strength to call your guides, the wolves, to carry a message to your brother."

Tesoro opened her eyes wide to the blackness surrounding her, calming herself to conserve oxygen. She understood her grandmother's message from beyond, a message clearer than anything she had ever understood from the living. She began to hum on each shallow out breath, calming her mind and centering her focus on her boulder turquoise necklace. The same pendant worn by her grandmother that Tino brought back from the hospital after her grandparents died...the stone with the image of a wolf naturally occurring from brown spots veining through the blue. Tesoro longed to place her fingers on the cool turquoise, but she could not risk moving lest her cocoon cave in.

As she concentrated on the image of the wolf, Tesoro's mind opened up once more. Two glowing silver specks of light appeared in front of her open eyes in the darkness. The dots of light zoomed directly in front of her, growing in dimension as they came closer and closer, morphing into two beautiful silver wolves, taking up her entire field of vision. They stood tall with their heads up, ears pricked, pupils small and tails slowly sweeping in a curled wag across their lower backs. Tears welled in Tesoro's eyes at the sight of them.

She whispered, "Lead Tino to me...hurry."

As quickly as the wolves had appeared, they vanished

into the same blackness as pinpoints of silvery light. The tears fell from her eyes and across the side of her face mixed with dust and grime. The warmth from the tear reminded Tesoro of Alonso's lips on her face. Another tear, more tender than the first, moved across her face as a wave of strong emotion and longing for Alonso consumed her. Softly, the words of e.e.cummings escaped from her lips:

"love is the voice under all silences, the hope which has no opposite in fear: the strength so strong mere force is feebleness: the truth more first than sun more last than star..." She drifted off into a shallow, unconscious place.

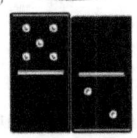

CHAPTER FIFTY-TWO

Guardians and Gates

"She's not there," Alonso said, shutting the door to the Impala behind Tino and jumped in on the other side.

"So, what do you guys want to do now?" Patricio asked.

"She was at Brett's party last," Tino said from the backseat.

"Let's go there. Where is it?" Mauricio asked.

"Patricio, go by tío Frank's house. I need Sombra to come with us." Alonso placed his hand on Patricio's shoulder.

"Say what?"

"I need my dog."

"Why?"

"I don't know. I just know I do."

"Chingado. Which is it, the party house or the dog house?" Patricio asked.

"The dog," Tino said.

"I thought Mauricio was muy loco. He's nothin' compared to you two." Patricio pointed the nose of the car in the direction of Frank and Ruby Garza's home.

"I thought I told you to lay off," Mauricio said.

"Then you lay off cheating."

Silence endured for the rest of the ride.

~

"C'mon, get in the car!" Patricio yelled. Sombra squeezed by Alonso's legs, exiting the Garza home. The black dog tore through the yard, stopping only to lift his leg on a shrub.

"Sombra!" Alonso yelled. Sombra put his back leg down and jumped into the car, right across Tino's legs.

"Hey, who are you?" Tino gave Sombra a pat on the head. Sombra gave Tino a wet kiss on his chin and moved further onto his lap. Tino searched for the Merrick address and then punched in the GPS coordinates.

"Here." Tino handed his phone to Mauricio. "Brett's address."

"Let's do it." Patricio placed the phone on his right leg and drove off.

"How fortunate...the gate's open." Patricio glided the Impala onto the large stone driveway in front of the Merrick home.

"The garage is, too." Mauricio pointed to the open garage door.

"Funny, it's empty?"

"Someone left in a hurry," Tino said. Alonso was out the door pulling Tino's wheelchair from the trunk.

Patricio and Mauricio, already in the garage, moved to the door leading into the house. It was cracked open and light streamed through. In the distance they could hear a television. Mauricio knocked on the door, causing it to swing wide open.

"Anyone home?" he yelled, stepping into the hallway.

"What do you want?" Brett, still fully dressed from the party, walked into the same hall.

Tino wheeled around Mauricio. "What happened to Tesoro?"

"Who?" Brett asked.

"Tesoro, my sister."

"Don't play dumb." Alonso stepped out of the dark garage, past Tino and Mauricio.

"Get the HELL out of my house," Brett yelled. Alonso held his ground.

"What happened to my sister?" Tino asked.

"She left with some guy."

"Who?" Alonso asked.

"Joey," Brett said. Alonso and Tino exchanged glances.

"Call him," Tino said firmly.

"Outside, go outside," Brett moved to the garage door and hurried the entourage past the container he left Tesoro in not glancing back. In the driveway, he fake dialed his phone.

"Hey Joey, dude! Did you leave with some chick named Tesoro? Yeah, thanks man."

"He took her home," Brett said.

Merrick's truck pulled through the gate. He slowed to look at the Impala in the drive, pulled into the open garage and leapt out.

"Brett, who are these guys?"

"We're just finishing up, right?" Brett looked directly at Alonso.

"Don't I know you?" Merrick eyed Alonso and Tino. The bright party lights from the trees put them in plain sight.

"We're leaving," Patricio said. They moved past Merrick to the Impala. Brett and his dad followed.

"Get your Mexican ass off my lawn!" Brett yelled.

Alonso turned to face Brett, "When did he take her

home?"

"Do we have a problem here?" Merrick asked.

"Yeah, we do. These guys weren't invited, they're trespassing," Brett said.

"You boys need to get off my property right now."

"When did he take her home?" Alonso moved closer to Brett, fists shaking by his side.

"Alonso, c'mon, we need to go," Patricio said. It was too late. Brett flat hand shoved Alonso in the chest and onto the grass. Mauricio lunged at Brett, forcing him to stumble backward and fall. Alonso steamrolled Brett on the ground, pinning his arms with his legs as he punched him, left, right, and again in the face.

Brett brought his knees up and hit Alonso hard in the back, escaping his hold. Alonso rolled on the grass, started to rise up and Brett kicked Alonso back down.

Mauricio quickly approached Brett and smacked him in the chest.

"How does that feel...gringo? Hurts, right?"

Alonso back flipped, reached out, grabbed Brett by the ankles and pulled him to the grass. Mauricio threw himself onto Brett's legs and Alonso jumped on his chest, taking swings at his face.

Merrick pulled the shovel from his truck bed and ran to the fight. Patricio grabbed the shovel, trying to wrestle the tool from his grip. Merrick shoved the handle of the shovel into Patricio's shoulder, knocking him back on the stone driveway. Looming over Alonso, he brought the shovel over his shoulders. But right before he could swing to hit Alonso, Tino grabbed the shovel handle. Merrick, full force, pulled it forward, lifting Tino out of his wheelchair and onto the ground with the shovel beside him. Merrick jumped on Alonso's back, wrapping his arms around his chest and pulled him off his son.

Patricio scrambled to Tino's side, lifting him into his chair and wheeled him fast to the Impala.

He starting the engine and honked. Mauricio high-kicked Merrick, knocking him on the side of the head; he released his grip on Alonso. Alonso and Mauricio raced to the car, diving through the open windows as Patricio backed out through the gate. Merrick ran at them with the shovel raised in the air and with Brett, bloody faced, close behind.

"He buried Tesoro alive," Tino said.

"What?" Alonso yelled.

"I saw it when I grabbed the shovel. He shoveled rocks on her."

"What?" Patricio asked.

"Psychometry...when I touched the shovel I saw Tesoro being buried with it."

"Right..." Patricio glanced over his shoulder after squeaking through a hairpin curve in the sleepy neighborhood.

"Alonso, that place your dad worked, what was it again?" Tino asked.

"Mansiones de Piedra Blanca."

CHAPTER FIFTY-THREE

Spoons and Balloons

"**W**hat do you mean the cement mixer will not be ready to go 'till ten? I need you on the job site immediately...yes, right away...before five like I've told you all along...get on it!" Merrick screamed into the phone.

"Do I need to come do it myself? It's going to rain later today. You have to get out there, NOW!"

"Dad, what's going on?" Brett rounded the corner of his Dad's office, wiping the last of the blood from around his nose.

"What?" Merrick was busy gathering up his truck keys and paperwork, placing everything in his jacket pocket.

"Where are you going? I need to talk...that girl."

Merrick glanced up quickly and back down at his desk as if he were forgetting something.

"I'm having job site issues with one of my concrete pours. They can't get anything right. I need to leave to wake up the crew."

"Now?"

"Now...aren't you supposed to be asleep like a good little boy?"

"Dad...shit...I drugged a girl...you saw...those hoodwinks have a price on my life."

"Go get in the truck. This is good training for you. Owning a company means the work never stops. There's a lesson in this for you when you inherit my businesses."

Brett buckled up in the passenger seat.

"Why did you do it, Brett? There's plenty of girls who give it up easily. Why did you need to drug one?"

Merrick shut the heavy iron gate glancing behind to make certain it closed. "You're tampering with life and death when you drug someone. You know that, don't you?"

"She doesn't like me...she would never let me..." Brett said, his voice trailing off.

"...have sex with you?" Merrick glanced sideways at his son. "Brett, I need to talk with you, seriously." Merrick sped up as they entered the interstate ramp. "I found your drugged girl." Merrick's eyes fixed on the empty nighttime highway. "She's dead, Brett. I found her on the side lawn by the garage," Merrick lied.

"What?"

"Your phone call...you told me you drugged her...I came right home. I pulled up and saw her by the side garage door, dead beside the trash bins. I didn't know what else to do, so I threw her into the back of the truck, she was covered in vomit. She's buried now."

"Holy crap Dad. What does this mean?"

"It means I covered your ass. That's why I don't want you to talk about this, ever again, to no one. Understand?"

"Where...where is she?"

"Can't tell you that." Merrick rounded the corner to his South Side Concrete Company's entrance gate and pulled up to the dimly lit office surrounded by concrete trucks.

"Dad, I'll take the heat for this, I'm a minor. They will not send me to jail for as long as they would send you. I need to know where she's at so I can say I did it."

"You don't drive, it would never go over."

"I can say I stole your truck."

"Who's going to find out?" Merrick turned the truck off. "She's just another missing, troubled teen. There'll be an 'Amber Alert' then we'll see her on the news, next her picture will be on a milk carton. The next big thing will come up and everyone will forget about her, thinking she ran away. That's how it works."

"What if we're questioned?"

"I know about your party, Brett. You lied to me about this. How many people were there?"

"Over one hundred."

"Good, what did you tell people about this girl?"

"That she was seen leaving with Joey."

"Okay, so they will question Joey and then us. Did anything else happen that I need to know about?"

"A few people saw me go into the back hall by the garage with her. She was passing out on me."

"Tell them you took her to the bathroom and then she was fine. She was last seen leaving with Joey. Do you understand what to say?"

"Yes sir."

"We're good on the story?"

"Yes sir. Dad, I liked this girl."

"Get a grip." Merrick jumped out of the truck and banged on the office door.

"Get out of the backroom, Jorge!" he yelled through the thin door.

"H...E...L...L..." He started to yell 'hello' as the door slammed outward. It was Jorge Cobos, the tattooed man.

"Put the blasted needles up and get out here now,"

Merrick said. Cobos had a belt wrapped tight around the upper part of his arm, a spoon in one hand a syringe in the other.

"You better be straight enough to pour concrete tonight. Did you find anyone to help?" Merrick followed Jorge Cobos into the back room.

"No. Looks like you brought help." His words slurred through his thick accent as he pointed to Brett, still in the open doorway.

"I'll let you off the hook this time. Brett and I will go to the job site with you. Is a truck ready?"

"Sí." Cobos pointed to a truck closest to the office and he reached up to vigorously rub his nose from side to side with the back of his hand.

"Hey, get it together. I need to rinse off my truck."

He turned to Brett. "Help me wash the truck."

Brett followed his dad outside, found a hose and a broom used to clean the concrete trucks.

"How did so much mud get back here?" Brett asked.

"Your girlfriend...go grab that broom. I'll hose and you sweep."

Merrick jumped into the bed of his truck and rolled up the legs of his custom Italian slacks.

"There's puke everywhere!" Brett exclaimed.

"Sweep it out."

"Dad, that was from Tesoro...right?"

"Just sweep."

"She's really dead?"

"Sweep!"

"I...I can't do this..."

"Then get out of the truck."

He jumped from the bed of the truck and threw up in a puddle, his face reflected back at him in the moonlight from the dark pool below. He picked up a block of hardened concrete and threw it into his reflection in the water.

"Easy there. Go get cleaned up in the bathroom, we need to go. Quick."

Brett raced into the building, past Cobos in the doorway. The bathroom was filthy. The sink had rust stains all over with soap scum and lime lined on the inside. The toilet had a thick ring of dark residue and the seat was missing. There were no paper towels, no toilet paper and no mirror. Brett urinated, rinsed his hands and wiped them on his shirt to dry.

A large cockroach scurried across the floor by a hole in the wall at the base of the toilet. Brett reached his hand past the toilet and pulled a shoe box out of the hole. It contained needles, spoons, a lighter, a cut-off straw and a red balloon with powder inside--Jorge's heroin stash.

Brett slowly opened the red balloon and poured out a small amount of the light brown powder into the palm of his hand. He moved it around with his finger tip and tasted it. It smelled and tasted like coffee. He put his nostril close, placing the straw to the powder and inhaled quickly. The substance rushed into his sinuses and burned the inside of his nose. He swallowed hard.

"Damn..."

Brett pulled his finger and thumb down the length of his nose. The powerful drug quickly took effect. He blinked slowly and rubbed his nose in circles. His body swayed front to back, and front to back again. Sliding his hand down the wall for balance, he sat down on the filthy toilet rim, bending forward to place his face in his hands. A sea sickness, slow and sticky, rocked him back and forth.

"...damn."

Brett picked up the syringe, rolling it between his fingers first and then placing it back into the box. He picked up the lighter and the spoon, flicked the lighter and watched the flame wrap around the convex curve of the spoon. Turning the faucet, he poured water in the spoon and lit it up again, watching the water mix with the residue of heroin left behind. Putting the paraphernalia back in the box, he picked up the red balloon, poured another line and snorted.

"What's taking you? We need to go pour concrete," Merrick yelled into the night air.

Brett tied the neck of the balloon into a knot and crammed it deep into his front pocket.

CHAPTER FIFTY-FOUR

Hairpin Curves and Mud

Alonso briefly fell asleep in the backseat of the Impala as Patricio cruised cross town. Suddenly, his entire body jolted and he drew in his breath, waking with a start.

Tino looked at him, "You alright?"

"Yeah, just had a dream about that place where I met you, think I got some kind of a message from it."

"What was the message?" Tino said, getting right to the point.

"It was weird, like it always is…it was as if I'd been there forever looking at the two suns and stars sparkling through the violet sky." Alonso recounted his dream.

"What was the message, get to the point."

"Yeah, this guy, his name is Sha, he told me to 'follow the wolves,'" Alonso said.

"Follow the wolves," Tino repeated, looking out the window as street lamps from the highway raced by. For a split second, Tino caught a glimpse of what he thought was his grandmother's face as a passenger in the backseat of an SUV right beside them. She slowly turned her head and looked Tino straight in the eye and pointed to the traffic ahead. Running right in front of the Impala, Tino could make out the silvery wisps of two wolves.

"Hurry!" He was filled with a sudden sense of urgency with this sight. He reached over and placed his hand on

Patricio's shoulder. "Hurry!"

Patricio maneuvered the large car through the side roads leading up to the closed gate at Mansiones de Piedra Blanca.

"Hang on." Alonso jumped out and punched in the entry code he had memorized from his papá working at this job site. The light by the electronic keypad flashed green and the gate slowly opened.

"Go." Alonso jumped back into the car.

"Where do we go now that we're in?" Patricio asked.

"I'll tell you," Tino said. He could still see the silvery wolves leading the way.

Without warning, Sombra leapt across Alonso's lap and out the window.

"Not again!" Alonso cried. Patricio hit the brakes as Sombra ran directly in front of the Impala. Tino could see Sombra running tight and fast, right between the two silver wolves.

Alonso started to leap out the window, too. Tino grabbed his shirt tail.

"Don't! We need to follow him. I can see the wolves, Sombra's running with them. They will take us to my sister."

"Say what? You crazy, muy loco!" Mauricio said.

"Just go, follow the dog," Tino said.

With no street lights, it was almost impossible for Patricio to see Sombra in the dark, out of reach of the headlights. Sombra zipped through a hairpin curve and raced into a new section of Mansiones de Piedra Blanca, wolves on either side.

"Dang...I'm going to run over him!" Patricio said.

"Just keep going, don't slow down," Tino said. He too, could no longer see Sombra, only the glow of the silver wolves running with heads pointed forward, tails out and feet flying just above the pavement.

"Here, turn right here! Okay, stop!"

The Impala rested right in front of several undeveloped lots.

"Why here?" Alonso said.

"Look, they're running across the field to the next road." Tino pointed past the partially framed homes to a field just beyond.

"I can't drive through there."

"No, but a F150 truck could," Patricio said.

"Hurry, we're following on foot now." Tino unbuckled his seatbelt and threw the door open. Alonso jumped out the window and pulled Tino's wheelchair out of the trunk.

"Hey, I can't push you through the mud," Alonso said.

"Just go! Run, follow Sombra!" Tino yelled. He leaned so far forward in his wheelchair that he almost fell out.

Alonso raced through the mud with Patricio and Mauricio close behind. Tino strained to watch the wolves, but he lost them and his heart grew heavy.

Alonso placed two fingers in his mouth to whistle, penetrating the silence. Sombra, who had slipped out of sight, stopped and dutifully ran back.

"Good boy, good boy!" He leashed up Sombra.

"Take us to Tesoro." Sombra pulled toward the wolves.

"You owe me for this one. There's mud all over my new kicks," Mauricio said.

"C'mon, hurry," Alonso said.

"Ésto es una locura." (*This is crazy.*) Mauricio shook his head and picked up the pace behind Alonso.

"Yeah, how do we know Sombra's not just having fun? He's led you on wild goose chases before," Patricio said.

Alonso quickened his pace behind the black dog.

Sombra leapt over a curb that had been poured at the edge of the muddy road. He ran to a homesite that was formed-up and ready for a foundation pour. The dog leapt onto the gravel of the soon-to-be slab, ran past pipes protruding out of the ground and sniffed the ground furiously.

Patricio and Mauricio jumped up onto the gravel to join Alonso and Sombra. Something smelled terrible, a cross between a rotten egg and the pungent smell of raw hamburger meat that's been left out on the counter too long, then cooked. Alonso pulled his arm over his nose and Patricio and Mauricio backed up. The stench of rotten material reeked through the gravel. Alonso placed his hand over his mouth and gagged, almost throwing up. It smelled like sickly death.

Sombra ran in circles around one spot, kicking up the rubble with his paws.

"We have to dig here," Alonso said.

"Uh-uh, there's no way," Mauricio said, gagging. "I'm outta here."

"Alonso bent down and began throwing gravel stones off to the side. Sombra tried to dig beside him, but his paws were not strong enough to move the large gravel stones.

Mauricio had walked away. A glimmer of something on a white PVC pipe caught his eye. Bending down, he saw a few singular strands of long black hair shimmering in the moonlight.

"Alonso, what color hair does she have?"

"Black." Mauricio showed the hair to Patricio. They turned around and wordlessly helped Alonso dig.

"What's this?" Patricio pulled out a bag from the gravel.

He looked closer: used syringes and other used medical supplies.

"Here's another one!" Mauricio said. It was filled with bloody gauze and bits and pieces of things pulled from people during surgeries.

"Sick, that's sick!" Mauricio stood up and threw the bag to the side.

"Who the hell would bury medical waste under a house?" Patricio said.

Alonso kept digging; Sombra kept sniffing and whimpering. He picked up a rock and held it for a moment. "This rock, it's warm. She's under here, I'm sure." He cautiously picked up rocks one at a time. "Careful, we don't want to hurt her."

"Hurt her? How could anyone be alive under this?" Patricio asked.

"Just dig." Alonso didn't look up. He pulled up the rocks faster and faster.

"Stop!" He slowly moved his hand across what seemed to be fabric. It looked wet in the moonlight.

"She's here! I think I've found her leg!" Alonso furiously threw gravel aside. Patricio and Mauricio joined him in the frenzy.

Sombra raced about barking, avoiding the flying rocks.

"Tesoro…" Her crumpled body was covered in dust, mud and vomit. She was curled up in the fetal position.

He reached down and pulled her limp arm to expose her face. He reached under her other arm and pulled her up. Patricio and Mauricio grabbed onto her waist and legs to lift her out, limp and lifeless--were they too late?

"Tesoro…" Alonso took her in his arms and carried her over the gravel, through the mud and back to the Impala. Her face was dark with a thin layer of dirt, sweat and tears once cried.

Tino could make out the silhouette of Alonso carrying Tesoro and his heart raced--she looked lifeless in his arms. He put the brakes on his wheelchair and with all of his might, stood up. He tried to take a step toward Tesoro, but fell back into his chair.

Patricio raced ahead of Alonso with Sombra by his side.

"We need to hurry!" Patricio said. Tino loosened the brake and let Patricio wheel him at a fast pace back to the Impala. Sombra jumped into the backseat beside Tino and licked his hand.

Just as Alonso reached the Impala, headlights cut through the black night and hit him directly in his eyes. The truck was moving toward them with its blinding lights. Behind the truck a noisy concrete truck rambled closer.

Alonso and Mauricio lowered Tesoro into the Impala, gently laying her head down on her twin's lap. She let out a low moan. Tino cried and started to gently clean the mud off of his sister's face with the tail of his shirt. Sombra licked Tesoro's face and hands. For a split second, Tino thought he saw the wolves licking Tesoro, too. Alonso sat down in the backseat, gently lifting up Tesoro's long legs and placing them on his lap.

Where's Mauricio?" Alonso asked.

"Cleaning the mud off his shoes, over there." Patricio pointed at his brother.

"Go, go now." Alonso said. The truck with the high beams was moving in closer. "He'll get in when he see's we're moving."

Mauricio ran to the Impala and jumped through the open window into the front passenger seat.

From the rearview mirror, Patricio could see that the concrete truck had turned off its lights. A skinny man was running from the concrete truck to the pickup. The pickup truck moved toward the Impala and Patricio stomped his foot onto the accelerator, peeling out. He raced to the built up section of Mansiones de Piedra Blanca with the truck in pursuit all the way to the front gate. Alonso jumped out and punched in the code. Alonso looked behind him at the truck as it rounded the corner. He ran back to the Impala and jumped through the back window, just missing Tesoro's legs.

"Move--it's Brett and his dad. Someone else I don't recognize," Alonso said.

Mauricio turned all of the way around in his seat and stared hard at the truck just behind them.

"No way! It's Jorge Cobos...what's up with that?"

"Get to the hospital--fast. She's not waking up," Tino was filled with a flash panic; his sister's fate may be the same as Lilianna's. He pulled Tesoro's hair from her face and gently patted her cheeks.

"Tesoro, wake up." The Impala roared onto Interstate 10 with the black truck close behind.

"Can't you lose them?" Alonso said. The truck would sometimes fall a few cars back and suddenly reappear, tailgating.

"This isn't a formula car. It's a pimped-out ride for show only!" Patricio said, glancing at Alonso. "You've driven it."

"Shake them," Alonso said.

The highway lights rhythmically raced across Tesoro's silent face.

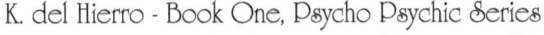

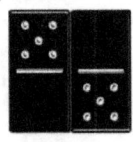

CHAPTER FIFTY-FIVE

Emergency Rooms and Flat Tires

"**W**hha, what...where am I?" Tesoro grabbed the side of her head. "Owweee."

"It's okay, baby girl," Tino leaned over so she could see his face.

"Tino?"

"Yeah, it's me. Just rest, we're taking you to the hospital."

"My head." She looked up.

"Alonso?"

"It's me." He reached his hand out to hers and held it. "You're going to be okay." Alonso smiled warmly at Tesoro.

A tear formed in the corner of her eye. "Why are you here? Where are we?"

"We pulled you out from under some gravel. Do you know how you got there?"

"Owwhh..." Tesoro pulled her hand away from Alonso's and reached up to her head again.

"I was drugged."

"Drugged? By who?" Tino asked.

"Brett's dad." She tried to push herself off her brother's lap, but collapsed. Reaching up, she rubbed her neck where the needle had gone in. There was a bump and she ran her fingers across the bruised area.

"Just stay still--rest," Tino said.

"No, I need to sit up." Tesoro struggled to rise upright between her brother and Alonso.

"So dizzy..." She closed her eyes and grabbed the sides of her head with both hands.

Patricio pulled off the interstate and drove through the hospital parking lot under the road. The black truck was on the exit ramp. Patricio pulled behind a concrete beam and quickly turned off his lights. Alonso hoped they would not spot the car. Wrong. The truck pulled directly in front of them with the high beams shining into the front seat of the Impala. Cobos jumped out of the truck holding a big .357 magnum. He walked up to Patricio's window and tapped on the glass with the gun.

Patricio slammed the Impala in reverse and squealed the old car backwards.

The truck followed, Cobos jumping into the bed as it moved past them. He stood up with one hand hooked in the open sliding glass window and the other hand pointing the pistol at the Impala.

Patricio hit the brakes and spun the Impala into a forward position as he slung the gear into drive. He took off quickly without burning rubber so the tires would not stick to the pavement.

"Tino, unbraid your hair, like your sister's hair," Mauricio said. Tino immediately untwisted his braids, allowing his long black hair to flow over his shoulders.

Alonso understood also. He reached over and pulled Tesoro down into his lap.

"Stay low..." he whispered. She turned over, looked at his face and smiled. He smiled back and bent down to gently kiss her forehead. Tesoro reached up to touch the side of his face, more tears forming in her eyes.

"I thought..." she started...

"...that you wouldn't see me again," Alonso finished, reaching his fingers over to touch her quivering lips.

"Turn into the emergency room entrance," Mauricio said. The car squealed to a stop at the front doors of ER.

Mauricio jumped out, opened the back door, picked up Tino and carried him to the entrance. Alonso had already laid down in the backseat of the Impala beside Tesoro.

The truck rounded the corner. Cobos put the gun down and sat in the bed of the truck.

"The girl's in the car," he yelled into the truck cab.

"I know," Merrick said.

The truck raced their way.

"Chingado, they weren't fooled."

Patricio quickly turned off the headlights and jumped the curb, the Impala's undercarriage scraping loudly as he navigated the sidewalk. He drove into the park and past the Piazza Italia fountain in the courtyard. Maneuvering beside the San Francesco di Paola Church, he plowed the old car right through the field, just past the church--the truck was gone.

"Ha, losers!" he yelled, holding up his index finger and thumb to make the letter "L" in the air.

Patricio steered the car slowly through the parking lot on the north side of the park and shimmied the car off the curb onto San Saba Street.

"I know this place--I have an idea," Patricio said. He drove down Quincy Street, under the interstate interchange of 35 and 10.

"There it is." Patricio pointed.

"That's the manhole we tried to follow Cobos down," Alonso said.

"Exactly, get out on the right-hand door and jump down.

Quick!"

Alonso grabbed his backpack from the floorboard by Sombra and opened the door; Tesoro followed.

Lifting the heavy lid up from the storm sewer, Alonso waved Tesoro over and helped her down into the drain. She grabbed onto the rebar sticking out as a ladder and shimmied down the hole. With trembling hands, she used all her strength to hold on. Her feet missed rungs and she slipped as they descended into the dark abyss.

A strong light beamed into the Impala. The truck was racing right at Patricio. He quickly pulled away from the sewer drain and raced under the interstate, plowing over a cardboard box.

"Jesus, Maria, y Jose. Hope no one was sleeping in there," Patricio said. The box flew into the air behind the Impala and smacked the windshield of the truck. The truck screeched to a halt; Cobos jumped out and pulled the cardboard off the windshield. The truck took off after the Impala again, only this time Cobos was running in the opposite direction, back toward the sewer drain, .357 magnum in hand.

"¡Chingado, Alonso, Tesoro!" Patricio jumped the car onto Cameron Street. From behind, the shadowy figure of Cobos dip into the manhole.

The truck gained on Patricio and bumped him hard from the rear.

"¡Chales!" He lowered himself behind the wheel and pressed the gas pedal all the way to the floor. The Impala responded better than he expected as he raced the wrong way down a one-way street back to the interstate entrance ramp.

A loud shot rang through the night air. The Impala swerved out of control; the back tire had been shot out.

"My rims!" He pounded the steering wheel. "¡Me la van a pagar los condenados!" (*They'll pay for this!*)

Patricio drove to the side of the road, rolled up the window and locked the doors from outside. He sprinted into the barrio just northeast of the interstate exchange--old-school Crips territory. This barrio was different in the dark. The graffiti painted on the dilapidated homes were covered with a long history of territorial disputes and claims.

Another gunshot winged past him. Rounding the corner of a small home he ran smack into Brett, who knocked him to the ground. Merrick was by his son's side, pointing a gun directly at Patricio's head.

"Get up. You're coming with us."

"My ride, nothing will be left, it will be stripped. This barrio is bad news."

"That's the least of your concerns." Merrick pulled Patricio toward him and locked his arm behind his back. The cold metal edge of the gun pointed at Patricio's heart from behind.

Sombra's growls and barks were muffled by the closed windows of the locked car. Patricio turned to look, struggling against the pull of Merrick's strong grip.

"Culeros," he spat.

"Shut the hell up." Merrick shoved the mouth of the gun further into Patricio's back.

"Get in."

CHAPTER FIFTY-SIX

Tunnels and Triage

Alonso pulled Tesoro's hand a little harder and they moved away from the light coming through the manhole.

"Footsteps," Tesoro whispered.

"Hold onto my backpack loops...here." In the darkness, he guided her hand to a loop on his backpack. "Hold on no matter what." He could feel her grappling with her other hand, moving it across the top of his low jeans to find another handle. He wanted to clear his throat, but he couldn't risk being heard.

A light flickered behind them in the distance and he knew to move swiftly. Taking Tesoro deeper into the darkness, Alonso placed his hands on both sides of the damp, sticky tunnel to feel his way through the dark. With limited sight, he swiftly placed one foot in front of the other putting distance between them and the light.

His right hand slipped and he stumbled, causing Tesoro to stumble with him. They had reached a junction in the tunnel. Feeling his way around the edge, he slowly stepped into it with Tesoro holding on tightly. Alonso's hands slid along the dank, slimy concrete pathways tucked deep under downtown San Antonio. At each junction he turned left, knowing he could turn right each time to get back. They no longer heard footsteps.

"They're gone," Alonso whispered.

"Where are we?"

"I have no idea...an amusement water park?" Alonso

slowly turned around and felt for Tesoro's shoulders. He pulled her in close.

"I'm scared." The drugs had worn off and she was thinking clearly again.

"Just hold me." She nuzzled her head into Alonso's chest.

"It's too soon to go back. They'll find us."

"So what do we do?"

"Let me think…" Alonso pulled his backpack off his shoulder and placed it at his feet. He dropped to his knees and unzipped his backpack locating a water bottle among the contents, "Thirsty?"

"Yes, terribly so." Tesoro reached out and placed her hand on Alonso's shoulder to avoid losing physical contact with him in the dark.

Reaching up into the dark tunnel, Alonso ran his hand down Tesoro's arm and placed the water bottle in her hand. He reached into his backpack again, locating the shoe he meant to show Mrs. Weaver. His hand lingered on the shoe for a moment; he felt the cable still attached at the side of the shoe.

"Hey, where's your phone?" he asked.

"The battery's dead."

"Let me have it." Alonso reached up and accidently brushed Tesoro's upper thigh. He heard her catch her breath.

"Sorry, that was an accident." There was a long silence. Alonso broke it by clearing his throat.

This touch in an unexpected place filled Alonso with tingling electricity. He felt her move her hand from his shoulder, up his neck and to his hair. She traced the shape of his ear with her finger tip--neither of them daring to breathe.

Alonso reached his hand up from his backpack, moving Tesoro's hand into his lips and kissed the inside of her palm. She fell to her knees in front of him; he pulled her close and kissed her hard. He could taste the dirt from her burial site on her face and he could feel the heat coming off of her body; more than physical heat, an intense magnetic energy...polar opposites irresistibly attracted.

He wanted to inhale her in the dark tunnel, to breathe her in. He reached his hands tightly around her lower waist and pulled her in close as they kissed again. He was overwhelmed with the desire to touch her skin and started to pull her shirt up over her jeans. As he reached to her front, he felt something in her jeans pocket. He slipped his hand in and Tesoro pulled back.

"Alonso, no..." she pushed away from him. As she did this he pulled the phone out of her front pocket and held it tightly.

"I could have gotten that for you."

"Here, hold onto my shoulder," he said, moving his hands about quickly in the darkness, only this time not on her.

Alonso put his science project shoe on and plugged Tesoro's phone into the cable.

"What are you doing?"

"Hang onto me." He reached under her arm and helped her stand up. Tesoro took hold of his backpack straps and they walked in the dark tunnel. Tesoro's phone began to light up in Alonso's hand.

"You got it to work! Here, let me see it...I have a flashlight app." She grabbed the phone from Alonso's hand, nearly disconnecting it from his shoe.

"Careful there," he said. In moments, the entire concrete tunnel was illuminated from the phone.

"Where are we?" she asked.

"I don't know..." He looked at the tube stretching out infinitely. He could see Tesoro clearly in the reflected light that bounced from the wet walls.

"You're beautiful," he whispered, moving in close.

"I'm filthy."

"I don't care." Alonso reached the back of his hand slowly to her cheek and let it slide down her face ever so softly. He lifted her chin with his curved fingers; she shut her eyes. He kissed her again, soft and gentle, pulling back to look at her. He felt the same magnetic pull as before only this time without being in direct physical contact with her body. He could see the soft pink sparkles of light emanating from her. He moved his hand inches away from her arm and the pink light became stronger. He could feel the pull of magnetic energy tingling through the palm of his hand. It seemed to be connected directly to his heart.

"You're beautiful..." he said again, looking into her eyes.

"Alonso, what are we going to do?"

"What I want to do is kiss you again. What we need to do is keep walking to find a way out of here."

"Is there a signal down here?" Tesoro looked at her phone.

"No, I already checked that."

"I have GPS. Is that working?"

"Not without a signal to locate us."

"Oh." She sighed, grabbed onto his backpack strap and followed him through the underground.

Alonso felt a familiar cold chill shooting down his spine. He turned and for a split second saw a grayish haze in the distance.

"What, did you hear something?"

"No...just keep moving."

"Now you're creeping me out," she said. Alonso's pace quickened.

"Hey, look at that." He pointed to rebar coming out of the wall in front of them. There was a tunnel going up.

"Let's do it." Tesoro said. She jumped in front of Alonso and started to ascend. Alonso followed.

"Good idea." Alonso stood back and watched Tesoro climb, shining the phone right on her. One of the rusty rebar handles broke in her hand and she fell backward. Alonso broke part of her fall with his arms, but not all of it. The shoe he invented sent him off balance and they both crumpled to the ground. Tesoro's foot twisted underneath her.

"Oh, I think it's sprained," she cried.

"Uh, oh." Alonso bent down to look at her ankle and took her shoe off.

"That's in case it swells." He placed the shoe in his backpack.

"Can you walk?"

"I don't know, it hurts pretty bad." Tesoro blinked back tears.

"Here..." Alonso pulled off his flannel shirt, bit into it and ripped off the sleeve. He wrapped her ankle and tied the sleeve together on the top of her foot.

"Try to stand." He reached down and took her wrists, pulling her up.

"How is it?" Alonso reached his arm around Tesoro's waist. She slowly put her foot on the ground, introducing weight to it.

"Not bad! Your triage worked."

"Good. Do you think you can try to climb again? You were almost to the next level."

"I need to rest and put my foot up for a little while before trying that again."

Alonso picked up Tesoro and placed her into a tunnel elevated on the opposite side of the rebar ladder.

"I can't stand up in here."

"Move back." Alonso lifted his body into the tunnel and crawled next to her.

"Here," he bundled his ripped shirt, making a pillow. "Lie down on this."

Tesoro placed her head on the shirt, still warm from Alonso's body heat. He moved his body next to hers: she was shivering. He reached his arms around her and pulled her in close, placing one leg over her two legs to keep her warm. The curve of this small tunnel forced them into each other. Tesoro brought both of her arms in tight, bent at the elbows, to the front of her body for additional warmth.

"There now." He kissed her forehead, finding it difficult to believe he was holding her in his arms. "There now," he whispered as she fell asleep.

The power from the phone battery died out and all went back into black. Something wasn't right. The skin on the back of Alonso's neck crawled and he felt oddly cold. A foul smell hit his nostrils--the smell of decay and death. Directly in front of him, Alonso could make out the form of the construction worker surrounded by a glowing gray haze. The construction worker held out his arms to reveal deeply infected needle tracts.

CHAPTER FIFTY-SEVEN

Backyards and Playscapes

"**H**ere, don't let him go anywhere." Merrick handed the gun to Brett. Patricio watched Brett carefully. He didn't know how to hold the weapon.

As the black truck pulled around the hospital the sunlight reflected off the tiles on the mural on the side of the building. It sparkled brilliantly. The sunrise in the sky and the sunrise depicted on the mural mirrored each other, light rising from the heavens in waves of yellow, softest orange and violet. Patricio turned around in the back of the cab to watch as the two images intersected.

Merrick pulled a plastic ID tag out of his center console and placed it on the rearview mirror. He parked right in front of Christus Santa Rosa hospital in employee parking.

"Stay here with him and don't let anything happen," Merrick said. Brett had the gun pointed at Patricio.

"I'll be right back." Merrick dusted off his Italian suit, buttoned his shirt, pulled his tie out of his pocket and slipped it over his head. He ran his fingers through his hair and walked into the building. The security guard greeted him by name and he walked directly toward the emergency room. At the nurses' station he picked up a clipboard and read the entries.

"Hey, you can't do that." A nurse walked over and smiled as she gently took the clipboard out of his hand. "Is there something I can help you with?"

"Yes," Merrick pulled out his hospital vendor

identification badge and flashed it at her.

"My nephew, he was in an accident last night. He's a teenager with long dark hair. Do you recall checking him in? Within the last hour?"

"No teenage boys."

"Okay." Merrick smiled at the nurse. "You know teens these days. He's probably not hurt as badly as they made it sound on the phone. Probably didn't make it here."

His phone rang. "Merrick...Yes, I'm at the hospital...I'll be right there." He jogged out of the hospital and back to his truck, jumping effortlessly into the driver's seat.

"Dad, what's up?"

"Business...keep your eye on him and lower that damn gun."

Pulling to a side entrance, Merrick exited the truck and approached a loading dock. Patricio could see him talking with a man on the dock. They picked up boxes with "Biological Hazard" markings and placed them in the bed of his truck. The men shook hands and exchanged a yellow tennis ball.

Merrick jumped into the truck and reached across Brett, placing the tennis ball into the glove box. He pulled away from the hospital and started north on Interstate 10. Brett kept the gun pointed at Patricio.

"Where are you taking me?" Patricio asked.

"Shut up."

"Culeros." Patricio spat on the leather seat of the truck.

"I said SHUT UP!"

Merrick reached up to his rearview mirror and pressed a button. The gate to Mansiones de Piedra Blanca opened. Patricio squirmed in the backseat and tried to loosen the rope around his wrists, using the spit on the seat as a lubricant. The knot gave a little and his hand pulled free. He held the loose ropes in place.

Merrick pulled up to the muddy job site. In the morning light, Patricio could see the drum of the abandoned concrete truck still turning.

"Stay in the truck," Merrick said. "Keep a close eye on him."

Lifting the boxes from the truck, Merrick carried them to the home site, emptying the contents into the gravel hole. Merrick climbed into the concrete truck and drove it through the mud to the edge of the wooden forms. The back of the truck churned in low, grinding circles as the concrete mixed inside. Merrick maneuvered the discharge chute of the concrete truck over the gravel.

Brett was preoccupied with the red balloon filled with heroin. He placed the gun on his lap and poured a small amount of the brown powder onto his hand, snorting it up with a straw. Patricio watched and pushed the ropes off his wrists. Brett leaned into the headrest and shut his eyes. Patricio grabbed the gun off Brett's lap and held it to his head sideways, gangster style.

"Open the door--NOW!" Brett complied.

Patricio rolled out of the truck cab onto the ground. Scrambling, he ran hard, the gun steady in his right hand. Dodging between homes that were almost complete, Patricio stayed in the long shadows. He hurdled a wooden privacy fence and landed in a well-landscaped back yard. Ducking down, he turned the lock on the gun and placed it down the front of his pants.

The back corner of the yard, where he landed, housed a wooden playscape, swings and a large metal slide with a small room under it. The swimming pool was covered with a tarp for the winter. Staying low, Patricio made his way to the playscape and crawled inside the small room. The play room had windows, a bookcase with a faded chalkboard and cobwebs in the shelves. Patricio opened a book on baseball, wrinkled and worn from rain and sun. Flipping to the page back page he read aloud: "To Skye on your 10th Birthday, Love YOU Always, Gee Gee."

He moved his fingertips across the words and repeated, "Gee Gee."

The back door to the main home opened and within seconds a small Yorkshire terrier was barking, growling and sniffing around the perimeter of the playhouse.

"Digger, shush!" A female voice sounded and the door shut.

"Perro rasca güevos callate." (*Hey dog, go scratch yourself.*) Patricio hissed through the small window at the Yorkie.

Inside the house, a woman walked to the buffet covered with wilted flower arrangments and picked up a picture of a boy: her son, Skye. She ran her fingers down the front of the photo and tears dropped freely from her eyes down her rosy round cheeks. Clutching the picture to her chest, she moved to the back window and watched the dog race around the playhouse.

"Digger, Skye's not playing in there anymore," she said and placed the picture back on the buffet.

Patricio ducked down a little deeper into the play house. Digger found a small crack and placed his nose in the structure, sniffing hard. Patricio reached over, letting Digger sniff his hand. He felt the cold wet dog nose and smiled. Shivering, he pulled his jacket tight around his middle, wrapping his hands up into the sleeves.

The wind hit the side of the playhouse and whistled through the swings, causing them to creak and move. Patricio looked through the window and saw a teen, maybe fourteen years old, swinging to and fro. He had a baseball cap on over his bald head with earbuds in; he was singing and his low voice eerily mixed with the whistling wind. Patricio quickly pulled his head back into the playhouse, afraid he would see him. When Patricio peered outside again the only thing he could make out were the swings swaying in the breeze.

"Ohhh, I didn't get enough sleep." Patricio rubbed his eyes, curled up in a tight ball on the floor and drifted off.

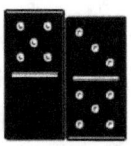

CHAPTER FIFTY-EIGHT

Bright Lights and Love Birds

"**M**ira nomáááás, lo que me encontré!" (*Look at what I found!*)

Alonso jumped away from Tesoro, whacking his head on the side of the tunnel. He could not see anything; a blinding light shone directly in his eyes.

"Los tortolitos." (*The love birds.*) A voice hissed.

Alonso pulled Tesoro behind him, turned around and whispered, "Run."

"You think you can escape me?"

Alonso grabbed his backpack and rapidly crawled after her.

He glanced behind to see Cobos crawling up into the drain pipe. His eyes were narrow slits that glowed red from his gaunt face.

"Go, go." Alonso stole a glance behind him again. For a fast second he saw black cockroaches filling the walls on either side of Cobos, who seemed to be moving with super human agility.

"Hurry." Tesoro pulled herself through the tunnel, breathing hard.

Cobos grabbed at Alonso's ankle, pulling the spring-powered shoe right off his foot, snapping the cable from the phone Alonso clutched. Alonso donkey kicked, trying to hit

Jorge with his other foot. Cobos tried to pull that shoe off, also.

Cobos shined the flashlight at the shoe he had ripped from Alonso's foot and quickly tied it onto his belt.

"¡Rata!" (*Thief!*) Alonso yelled, fearing that was the last he would see of his invention. "I'm taking you down for that, Cobos."

"Tesoro, up, go up, climb, fast!" He saw rebar coming out of another upward tunnel.

"Rápido!" He pushed up on her rear as she climbed using only her upper body strength and uninjured foot. Alonso marveled at her agility, athleticism and the shape of her nalgas as she ascended. Cobos was close behind, holding the halogen light in between his teeth.

"I don't think so…" Alonso paused for a moment, just enough to let Cobos catch up to him. Timing precisely, he delivered a swift, punishing kick to the hand that grasped the rebar. Cobos screamed and tumbled down, landing with a resounding thud at the level below.

"This is our break Tesoro…rápido!" Tesoro pulled herself to a narrow passageway on the right, head first. Alonso could hear her screech as she disappeared. He followed her in and zoomed down a steep, slippery tunnel. He crossed his hands over his chest and tucking his chin, moving at high speed, he braced for impact.

"Aaauuggghh…" He could hear Tesoro's cries, just ahead of him…then a splash. He was suddenly airborne, free flying in black space and then boom, submersed. Alonso fought to find the top of the water. He was terribly disoriented and could not tell which way was up. He let his body go limp for a moment to float, seeking the surface. He felt it-kicked hard in that direction-broke the surface and gasped for air.

"Tesoro! Tesoro!" he yelled, echoing into the dark. He heard a splash and quickly swam toward it.

"Alonso!" she cried as he grabbed onto her.

A flickering light shone far above their heads. Cobos was searching for them. Alonso put his hand over Tesoro's mouth. He hooked his arm under her neck and started to swim without making a sound, moving his feet and one free arm under the waves.

The current picked up momentum and carried them swiftly away. Alonso relaxed into the pull. It had to be leading to a way out.

Alonso felt a wall, slippery and mossy. He could not hold onto it, but he let his hand glide along until there was a crack and he held on fast. Their feet were being pulled upward by the current. Tesoro held tight to Alonso with one arm and with the other she took hold of a corner of another opening.

Grasping around the slippery edges, she pulled herself up into it.

"C'mon," Tesoro said.

This tunnel was smaller. Tesoro's feet touched the bottom, the water gushing up to her waist as she stood upright with her hands on either wall for balance. Alonso passed her his backpack and followed her in. He turned to face Tesoro, wrapped his arms tightly around her waist and nuzzled his face into her wet hair.

"Shhhh, shhhh, it's okay, it's okay now. We'll get outta here, I promise," Alonso whispered.

He could feel Tesoro melting into his hold, his warm, hard body pressed against the length of hers. She let out a deep moan and Alonso pulled her in even tighter. Alonso stepped forward to get closer yet to Tesoro. He lost his footing and they were both pulled downward into the current. They caught their breath as they were sucked into a water-filled tube, narrower than the last. In an instant they shot mid-air into blinding daylight and landed with a loud splash directly in the San Antonio Riverwalk waterway.

"Oh my, oh my..." The voice of a woman called as he surfaced. He could see Tesoro being helped into a Rio water taxi just under West Crockett Street. A rather rotund woman, with flushed cheeks and wearing a sun visor, was pulling her aboard. Alonso swam over to the cab and a man reached over the rim of the red, white and blue boat to haul him in.

"Oh you poor dears, what happened?" The woman asked.

"We were lost..." Tesoro trembled. The cold winter air hit her wet skin. The woman removed her coat and wrapped it around Tesoro's shivering body. The man offered his coat to Alonso, but he held his hand out, shaking his head no.

"I'm fine."

"Go ahead, take the coat from him dear," the woman insisted. The man rose and placed the warm coat around Alonso's shoulders.

"Thank you, but I'm fine, really," Alonso said.

"Here's your jacket. Thank you," Tesoro said and handed the jacket back to the woman.

"We're almost at the mall. Can we get you two a cup of coffee?" They nodded yes.

"Great then, there's a coffee shop right inside on the first floor." They exited the parked boat and went into the well-lit mall, which seemed extremely bright and shimmering to Alonso and Tesoro after being in the dark for so long.

As they settled down to a table, the woman asked, "How do two such adorable young people get so lost that they come flying out of the storm drainage system in this town?"

Alonso reached down and wrapped both of his hands around the coffee cup, savoring its warmth. He shrugged and stood up, his dark bangs stuck to his forehead in jagged lines.

"Leaving so soon?" The man said.

"Yes, thank you for the coffee...we're okay." Alonso

reached over to Tesoro's hand and gave it a squeeze.

"Yes, thank you for your kindness." Tesoro reached over to shake the woman's hand.

"Cobos took my shoe, my project for Mrs. Weaver's science class. I'll fail her class now." Alonso said as they walked out of the coffee shop.

"Do you still have your other shoes in your backpack? You should have my shoes in there, too?" Tesoro asked.

"Yeah."

"Maybe we should go outside to put them on," Tesoro said. "Can you make another project for science class?"

"Not like that one, it took me all night." Alonso reached over to hold Tesoro's hand and they walked outside of the mall.

"I could help you stay up all night to build another project," Tesoro said with a wink.

"That works for me," Alonso said, gently brushing the side of her face with the back of his hand. She kissed his fingers as they passed close to her mouth.

"You don't need that shoe to produce electricity." She took his hand in her own and pushed it against her fast beating-heart. They looked deeply into each other eyes as crowds of people moved around them.

"Brrrr! My feet are cold!" Tesoro shivered." There are chairs by that restaurant we can use to put our shoes on," she said pointing to black metal chairs close to the edge of the water.

As they put on their wet shoes, a band of mariachi players appeared with a crowd of flamenco dancers close behind. The music was loud and fast. Two men dressed in black and white formal attire moved around Alonso and Tesoro playing their guitars. The women swirled their colorful skirts and madly tapped their feet, creating a pulsating rhythm of activity on the hard pavement of the Riverwalk.

After the flamenco dancers, a crowd of people, dancing and celebrating, followed the music up the sidewalk, pulling Tesoro and Alonso deep into the crowd. They became caught up in the moment of music and celebration and moved in the same rhythm, holding each other and dancing to the beat.

Alonso took charge of the dance and moved Tesoro gracefully beside him, dipping her low and then twirling her around by her hand. She balanced on her uninjured foot. He slowed down for a moment, looked deeply into her laughing eyes and bent down to kiss her. Her laughter was suddenly stifled. Beyond the crowd, on the opposite side of the river, Cobos stared coldly.

The word "run" barely squeezed from her lips just as Alonso's lips met hers.

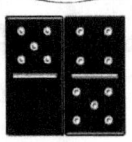

CHAPTER FIFTY-NINE

Stolen Ride and the Fight

Patricio peered from the small playhouse at the large warm home. He could see the woman moving around in the house. He wondered if he could approach her. He tried to visualize what this would look like and it never had a good ending. Each time he played different scenarios in his imagination, she became frightened and called the police. He mumbled, "Soy mexicano." He let out a deep sigh fearing their cultural differences would create a communication barrier. He decided to wait it out in the playhouse. He just was not sure how to get home and needed a friend.

He was just getting comfortable when the garage door opened and a car started. Patricio looked back into the house and could not see the woman. The lights were out in the home and it appeared empty.

"¡Chale por fin!" (*You're kidding, at last!*)

Opening the wooden door to the playhouse Patricio ran to the fence. Through a crack in the side gate he saw the woman as she walked back to the house. She had left the car door slightly open with the engine running.

Patricio hurdled the fence and jumped in the car, quickly throwing it into reverse and driving away. The woman was nowhere in sight as the taupe Lexus flew down the street.

"I'm outta here!" Patricio ducked low at the automatically opening gate to avoid the security cameras, pulling his black beanie cap over his face. He was barely able to see through the knit fabric. He raced directly to Interstate 10 and pointed the car toward downtown San Antonio. Desperate to get to his Impala-and Sombra-before anyone else did.

"Lady, I promise you will get your car back, unharmed." He patted the dash board and sunk even lower in the seat. Glancing down at the speedometer, he noticed two small pictures of a young boy: a thin healthy boy in a Cub Scout uniform with a snaggletooth smile...the other, the same boy, older, with black circles under his eyes, no hair...obviously a cancer patient.

"I just jacked the car of a mamá whose baby died. ¡Me lleva la chingada!" He now understood the abandoned playscape and that he had seen the boy's ghost. He moved even lower in the seat, this time out of guilt and fear.

"Damn if I'm not going to juvie on this one. The judge will have no mercy. Can't even blame Mauricio for this one. Damn." He shook his head back and forth.

With the hospital in sight, Patricio maneuvered the new Lexus under the Interstate 10 parking lot, careful to avoid the cameras at the intersections. He used his shirt to wipe his fingerprints from the steering wheel and gear shift. He locked the car and placed the key ring in his front Dickies pocket.

"That should do it." He ran hard to the Impala parked only a few blocks away, holding the gun under his belt so it wouldn't fall out. A siren sounded in the background. Fearing the worst, he cut through the trees in Columbus Park, just north of the hospital.

On Cameron Street the Impala stood out, glowing in the winter Texas sunshine. Sombra was barking, his tail was wagging and his front paws were scratching at the front window as Patricio approached the car.

"You're gonna rip up my ride!" Patricio ran even harder, his head down. Opening the trunk he found a bungee cord. Patricio opened the front door. Sombra lunged at him and he swiftly looped the bungee cord through the dog's collar as a temporary leash. Sombra didn't make it to a grassy spot to do his business. He lifted his leg and urinated on the Impala's flat tire.

"Sombra, rápido!" Patricio tugged on the bungee cord and led Sombra to the dormant grass by the side of Cameron Street.

"¡Sombra, arriba del carro, ÓRALE!" (*Sombra, get in the car, NOW!*)

Patricio removed the bungee cord and Sombra jumped back in, tail wagging. He opened the trunk and pulled out Tino's wheelchair, carefully placing it beside the car. Digging a little deeper, under the carpet and trunk deck, he pulled the jack and spare tire out. With professional efficiency, he used the tire iron to loosen all of the lug nuts and he slipped the jack underneath the metal frame to raise the Impala. He pulled the flat tire off and pushed the smaller spare on. He retightened the lug nuts, careful not to cross-thread them.

The Impala fired right up and Patricio drove to the hospital parking lot, a safe distance away from the stolen Lexus. He walked across the access road, pushing Tino's wheelchair to the main entrance. He knew where to find his brother--with Lilianna in her room.

"What took you so long?" Mauricio jumped up when Patricio entered. Tino waved from the reclining hospital chair beside Lilianna's bed.

"I was shot at and kidnapped, that's what took me so long, fool! Yeah, that's right...that's right...you go ahead and laugh...all the time you're here, all relaxed and all!"

"You for real?" Mauricio asked. "Dawg!"

"Don't come near me, fool!" Patricio took a step backward as Mauricio removed his baseball cap and cupped it in his hand. Before Patricio could take another step back, Mauricio slapped him across the ear with his cap. Patricio grabbed his wrist as he pulled back...and the fight was on.

Mauricio took his other arm and slammed Patricio down to the floor from behind the neck. Patricio raised his legs and scissor-wrapped them around his brother's knees, pulling him to the ground with him.

Patricio jumped on his brother's back, locked his arms in place and put Mauricio in a chin lock.

"¡La de a Caballo! ¡No!" Mauricio screamed out kicking at the floor. Tino laughed loud, doubled over in the hospital recliner. He leaned forward and toppled out of the chair, curled on the floor and cracked up with zealous laughter.

"What the..." Jon, the nurse, stepped through the open door. The fighting was over as quickly as it had started. Patricio jumped off of Mauricio, who was still on the floor groaning.

"Sorry, were we being loud?" Patricio smiled at Jon.

"Loud enough to get me down the hall quickly." Jon gave Mauricio a hand up. "This is what I get for helping you guys out in a pinch?"

"Thanks, man. Really, thanks for letting us stay up here."

Tino pulled up from the floor to the chair.

"Hey, can someone bring my chair over?"

"Yeah, yeah man!" Patricio raced to retrieve his chair from just outside the doorway.

"My shift is almost up; it's time for you guys to leave. Do you need a ride?" Jon asked.

"No, I've got my ride," Patricio said. He wheeled Tino in a tight circle.

"You guys are crazy," Tino said.

"Yeah. He's the crazy one," Patricio motioned to his brother.

"C'mon, we need to get back to civilization." Patricio

pushed Tino to the elevator and out to the parking lot.

"Hey, what's with the chotas?" Mauricio pointed to a taupe Lexus being loaded onto a tow truck. There were two police cars and officers were scrambling around the scene, writing furiously and taking photos. Patricio slowed down and positioned himself behind his brother, trying to make himself invisible to the police officers.

"That's the car I jacked!"

"Say what?" Mauricio turned around and gave his brother a look of disbelief.

"Hide me." Patricio had his head down, guiding Tino in his chair.

They reached the Impala and were met by an anxious Sombra at the front window.

"Man, that dog's gonna ruin my ride." Patricio slowly opened the front door.

"Sombra, back!" The dog jumped in the backseat, wagging his tail.

"Buckle up. I don't want to get pulled over for one of you not wearing your seatbelts."

Patricio slowly maneuvered the Impala from the view of the officers busily inspecting the stolen car.

"Pendejo, you goin' to juvie, for real man." Mauricio said.

"I had to get here," Patricio said. "They shot out the back tire of the Impala on Cameron. They took me back to mansion land, they were going to shoot me and bury me in the same hole they dug for Tesoro."

"Damn." Mauricio whispered long and slow under his breath.

"You got away," Tino said. "That's all that matters."

CHAPTER SIXTY

Segways and the Alamo

On the opposite side of the river, Cobos was running into people and knocking over restaurant tables that flanked the river banks. Tesoro's ankle still swollen from the sprain caused her difficulty with running. She ran a little, then hopped on one foot, then ran a little.

"Here, jump on my back." Alonso stopped and passed Tesoro his backpack. He bent down just enough for Tesoro to leap onto his back. She wrapped her lean legs around his waist and Alonso moved as quickly as possible. People stared and moved out of their way.

Alonso pushed hard on the glass doorway leading into the mall's main level.

"Here, hop down." She slid gently off his back. He took hold of her hand and pulled her quickly through the crowd of morning shoppers toward the escalator.

"Get down low." They ascended to the next level of the large mall. As they rose, Alonso could see Cobos opening the glass door on the opposite side of their entry point. Cobos looked furtively from side to side. As if suddenly aware of his surroundings, he smoothed his jacket and ran his hands through his stringy dark hair. He placed his hands deep in his front pockets, put his head down and walked quickly toward the coffee shop.

Alonso slowly stood up on the escalator as Cobos entered the shop. Alonso's shoe invention was still tied to his belt loop. A girl younger than Alonso held her phone over the railing of the escalator going down, opposite of him, right within reaching distance. Alonso swiftly plucked the phone from her hand.

"Hey!" she screeched.

Alonso took the escalator steps three at a time, simultaneously dialing his tío Luis' home number.

"¿Hola?"

"Mauricio, listen to me...pick Tesoro and me up at the Alamo as soon as you can...the corner of Houston and Alamo Street. ¡Rápido!"

Tesoro lagged behind Alonso, not moving very quickly. She appeared casual in the crowd of well dressed shoppers. What set her apart was her stringy, wet hair and unkempt wrinkled clothing.

Alsono hung up the phone and quickly deleted his tío's number from call history. He peered over the railing. Cobos was not in sight. Alonso stood all of the way up.

"There he is!" The girl yelled out to her friends coming up the down escalator after him.

Alonso flashed a handsome smile at her and held up the phone.

"Catch," he said and threw the phone directly to the girl. She caught it with ease and made certain it was okay.

"OMG, he's cute. Did you see him?" Through the crowd, Alonso could hear the girl's high pitched chatter to her friends. The girl looked back at Alonso who placed his finger to his mouth in a gesture for her to remain silent. The girl winked, giggled and faded into the crowd with her friends.

"What did you just do?" Tesoro limped over to Alonso. "Who did you call?"

"We need to get to the Alamo. I have a ride lined up." He took Tesoro's face in his hands and kissed her on the forehead.

"Here, hop on my back again." Alonso bent down. She nestled her face into his neck as he walked at a normal pace through the mall. She felt amazingly light to him; her breath on the side of his neck was giving him goose bumps.

Alonso carried Tesoro out of the mall and onto Crockett Street. He crossed over and walked alongside the Crockett Hotel. He had heard the hotel was extremely haunted and wished to see if he could sense any activity.

"Alonso, where are you going? The Alamo is across the street?"

"I like this hotel." He could feel a heaviness in the air and fought the urge to enter the hotel. He moved across busy Bonham Road to the outer walls of the Alamo, through the back entrance of the mission complex.

They walked through the gardens, past the main mission and through the many tourists taking pictures of the famous facade.

"We're early, they didn't have time to make it here yet." He let Tesoro down from his back.

"Who's they?"

"My cousins and their gold Impala."

"Those guys are your cousins?"

"Yeah." Alonso turned his attention on the traffic. He felt a chill directly behind him and turned only to see tourists everywhere. A glimmer of light caught the corner of his eye and he looked in its direction. From the top side window of the Alamo, Alonso could make out the faint image of a man in a military uniform sticking his head out the window and looking right at him, then disappearing. An apparition. He had heard stories about the Alamo being haunted. Now he had proof.

He gave Tesoro's hand a tight squeeze. "I'm hungry. How about you?"

"I'm hungry, too. I could eat an entire pizza all by myself right now." He held her hand a little tighter. They locked gazes, looking deeply into each other's eyes.

"You're beautiful when you want pizza," he said in a soft tone and moved in closer. He could feel her gentle energy and wanted to hold her in his arms. Tesoro shut her eyes for an instant. Alonso leaned down to kiss her forehead.

"His timing sucks!" Alonso pulled Tesoro quickly up the sidewalk toward Houston Street.

"The man with the tattoos?"

"Yes, he's in front of the wax museum. I think he just saw us." Alonso tried to hide behind the crowd of people on the sidewalk. It didn't work. Cobos bolted around the moving cars on Alamo Plaza. Horns honked and drivers yelled as he jumped over their bumpers like they were hurdles on a track.

A tour group on Segways whirred past Alonso and Tesoro, nearly running them down. Alonso glanced across the traffic. Cobos had somehow moved ahead and was coming right at them.

A straggler on the Segway tour collided with Alonso and they tumbled onto the hard sidewalk. Alonso snagged the Segway. Tesoro jumped on and wrapped her arms around his waist.

"I'll bring it back to you, I promise!"

Cobos tripped over the man on the sidewalk as he was trying to get up.

Alonso zipped the Segway right through the front doors of the Alamo mission, right past the guards and the multitudes of tourists inside the building. People screamed and scrambled out of the way as Alonso maneuvered the Segway across the old stone floor.

Alonso glanced behind. To his amazement, Cobos had stopped dead in his tracks at the entrance of the Alamo. Right in front of Cobos a large apparition of a man appeared holding balls of white and blue fire in both hands. Alonso could see Cobos rubbing his eyes as if he were hallucinating. People yelled and screamed at Alonso and Tesoro on the Segway as they zoomed toward the back of the building.

Alonso felt cold. He had the chills worse than he could ever remember. He stopped the Segway and completely turned around. The walls themselves appeared to be moving slowly, as if breathing. Alonso was able to get a better look at the sparking electrical form of a cowboy wearing a wet black duster and cowboy hat. The cowboy was blocking Cobos from entering the building any further. The ghost was dripping wet as if he just emerged from a great thunder storm.

"He stopped chasing us!" Tesoro said.

"Do you see what's holding him back?" Alonso asked.

"What? He looks sick. He's white as a ghost."

"Do you see a cowboy?"

"C'mon, we're in Texas, cowboys are everywhere!"

"In a black duster?"

"Huh?" Tesoro squinted her eyes and looked deep into the crowd of the historic building. "No?"

Cobos turned away from the cowboy and faced another apparition in the doorway. An almost entirely nude Native American stopped Cobos from bolting out the front door. The large Native had his arms crossed over his broad bare chest, his eyes glowing, white orbs. Cobos did not move. He had shut his eyes tight in a cold sweat. He was as white as the eyes of the ghost directly in front of him. Cobos could not escape--he held a paralyzed position.

"Let's get outta here!" Alonso said. "Hang on tight!"

He maneuvered the Segway through the back entrance and traced the side of the mission building to the front of the building, arriving back at the Alamo Plaza. He did not turn around to look at the front entranceway at all.

"Great, there you are. Here's your ride, just like I promised!" Alonso handed the Segway over to the bewildered man whose tour group was coming back to get him. A horn sounded. The Impala was moving south from Houston Street on Alamo Plaza, glistening in the bright winter sun. To Alonso it was a most beautiful sight--a Roman chariot coming to their rescue.

"Tesoro, jump on my back again." She moved faster this time and landed firmly on his back, clasping her arms and legs around his torso. Tino leaned across the seat and held the back door open. Patricio slowed the car to a crawl in the middle of honking city traffic. Tesoro and Alonso climbed in right next to Tino and Sombra.

CHAPTER SIXTY-ONE

Hydraulics and Toothy Grins

"¡**P**rimos…Tino!" Alonso settled into the large backseat of the Impala. "Muchas gracias!"

"No hay de qué." (*No big deal.*) Mauricio turned around and slapped Alonso across the knee with his baseball cap.

"Let's get outta here." Alonso looked back at the Alamo and saw the large, slightly translucent Native American man, without a shirt, smiling and nodding at him. Alonso nodded back.

"Who was that?" Tino asked.

"You saw him, too?"

"He looked like a chief, from about two hundred years ago." Tino glanced back.

"I don't know who he is, or was…I think he held back Cobos at the gate so we could make our break," Alonso said. "He never made it out of the Alamo. It seems we had…protection."

"Yeah, it's good to have friends on the other side," Tino said.

"What are you guys talking about?" Tesoro patted her brother's knee.

"Ghosts, Tesoro--boo."

"Oh yeah, right!" They laughed.

"Mauricio, do you have your phone?" Alonso asked.

"Yeah, what do you need it for?" "Quiero llamar a la policía." (*I want to call the police.*)

"No es una buena idea." (*Not a good idea.*) Patricio glanced in the rearview mirror and made eye contact with Alonso.

"¿Por qué no?" (*Why not?*)

"Acuérdate, estamos en *probation*." (*Remember, we're on probation.*) "Father Fuentes..."

"Órale." Alonso looked out the side window.

"¿Qué vamos a hacer? ¿Cómo vamos a permanecer seguros?" (*What are we going to do? How are we going to stay safe?*)

"No te preocupes, güey." (*Dude, don't worry.*) Mauricio turned around to talk to Alonso.

"Los Royal Riderz, son buena onda primo. Estamos más seguros con ellos que con la chota." (*The Royal Riderz are cool, primo. We are a lot safer with them, than with the cops.*)

"What are you talking about? The only thing I got from that was 'Royal Riderz.' Everyone's heard of them," Tesoro said.

"Everything is going to be okay--I'll tell you later." Alonso reached over to hold Tesoro's hand; she pulled back from him.

"Hey...I didn't understand."

"I'll explain later." Alonso moved closer to place his arm around her shoulders and gave her a squeeze.

"There's a dance, tonight..." Mauricio turned and flashed a wide, toothy grin, his bushy eyebrows raised. "...it's a Quiñce Anos for Marisa."

"Who's Marisa?" Alonso asked.

"She's from school, someone from the barrio," Patricio said. "She's been at the house. You don't remember her?

Mauricio remembers her, right Mauricio?"

Mauricio made an a-okay sign with his hands and nodded yes.

"I don't remember her." Alonso gave Tesoro another squeeze.

He pushed his mouth into her hair. "Would you like to go to a dance with me tonight?" he whispered.

Her answer was a simple kiss on the cheek, a nod yes and a smile.

"What time does it start?" Alonso asked.

"Six. Are you two in?" Mauricio asked.

"Can you take me home to get cleaned up first?" Tesoro pulled her stained shirt up from her stomach.

"You stink, you smell like a sewer." Tino pretended to sniff the air like a dog and he curled up his nose when he reached his sister's shoulder.

"Stop that!" Tesoro laughed and pushed her brother away.

"You two aren't Mexican, are you?" Mauricio glanced back at Tino and Tesoro.

"What do you think we are?" Tino asked.

"I don't know, Cuban maybe? You have dark hair and black eyes. Maybe Puerto Rican? I don't know? Further south, like Chile maybe?"

"Now you're just guessing, fool!" Patricio announced loudly. "We're Mexican. Seriously, where are you two from?"

Tino shot a glance at Tesoro before speaking. "Have you ever heard of the Tonkawa? The 'real people' of the land we are on?"

"No," Mauricio turned all of the way around in his seat. "What do you mean, by 'real people'?"

"Mauricio, he's saying they're Native American."

"Thanks Alonso, our tribe was the first to live in San Antonio. In fact, we inhabited a good part of central Texas. There aren't very many of us left and most of our people are in Oklahoma now, on the reservation."

"We're full blood," Tesoro said. "That's rare. There are fewer than six hundred Tonkawa left and only one hundred live outside of Oklahoma."

"Hey, I just remembered my papá saying he has Indian blood in him," Alonso said. "From Mexico, the Indians from Mexico."

"Some of our people went to Mexico during the early 1800's. They tried to get away from the American settlers," Tino said.

"So...we could be related, then?" Alonso laughed.

"Not funny!" Tesoro slapped him across the leg. "I don't want you to be my cousin."

The car went quiet. The crescendo of Tesoro's ring tone broke the silence. She picked up the call.

"Hello...Sarah...yeah, I'm doing great, never better!" She shot a smile at Alonso. "You're kidding? Brett?...That must have just happened...They got him on possession charges? What was he possessing?...Heroin?...Really?...How long will he be in juvie?...Are you okay?...Great...wow news travels fast. Thanks for letting me know...bye."

"Tesoro, sorry to be listening in, but did I just hear you say Brett got arrested for possession?" Tino asked.

"Yeah, what's up with that?" Alonso couldn't wipe the smile off his face if he tried.

"He's under lock and key as we speak. He had heroin on him. I didn't know he used!" Tesoro said, befuddled.

"Yeah, I thought he just dealt," Alonso added. Tesoro shot

him a sideways glance of surprise.

"Don't need to worry about that joker anymore," Patricio said looking into the rearview mirror.

"Nope," Alonso laughed out loud.

"Tino, do you have your seatbelt on?" Patricio peered mischievously into the rearview mirror.

"Yeah, why?"

Pulling up to a red light next to a car full of girls, Mauricio turned up the music, rolled down the windows and crouched in his seat in an attempt to look cool.

"Oh no you don't!" Alonso yelled. Patricio's hand hit the levers to activate the front end hydraulics.

"Hold on everyone!" Alonso quickly shoved Sombra to the floorboard and placed his legs gently over the nervous dog.

The car's front tires bounced up and down furiously and rhythmically.

"Ya man, that's what I'm talkin' about!" Mauricio sang out. "Ha!"

The girls were wiggling, giggling and pointing. Two girls in the backseat jumped out and started to dance between the cars; they grinded to the loud rap rhythm coming out of the big bass speaker in the trunk of the Impala.

"Impromptu partay! Woot woot!" Mauricio screamed. He placed his arm outside the car window and tapped the rhythm on the cold gold metal.

"Don't scratch the ride," Patricio said.

"Just movin' to da beat, dancin' 'n my seat!" Mauricio placed both arms above his head, allowing the bouncing to move him from side to side.

"Muy loco!" Laughing, Tino held his arms up, too. The jumping car whipped him between the door and his sister.

Alonso and Tesoro held onto each other as the car bounced them around the backseat. They laughed and tangled their legs and arms around each other. Sombra clawed into the carpet and hung on for dear life.

"That's too much of a party!" Tino said, noticing Alonso entwined with his sister. Alonso cleared his throat and untangled his legs from Tesoro.

The car stopped bouncing and Tesoro's eyes glittered with delight. Alonso wrapped his arm around her and she moved into his hold.

"I almost died," she whispered.

"I'm glad you didn't."

"This is the most alive I've ever felt in my life." In spite of Tino's hard stare, Tesoro placed both of her hands on either side of Alonso's face, he pulled her in and they kissed without looking up.

CHAPTER SIXTY-TWO

Ghosts and Royal Riderz

"¡**A**lonso! ¡Mia Chamberlán!" Laurencia Castillo's voice pierced the music and the crowd at la Quince Años. She ran to Alonso and wrapped her arms around him, planting a big kiss on his cheek. She completely ignored Tesoro standing right next to him.

She held his blushing face in her hands.

"It's so good to see you. I'm so glad you're here. Let's dance!"

Bursting with excitement, her dark curly hair danced around her fevered cheeks.

"Laurencia, there's someone I would like you to meet." Alonso looked at Tesoro.

"This is my girlfriend, Tesoro."

"Oh." Laurencia offered a fake smile that curled unnaturally under her very red, sparkly lip gloss. She extended her hand to Tesoro.

"Nice to meet you, I'm Laurencia."

"Hola preciosa, I'll dance with you." Patricio stepped forward with a large smile on his face.

"Patricio!" Laurencia screamed with the same exuberance she had shown Alonso.

"Wow, she's pretty," Tesoro said.

"Would you like to dance?" Alonso asked.

"With my boyfriend?" Tesoro teased, glancing back at Alonso as she navigated ahead of him through the crowd. Alonso laughed, watching her lithe athletic movements as she started to dance to the pounding rhythm. He felt a strong urge to place his hands on either side of her small waist and squeeze her there.

"Move faster if you can. I need to keep my sister in sight." Mauricio guided Tino in his chair, just behind Alonso.

"Yeah, yeah. No worries, Alonso has your sister in sight," Mauricio said, tilting Tino's chair back. He put his face inches from Tino's and made exaggerated lip smacking sounds.

"That's what I'm worried about!" Tino said. "Hurry, fool!"

"Look at that!" Maurico pointed at a girl in the crowd. It was the Quinceañera, Marisa.

"Chingado. She looks good tonight." Mauricio stood up straight and ran his fingers back through his hair, an impromptu styling attempt to tame his wavy locks.

"Go talk to her," Tino said, "I'm fine. Just push me closer to the dance floor so I can see Tesoro."

"I'll push you right onto the dance floor and you'll see more than that." With that, Mauricio pushed Tino directly in front of a girl dancing in a very tight short skirt.

"I can't see my...sister...from here...oh, God..." he looked directly at the girl dancing in the tight skirt. She moved her round hips around sensuously to the bass beat. Leaning forward, his jaw dropped open slightly and his eyes followed the rhythm of her movements. He put his hands down on top of the wheels and moved closer to the gyrating dancer.

With a wide smile he leaned forward tapped her on the back. She turned around and smiled at Tino, taking his hands and wheeling him across the dance floor as she continued to grind. Dancers caught on quickly and pulled up behind the girl, grabbing each other by the waist and grinding with Tino at the front of the line, facing everyone.

"Hey, that's my brother over there!" Tesoro stopped dancing and pointed to her brother dancing with the others.

"Alonso look!" She fell into a fit of laughter at the sight.

Alonso noticed Tino and grinned. Just behind Tino something else caught his attention: a group of guys around a table. They were well dressed in dark clothes.

"Come with me," Tesoro took Alonso's hand and they moved through the crowd toward Tino.

"Tino!" Tesoro reached down to give her brother a hug around the neck and joined in with his dance line up.

Alonso looked again at the table of men. They were being joined by another man who bore a tattoo of a skeleton with a sombrero on his forearm. Static raced up Alonso's spine. A teen with curly hair rose to shake hands with the man who had just walked up. Alonso focused and could hear them. The one who stood up introduced himself as Santiago Navarro.

Santiago was not much older than Alonso, about the same height and build. He had a friendly face with a welcoming smile. Alonso wondered what he was doing with his current company. Santiago glanced over and made fast acknowledgement of Alonso's stare. He quickly went back to his seemingly casual banter.

"No good," Alonso muttered and turned around to refocus his attention on Tesoro who stopped dancing and looked in the same direction.

"What's Lindsey doing here?" Tesoro pointed through the crowd. "Look Tino, it's Lindsey from Flores!"

"Lindsey?" Tino whirled around in his chair. Tino wheeled away from the dancing girl, his sister and Alonso, past the table with Santiago and bee-lined across the hall toward Lindsey.

"Who's Lindsey?" Alonso asked.

"Our friend...well, more like my brother's friend." Tesoro smiled and took Alonso's hand, moving her body to the uptempo song the DJ was playing. Alonso couldn't resist any longer. He reached out and placed his hands on either side of Tesoro's small waist and squeezed tightly.

"That tickles..." Tesoro giggled, her eyes shining and her smile wide.

"I know." Alonso pulled Tesoro close to him and held her in a tight embrace.

"This is a fast song. Dance with me." Tesoro pushed away and twirled to the rhythm. Alonso took a step back and watched her.

Tesoro stopped dancing; she locked eyes with Alonso's penetrating gaze. She started to laugh and then ran swiftly to the door of the hall. Alonso stumbled through the crowd and by the time he was at the front door Tesoro was halfway across the parking lot.

"That girl's fast!" Tesoro removed her sweater wrap as she ran, balled it up and threw it to the ground. She hopped and skipped as she reached around to her feet and pulled her shoes off.

Alonso tracked her, slowing down, sure in his steps. His look was dark and intense as he locked in on his target moving off into the distant parking lot. He could feel his heart beating slow, steady and hard. His neck and temples throbbed with his pulse.

Tesoro stopped running and leaned against the Impala. She looked right at him and smiled. In the back window of the Impala something glimmered--a golden sign that bore the logo of the Royal Riderz. His cousins had switched car clubs and were now aligned with San Antonio's finest.

Alonso's attention turned quickly back to Tesoro. She

looked exactly the same as the dream he had of her in the hospital, the dream Jon awoke him from. She was wearing tight fitting jeans and the same loose, pale lavender blouse. For a moment, he forgot to breathe. The wind blew a lock of her hair over her face and she slowly reached to push it down.

She was breathing heavily from the run. The boulder turquoise pendant of the wolf rose and fell with each breath. He knew what was coming next: she would pull the note from her pocket.

"This is not happening..." he murmured. She reached into her back pocket. He walked to her and she handed him the note. It read: "xxoo." He pushed her against the Impala and kissed her hard on the mouth. Reaching his hands around her waist, he gathered the fabric and moved his hands slowly, deliberately, across the bare skin of her back. He could not stop. He knew what was about to happen. He felt a rush of emotions overwhelm him, and for the first time in his life understood what it was like to be in love. He ached to tell her.

He reached around to the back door handle and opened it. He wanted her alone and in silence; he did not want to hear the pounding music from the hall. Lowering her onto the car seat he closed the door behind them and kissed her gently, gently.

"You're beautiful," he said. Everything was happening exactly as it did in the dream. There was nothing he could do to stop it...nor did he wish to.

They moved further back onto the car seat. Alonso untied her lavender blouse. She did nothing to stop him--she was trying to take his shirt off, too. Her trembling hands grasped at his buttons and pulled at his shirt tail.

Alonso straightened up and pulled his buttoned shirt over his head, exposing his lean, muscular build. Tesoro ran her hands across his chest, down his stomach. Alonso shuddered-this was much more intense than his dream-much better.

Tesoro reached her hands into Alonso's hair and pushed it away from his face; it fell through her fingers. Looking deeply into her dark, almond-shaped eyes, he reached down and unbuckled his belt, pulling it off. She placed one hand flat on his stomach, as if to hold him back. Her hand felt as if it were fire burning right through to his core.

Reaching down, Alonso pushed her blouse just off her shoulders. He placed his full weight on top of her and kissed the top of her chest. He could hear and feel her breathing. He moved up her neck to her mouth. He kissed her deeply, their breath intermingling as the windows of the old car began to fog.

"Tap tap." Alonso jumped at the unexpected sound. He could not see out of the glass window because of the fog.

"Tap tap," came the sound again, only this time from the other side of the car. He took his perspiring hand and wiped a circle shape clear on the window. The faces of the dead construction worker...and Skye...stared through the foggy glass. Skye was shaking his head. The worker turned around and pointed into the parking lot. Tesoro pulled herself closer to the window behind Alonso and strained to look outside.

Suddenly their faces vanished--exposing the strung-out face of Jorge Cobos, the tattooed man, moving quickly toward the gold Impala.

"Los tortolitos," he yelled in a taunting voice that pierced the night, loud enough for Alonso and Tesoro to hear through the closed windows.

"Los tortolitos!"

Look for K. del Hierro's 2ⁿᵈ novel in the Psycho Psychic
series. "Day of the Dead, Día de los Muertos"
racing your way soon!

About the Author, K. del Hierro

Kathie del Hierro calls Austin, Texas home with her husband, two rescue dogs and a bird that landed on her head one day and stayed-- appropriately named Lucky for not being a cat snack. She is a traveler, born in Cambridge, England and grew up the daughter of an American telecommunication spy. She lived in 18 different places by the time she was 17 years old. K. del Hierro inherited her father's keen observation skills and this is what drives her to write.

K. del Hierro has always been an artist. Her first love was the piano, but a family move left the piano an ocean away. At age 14 her hands left the keyboard to write poetry and paint. Her oil paintings are sold and shown professionally. Her first book, "Riding Polluto" an epic adventure with an environmental twist, has her original artwork on the cover. Over the past 12 years, she's worked as a teacher in Austin. She loves being around her teenage students, "My classes are hilarious. We laugh together every day."

She is currently working on her second novel in the Psycho Psychic Series, Day of the Dead...

www.kdelhierro.com or
www.google.com/sites/kdelhierro/
kdelhierro@gmail.com Facebook, Google+, Twitter

Skype author talks are welcomed, please email
kdelhierro@gmail.com to set up a date & time.

Here's a sneak preview of "Day of the Dead, Día de los Muertos"
The 2nd novel in the Psycho Psychic series by K. del Hierro

Chapter One ~ Chicada's and Purple Skulls

Lowriders lined both sides of Fennel Drive leading up to tío Luis' home in the barrio. The tree lined street was heavily pregnant with dense foliage from the unusual heavy rains and heat of early August in Texas. The evening air was quiet the only sound was the cicada's rhythmic chirping from deep inside the green leaves of the trees.

"This is for Lilianna." Mauricio announced to the crowd of Royal Riderz car club members gathered in the front yard. Patricio pulled off the white sheets that covered the Impala to reveal a lustrous, purple paint job. The hood of the car portrayed a large skull designed with air brushed flower, paisley and swirl motifs. Howls and hoots resonated through the neighborhood momentarily drowning out the cicadas. Mauricio opened the door to reveal swiveling bucket seats in purple velvet and silver leather. The small chain steering wheel matched the new silver hydraulics switch box and shiny rims. A tiny skeleton figurine hung from the rear view mirror by a silver chain. The windows, tinted dark far beyond the legal limit, with "Royal Riderz" printed neatly in silver, gothic text across the back glass.

Camera's flashed and a lead member of Royal Riderz, accompanied by two scantily clad girls, stepped forward to shake Patricio and Mauricio's hands. As he did this, he passed a key chain bearing the Royal Riderz logo. The metal letters glimmered with each camera flash. The crowd clapped and cheered loudly until the car club leader raised his hand flashing a peace sign. They quickly became quiet and he held up his hand in an "I love you" gesture, holding up his index and pinky fingers with his thumb extruded. The sound of the cicadas prevailed, humming low and slow. Mauricio slipped the Impala keys onto the key chain and handed them to Patricio.